ISBN: 978-1-942500-98-8

Boulevard Books
The New Face of Publishing

A SERGEANT MARKIE MYSTERY

THE CASE OF THE MISSING SOLE

Anthony Celano

DEDICATION

This book, my 8th in the Sergeant Markie Mystery Series, is dedicated to the loving memory of those who influenced me without ever realizing how much:

GRACE PAPARELLA CELANO, a strong mother who faced problems head on.

ENRICO CELANO, a father who always had the back of his children, right or wrong.

EDWARD CELANO, a brother who served as the perfect role model.

CAROL CELANO MAZZA and LORRAINE CELANO MENIST, two wonderful, caring sisters.

THOMAS AND HELEN KAVANAGH, in-laws who were the epidemy of decency and kindness.

BIOGRAPHY

ANTHONY CELANO is a former NYPD Detective and Detective Squad Commander. His law enforcement assignments as a detective included the Queens District Attorney's Office Squad, the Organized Crime Control Bureau/Brooklyn North Narcotics and the DEA Joint Task Force. The author was also a Special Investigator for the NY State Prosecutors Office-Nursing Home Investigation.

The author was the Squad Commander of several Brooklyn precincts. He was also assigned to the Colombo Organized Crime Task Force during the Colombo war of the 1990's.

Mr. Celano was the Co-Founder, Owner and CEO of Full Security, Incorporated, a Midtown Manhattan Investigative firm, for 17 years. After his retirement from FSI the author began writing novels. He is currently in the process of writing The Case of the Yearbook Killer, his 9th offering in his Sergeant Markie Mystery Series.

Author's Website: anthony-celano.com

1

A Genius Snaps

AS SOON AS DARIO TENGO TOOK POSSESSION OF the paper bag that contained the five-shot .38 caliber Smith & Wesson detective special, he stuffed it in the inner pocket of his coat. He couldn't wait to get home with his newly purchased equalizer. Once in the privacy of his apartment Dario proceeded to closely examine the illegal handgun with the crudely filed off serial number.

Dario sat on the edge of his bed and removed the gun from the bag. Never having held a handgun before, Dario found the loaded revolver to be heavier than anticipated. When he jiggled the gun he heard the bullets rattle in the chamber. He hadn't expected this. It seemed to make the weapon somehow fragile.

Dario pointed the revolver at the water pitcher that rested atop the end table next to his bed. He then lowered the gun, opened the chamber and examined each bullet. Having only the ammunition in the gun he wondered how hard it would be to get more bullets if necessary. This thought was short lived. He'd have to worry about that if and when the time came.

Careful to keep his finger off the trigger, Dario raised the gun to his eye and looked into the 2-inch barrel of the revolver. He frowned when he saw the dust accumulation. Also disappointing were the small traces of rusting he noticed above the grip. For the money he paid Dario had assumed that the gun would be in pristine condition. Even the banana shaped grip appeared weathered. These imperfections were things Dario didn't anticipate.

In the end, Dario accepted the condition of the weapon. At least he had what he wanted, a gun that presumably worked. However, the more Dario handled the gun the more dissatisfied he became with the banana grip. The wooden grip just didn't seem to fit his hand right.

Improvising, Dario fished out the black electrical tape that he had in a drawer. He wrapped the black tape around the grip to fatten it. He had seen this done once in a movie. Once the grip was thickened to his liking, the feel of the weapon in his hand felt more comfortable.

The novice gun owner stood in front of the mirror over his dresser. He tucked the gun into his waistband and stared into the glass to evaluate how he looked. He then donned a loose-fitting blue blazer and buttoned it to see if there would be a noticeable bulge. There wasn't thanks to Dario being a trim man.

I may want to keep my jacket open sometime, Dario thought.

With this in mind, Dario shifted the weapon to his hip. This didn't feel right to him. He then put the gun in his pants pocket to see how that felt. Not satisfied, he placed the gun in the side pocket of his blazer. Since he had no bulky holster, he found this to be an acceptable option.

Aware that there were strict laws pertaining to guns, Dario carried the revolver on his person only when he felt there was a need to. His location, and the time, was the determining factor on whether or not to arm himself. Most of the time, Dario's equalizer remained in the glove compartment of his car.

The first time Dario left his apartment packing the gun he did so with a swagger. The feeling of invincibility was written on his face. Being armed gave the Italian born Dario the confidence he required to navigate the streets of New York City unafraid.

Dario had relocated to America from Italy with Victor Spinello. They had worked together in a Milan shoe factory. Victor, an exceptionally creative man, invented a shoe accessory that his co-worker saw potential value in. Dario, a conniver with big dreams, recognized that Victor lacked talent when it came to business. Taking advantage of this, he persuaded Victor to enter into an equal partnership.

Dario explained to Victor that he was soon to attend his brother's wedding where he would meet his brother's future father-in-law. He indicated that his physician brother was marrying the physician daughter of a shoe man from America. "Victor, listen to me," said Dario in his most convincing voice. "If you agree to get together with me, I'll pitch our new sole to my brother's father-in-law at the wedding." Victor, a naïve man when it came to trusting Dario, agreed to the proposed partnership with Dario.

As planned, Dario met with the bride's father, Richard Frantellini, at the wedding. Frantellini, a shoemaker with a small real estate portfolio, listened to Dario's pitch with interest. He liked what he was hearing.

The shoemaker conveyed that if the new product met expectations, he would be interested in forming a corporation with Dario and Victor. Financed by Frantellini, the trio could then further develop the new product in America, offering it to the public as The Frantellini Sole.

Dario was so excited over this proposition that he immediately agreed without first conferring with Victor. As anticipated, Victor went along with Dario, who he thought much of in terms of business acumen.

Dario and Victor relocated to New York City where papers were drawn up. Overwhelmed with enthusiasm, neither Dario nor Victor read the fine print contained in their contract.

Limited in their command of English, they were under the impression that they were equal partners with Richard Frantellini in the newly formed corporation. In this they were very mistaken.

Victor Spinello's creation went on to generate huge interest. A cinch to be a financial success, the corporation Richard formed morphed into the successful Frantellini Shoe Factory. It was at this point that Dario and Victor came to realize that they only possessed a minority interest in the entity. Now seeing that he had been tricked by a slicker man than he, Dario vowed to one day take revenge. Having no money for lawyers, Dario was compelled to wait.

Dario's opportunity finally came when Victor informed him that he was in the process of developing a new product that would rival the sole he had previously created. Victor explained that the new product would alleviate the discomfort related to neuropathy. The creative genius predicted that the new product, which he called The Dynamic Shoe, was going to be an even greater success than the sole that bore the Frantellini name.

"Have you told anyone about this?" Dario asked.

"Only you," answered Victor.

"Excellent. Let's keep it that way, my friend."

Armed with this knowledge, the wheels in the head of the scheming Dario began turning. The manipulative Dario now envisioned a way to avenge his being lured into a one-sided business venture with Richard Frantellini.

***

DARIO HELD THE GUN in his hand tightly as he pondered things. His look was one of determination. The time had finally come to convince Victor Spinello of what they needed to do. Since Victor was not a resentful person, selling the idea Dario had in mind might prove difficult. Victor's only interest was in creating new products, not taking revenge.

For Dario to move ahead with the double cross he plotted, he needed Victor's cooperation. Without Victor and The Dynamic Shoe, there would be no deal to cut with Chen Lowe, a major competitor of the Frantellini Shoe Factory.

Since Victor was a moral man of integrity, Dario knew enough to keep Victor in the dark regarding some aspects of his plan. Victor needn't know about Dario's other venture, the one that consisted of his opening a boutique gentleman's club with a stripper partner.

The projected club could more accurately be described as a high-end, by appointment only, brothel. The working women at Dario's house of sin would be restricted to those who bore a striking resemblance to celebrities.

Dario intended to impress upon Victor that it was their creation, The Frantellini Sole, that established the Frantellini Shoe Factory as a major entity. Actually, claiming that the sole was their creation was a stretch. The sole was strictly the brainchild of the brilliant Victor. Dario just happened to be slick enough to hitch his wagon to the rising star.

Once I open Victor's eyes and point out that Frantellini and his family are receiving the lion's share of the profit being made off of our sole, he'll have to see things my way, thought Dario.

In order to soften Victor up Dario extended an invitation that the two have dinner together. The plan was to follow dinner with a viewing of the Italian movie, Il Mostro (The Monster), a new Roberto Benigni movie being shown at a movie theater on the upper west side of Manhattan.

"Are you sure that you want to go out tonight?" asked Victor.

"We have work tomorrow."

"We won't be late, Victor. We have to eat, and besides, this movie is supposed to be really funny. It's about the police believing that Roberto is a serial killer. C'mon, you love Roberto."

Victor consented to go along because he really did enjoy the movies of the Italian comedian.

On the drive home after the movie, Dario could see that Victor was in good spirits. It was at this point that he outlined how they had been taken advantage of by Richard Frantellini. He then broached the idea of their propositioning Chen Lowe.

Dario neglected to make any mention of the brothel he was planning to open. "But Dario, once my Dynamic Shoe is perfected, they're probably going to call it the Frantellini Dynamic Shoe. How could we possibly involve ourselves with Lowe's Connecticut company?"

"Because we aren't locked into Frantellini with the new shoe product. Our deal with Richard only applies to the Frantellini Sole. Listen to me, Victor. Just go along with what I say, and we'll collect from both ends."

"We're still going to be working at the Frantellini Shoe Factory?" "No, we'll be practically done with Richard Frantellini and his whole family. We're going to be partners with Chen Lowe and working in his place in Connecticut."

"But what about Richard?"

"We'll always have that small piece of the Frantellini Shoe Factory. We'll be collecting that money forever, unless he buys us out. Which I think he's going to want to do."

Victor took a moment to digest this before responding. "I don't know, Dario," he finally said.

"What don't you know?"

"Richard has been good to me," replied Victor. "I have some equity in the company. I receive a nice salary. And I have a nice office. I am even free to work on my new shoe. What more can I want?"

Dario was now growing frustrated. "You're talking peanuts, compared to the money we can make off The Dynamic Shoe. All we need to do is hitch out wagon to Chen. He'll give us a bigger piece of the pie."

"Why don't we just ask Richard for more money when I perfect my shoe?" Victor questioned.

"What! And give that bastard a present after what he did to us? Never!"

"But I'm content at the Frantellini Shoe Factory and I'm happy living in an apartment with you above the factory. There is a lot to be said for being content."

"Are you crazy? What do you think happens to us when Richard goes?" "Goes where?" "If Richard drops dead tomorrow, we'll both be under the thumb of that bitch daughter and that new wife of his."

"Oh, I don't know, Dario," countered Victor, "I get along with both of them."

Dario exploded internally after hearing this remark. Without saying a word, he adjusted his route. Dario drove to a secluded area in Washington Heights that overlooked the Hudson River Drive. It was an infrequently traveled location that he knew of. Once parked, things turned nasty.

Unable to sway Victor with words, Dario resorted to intimidation. He used his size advantage and slapped the smaller man's face as a way to force compliance. The first stinging blow shocked Victor. The open-mouthed Victor placed his own hand to his face and stared at Dario in disbelief.

The barrage of smacks that followed caused Victor to cover his face with his hands. Victor fell back against the car door and lifted both feet in an attempt to prevent further blows from striking him. The assault victim pushed Daro back with his feet. This defense tactic not only dirtied the aggressor's clothes, but it also enraged him. Dario reacted by shoving Victor's legs to one side. At this point Dario resorted to throwing heavy punches.

"You're going in with me!" shouted Dario as he swung away.

"If you don't, you're not leaving this car alive!"

Finally, under the pounding, the dazed Victor relented. "BASTA!" Victor screamed, indicating in Italian that he had enough. "I'll go along with whatever you want."

With calm now restored, Dario backed off. He let out a deep breath as he patted the dirt off his jacket. Dario began to slowly shake his head as he watched Victor, head bowed, begin to wipe the blood from his split lip and nose with a white handkerchief. The man behind the wheel of the BMW never got to see the bug-eyed maniacal look behind the handkerchief.

Believing that things were now under control, Dario took out his comb and began fixing his hair. He spoke calmly as he groomed himself while peering into the car's rear-view mirror. "All this was unnecessary, Victor," said Dario. "I'm sorry that I had to hit you, but you will thank me later, my friend. Trust me, I know what is best for us." Victor offered no response. The silence was eerie.

When Dario reached into his pocket for a cigarette he found the soft pack crushed as a result of the skirmish he had with Victor. Dario asked Victor to hand him the pack of cigarettes contained in the car glove compartment. Unfortunately for Dario, he had forgotten all about the revolver he housed there.

Seeing his chance, Victor seized the gun. Dario was now on the business end of the firearm held by the crazed Victor. Without hesitation Victor fired two shots off. Both bullets hit home. The round entering Dario's forehead was not survivable. He was gone in seconds.

"You want my products?" bellowed Victor. "Well here, take this one!" Victor shouted as he removed the inner sole from his shoe. He then jammed the Frantellini Sole into the mouth of the man he killed. He capped his wrath by beating Dario about his head with his shoe until he exhausted himself.

Once his rage was released, Victor entered into a dazed state. Nevertheless, he was able to realize that he needed to get away from the scene of crime he committed. Victor slipped his foot into his blood-stained shoe and walked off into the night. In his haste he left behind the gun on the passenger seat of the car.

***

WHEN NEITHER DARIO NOR VICTOR showed up for work at the Frantellini Shoe Factory, Richard Frantellini wondered why. The CEO's concern rested more with the absence of Victor, because he was the more valuable of the two unaccounted for men.

"Maria, see if you could get Victor on the phone, " Richard said.

"I already tried, he's not picking up," replied the daughter, who worked for her father as the company chief financial officer.

"What about Dario?"

"He's not answering his phone either."

"Go upstairs to their apartment and see if they are there."

"I already told her that she should do that," chimed in Ronnie, who was Richard's new wife.

"It's not your place to tell me what to do," voiced the annoyed stepdaughter. "Why didn't you go and do it yourself?"

"See what I mean," said Ronnie, addressing her husband. "There is no working peacefully with her, Richard."

"No working with me!" shouted Maria. "You're the one…."

"Maria," said Richard sternly, cutting his daughter off mid-sentence. "Just go upstairs to the apartment and see if they are there."

After a few minutes Maria reported back. "No one answers the door."

"That's strange," said Richard. "They probably went out last night and had a big time for themselves."

"A big time?" questioned Maria.

"It happens, you know," added Ronnie, her voice laced with sarcasm.

"Boys will be boys."

2

Birth Of An Empire

THE TRAIL LEADING TO the murder of Dario Tengo had a beginning. It all started with Richard Frantelli, the son of a self-employed Italian born shoemaker. The father and son lived in the rear of the store they rented. Richard, an only child who lost his mother at an early age, spent lots of time working for his father. Thanks to Frantellini senior the son learned much more than the shoe trade.

Not one for extravagances, Richard's father was a thrifty man who knew how to hang on to his money. Frugalness was something he impressed upon his son. Richard proved to be an apple that didn't fall far from the tree. Not one to challenge a proven track record when it came to money, he appreciated his father's formula.

Richard saw in his father an independent man who answered to no one. The father had no boss, no wife and no one he owed money to. Never wanting to be far from his cash, Richard's dad kept the bulk of his currency stashed away in an old travel trunk buried under dozens of loose shoes. The small business owner did keep some money in a bank located within walking distance of his shop.

The thought of one day operating the family business was appealing to Richard. Having seen once or twice the interior of the old trunk, the heir apparent appreciated the upside of running a cash business.

As Richard matured he began to see the value in education. This prompted him to pursue a degree in business management. While attending a city college at night, Richard continued to work alongside his father each day in the shoe shop. While in college Richard became friendly with a classmate who came from a family that invested heavily in real estate. Through his friend, Richard learned of the financial benefits to being a property owner. He also learned a few tricks when it came to the real estate business.

Richard's classmate mentioned that his family had been looking at a commercial/residential property on 10th Avenue that was owned by an elderly Italian widow. The student explained that the woman was no longer able to cope with the responsibilities involved in being a landlord. The friend noted that no real estate brokers were involved.

Richard gathered that the negotiations for the sale of the property were stalled due to a language barrier. This got Richard thinking. Particularly attractive was that the property in question was not far from his father's shoe shop.

Richard, armed with this intelligence, went to see the property. He found the commercial/residential building to be impressive. Richard, who knew enough Italian to communicate with the building owner, introduced himself. Their conversation was so productive that the white-haired senior citizen insisted on feeding Richard her homemade pizza.

After he finished the pizza he advised the property owner that he would return that evening with his father. Confident that he was on the verge of putting together a good deal, Richard approached his father concerning the opportunity to buy the building. Richard efforts to convince his father of the investment opportunity was lukewarm. Even after explaining that the property in question could house the family business and several residential apartments the father still remained unsold on the idea.

What finally swayed the father was being told that the property could be obtained at a reduced price, if some of the money was paid in cash under the table. While the father hated to part with any of his cash, the opportunity seemed attractive enough to consider. When told that the seller was born in Italy, the senior Frantellini finally agreed to go and see her.

When Richard introduced his father to the woman they immediately began conversing in Italian. The two soon found common ground in their recollections of their childhood in Italy. Furthering their bond was their conversation concerning the loss of their respective spouses. This time there was no pizza. The seller insisted on cooking a full dinner for both the father and son. She enjoyed the company enough to want to do business with her visitors.

"You like to cook?" asked the father in English. The reply came in English.

"Ah, sure. Why make-a-the restaurants rich?"

As the building owner toiled over the stove she began to talk of her plans. She conveyed that once her property was sold, she planned to return to Venice to live with her sister.

"So, you wanna buy-a-my house?"

"Quanto costa?" Richard's father asked, inquiring about the price.

"You no worry, I give-a-you a break."

"Yeah?"

"Ah, sure, My Pino leave-a me plenty. You gotta some cash?"

The end result was that the widow's property was sold to the senior Frantellini. The seller was glad to accept the cash offered under the table and sell her building to someone she had lots in common with.

The father and son relocated their family business to the newly acquired building. The residential apartments over the shop were renovated one by one and rented. As a result of their investment, greater prosperity came with each passing year. After the death of Richard's father several years later, Richard came into a substantial inheritance. He used the money to venture forward with other property acquisitions. These proved to be fruitful investments, giving Richard an impressive real estate portfolio.

Richard continued to operate the family shoe shop, a business that he had grown to be profitable enough to hire workers. Richard, who was still single, made things convenient for himself by converting the top floor of the building that housed the shoe shop for himself. Upon completion of the work, he had a penthouse apartment that came with a roof deck for entertaining.

By his late thirties, Richard was financially secure. Over the years Richard had struck up a close friendship with Father Fiorello St. Denis. The parish priest was about the same age as Richard. It was St. Denis who mentioned to Richard that he knew of a fine woman who would make some lucky man a terrific spouse.

Since Richard wanted a family at this point, he was eager to meet someone who could give him children. It was at a church mixer that Father St. Denis introduced Richard to Angela DeCarlo, a raven-haired woman who was twelve years his junior. Richard liked what he saw.

Angela also approved of Richard who, with his full head of dark curly hair and being only a few pounds overweight, made a good appearance. The two proved well suited for each other. Both were God-fearing people who wanted to start a family. Within a year, the two married, taking up residence in Richard's penthouse apartment. Their union was destined to last.

Angela, aside from being a fine wife and mother, was an intelligent lady with a head for business. Her suggestion that the shoe shop deliver repaired shoes to the home or business of customers was well received by a clientele who appreciated having their life made easier. She also saw the value in broadening the Frantellini real estate footprint.

While spending money did not come easy for Richard, he gave in to Angela's suggestion that they add to their real estate portfolio. As a favor to Father St. Denis, Frantellini ads were placed in The Tablet, a Catholic newspaper. The priest had become a regular dinner guest at the Frantellini household. The family attended the priest's Sunday Masses, confessed their sins to him, and generously donated to his church. It was Father St. Denis who baptized the two Frantellini daughters, who were born two years apart.

Richard Frantellini had always encouraged his girls to display an interest in the family business. In this endeavor he was just partially successful, with only his youngest girl embracing involvement in the family holdings.

Caroline Frantellini, the oldest daughter, had a calling of a different nature. An excellent student, she set on a path to be a doctor. Resilient in this regard, she fought off her father's urging that she become a businessperson. Her passion for medicine was not one to be derailed.

Since Caroline had the grades necessary, she garnered support from her mother, who viewed her daughter's quest to be a physician an admirable one. Richard, although a bit disappointed at Caroline's decision to pursue a costly medical career, eventually consented to support his daughter's dream. When Caroline announced that she was accepted at The University of Milan in Italy, Richard was staggered by the price tag connected to studying overseas. His suggestion that there were cheaper alternatives to consider was ignored by both his wife and Caroline.

Angela, after doing her homework, drew a line in the sand. She argued that Milan made sense for their daughter. She detailed how the university's reputation for excellence, particularly in the area of medical research, was outstanding.

Once the shock of the price wore off, Richard had to admit that having a doctor in the family wasn't the worst thing. To keep peace, Richard ceased to voice his objections. He was thinking that in the long run divorce would cost him more money than medical school. With the financial backing of her parents, Caroline's aspiration to attend medical school in Italy became a reality.

While in Milan Caroline became smitten with an Italian born classmate. Although both were serious career-oriented medical students, the call of romance found a place in their lives. The only thing that could tear Ettore Tengo away from his medical books was the scent of Caroline Frantellini. The reverse could also be said.

Upon graduation and a year of living together, the Frantellini-Tengo union became official. The announcement of wedding bells delighted the parents on both sides of the ocean. While the Frantellini side was a bit sad that their daughter was remaining in Italy to be with her husband, they conceded that Ettore was a good man for Caroline to build a future with.

Richard and Angela flew to Milan to assist in the planning of their daughter's wedding. Accompanying them was their youngest daughter Maria, who served as the maid of honor. Father Fiorello St. Denis, who was to participate in the wedding ceremony, also went along.

While in Milan, Richard and his wife got to meet the groom's brother, who was the best man in the wedding party. Richard Frantellini found Dario Tengo interesting because he worked in an Italian shoe factory outside of Milan.

Angela and Maria Frantellini thought that Dario was the handsomer of the two brothers. The Tengo siblings were nicely built men of above average height. The Frantellini family came to learn that Dario Tengo had married at eighteen after impregnating the sixteen-year-old Gia Marcello.

Birthing and caring for three children was hard on Gia, who showed signs of wear and tear. Having children had no apparent physical effect on Dario. Appearance-wise the husband never changed.

"So how is the shoe business here, Dario?" asked Richard, making conversation during the wedding festivities.

"To be honest, it's been a little frustrating for me," replied the best man, who spoke perfect English.

"In what way?"

"I have developed a new product that I know has the potential to be tremendously successful. Unfortunately, I work for a shortsighted man you can't tell anything to. He knows it all."

"What's the product?'" asked Angela, who expressed an interest in learning more.

"I want to introduce to the market a breakthrough inner sole for shoes."

"But they have that already."

"There is nothing like what I'm talking about, Angela. This product is a beautiful black innersole crafted with a material that not just increases height and is comfortable, it also contributes to foot relief."

"How can that be?" asked Richard, who remained skeptical.

"It's true, my brother Ettore didn't believe it possible either. He and his doctor friends were astounded after examining my product."

"The doctors evaluated the sole?"

"Yes, several of them did."

"So, what's stopping you from putting it out on the market yourself?" queried Richard.

"The one thing preventing that is the lack of financing. Neither my partner nor I have the money."

"You have a partner?" asked Angela.

"Yes, I do."

"Do you need him?"

"Yes, he is the genius instrumental in making the sole. I handle the business end. We work at the factory here. He, also has no money."

"Is there a patent?"

"Yes, we're protected. We are listed as co-inventers in the patent."

"How did you manage that?" asked Angela.

"Let's just say that my partner recognizes my value."

"Our meeting you is fortuitous, Dario," said Angela, apparently having ideas. "Isn't that right, Richard?"

"If this product is for real," replied Richard, "every short man with bad feet would go out and buy these soles."

"That's exactly what I've been telling people," Dario voiced enthusiastically.

"My husband and I know how to promote this," advised Angela. "We can start our own factory. We have the space for it."

"Hold up a second, Angela," said Richard, sounding a bit annoyed.

"There are no more shoe factories in New York. There is a Chinese guy named Chen Lowe who is taking over the industry."

"So what? We're introducing a new product," shot back Angela. "You're good at handling negotiations, Richard. Think long term."

Richard comprehended what his wife was thinking. If I could grow a shoe factory, thought Richard, I could probably sell out to Chen Lowe for a bundle down the road.

Richard then turned to Dario to ask, "How much to get you guys to New York where we could start up a business?"

"My partner and I would require a half interest," answered Dario. Richard flinched at the thought of giving up half. Dario could tell by Richard's reaction that he was asking for too much equity. "What do you think is fair, Richard?" he asked, easing his demand.

"You have an idea, but no money. I have the money, I know how to promote the product and I'm the one taking the financial risk. With that said, you and your partner will draw spending money until we become profitable."

"Where will we live?"

"I'll get you both fixed up in an apartment in my building. You'll live rent free until we get on our feet. How does that sound?"

"What is our percentage of the company?"

"Ten percent each."

"Give me 15 percent," replied Dario, adding, "Victor will accept 5 percent."

Richard did a double take. "Are you sure your partner is going be okay about that?"

"I'm sure. He leaves all business decisions to me."

"What's your partner's full name?" queried Angela.

"Victor Spinello."

"Are you sure that he's all that brilliant?" Richard questioned.

"He is in most things, just not with money."

"Okay, Dario, I'll have my lawyer draw up the papers."

When alone Richard and Angela Frantellini admitted that they were high on the idea of a cutting-edge inner sole. They agreed, providing the sole was what Dario claimed it was, that the cost of expanding their shoemaker shop into a shoe factory was a safe gamble.

"What about Dario's wife and children, Richard?" Angela asked.

"He can send for them when he can afford to make his own arrangements," answered Richard.

"You know what else we could do?"

"Is this going to cost me more money, Angela?"

"We can have the name Frantellini printed in gold lettering on black inner soles."

"That's a great idea," acknowledged Richard.

"What do you want to call the new business?"

"The Frantellini Shoe Factory," announced Richard proudly. "I'll plaster that name in gold on every black sole we sell!"

"Yes!" Angela agreed. "But how fair is all this regarding poor Victor?"

"This is business, Angela. Besides, if this deal works out there will be enough money to go around that poor Victor won't be so poor."

Richard and Angela Frantellini pursued their new venture with great vigor. While they forged ahead without the involvement of their oldest daughter, they found ample willingness to participate coming from Maria, their younger girl. It had become clear to Richard and Angela that Maria Frantellini represented the future of the family businesses. No one had any reason to suspect otherwise.

3

All In The Family

THE GROWTH OF THE FRANTELLINI SHOE FACTORY exceeded expectations. The decision of Richard and Angela Frantellini to open the factory proved to be the wisest business decision they ever made. The gratification they received from their success was as pleasurable as the monetary rewards.

Sceptics thought it foolish for them to invest in what was considered by many to be a dying industry. Shoe factories had been spiraling downward in New York City due to increased import competition and labor costs. Yet, despite the naysayers, Richard and Angela remained firm in their belief that the newly developed Frantellini Sole would justify the expense. Knowing that they were right fueled further ambition.

Fortunately, the sole gained popularity with the public almost immediately. As the factory flourished Angela thought it a good idea to invest the revenue gained. Richard, who by now had great faith in Angela, agreed. The couple decided to invest in more real estate, which was generally considered a safe investment. For the Frantellini family, it was.

Richard kept an eye on every aspect connected to their finances. He was so diligent when it came to his assets that his overwork led to a heart attack. Angela's focus, in addition to now having to monitor their business interests, was to serve as her husband's caretaker. Luckily, their daughter Maria was there to assume more responsibility in operating the business. A graduate of Pace University, Maria's education included an accounting degree and a master's degree in business administration. These credentials prepared her well for the chief financial officer's role she assumed in the family businesses.

Maria assumed her CFO role passionately. In addition to the sound judgment of her parents, Maria inherited Richard's tendency to be frugal. A self-starter, she tore into her work. Her vigorous examination of how company money was being spent was revealing.

Disturbing to Maria was the cost connected to employee-related litigation. Another concern had to do the invoices paid to certain vendors by minority partner Dario Tengo. These seemed inflated to her, as did Dario's personal expenses. A check of Victor Spinello's expenses reflected no irregularities.

Prior to taking steps Maria took time to review the agreement between her father and the minority partners. She was impressed. She hadn't realized just how much of an upper hand her father had on Victor Spinello and Dario Tengo contractually.

"I could learn a lot about contracts from dad," she commented to her mother one day.

"You certainly could dear, especially when it comes to money," agreed Angela. "But to be honest, having a shrewd lawyer helps."

Maria began to work closely with the company lawyer, who worked off site on a retainer. Together they created an employee handbook designed to protect the company. Maria squared matters pertaining to recruitment, retention and employee termination procedures. She then addressed Dario Tengo's expense report submissions. It was here that she ran into resistance.

Maria brought Dario's abuse to the attention of her father once he returned to work. Richard nodded, almost as if he wasn't surprised. He inquired about his other minority partner, Victor Spinello. Richard was told that the expenses of the inventor of The Frantellini Sole were practically non-existent. He was informed that the only money Victor spent pertained to a new product he was developing.

"What product is that?" Richard asked.

"Some kind of shoe product," answered Maria. "Supposedly when its perfected, it will outdo anything currently on the market when it comes to alleviating foot discomfort."

"Neuropathy?"

"I believe so."

What remained unknown to the Frantellini family was that Victor Spinello had problems with his own feet. His foot difficulty, along with his short stature, was what prompted him to create the highly successful Frantellini Sole. Since Victor did well with the inner sole he created, he was confident in his quest to develop footwear that would substantially reduce most forms of foot pain. He called his new product The Dynamic Shoe.

Richard Frantellini saw Victor's new creation as a potential goldmine. He envisioned that one day they'd be producing a product he intended to rename The Frantellini Dynamic Shoe.

"Let's leave Victor to his work," advised Richard to his wife and daughter. "Let the man have whatever support he needs. We just need to monitor the progress he's making. I want to know when he's getting close to completion."

"What do you want me to do about Dario?" Maria asked. "Clip his wings if you have to," replied Richard. "The guy brings no value to the table. He's just a sponge. The other guy is the real asset."

With his daughter Maria proving herself capable, Richard Frantellini began to scale back his involvement in the day-to-day operation of his business interests. Finding his heart attack to be an eyeopener, Richard intended to spend more time relaxing.

With no interests other than work, Maria Frantellini welcomed the added responsibility given to her. Her idea of having a good time was troubleshooting and problem solving. Her love of work left her little time for a social life.

As part of her routine to stay abreast of what was going on, Maria became something of a snoop. She regularly monitored the private offices of the shoe factory's minority partners. She suspected that Dario Tengo, in particular, required close watching. Before confronting

Dario, she wanted to gather more information.

Handsome and always sharply dressed, Dario's had the look of someone to be suspicious of. Dario, who had a wife and children back in Milan, was a man with plenty to conceal.

Maria noticed that whenever Dario was on the office telephone or his cellular phone, he spoke with his hand covering his mouth. This peculiarity prompted Maria, who paid both phone expenses, to examine the telephone records. She was upset to discover the frequency in which Dario telephoned Italy to speak to his wife Gia and their children.

Seeing two frequently called local numbers dialed from Dario's office line, Maria called the numbers out of curiosity. One call resulted in a female named Mary advising on a recording to leave a message. The other was answered by someone working at the Kingly Castle Review, a Manhattan strip club. Maria didn't find this to be very surprising.

Since Dario brought nothing to the table, she agreed with her father that he was a drain on the company finances. Figuring out a way to oust Dario from the company altogether had become a priority.

When Maria clued in her father about Dario, Richard's only reaction was a shrug. With his eye on the potential of The Dynamic Shoe, Richard didn't want to hear about Dario's extracurricular activities as long as they didn't cost him a lot of money. Richard wasn't going to do anything that might upset the progress of the new product under development. Since Dario and Victor Spinello were close friends, Richard saw it in the Frantellini interest to keep a happy house regardless of what Dario's telephone costs were.

"Don't say anything to Dario right now," said Richard. "We'll handle Dario after the shoe is perfected."

"If we are going to buy Dario out, why not do it now?"

Richard Frantellini was cool to the suggestion.

"I don't want to risk upsetting Victor. Besides that, Dario won't go away cheap, Maria. This country smartened him up."

"So, won't he want more once work on the Dynamic Shoe is completed?"

"You just keep close tabs on him. Dario's a married man with a wife and children in Milan. When the time comes, we'll remind him of what it'll cost him once his wife learns of what he's been up to. He'll be more amenable to reasonably coming to terms with us."

"So, you don't want to do anything now?"

"Correct. I don't want to do anything that might upset Victor while he's perfecting that shoe of his," replied Richard. "Leaning on Dario might upset the applecart, so go slow."

"So that means Dario can spend whatever he wants? He's probably running around with a stripper on our time and money," voiced Maria.

"You know that for a fact?'

"No, I don't. I'm just speculating."

"If he is that'll be good for us."

"That's probably why he never sent for Gia and his kids to come to the United States. He's having too much fun. I never believed the story that Dario's wife prefers to live in Italy with their kids. He doesn't want her here!"

"That's none of our business, Maria. Let's just drop the subject as far as that goes. Just see if you can get us the leverage we need for down the road. Dario might even be doing something more than just womanizing.

"I wouldn't put anything past him!"

Since Maria got along well with Victor Spinello, she decided to have a word with him to see if she could gain insights about Dario. She found Victor hard at work in his office. When Maria asked if he had a moment to chat, Victor cordially stated that he did. After some small talk, Maria discreetly got around to discussing Dario.

Coming across as sincere, Victor seemed to know nothing about Dario's private affairs. Maria left Victor's office thinking that the minority partner was either covering up for his friend or just a very green apple.

Maria moved on to walk through the factory to observe her employees. This was something she often did. Her inspections were made in a mechanical way. She rarely actually engaged the workers who operated the machines in conversation. Those who made eye contact with the daughter of the owner would briefly smile before turning away to continue their cutting, sorting, and preparing of the leather, cloth, and synthetic materials.

Maria watched workers cut patterns on presses with sharp molds, and thin leather at the seams to make it easier to sew or glue. As an observer, she eyed the lining that was hot-pressed onto the pieces of material to be sewn. Aside from her suspicions of Dario, she came away thinking that the factory was operating smoothly and the Frantellini family was getting good production out of their employees.

***

WHILE HARD IN BUSINESS MATTERS, Richard Frantellini was actually a sentimentalist who worked at cloaking his sensitive side. Only his wife knew him to be a man who wept watching movies of a tearjerking nature. When tragedy came his way in the form of losing Angela, the love of his life, it had a devasting effect on him.

The grim reaper took Angela Frantellini in a cruel and unexpected way. She was run over by a delivery van while attempting to cross a street in the middle of a block. The subsequent police inquiry revealed that the driver had accidentally struck Angela while backing into a parking space.

News of Angela's death caused the still recuperating Richard to collapse emotionally. He entered into a state of depression severe enough to require intervention. Fortunately for him, there were support mechanisms in his life. Richard's daughter Maria bore the heavy lifting in the business. Aside from running the shoe factory and real estate holdings, she stepped up to take charge of all the funeral arrangements for her mother.

Spiritual guidance for Richard came by way of family friend Father Fiorello St. Denis. The priest's soothing talk of faith helped stabilize the depressed Richard. While Richard may have lost much of his ambition, at least there were no longer thoughts of suicide.

Father St. Denis suggested to Richard that it might be therapeutic if he spent time with his daughter Caroline and her husband in Milan. Both daughters, as well as Richard's physician son-in-law, thought this was an excellent suggestion.

Caroline and her husband, a childless couple, made it clear that they had more than enough room at their home to accommodate an extended stay. Richard's oldest daughter suggested that her father bring along Father St. Denis as a travel companion. All agreed that the trip would be financed by the Frantellini Shoe Company. Even Richard's youngest daughter, Maria, was on board with this.

When Richard and the priest arrived in the old county, Dr. Ettore Tengo's sister-in-law Gia visited Richard to offer her condolences on Angela' death. Richard thanked Dario Tengo's wife and conveyed that he preferred not to talk about his loss. When alone with Gia Tengo, Father St. Denis asked her when she planned to be with her husband in the United States. Gia answered him in a way that the priest found baffling.

"I've been waiting for Dario to send for us," advised Gia. "I'm hoping it won't be much longer before he makes enough money for us to reunite. The children need to know their father."

"You and the children are welcome to travel to America with us when we return," invited St. Denis. "We are planning to be in Milan for only month or so."

"I only wish that were possible, Father. But we haven't the money for that. Dario said that he is having a tough time saving money. He said that the shoe factory hasn't been making much of a profit yet."

"Dario told you that?" questioned the priest.

"Why yes, Father."

"Gia, I want to share something with you. Please, put on some coffee. We need to talk."

***

BACK IN NEW YORK CITY DARIO had begun to sense that Maria Frantellini had taken an interest in him. At first he presumed that her always looking at him had to do with a romantic attraction. His conceit made this seem entirely plausible.

Dario considered Maria to be an attractive woman who dressed well and took pride in her appearance. This made him wonder why she was without a paramour. *It can't be possible that her only passions are money and business,* thought Dario. *But yet it seems that way. Maybe she is shy.*

Dario tested the waters with Maria by making an overture that came across as something more than just friendly. He soon found out that Maria possessed no amorous feelings for him. He attributed this to her likely preferring women. Dario's ego wouldn't permit him to think otherwise. Dario's advance toward Maria triggered a response. Ignoring her father's words, Maria set out to reel in Dario.

Whatever liberties he had been taking with expenses were halted. Dario found himself now answering questions about what he was spending company money on. A new policy was drawn up that required Maria's involvement on all vendor-related dealings.

As expected, Dario questioned Maria's authority while vehemently expressing his displeasure at her attempt to micromanage him. Since he was a partner in the business, Dario felt he was on firm ground. Maria scoffed when Dario reminded her of his part ownership in the shoe factory. Unfazed, Maria made it clear that a line had been drawn in the sand and that she wasn't budging. Their conversation didn't end well. Dario began coming to work late on a regular basis. Not wanting to involve her father, Maria faced the challenge of Dario alone. She began by probing into his activities.

Maria entered Dario's office after business hours to have a look around. What she found was disturbing. In Dario's desk was a copy of already prepared expense reports for future months. The minority partner obviously intended to submit bogus expenses. Listed were such things as parking fees, meals, and other miscellaneous items for reimbursement. Attached to the expense report were blank invoices that could be purchased at any office supply.

Maria's mouth opened wide after she found a spiral notebook in Dario's Desk. The entries reflected the following:

Mary Custer, Dancer, Kingly Castle Review
(Sharon Stone/Actress)

Hillary Martin, Dancer, The Evil Cove
(Claudia Schiffer, Actress)

Annette Rosado, Dancer, Stinky's Palace
(Demi Moore, Actress)

Irene Morely, Dancer, Lancer's Lounge
(Marilyn Monroe, Actress)

Melba Singleton, Dancer, Bert's Hideaway
(Lena Horne, Actress)

Lois Gale, Dancer, Nick's Cosey Cottage
(Jackie Kennedy, Former First Lady)

What is all this? Maria wondered, as she perused the names on the list. No wonder he never sent for his wife and kids! I have to find out what he's up to, and if he is alone in his scheming. I have a business to protect! Upset over the document she read, the chief financial officer next entered the office of Victor Spinello, the minority partner with the smallest interest in the shoe factory. Maria wanted to see if there was evidence that suggested that Victor was involved in Dario's activities.

He just might be clever, thought the CFO of Victor. It's the quiet *ones you have to watch closest.*

Maria perused the items left on Victor's desk. When satisfied that there was nothing for her to be concerned about, Maria went through Victor's desk drawers. As far as the CFO could see, Victor was ardently working on the new product he referred to as his Dynamic Shoe. She was happy to find no evidence that Victor was engaged in anything irregular with Dario Tengo.

4

Sleazy Beasley

IT WAS 8:15 A.M. WHEN MARIA FRANTELLINI entered the shoe factory. An inspection of the work area, which she always conducted each morning, found the factory workers hard at work. With the exception of Victor Spinello, who was always the first to arrive at work, the corporate offices were vacant.

Since no one else was around the CFO took the opportunity to speak to Victor privately in his office. Her purpose was to gauge how strong a bond existed between Victor and Dario Tengo, the other minority partner.

Maria entered Victor's office flashing a warm smile. The pleasantry she projected was a false one, calculated to lower Victor's guard. The gentlemanly Victor rose from his desk to greet the CFO. Maria was taken aback at how short Victor seemed. She had always thought him to be a taller man. Her confusion was erased once Maria looked downward and saw that Victor was shoeless. Gazing at the floor around Victor she noticed a pair of black-laced shoes next to his chair. *Why,* thought the CFO, *those Frantellini Soles actually do make a difference in a person's height!*

Maria opened their conversation innocently enough. She casually inquired if Victor had seen Dario. It was a question that she already knew the answer to. Dario had fallen into the habit of not coming to the office before noon. To Maria's annoyance his routine was to stay a couple of hours and then leave. "I haven't seen him," advised Victor. "He should be in later." "You know Victor, I can't believe that we've never spent any time together. Let's plan on having lunch today," said Maria, not making an issue of Dario not being at work yet.

The creative genius was taken aback. He suspected that something might be wrong." "Is there a problem?" Victor asked. "No, of course not. I'm just curious as to the progress you're making on the new project and to see if you need anything in the way of support. After all, you're a valuable asset to the Frantellini family. We've invested lots of money in you." "Thank you," replied Victor, appreciating the sentiment. "Besides, it really is time that we get to know each other, Victor. Lunch will be my treat."

"Do you want Dario to join us?"

"No, let's just you and I get together."

Over lunch Maria was surprised to learn that the two men from Milan weren't as close as she suspected. When queried as to why this was so, Victor attributed the distance to his being a workaholic.

"It's my fault," advised Victor. "Since we've come to America I've been dedicated to my work. I have little time for socializing. Dario is much more engaging with people."

"The two of you share an apartment. How is that going?"

"We get along well because we're like two ships in the night. I go to bed early and rise early. Dario is the opposite."

As they lunched, Maria gathered all she needed to know about the relationship between the never-married Victor and the conniving Dario. After hearing their history Maria walked away seeing Victor as a grateful man of true integrity who was loyal to the Frantellini family. Her opinion of Dario was far less flattering.

Puzzling to Maria was how a brilliant man like Victor could be so totally lacking in business acumen. His ending up with the tiniest percentage of the shoe factory was proof of his business ineptitude. Maria couldn't prevent herself from asking the one obvious question.

"Victor, what was the need of your partnering with Dario?"

"What do you mean?" asked the inventor, unsure of what the CFO meant.

"It was you who created the sole that is making all the money. What did Dario bring to the table to earn a percentage?"

"You father has the kingly percentage," reminded Victor.

"Yes, that is true. But don't forget that my father was the one who took the risk. He put up the money."

"Your father had faith in us."

"Us? You created the product, Victor. Not Dario."

"Dario and I worked together like slaves in the shoe factory in Italy. Dario had faith in me when others thought I was a dreamer. He encouraged me."

"Dario was definitely astute in that respect," acknowledged Maria.

"I am a grateful person," said Victor. "Dario was the one who introduced me to your parents. Thanks to him, and your family, I am here in this country living well and doing the work that I love to do. This is something I'll never forget."

Maria simply nodded, withholding what she was really thinking.

You pathetic idiot, she thought, you've been cheated out of a product worth a fortune.

At this point Maria realized that Victor would never go against Dario. Once this was established, Maria truncated their meal. That evening, while alone in the penthouse apartment, Maria happened to be leafing through The Tablet, a religious newspaper that her father advertised in. As she sipped her wine she paused after coming across an ad that reflected the name of the Frantellini family lawyer. She thought the time had come to solicit the help of Thomas Beasley.

***

THOMAS BEASLEY'S LAW OFFICE was located on Court Street in Brooklyn. His reputation varied, depending on who you spoke to. To some he was an effective fixer of problems. To others, he was a shady ambulance chasing shyster in a pinstripe suit.

The majority of Beasley's clients were result-oriented people. As such they generally cared little about the methods used to resolve their issues, be they personal, corporate, criminal or civil. They paid generously for the peace of mind that came with a favorable outcome.

Beasley thrived knowing that there would always be a need for an unethical man like himself in the legal profession. Immune to public opinion, his skin was thick, his shell shatterproof. As long as he was earning money Beasley would continue to do whatever necessary to benefit himself and his clients.

The attorney routinely corrupted judges. He bribed law enforcement officers, and compromised jurors. He also provided alibis for those in need of one. Money or favors were used to sway the testimony of witnesses. Deploying these unethical methods garnered Beasley an impressive string of litigation victories. This record attracted the kind of attention that kept his services in demand.

In some ways Beasley was personable. He appealed to clients by coming across as being non-judgmental. There was no right or wrong with Beasley. Positive outcomes were all that mattered. Clients liked this about the lawyer. One client who fell into this category was Richard Frantellini.

Frantellini first retained Beasley to address a complicated matter involving a difficult tenant who resided in one of Richard's residential properties. This matter achieved a successful outcome without Frantellini ever learning that two goons had been hired by Beasley to convince the tenant to take the money offered and move.

Richard was so impressed that he went on to have Beasley represent the Frantellini family in both corporate and personal matters.

After assuming the CFO responsibility Maria Frantellini came to know the never-married Beasley well. As the two worked together through various corporate issues they grew close, sharing similar mindsets when it came to intimacy.

While Beasley was no poster boy in appearance, he could be very charming. His thinning hair and pot belly was an overlooked flaw because he was romantically convenient for Maria Frantellini. Their arrangement called for their meeting at the lawyer's office for weekly trysts. This union was an accommodation that suited both parties.

"Tommy, we need to talk," said Maria telephonically.

"I'm seeing you Thursday, right?" "No, I want to talk to you now."

***

THE EAR OF THOMAS BEASLEY'S PALE SKINNED SECRETARY was reddened due to her pressing it to the door of her boss's private office. Clara Calhoun chewed down a fingernail as she listened to the erotic vocalizations emanating from the other side of the door. Excited, the secretary closed her eyes and pictured herself as being in the mix.

The weekly sexual romps that took place in the lawyer's office was something the sex-starved Clara looked forward to as much as the participants. Without Beasley's weekly romantic interludes with Maria Frantellini, the only thing the secretary had to fulfill her desires came from the spicy novels she read.

The secretary understood what her boss saw in his client. Although somewhat snobbish, Maria Frantellini was still young, attractive and heir to a fortune. These attributes were more than enough to appeal to the attorney.

Clara grew accustomed to the boorish ways of her boss. She had no problem with Beasley's office shenanigans because of the pleasure her eavesdropping provided. Also to be considered was the fairly generous compensation she was receiving. Combined, these factors were sufficient in gaining her willingness to work for Beasley. When the romance quieted down inside the office between Beasley and Maria, they entered into a serious discussion. They spoke in a low voice, making it difficult for Clara to hear all of what they were saying. Nevertheless, the secretary was able to overhear parts of their conversation.

"So, I can count on you to take care of this?" Maria was heard asking. "Of course, you have nothing to worry about," replied the attorney.

"Remember, my father is to know nothing about this."

"Leave it to me," replied the attorney. "All I'll need is a photo and the type of car he drives."

"I have that with me."

"Excellent, let me have it," said the lawyer. A few seconds later he was heard stating, "We're all set, baby." This was followed by a short silence.

"Not now, Tommy," finally said Maria. "I have to go."

"Until next week?" Beasley asked.

"Yes, I'll be by then. Will I be getting an invoice?"

"Do you really want one?"

"No, of course not. I prefer not to have any record. I'll pay you in cash."

"That'll be fine. And let's not forget my bonus," reminded the attorney with a wink. Maria displayed a half smile upon hearing this.

"That's fine," she replied.

Maria reached into her purse and removed a small brown paper bag. She held the bag out for the attorney to take. Inside the bag were Frantellini Soles. "Here, this is for you."

"Thanks, I've been waiting for these," said the lawyer as he examined the gift. "These inner soles are the best on the market."

"I'll bring more next week."

"I got plenty of clients who could use them."

"Your clients could afford to buy them," stated Maria tartly.

Aware that the meeting was concluding, Clara hurriedly returned to her station, which was located just outside the office of her boss. In an effort to appear busy the secretary began to shuffle documents that were on her desk.

Clara watched as the chief financial officer of the Frantellini Shoe Factory strolled past without acknowledging her. *Look at* her, thought the secretary. *She really thinks who she is! If it weren't for her money she wouldn't be so hot!*

***

TEDDY LEONARD WAS A FORMER NYPD POLICE DETECTIVE who retired from the department under a cloud after twenty-five years of service. The detective's sudden exit stemmed from his belief that he was in jeopardy of losing his pension. The incident that put him in harm's way occurred late one evening when walking to the precinct after visiting the home of a complainant. While strolling Leonard heard a crash near where he was walking. Responding to the boom, he came upon a vehicle accident. A young man had crashed the car he was driving into a parked car, causing property damage.

Leonard approached the driver's side of the vehicle. It soon became clear to the detective that the operator was intoxicated. Leonard recognized the drunk driver as the son of a purported drug dealer who owned a pizzeria located within the confines of the precinct.

Seeing opportunity, Leonard wasted little time in taking steps. After assessing the damage to the vehicles, he repositioned the inebriated driver to the passenger side of his vehicle. The drunk man's protests were met with a stiff slap to the face, putting an end to further resistance. The detective then got behind the wheel of the drunk man's car.

Leonard drove several blocks before pulling over in a desolate area. The detective then searched the vehicle. To his delight, in the glove compartment he discovered two ounces of white powder that he believed to be cocaine. His search for a gun in the vehicle proved negative.

With the son and cocaine in tow, Leonard drove to the family-owned business where he engaged the father. The mob connected patriarch was grateful for the return of his car, son and the cocaine, which was referred to by Leonard as something in the glove compartment of interest.

After receiving payment for his covering up the trouble, the father had an employee of the pizzeria drive Leonard back to the scene of the accident. Once there, Leonard interacted with the responding police officers who were called to the scene. The police accident report ultimately reflected the incident to be a hit and run affair.

The following day Detective Leonard was questioned by the precinct integrity control officer, who began asking questions about the hit and run report prepared by the uniformed officers. Leonard got nervous because the lieutenant was known to be a bulldog whenever he sunk his teeth into something.

Thinking of the worst possibility, Leonard feared that a witness may have seen what he did and turned him into the lieutenant. If this was the case, it meant that Leonard was running the risk of losing his job and pension. There was also the possibility that the lieutenant was out for a piece of the money he received for his corrupt act. Both scenarios weren't good. Since Leonard was eligible for retirement, he wasn't taking any chances. The detective put his papers in and called it a career.

Once officially out of the police department, Leonard secured a private investigator's license. Working from his house, he had business cards made up that reflected his name, title and contact information. Leonard saw no need to advertise his services. His familiarity with attorneys included Thomas Beasley, who provided him with more than enough work.

When the private investigator was notified by Beasley's secretary that he was wanted at the lawyer's office, Leonard let no grass grow under his feet. He hurried to see Beasley without delay. "I have a surveillance job for you, Teddy," advised the attorney.

"No problem, who is the client?"

"The Frantellini Shoe Factory."

"What's the problem, a wayward employee?"

"Something like that."

"The usual pay?"

"Yeah, same as always."

"What are the details?"

"Meet me tonight at Parnelli's Roost on Tenth Avenue. Say, 8:00 PM? I'll have money and details for you then."

"That works."

5

Gumshoe Glee, And All Free

AS ARRANGED, THOMAS BEASLEY was at Parnelli's Roost waiting for the arrival of his investigator. The bar was a gathering place for people on the prowl for company. The attorney, who was a regular there, had arrived early. He was sitting at the bar talking to a woman when Teddy Leonard arrived. The lawyer's suit jacket was hanging off the back of his chair. The red suspenders that held up his trousers stood out prominently against his white shirt and loosened black tie.

Leonard, seeing that the attorney was engrossed in conversation, didn't advance. The private investigator waited until he was noticed by the lawyer. Recognition came when Beasley ordered a martini and a drink for the lady.

Beasley noticed Leonard when he glanced over the shoulder of his new acquaintance. They had just touched glasses. After spotting Leonard, the lawyer removed a yellow manilla envelope from the brown satchel he had with him. Beasley then excused himself from the conversation he was having. He walked over to the investigator and handed him the envelope that contained his cash retainer, and the information needed to conduct surveillance. No words were exchanged. Leonard simply took the envelope, nodded and left Beasley to his new friend.

Armed with a photograph of Dario Tengo, his work/home address and information regarding the car he drove, Teddy Leonard would have no problem identifying the man he was being paid to shadow.

***

THE PRIVATE INVESTIGATOR COMMENCED his surveillance at the Frantellini Shoe Factory. He sat in his parked car having coffee and a bagel an hour before the factory was to open. As workers began arriving Leonard had no expectation that he'd be seeing his subject among them. This was because Dario Tengo resided in an upper floor apartment in the same building as the factory.

Dario emerged from the building around noon. The weather was above average for the time of year. Neatly dressed in high-end clothing, the handsome Dario looked like a man of affluence. Clean-shaven and trim, he was attired in black slacks that held a sharp crease. A white turtleneck was visible beneath the black cashmere cardigan sweater he wore. Dario's hair was combed back, with every strand falling perfectly. The black sunglasses he wore gave him the look of a thespian trying to conceal his identity. His index finger hooked the inside loop of the brown tweed overcoat that hung down his back.

Leonard observed his target as he walked along the sidewalk. Dario's strut made him memorable enough for the private investigator to comment aloud, "The conceit just oozes out of the ears of this guy." Leonard followed Dario to a nearby parking garage. After a few minutes Dario emerged from the garage behind the wheel of his car. The investigator tailed Tengo to a weathered brownstone on West 51st Street off 9th Avenue. The 110-year-old building was in obvious need of a cosmetic overhaul.

Dario double parked, got out of the car and walked up the front steps of the brownstone. Leaning over the black wrought iron handrail he began tapping on the front window of the second-floor apartment. From his vehicle Leonard was able to see a woman come to the window. She raised her hand while extending her fingers, indicating that she would be out in five minutes. Dario acknowledged this with a nod and returned to his car.

When the woman exited her building, she joined Dario in his vehicle. In terms of appearance, she was the equivalent of Dario. She was in her late 20's, tall, blond and beautiful. There was something about her that looked familiar to Leonard, who thought, *What a peacherino this one is!*

The investigator tailed the couple to The Old Homestead Steakhouse. After Dario parked his car, Leonard did the same. The former NYPD detective followed the couple on foot to the restaurant. Once they were seated Leonard entered the restaurant in order to get a better view of the woman.

This babe looks just like Sharon Stone, thought Leonard, who had been a fan of the actress ever since seeing her in the movie, *Basic Instinct.* The private investigator proceeded to the restroom. When he came out, he could see that Dario and the woman were engrossed in what seemed like a serious conversation. Leonard left the restaurant and returned to the West 51 Street brownstone where the woman had been picked up. Once there he checked the mail contained in the exterior mailbox. He noted that the name associated with apartment number two was Mary Custer.

Leonard rang the bell to the first floor. A toothless older woman answered the door. Leonard flashed the duplicate gold shield he had made prior to retiring from the NYPD. The woman identified herself as the owner of the brownstone. It was obvious that she was a leftover in a neighborhood that was undergoing transition.

Using a pretext, Leonard told the landlord that he was a detective from the NYPD Missing Person Squad. He explained that he was endeavoring to locate someone, noting that he received information that the missing person might be staying at the landlord's address.

When the private eye asked who her tenants were, the landlord informed him of their identity and occupation. The senior citizen identified the second-floor tenant as Mary Custer, adding that Custer worked at the Kingly Castle Review on 8th Avenue. Leonard was familiar with the establishment, having often driven by the strip club.

To make things look good, Leonard showed the landlord a photo of his ex-wife, passing her off as the missing person he was looking for. The landlord indicated that she had never seen the person in the photograph. Leonard thanked her and returned to his vehicle.

The private investigator returned to the Old Homestead and waited outside in his car for Dario and Mary Custer to finish their lunch. When they did Leonard followed the couple to the Kingly Castle Review. After dropping his lunch date off at the Kingly Castle, Dario proceeded to his place of business/residence. At this point Leonard terminated the surveillance.

After telephonically posting Thomas Beasley of the information gathered, the attorney authorized Leonard to see what he could find out about Mary Custer. It was agreed that Leonard should later go to the Kingly Castle. Since he was going to be reimbursed for any expenses he ran up, the private investigator looked ahead to what he believed to be an enjoyable evening. Once inside the Kingly Castle the private investigator established that Mary Custer was a dancer at the strip club.

Leonard wasted no time buying drinks and enjoying Custer's lap dances. Healthy tips led Mary to believe that Leonard was a big spender who took a shine to her. She did her utmost to accommodate her new client. She was in no hurry to leave the side of such a generous customer.

As the drinks and money flowed, the private investigator began to discreetly ask Custer questions about herself. Leonard was effective in pretending that he had a sincere interest in Mary. Before he got around to figuring out a way to ask about Custer's connection to Dario Tengo, Leonard mentioned her resemblance to the actress Sharon Stone.

"I get that all the time," said Custer. "Do you like Sharon Stone?"

"What's not to like," answered Leonard, then asking for another lap dance.

"How much do you like Sharon Stone, honey?" asked the dancer.

"Plenty."

"Enough to pay for a date with her?"

Custer's come-hither proposition was tempting. After receiving payment for her dance Custer remained with Leonard. "Another go?" she asked.

"By all means," replied Leonard.

Custer mounted Leonard with a renewed passion. As the music played a deeper connection began to form.

"So, what do you do for a living, honey?" Custer asked after the song ended. She was trying to determine just how well off her client was.

"I dabble in a lot of things," answered the investigator vaguely. At this point Mary Custer noticed something on Leonard's ankle. A closer look caused her to realize that he was wearing an ankle holster.

"Are you a cop?" asked the dancer, pulling back.

"I'm no cop, sweetheart," laughed Leonard. "That's a hot one."

Leonard played his role perfectly, leading Mary to believe that he was connected to the mob. Once under this impression Custer asked no more questions. Now comfortable, Mary expressed that she was tired, noting that she hadn't had much sleep the night prior.

"So, sit down next to me and take a load off if you're tired," said Leonard.

"I can't, I have to make money."

"I'll pay for your time."

"You don't mind?" asked Custer, who liked the idea of being paid for her idleness. She had never experienced such consideration before from a customer.

"Nah, I don't mind. Take a blow, I'll pay for your time. I enjoy your company."

"Really?"

"Sure, I don't get to talk to a lot of movie stars."

"You like movie stars?"

"Sure, why not? I already told you that I like Sharon Stone.

"What's you name anyway?"

"I'm Mary. What's yours?"

"Everybody calls me Steady Teddy," answered Leonard. This amused the dancer.

"Can you keep a secret?" she asked, lowering her voice as she looked around her.

"Certainly. Shoot."

"I'm going to be opening up my own place pretty soon."

"What kind of place?"

"A private club for men where a member can spend time with sporting girls."

"Sporting girls, now that's an old term for it."

"It's going to be a high-class place in a brownstone not far from here. Everything will be done strictly by appointment. All the girls are going to look like famous people. You know, actresses, public figures, and people like that. We already have celebrity lookalikes just waiting to work for us."

"We?"

"I have a partner."

"Guy or girl?"

"A guy."

"Is he your boyfriend?"

"Not really," lied Mary, "he's just a good friend."

"Is he with people?" Leonard asked, referring to organized crime associations.

"Oh, no. He's a businessman." "What kind of business?" "He's in the shoe business."

"He must have money."

"Well, yes and no. He can pull some money out of the shoe business, but we need more."

"A good businessman never spends his own money," voiced Leonard.

"I've heard that. So, are you ever going to tell me what you do for money?"

"I'm in the private carting business," lied Leonard. "I got a lot of the big buildings in the city as clients." The ex-cop was fluid enough in his story to seem credible. "Tell me more about this partner friend of yours," said Leonard.

"Why?"

"If you need money, I may be willing to invest with you." Leonard's remark caused Custer to now see the investigator in a more promising light.

"He's a successful businessman from Italy, so he knows business. I know the rest and have the girls."

"His business is in Italy?"

"No, he owns a factory here in Manhattan. Are you serious about having an interest in financing us?"

"I'm willing to think about it."

"Well, while you think, I'm going to give you the lap dance of your life," announced the newly energized stripper, who whipped off her top and mounted her new friend.

***

TEDDY LEONARD WAS IN THE OFFICE of Thomas Beasley the following afternoon. Arriving at the lawyer's office unannounced, he was anxious to report what he had learned from Mary Custer. The private investigator headed directly to Beasley private office.

"Excuse me," said Beasley's secretary, who knew who Leonard was. "Do you have an appointment?"

"Chill out, sweetheart," advised the private investigator. "Just let the boss know I'm here."

Clara disliked Leonard. She resented being called sweetheart and being told to chill out. After checking with her boss, she gave him the green light to enter Beasley's office.

"Go in," advised Clara.

"And you were worried," said the smug investigator as he passed the secretary's desk. Clara's half smile smacked of antipathy.

"That's a real prize you got working for you out there," said Leonard, upon entering the lawyer's private office.

"Who, Clara?"

"How does she travel around, by broom?"

"Never mind her," said Beasley. "Tell me how you made out." "I got good results."

"Give me the recap and start from the beginning."

"Dario is in solid with a stripper named Mary Custer. He picked her up at home and took her for eats at The Old Homestead."

"Where does she live?"

"In a brownstone in Hells Kitchen. After lunch, he drops her off at the Kingly Castle Review where she works. Then our boy goes home, or to work, and I break it off."

"And later?"

"Later I go to the strip club and get friendly with Mary Custer. Now remember, lap dances cost money."

"Go on."

"Dario and this stripper are planning to open up a private club together."

"Really? What kind of a club?"

"A whore house club. They need money to pull this off. Dario intends to tap into the shoe factory bankroll."

"How does he propose to do that?"

"That you'll have to ask him. To tell you the truth, this club their planning doesn't sound like a bad idea. All the hookers are going be celebrity lookalikes. This Custer is a dead ringer for Sharon Stone."

"It does sound like a good idea," agreed Beasley.

"I could go back and get deeper into this if you like. The girl thinks I'm a potential investor."

If I could get an underage kid working for them in their brothel, I could drop a dime, thought Beasley. That'll get Dario scooting back to the old country with his tail between his legs for sure.

"Hold off on that," said the attorney. "I want to confer with the client."

"Whatever you say, Tommy."

"You did a good job, Teddy. What's the damage at the end of the day?" After learning the balance of what he owed, the attorney opened his office safe and made a cash payment without balking. Their business relationship was longstanding, thus erasing the need of invoices or the breakdown of expenses. While the cost was high, the information gathered was believed by Beasley to be worth the money.

"You know that secretary you got gave me an earful for not calling for an appointment."

"Leave her alone, she's good at her job," said the lawyer. "Besides, you should call first."

"If I were you, I'd look to upgrade my help. That secretary isn't nothing to write home about."

Clara, who had her ear to the door, heard this remark. Sensitive to her appearance, a tear began to journey down her cheek. That bastard has a lot of nerve, she thought as she rushed to her station.

Later that day, after getting over what she overheard, the offended secretary got around to wondering why Maria Frantellini wanted the crude private eye to shadow Dario Tengo.

6

New Mama Drama

THE TIME THAT RICHARD FRANTELLINI spent in Milan was helpful to his mental state. Both he and Father St. Denis found it comfortable staying within Milan's Centro Storico, at the spacious home of Richard's physician daughter and her husband, Dr. Ettore Tengo.

While Caroline and Ettore were tending to their patients, the priest urged Richard to join him in exploring the historical center. At first Richard was reluctant to venture beyond his daughter's home. However, eventually he began to get bored. It was at this point that Richard went along with the priest.

The historical center had lots to offer with its history and landmarks. Father St. Denis in particular thoroughly enjoyed the time they spent at the Duomo Cathedral, one of the world's largest churches. An unforeseen low point for Richard came during their visit to Via Montenapoleone, a Milan street known for its high-end boutiques and luxury brands. The flagship stores caused Richard to think of his late wife. He grew emotional as he recalled how, citing expensiveness, he discouraged the late Angela out of shopping there.

As the weeks passed things began to improve for Richard, who was slowly regaining some of his prior form. As he came to grips with Angela's death, he began to restore emotionally. At this juncture both Richard and the priest knew that the time had come for them to journey home to

America.

Richard and Father St. Denis embarked on their journey home with enthusiasm. Richard was anxious to see how his business was doing. Father St. Denis had the same thought regarding his church.

Richard sat on the airplane between Father St. Denis and a highly attractive, well styled woman who appeared to be substantially younger than Richard. The flight into Kennedy Airport was practically turbulence free, thus relieving any apprehension about being in the air. The smoothness of the journey enabled Richard and the priest to speak freely. They never realized the attention they generated from the woman seated next to Richard.

After gathering that the man seated next to her was an affluent widower who owned the Frantellini Shoe Factory, the interest of the female passenger spiked. As a resident of Manhattan, the woman was familiar with the successful entity. This knowledge prompted her to improve her appearance. She removed lipstick and a small mirror from her purse. The passenger then shifted her body toward Richard as she applied the lipstick.

Once satisfied that she was appearing her best, she began looking through the catalogue she removed from the storage compartment of the seat in front of her. Pretending to be reading the catalogue, she was actually listening to the men seated beside her.

Perceiving Richard to be a potential sugar daddy, she glanced over at Richard several times and smiled sweetly. Both Frantellini and Father St. Denis were too absorbed in their conversation to realize they were being targeted for conversation. When mention was made of the financial potential connected to The Dynamic Shoe that was under development at the shoe factory, the woman next to Richard tired of waiting. Perking up, she made the overture to engage Richard in conversation.

"Excuse me," she began in her sweetest voice, "but I couldn't help but overhear what you gentlemen were talking about. With you being a businessman, I'd like to ask your opinion on something. Do you mind?"

Turning to look at the stranger, Richard was taken aback. Coming face to face with someone he considered a ravishing beauty caused him to pause before answering.

"Why, of course I don't mind," he finally replied. "How can I help you?"

Richard heard nothing of the question posed. The widower was fixed on the smiling woman's wealth of light brown hair and striking blue eyes. Richard estimated her to be about twenty-five years his junior. Intimidated by beauty, little did he know that beneath the facade of loveliness rested a vixen well versed in using her physical attributes to charm men into doing whatever she wanted.

"Did you hear my question?" she asked when Richard failed to reply. Realizing the effect she was having on Richard, her smile broadened. She was genuinely pleased.

"Why no, could you please repeat that," Richard finally managed to utter. After Richard provided an answer to the question posed, his new acquaintance zeroed in.

"My name is Rhonda, but my friends call me Ronnie."

"Pleased to meet you," answered Richard.

"And you are?"

"I'm Richard Frantellini."

As they continued to converse, Richard's new friend removed the jacket she was wearing.

"It's awful warm in here, isn't it?" Ronnie asked, justifying her shedding of the jacket.

"Yes, it is," answered Richard, while sneaking glances at Ronnie's ample breasts.

Ronnie could see that the treasures displayed before Richard were effective in gaining his attention. Their conversation went on to be lengthy. As Father St. Denis napped in his seat dreaming of one day being a Monsignor, Richard was ensnared in a well-set trap that was to culminate in marriage months later following a whirlwind romance.

As things turned out, Ronnie's influence proved to be a remedy for Richard's blues. Her antidote proved to be far more effective than anything that Father Fiorello St. Denis or the physicians in Milan conjured up.

***

RONNIE BORDEN HAD GROWN UP in the Inwood section of northern Manhattan without the benefit of a mother. She was raised by raised by a self-employed father with a weakness for alcohol. His weakness for John Barleycorn restricted the plumber to only taking on small jobs. On occasions when in need of support, Mr. Borden took on a helper. More often than not the helper, a fellow alcoholic, was only too happy to work off the books.

When the time for compensation arrived for completed work the father paid his helper the cash due him. The majority of the money they made was then spent drinking in a sawdust saloon frequented by similar types. Once their funds diminished, the intoxicated duo would then make their way to the Borden apartment where they would resume drinking in front of the plumber's waiting young daughter.

As she matured, Ronnie's routine only became more problematic. Whenever her father passed out, Ronnie found herself fending off advances made by men her father took home to drink with him. The scarred Ronnie was barely eighteen years old when her father died of cirrhosis of the liver. By that time, she was well attuned to the dark side of life. Left to navigate the world alone at an early age, Ronnie was a hardened woman who gave no quarter in her dealings with people.

Ronnie's early exposure left her with a blurred perception of right and wrong. For Ronnie, life was a matter of looking out for number one. The code of conduct she followed was a selfish and unethical one. All was fair in order to achieve the end result desired, which was acquiring enough money to sustain herself in comfort.

Ronnie came to rely on her beauty to see her through. She weaponized this God given gift, using it as a tool to exploit men. Ronnie's adult history was comprised of a litany of financial settlements. Whenever money ran short, she'd find herself another mark that she could compromise and then extort.

The plane ride from Italy to New York was a heaven-sent gift for Ronnie. Richard proved to be putty in the hands of Ronnie. The business owner was so smitten that he was too blind to even inquire about Ronnie's past. As far as Richard was concerned, Ronnie made him feel invigorated, and that was all that mattered. Even the early warnings of Father St. Denis to tread carefully had little impact.

Ronnie went on to exert Svengali-like control over Richard that culminated with their marrying. Her power over the business owner was of a magnitude once not thought possible. Most amazing was Ronnie's ability to make Richard forget all about his aversion to spending money frivolously. All the second Mrs. Frantellini had to do was ask, and she got whatever it was that she wanted.

Once settled in as Mrs. Frantellini, Ronnie's set a new goal for herself. Her aim was to secure solid footing in all of the Frantellini enterprises. In answer to her want, Richard appeased his wife by giving her a high-level position at the shoe factory.

As a senior vice president with unexplained duties, Ronnie had made inroads into the Frantellini fortune. With Ronnie's new title came a salary, a company car and an expense account. The company American Express card was used liberally by Ronnie. Her clothes, spa treatments and whatever else she wanted were charged.

Ronnie's lavish spending eventually found her at odds with Maria Frantellini, Richard's youngest daughter. Maria took her role as chief financial officer seriously. She saw her stepmother as an even larger drain on the family business than Dario Tengo. Desperate to diminish Ronnie's power, Maria telephoned her sister in Milan.

Dr. Caroline Frantellini Tengo, content with the good life in Italy she was leading with her physician husband, expressed little interest in the doings of the Frantellini enterprises. When it came to her father, she conveyed that if Ronnie was making Richard happy, that was all that mattered. Caroline's attitude infuriated Maria, who abruptly hung up on her sister.

The tumultuous relationship between Maria and her stepmother finally came to a head during the tax season. Aware that Ronnie's spending habits would be a red flag to the Internal Revenue Service, Maria informed her stepmother that her spending needed to be curbed. This resulted in an intense argument between the two women. Eventually the power struggle escalated. Richard, hearing the ruckus from his private office, threw the newspaper he was reading down on his desk. He then hurried into the hall to investigate the cause of the disturbance.

In restoring civility, Richard had listened to both sides of the argument. He then made the decision to side with his second wife over his daughter. "Take it easy, Maria," said Richard. "Let the accountant worry about it."

Once Ronnie gained the upper hand, there was no discouraging her authority. She even got Richard to secretly amend his will to where it read that after he died, Ronnie was to inherit half of all he owned, this included the shoe factory and the real estate portfolio.

With the will amended, Ronnie set out to learn all aspects of the Frantellini business interests. Richard's new wife licked her lips as her husband spoke of the projected profits to be made with The Dynamic Shoe that was close to being perfected. Ronnie found the money to be made on the new product to be staggering. The anticipated windfall that was to come one day caused Ronnie to see value in getting close to Victor Spinello, the creative minority partner. By controlling Victor, Ronnie imagined herself as one day being the supreme power behind the Frantellini empire.

Ronnie immediately recognized Dario Tengo for what he was, a shifty man who had taken advantage of the naïve Victor Spinello. Ronnie planned to one day remove Dario from the equation by either buying him out or resorting to whatever means necessary.

Richard's wife saw her stepdaughters, who one day would come into the other half of Richard's assets, as the only true complication when it came to her reigning supreme. With Caroline, the doctor rooted in Italy, Ronnie didn't see much of a threat. Distance, Ronnie believed, would provide her with the upper hand. The younger daughter, Maria, on the other hand was a different story. Maria was a force that would have to be neutralized.

***

MARIA FRANTELLINI WAS so upset over the situation with her

stepmother that she couldn't concentrate on dealing with the antics of minority partner Dario Tengo. The treatment she received from her father Richard after her altercation with Ronnie left her feeling betrayed. *The hell with him*, she thought in a moment of anger, referring to her father. *If he is too stupid to see things, let him learn his lesson the hard way!*

Maria didn't actually believe what she was thinking. She knew down deep, that after time passed, she'd cool off. At that point she'd figure out a way to secure her place as the heir apparent to the Frantellini empire.

Richard's youngest daughter telephoned the attorney Thomas Beasley to inform him to suspend his investigation into Dario Tengo for the time being. Beasley was surprised to hear this. "Why the change of heart?" asked the attorney.

"There are things going on with my stepmother," replied Maria. "I just can't deal with Dario right now. There are bigger fish that require frying."

"But we were making headway in finding out about Dario."

"Let it go, Tommy. I just can't be bothered with Dario right now."

"Think this over. If Dario is doing what he's doing, it's he's got other big ideas," warned the lawyer. "I'm telling you, Maria. this guy Dario needs to be watched."

"AND I'M TELLING YOU, NOT NOW!" Maria shouted.

Beasley realized that he overstepped. "Okay, don't get excited, Maria. I'm just trying to look out for you."

"I'll talk to you later, Tom, goodbye." "Wait a second, there is something you need to know. Your father and his new wife in here to amend his will. Ronnie now gets half of everything when your father goes."

"Half of the shoe factory and real estate?"

"The works." The line went silent as Marie digested this information. "Are you still there?" asked Beasley.

"I have to go."

"When are you coming to my office?"

When the attorney heard the line go dead, he knew the answer to his question.

7

Dario Gets Ambitious

IT WAS 4:50 A.M. WHEN A TIRED DARIO TENGO tiptoed into the apartment he shared with Victor Spinello. Having just returned from hours of passion with Mary Custer he was anxious to go to bed. Moving quietly, he was respectful enough not to disturb Victor, who was asleep in his room.

Dario tore a page off the spiral pad that was on the kitchen counter and scribbled a note to Victor. The message indicated that he wouldn't be at work that day. He then went to brush his teeth. After finishing he taped the note to the mirror over the bathroom sink for Victor to see.

Dario quickly undressed and slipped into a pair of white silk pajamas. After checking the time, he decided to call his wife in Italy before turning in. He lit a cigarette and sat in a chair while waiting to make the call. At 5:00 A.M. he began dialing. It was 11:00 A.M. in the old country.

Dario was blowing smoke rings as he waited for his wife to answer his long-distance call. While he longed for his children a little, the same couldn't be said of his wife Gia. Frolicking with Mary Custer was a sufficient enough distraction for him to seldom think of the woman four thousand miles away on the other side of the Atlantic.

When Gia answered the phone, she proved to be true to form. Weary of the loneliness of being without her husband, she began questioning Dario about when she and their children would be allowed to come to America.

This request was out of the question as far as Dario was concerned. He was having too much fun living the life of a single man to be anchored by children and a wife who would keep an eye on his every move. Besides that, there was the brothel venture with Custer to think about. That was an enterprise that Gia would surely stand in the way of. These things dampened any notion of Dario reuniting with his wife in New York.

To eliminate the chance of Gia ever showing up in New York with their children unannounced, Tengo limited the amount of money he sent to her. He justified this by maintaining that business at the shoe factory was bad.

"We can't afford to have you come over right now, Gia."

"Don't lie to me, Dario!" Gia shouted with great emotion. "I'm not your fool any longer. I know you have lots of money. The priest told me how well the shoe factory is doing!"

"What priest?"

"Father St. Denis."

"You can't believe everything you hear, Gia."

"Father told me everything. I know all about the great success of the Frantellini Sole in America. Father wouldn't lie to me."

"No, of course not. But appearances can be deceiving. This priest has no idea of the overhead connected to operating a factory. There are expenses."

"The children and I are coming to America, Dario. Even if I have to borrow the money, we are coming."

"What has gotten into you, Gia?"

"If you don't send me the money, I'm going to see my uncle. He has friends in America that will know how to straighten things out for me."

"Which uncle?" Dario asked, taking this as a threat.

"You know which uncle....Pasqualino."

The mention of Gia's mafia connected uncle gave Dario pause. "Are you crazy, Gia? You don't need to involve him in our affairs."

"Then send me the money."

"If it's so important to you, of course I will. Just give me some time to scrape up the money and I'll send it to you."

"Don't give me that, Dario! I know that you have the money!"

At this juncture Dario backed off. He fabricated a tale that flowed easily from his mouth. Dario explained that he had a good reason for preventing his family from coming to America. He articulated that he couldn't risk being distracted by family demands. He advised that he was absorbed in putting together a lucrative business deal that would leave them financially set once it came to fruition. Gia accepted this explanation not because Dario was convincing, but rather, she wanted his words to be true. It made reconciliation easier.

Before hanging up the two spoke of purchasing a luxurious family home once Dario's ship came in. The husband neglected to point out that the home was going to be located somewhere in New Jersey. A distance great enough to allow him to continue living as if he were a single man when in Manhattan.

After an unsound night's sleep, Dario changed his mind about not going to his office at the Frantellini Shoe Factory. On his way to the factory kitchen to get a cup of coffee, he ran into Maria Frantellini. The look she gave him was a cool one. The iciness of Richard Frantellini's youngest daughter made it vividly clear that she was upset with Dario. As to why this was so, Dario didn't know for sure.

This spoiled brat, thought Dario of Maria as he put sugar in his coffee. I'm the one who should be bitter. I'm the one who was cheated by her father! After taking a sip of coffee Dario continued to work himself up. *After all, I was the one responsible for bringing the Frantellini Sole to the table, reasoned Dario. It should really be called the Tengo-Spinello Sole!*

Once in his office Dario's malcontent was further fueled by thoughts of Maria exerting her authority as the chief financial officer. Maria's appointment, and the emergence of Richard Frantellini's new wife as an additional layer of authority, added to Dario's displeasure. Why the two women were awarded such positions was baffling to the chauvinistic Dario.

Dario sat in his office perusing the newspaper in an effort to take his mind off the doings at the factory. The crime-related accounts he read only further disturbed him. Home invasions, murders and the like were so frequent in New York City that he saw a need to have protection in the form of a gun. Then there was the concern of his wife's uncle coming after him one day. Later that evening he turned to his American lover, Mary Custer for relief.

"Mary, I need a favor," said Dario over an early dinner at Tio Pepe, a West Village restaurant.

"Sure, sweetie, what's the favor?" Mary asked pleasantly. Seeing Mary chew her food caused Dario to momentarily take his mind off what he was doing.

"I, uh, forgot what I was going to say." *Jesus,* he thought, *her resemblance to Sharon Stone really is amazing. I can't even think straight!*

"It can't be that important then."

"Wait, I remember. I want a pistol," he answered. "Can you help me with that?"

"What do you need a gun for?"

"Protection."

"Protection from who?"

"Don't ask silly questions, Mary. I need a gun to protect both of us, especially now that we are going to be in business together. Do you have a connection that can get me one?"

"Maybe. What kind of a gun are you looking for?"

"I want a revolver. They are more dependable."

"I'll find out when I go into work later."

"Who are you seeing?"

"A connected guy." "Connected to who?"

"No names, Dario. Remember, curiosity killed the cat."

"I understand. Tell me, do you have a friend who looks like Sophia Loren?" he asked, thinking of his own personal fantasy woman.

"You want me to find you a Sophia Loren lookalike?"

"Well, not for me of course," answered Dario, taking the hand of his lover. "I'm content. This is for our business."

"Whatever," said Custer. "So, when are you seeing that Chinese man?"

"I have an appointment to see him this week in Connecticut."

"Do you think he'll back us?"

"Why wouldn't he?"

"How can you be so sure?"

"I have a shoe deal that he is going to want in on. Once I sell him on that, I'll make that deal contingent on his going in with us on our celebrity lookalike business."

"You just gave me an idea!" Custer said with great enthusiasm. "We could call our place the C.L.C. Club!"

"What are you talking about, Mary? What is C.L.C. supposed to stand for?'

"Celebrity Lookalike Club!"

"That's a catchy name. It might work."

***

THE SIXTY-TWO-YEAR-OLD CHEN LOWE was an exceedingly smart businessman. Born in Canton, Lowe settled in San Francisco where he worked in his uncle's restaurant as a cook. Taking morning classes, he pursued an education in business. Upon graduation Chen approached his uncle regarding an opportunity to gain experience in the shoe business. A sufferer of bad feet, the uncle wished Chen well, figuring that good shoes might do him some good. Two years later the uncle gambled and financed his nephew in a business of his own. Chen Lowe proved to be the best investment the uncle had ever made.

Chen's small business evolved into the Chen Lowe Footwear Company. Ever on the lookout for an opportunity to expand, Chen met with an accountant who had ties to a Russian entity that produced orthopedic shoes. This led to Chen opening a new factory in Bridgeport, Connecticut that specialized in orthopedic shoes.

Lowe, who had relocated to Connecticut, was always on the alert for new opportunities. He was receptive to meeting Dario Tengo once he learned that Dario held an interest in the Frantellini Shoe Factory. Lowe was hoping that the Frantellini organization might be looking to sell their shoe factory.

At their meeting in Chen Lowe's office in Bridgeport, Dario explained that he was on the verge of developing a groundbreaking product designed to combat foot issues. Chen, a short balding man who was impossible to read due to his poker face, listened quietly. When he finally did speak, he did so through his general counsel, who was present for the meeting. The lawyer's words were brief.

"Tell Mr. Lowe more about this new product," said the general counsel.

""It's a new type of shoe. We call it The Dynamic Shoe." Dario then expanded on the product.

"You developed this product on your own?"

"Not exactly. I have a partner who is a creative genius."

"Your partner also has an interest in the Frantellini Shoe Factory?"

"Yes, we both have a small amount of equity. We receive peanuts for creating the Frantellini Sole."

Remaining silent, this remark caused Chen Lowe to display a wry smile.

"That unfortunately is the price for making a bad deal, Mr. Tengo," said the general counsel.

"Well, we aren't making the same mistake with this Dynamic Shoe of ours."

"Aren't there contractual restrictions?"

"We are under no obligation when it comes to developing a new product."

At this point Chen Lowe said something to his general counsel in Chinese.

"Perhaps we could do business, Mr. Tengo," advised the general counsel, "providing that your product is capable of performing as you say it can. However, I must admit that I am a bit skeptical that it can do all that you say. Mr. Lowe will need to see proof."

"Once I prove to you that this product is all I say it is, what would our deal be?" Again, the general counsel and Lowe spoke in Chinese.

"Mr. Lowe proposes that a subsidiary be formed in which he holds sixty percent. You and your partner will divide the remaining forty percent. The new shoes will be produced here at the Bridgeport facility. I assume that's acceptable."

"That sounds fair. But there is a second opportunity that goes along with the first."

"And what is that?"

Dario went on to explain the gentleman's club vision he had with Mary Custer. The idea of celebrity lookalike hookers intrigued Chen who listened attentively. In his silence the businessman instantly thought of a way to enhance the idea. He had a friend in NYC's Chinatown area who could install poker machines in the proposed sex parlor.

"Have you a photograph of Ms. Custer?" asked Chen, finally speaking up. "I'd like to see exactly how much she looks like Sharon Stone."

"No, I don't. Are you available this evening? I'll take you to see her at the club where she works."

"I'll send my general counsel to go with you."

Acutely aware of the vices that attract men, Chen Lowe liked the idea of having an interest in a sex and gambling business in Manhattan. Once he received positive news from his general council regarding Mary Custer, Chen had his lawyer convey that there was an interest in doing business.

The general counsel sought clarification from Dario in one area. He wanted to know if Victor Spinello was involved in the brothel proposal. Dario assured him that the enterprise didn't involve Victor. The lawyer was happy to hear this. Having one less partner was good news for Chen.

At this point Dario Tengo was certain that he was on his way to achieving important things. All he needed to do now was let Victor in on his plans to double-cross the Frantellini family. With the money to be made, the conniving Dario was confident that he'd run into no resistance from his friend. In this assumption he was sadly mistaken.

8

News Travels Fast

IT WAS CLOSE TO 5:00 A.M. WHEN THE BODY of Dario Tengo was discovered in his car. An early riser who was going to work had been walking to his car when he noticed a parked vehicle with its engine running. Sensitive to climate change, the curious citizen was passionate in his dislike of vehicles releasing harmful pollutants and greenhouse gases. The activist approached the idling vehicle to remind the occupant of the harm he was doing to the environment.

Seeing the driver slumped over to one side of the vehicle caused the pedestrian to think that the motorist was either intoxicated or had taken ill. The pedestrian tapped on the driver's side window to gain the attention of the car occupant. Looking closer, he saw the blood. Unaccustomed to such gruesomeness, a pained expression came over the citizen's face. He took out his cell phone and failed 911. Between nervous gulps he advised the emergency dispatcher of his discovery. The man reluctantly agreed to the dispatcher's request that he remain at the scene until the police arrived.

Two detectives assigned to the Manhattan Night Watch were notified by the uniformed police officers who responded to the Washington Heights crime scene. The duties of the overnight investigators were limited. Their duty called for them to conduct an initial inquiry and get the investigative ball rolling. This entailed their safeguarding the crime scene, interviewing the discoverer of the body and calling for a forensic team to respond to the location. Before going home, they submitted a report regarding the results of the actions they took. Relief for the overnight investigators would come when the precinct detectives arrived for work and assumed responsibility.

By the time the precinct sleuths arrived the forensic team was well into their work. They had taken their photos, dusted the interior and exterior of the vehicle for fingerprints and discovered the handgun used to kill Dario Tengo. The weapon was also dusted for fingerprints. It was established that the prints lifted from the gun were of value. The chore now was to match the prints lifted off the gun to a person.

The precinct detectives conducted a canvass of the area while the crime scene unit continued their work. The forensic team met with a startling surprise when they got around to examining the body. They were stunned to see that the inner sole of a shoe was lodged in the dead man's mouth. This additional evidence was processed and vouchered along with the murder weapon.

Once back at the precinct the local detectives, a male and female team, went through the belongings of the dead man. The contents in the wallet of the victim identified him, his address and his place of employment.

"His name is Dario Tengo. He has an ID card from the Frantellini Shoe Factory," said the female detective to her partner.

"The car comes back to the shoe factory," indicated the male detective after researching the license plate. "The factory is located downtown."

"What do you make of this shoe sole jammed in his mouth?"

"I don't know." What's that printing on the shoe sole say?"

"It says, Frantellini Sole."

"Let's go to the factory after we finish vouchering this stuff. Somebody over there will probably know a family member to notify."

"The serial number on this gun is filed off. Maybe this was an organized crime hit," conjectured the female detective.

"That could be."

***

RICHARD FRANTELLINI WAS in his office chatting with Father Fiorello St. Denis. St. Denis was there to talk to Richard about his health. Frantellini had confided in his friend about the chest discomfort he'd been experiencing in recent weeks. St. Denis recommended that Richard take his health seriously and see his doctor.

"You're not a young man anymore, Richard," the priest reminded. "Don't forget that you suffer from high blood pressure and high cholesterol. And those other pills you take could also be having an adverse effect on you," said the priest. He was referring to Viagra.

"I need those pills to take care of Ronnie, Father. I told you about that."

"Forget your wife's needs, Richard," advised the priest. "You'll be of no use to anyone if you are dead."

"You take care of my soul, Father," was Richard's standard reply. "Let me worry about the rest."

When the detectives showed up at the shoe factory they were led to Richard's office by a factory supervisor. Once there they informed Richard that Dario Tengo had been murdered. Upon hearing the shocking news Richard grew visibly upset. He then suddenly felt that familiar pain that he attributed to heartburn. As in the past, the pain subsided.

Maria Frantellini took the news of Dario's demise much better than her father. The knowledge she gained as a result of having Dario shadowed fostered a callousness where the dead man was concerned. She preferred to see the upside to Dario's murder. With Dario gone, her only existing concern rested with Ronnie, her stepmother. She only wished that Ronnie Frantellini could have been found dead in the car alongside Dario.

Maria's cold-heartedness toward her stepmother was hardly surprising. She had always been suspicious of Ronnie's sincerity in loving her father. Maria considered her stepmother a shrewd manipulator who possessed an extraordinary influence over her father. Ronnie held a power that Maria was envious of.

As far as Dario's murder went, all in the Frantellini family thought alike. Each member now believed that Victor Spinello's absence from work was no coincidence. They harbored thoughts that Victor must have knowledge of, or involvement in, what happened to Dario. The Frantellini Sole found in the mouth of the victim convinced them of this.

For selfish reasons, not one Frantellini family member conveyed their suspicions to the authorities when interviewed. Victor was considered too valuable an asset to the Frantellini organization to run the risk of losing.

Whenever faced with a difficult decision, Richard inevitably turned to Father Fiorello St. Denis for counsel. The priest thought the Dario Tengo matter out minus emotional interference.

"The detectives said that you have to notify Dario's wife in Milan," said the priest.

"Please take care of that for me, Father. Gia is a true believer. I think that she'll take the news better hearing it from you."

"Of course, Richard," replied the man of the cloth. "I'll assume that responsibility."

"Maybe you could also call my daughter Caroline, and her husband, in Milan. Dario's brother Ettore needs to know."

"I'll notify them as well, so don't fret. Remember, you need to look after your health."

"Ettore will probably want the body shipped back to Milan."

"Don't worry about that, Richard. I'll tend to what needs to be done."

"Thank you, Father."

"You know, as a police department chaplain, I can get things done in terms of the investigation into Dario's death," advised the priest. "I can call the Chief of Detectives and have him look into this terrible situation. At least then we'll know that everything possible is being done."

"I suppose that's a good idea," said Richard, after letting out a deep sigh. It was clear that he was fatigued. Father St. Denis wasted no time calling Chief of Detectives Harry McCoy. McCoy, for political reasons, was a man who wanted to stay on the good side of the department chaplain. In answer to the priest's request, the chief assigned Detective Sergeant Al Markie to get involved in the murder investigation of Dario Tengo.

9

Duty Calls

THERE WAS MINIMAL TALK IN THE CAR on the drive to Washington Heights. Detective Oliver Von Hess drove slowly so that he wouldn't upset the hungover Al Markie's equilibrium. The sergeant sat quietly in the passenger front seat with his head back and his eyes closed. Whenever Von Hess inadvertently went over a bump in the pavement Markie let out a low groan.

"Easy, Ollie, you're killing me," advised the sergeant after Ollie stopped short at a light.

"Sorry, Sarge. How are you holding up."

"I'll live."

"Do you want me to pull over for a bit?" "No, keep going."

The sergeant was recovering from a recent drunk that challenged his recuperative abilities. His condition was fragile. The bender Markie had been on was severe enough to require additional time to restore himself to his usual form.

"How are you holding up, Sarge?" Von Hess again asked ten minutes later.

"I'll be okay, stop asking," replied Markie, who then turned his head to look out of the passenger side window. The supervisor sat motionless with his hands resting atop his thighs. A few minutes later he turned to Von Hess.

"I don't know how I allowed myself to fall so hard for that woman, Ollie."

"It, happens, Sarge. You're not the first guy who thought with his little head."

"Rochelle either slipped something in my drink or Cupid shot me in the ass with one of his arrows."

"It's better you found out about her now, rather than later. You just need a little time to forget her."

"Don't worry about me when it comes to that. I'll live without Rochelle Parish, that you can bank on."

Markie was putting on a false front. Despite the bravado, his feelings remained strong for Rochelle. Her favoring a married professional wrestler over him continued to pain the detective sergeant.

Markie again put his head back and rested his eyes. He immediately began reliving the past. He saw himself attending the Madison Square Garden wrestling matches with Rochelle. They always sat close enough to the ring to see the beads of sweat pour out of the battling contestants.

Markie vividly recalled Rochelle's glee as she thrilled at the antics of the performers in the squared circle. Envisioning her smile made him smile. Von Hess glanced over at Markie to see how he was doing. The detective wondered what his sergeant was so amused by.

He must be starting to improve, thought Von Hess.

Markie continued to dwell on yesterday. His smile evaporated once the face of the man Rochelle threw him over for came into focus. I don't get what Rochelle sees in that tomahawk toting phony Indian of hers, thought Markie. The sergeant began muttering something under his breath as he recollected the grappler in question breaking into a mid-ring war dance that came complete with his tapping his mouth with his fingers as he whooped."

"What did you say, Sarge?" asked Von Hess, who heard Markie's utterance.

"I was just clearing my throat," replied the boss. Once they arrived at the Washington Heights precinct Von Hess introduced himself and Markie to Detective Ellison, the female investigator assigned to investigate the Dario Tengo homicide. He then stated his purpose for being there.

"The chief of detectives has an interest in this homicide?"
Ellison asked

"Yeah, a big enough interest to send the sergeant and me here to pitch in," answered Von Hess.

Since working in a busy detective squad meant catching an endless flow of new cases, Ellison wasn't against receiving support. Her only reservation was the possibility of her being pushed aside in her own investigation. Her concern was addressed tactfully by Markie, who assured her that this would not be the case. With the air having been cleared, the detectives went on to work cohesively together.

After going over the facts of the case all agreed that there had to have been a reason why the Frantellini Sole was lodged in the mouth of the homicide victim. The detectives believed that the answer to the commission of such a vile act might be found at the Frantellini Shoe Factory.

Detective Ellison, a ten-year veteran of the force, indicated to Markie that she had spoken to the key principles at the shoe factory. She communicated that she learned little from them. She pointed out that she was told that the homicide victim had a minority interest in the factory.

"It's going to take a little work, Sarge," said Ellison. "But I'll get to the bottom of this." The detectives from headquarters found the detective's optimism to be admirable.

"No one at the factory had anything to say about the sole being stuffed in the dead man's mouth?" Von Hess asked.

"Not a thing," answered Ellison. "They all just looked at each other without saying a word."

"Was it a puzzled look or more like a knowing look?"

"That's hard to say."

"Did Dario Tengo have some kind of a personal connection to the sole?" Markie questioned.

"He did, Sarge. The victim invented the sole with a partner, Victor Spinello."

"That's somebody to talk to," said Markie. "Did you get to speak with Spinello?"

"Didn't get a chance. He didn't show up for work. I left word that he should contact me."

"Did you look at the dead man's cell phone?"

"Not yet, Sarge." "Let's do that now."

An examination of the victim's cell phone uncovered information that merited looking into. The numbers memorialized in the phone were accompanied by a name and/or a business. One noteworthy number was that belonging to Chen Lowe of the Connecticut based Chen Lowe Footwear Company. Another frequently called number was to a woman named Mary Custer. Next to Custers name in the cell phone contact list was the name of a strip club.

"How about we do this," said Markie, addressing Detective Ellison.

"Ollie and I will go out in the field and start digging. While we do this, how about you take care of what needs to be done from the office.

"That's fine, Sarge," stated Ellison. "You'll keep me posted, right?"

"Definitely. And if you hear from this Victor Spinello, give us a shout."

"Perfect."

"Did you by any chance go through Dario Tengo's office or where he lived?"

"No, Sarge. As far as where he lived, the victim shared an apartment with Victor Spinello over the shoe factory." "Now that's interesting," commented Markie.

"What do you make of the Chen Lowe Footwear Company connection, Sarge?" asked Von Hess, once He and the sergeant returned to their car.

"I don't know, Ollie. Maybe we'll need to go to Connecticut. But let's concentrate on that Manhattan strip club first."

"The Kingly Castle Review?"

"Yeah. Let's dig up this Mary Custer and see what she and Dario Tengo had going."

"I can hardly wait," commented Von Hess.

"You could tell your wife all about how you visited a strip club when you get home." Von Hess let out a booming laugh.

"Do you think I'm nuts?" he asked.

"Did you happen to take a good look at that sole they recovered from the mouth of the victim, Ollie?"

"Yeah, it was a black sole with gold lettering that reflected it was a Frantellini Sole."

"Did you notice how small that sole was?"

"Come to think of it, it was kind of small."

"Somewhere out there is a pair of shoes with only one inner sole, Ollie."

"Good point. How is you stomach holding up, Sarge?"

"Getting there. Do me a favor, let's stop someplace where I could get something solid in my stomach."

"Do you want to sit down?"

"No, I just want to pick up something."

"Righto, Sarge. I'll stop by Joe's, he's good."

"Perfect," answered Markie, knowing that Joe never charged cops for what they ordered."

Once Markie had something in his belly he improved. "I really needed that," said the sergeant, referring to what he had just eaten.

"That's good, Sarge. You might need your strength for the strip club." "Nah, I'm swearing off women for a while." "Are you forgetting what you always say?"

"What's that?"

"The cure to one woman, is another one."

Markie laughed. "I got that line out of that movie, Of Human Bondage. I'm talking about the original flick with Bette Davis. It was good advice then, and I guess now as well."

10

Custer's Proposition

THE KINGLY CASTLE REVIEW was an upscale gentleman's club as far as such places went. A large facility, the enterprise operated on two floors. The first floor had a large, raised platform on which topless pole dancers entertained while attired only in a G-string or thong. Customers who sat around the square platform drank and got their jollies by placing their money between the flimsy covering and the intimate area of the dancers.

The rest of the room was sprinkled with scantily clad women who engaged with customers seated at tables or standing at the bar. Laptop dances were offered for a flat fee. For those willing to pay the price, there was also a private area where more involved arrangements could be made.

The second floor boasted a wraparound dining area where those seated at tables had a fine dinner as they looked down at the first-floor activities. The Kingly Castle Review could be rated high when it came to the food they provided.

The detectives approached the front entrance of The Kingly Castle appearing official. A serious looking Von Hess flashed his shield at the two security men/bouncers posted at the front door.

"Are you guys here on business or for pleasure?" Von Hess was asked.

"Business," replied the first-grade detective. "We're here to see Mary Custer."

"Just a minute, I'll get the boss."

A short time later one of the men at the door returned with a man who identified himself as the club manager. The manager was about fifty years old. The tinted glasses he wore made him seem like someone mobbed up. Of average height, he was attired in a black button-down shirt, navy blue slacks, thin black socks and burgundy loafers.

"How can I help you?" asked the manager.

"We'd like to see Mary Custer," said Von Hess. "Is she around?"

"Yeah, she here. But she's working."

"She takes a break, doesn't she?" asked Markie.

"Yeah, but that won't be for a long time. She just came off one." "Why don't you just go and get her," said Markie.

"Can't you see her after work?" asked the manager, "Time is money. If I pull her off the floor, we both lose money."

"Would you rather see us hanging around here all night until she finishes?" Markie asked.

This was the last thing the manager wanted. Besides the presence of the law being a distraction that made people uncomfortable, there was the outside chance of the detectives seeing customers engage in illegal transactions.

"Is Mary in some kind of trouble?"

"No, she's not in any trouble. We just need to ask her a few questions," voiced Von Hess.

"Okay, have a drink at the bar. I'll get her." Markie, still recovering from his last interaction with alcohol, declined the offer of a drink. Von Hess echoed the sergeant's refusal to imbibe.

After a few minutes, Mary Custer was introduced to the detectives by the manager. The manager then escorted the Sharon Stone lookalike and the detectives to a small office where they could converse in private.

When Mary asked why the detectives wanted to speak with her she was told that her telephone number was found as a contact on Dario Tengo's cell phone.

"So?" Mary asked innocently.

Markie replied bluntly. "So, Dario was found shot dead in his car in Washington Heights."

Mary gasped at hearing this. "Dario is dead?"

"Yeah, I'm afraid so. Do you have any idea what he'd be doing in Washington Heights?"

It took time for Custer to digest that her lover and potential business partner was gone. Her state of remorse was two-folded. The lost opportunity of one day owning her own business equaled her anguish over losing someone she genuinely liked.

"I have no idea what he'd be doing in Washington Heights," Mary finally answered. "Who killed him?"

"That's what we're trying to find out, Mary," answered Von Hess.

"What was your relationship to Dario."

"We were good friends." Von Hess detected something more.

"How good?" queried the detective. "Look," said Mary, now annoyed. "We liked each other, okay. Do I need to spell it out for you?"

"No, I just wanted to establish your relationship to him."

"What for? Do you think I killed Dario?"

"Look," injected Markie firmly, having lost patience. "For all we know you might have a pimp who didn't like the idea of you having a good friend. He might've had a reason to off Dario." Mary stiffened at the sergeant's suggestion. "I have no pimp," said Mary defiantly.

"Okay, don't get your G-string twisted. So, what was this great bond between you two?"

"Dario liked me because I resemble Sharon Stone, the actress."

"You do look like her," acknowledged the sergeant.

"And why did you like him?" Von Hess asked.

Mary shrugged at the question asked before replying. "I don't know," she answered.

"Make things clear to us, Mary, so we can get out of here," stated Markie, looking to move things along. "We aren't here to stop you from making a living, and you aren't going to be telling us anything that'll shock us."

Mary let out a deep sigh before responding. "We were planning to go into business together," she advised, seeing no harm in being truthful.

"What kind of business?"

"A private gentleman's club that features girls who look like famous people."

"For dating?"

When no reply was forthcoming, Von Hess began reciting the female names that were contained in Dario's phone.

"Do these names ring a bell to you?" Von Hess asked.

"They are the girls who were going to work for us. They all look like celebrities."

"Was Dario having any problems with anyone?" questioned Markie. "You know, like wise guys trying to muscle their way into your new business?"

"No, we had no issues like that. All I know is that Dario wasn't happy at the shoe factory he worked at."

"The Frantellini Shoe Factory?"

"That's right."

"What was the problem over there?"

"Dario felt that they were cheated out of the money they should have been getting."

"Who is they?"

"Dario's had a partner. They invented a shoe sole that they came over here from Italy with."

"Do you know the partner's name?" questioned Markie.

"Victor something. He works at the shoe factory."

"What do you know about Victor?"

"Only what Dario told me. He said that Victor is a brilliant inventor."

"Did you ever meet Victor?"

"No, there was no reason for me to meet him. Victor has nothing to with the business we were planning to start."

"I see," said the sergeant. "So, you don't know what he looks like?"

"I saw him once on the street when Dario pointed him out to me."

"Describe him for us."

"He's average looking and about the same age as Dario I suppose. Dark hair.

"Was he a big man or a small man?" Markie asked, recalling the small size of the Frantellini Sole that was recovered from the mouth of the murder victim.

"He was pretty small for a man I suppose." "He was short?"

"Yes, he was about the size of a jockey."

"The last time you spoke to Dario, what did you two speak about?" Von Hess queried.

"He was going to see some Chinese businessman about backing us financially in the club we intended to start." "Chen Lowe?"

"How do you know that?"

"That was all Dario had going with Chen Lowe?" asked Markie, neglecting to reply to her question. "No, actually Dario also had another proposition for Chen. It had something to do with the shoe business. I wasn't involved in that."

"Did Dario carry a gun?" queried Von Hess.

Mary froze at the question posed. Since they knew about Chen Lowe, Mary wasn't sure exactly how much the detectives knew. She now appeared nervous. There was no way she was going to admit to facilitating Dario's acquisition of a revolver.

"I never saw Dario carrying a gun."

"Did he have one?"

"Not that I know of."

"Dario's fingerprints were all over the gun that killed him," informed Markie.

"Were they?"

"Thank you, Mary," said the sergeant, concluding the interview. "Come on, Ollie, let's let the young lady earn a living."

"Can I ask you a question, Sergeant?" asked Mary, now seeming relieved. She put forth the voice she used when wanting something from a man.

"What?"

"Would you happen to know of someone who would like to go into business with me?"

"Are you serious?"

"Of course I'm serious. Just because Dario is dead, that doesn't mean that my dream is dead. I mean, you must come across people with money in your line of work, somebody who may be interested in going in with me."

"I'm sorry, but I don't know anybody who would have such an interest."

"There are side benefits to my business, Sergeant. Consider that."

"Not a chance, Mary," advised Markie, shaking his head at her proposition.

After the detectives left the club, the Kingly Castle manager confronted the Sharon Stone lookalike. He appeared concerned. "So, what was all that about, Mary?" asked the manager.

"Somebody murdered one of our regular customers. He had my number in his phone, so the detectives came here to ask me questions."

"That's too bad. Which customer?"

"Dario, you know him."

"That's the pretty boy from Italy that I got that gun for?"

"Yeah, but don't worry, that never even came up."

"I guess he really had a need for the gun."

"Yeah, but what good did it do him?"

"I don't know, Mary. But will you do me a favor in the future?"

"What?"

"Don't involve me in your personal affairs anymore. I can get in trouble without any help from you."

"You aren't in any trouble."

"Yeah, I'm sure," commented the manager, not convinced of that.

"Just go out there and make these suckers spend money. And make sure you push the good booze."

***

MARKIE AND VON HESS FOUND their interview with Mary Custer to be fruitful. In particular, they were curious about Dario's wanting to do business with Chen Lowe. The detectives were thinking that perhaps there was a motive there for someone to kill Dario.

"What do make of it, Sarge?" Von Hess asked.

"I want to hear what Chen Lowe has to say."

"Want me to call him for an appointment?"

"No, let's catch him by surprise. Do me a favor, Ollie. phone the detective from the precinct and give her a courtesy call. Bring her up to speed."

Von Hess telephoned Detective Ellison as directed. After briefing her, he asked if she had heard from Victor Spinello. She hadn't.

"We'll be going off to Connecticut to talk to the guy who owns the shoe factory," informed Von Hess. "I'll call you afterward to let you know how we made out."

"Thanks, Ollie. I'll keep trying to catch up with this guy Victor," advised Ellison.

"You know, Sarge," said Von Hess after getting off the phone, "the more I think about it, the more I'm convinced that there must be a story surrounding that inner sole. Why else would someone stick something like that in somebody's mouth?"

"That's what I'm thinking," replied Markie. "You know, Ollie, they had celebrity lookalike hookers doing business in Hollywood way back in the day. Can you imagine how popular an escort service would be if a client could just make a call and order up a celebrity lookalike?"

"I know you're an old movie buff, Sarge. I'm curious, who would you order up?"

"ZaSu Pitts," answered Markie, trying to be funny.

"Who?" Von Hess asked. He was unfamiliar with the long-gone character actress.

11

Chen's Den

THE DETECTIVES WERE IMPRESSED by the massiveness of the Chen Lowe Footwear Company. The company building was about half the size of a NYC block. There was a parking lot, a loading dock and trucks. Upon entering the building, they found themselves in a large lobby. A neatly dressed woman sat at the small reception desk to greet visitors. Only a telephone was visible on the desk.

To the left of the desk was a waiting area where several chairs and a couch sat. In front of the couch was a coffee table on which magazines rested. On the other side of the reception desk was an elevator that led to the corporate offices.

Von Hess approached the receptionist. She was smiling politely. The detective presented his gold shield and indicated that he and Markie were there to speak with Chen Lowe. The receptionist's welcoming face quickly transformed to one of suspicion. She inquired as to the purpose of the detectives wanting to see the company owner.

The reply offered by Von Hess was a vague one. He informed the receptionist that he and the sergeant were there on official police business. Accepting the limited explanation, the wary woman reached for the telephone on her desk to make a call.

After a brief conversation with someone in Cantonese, the receptionist hung up the telephone. She then held up two fingers and pointed them to the elevator. Markie and Von Hess both understood that they were to go to the second floor.

When they got off the elevator, the detectives were greeted by a long dark-haired woman who, like the receptionist, smiled politely and nodded. She was about thirty, tall, and professionally attired in a black suit and long sleeve white ruffled shirt. Without words spoken, the woman led the detectives to Chen Lowe's office.

The office was impressive, consisting of two large rooms. One room housed a massive oak desk. Atop the desk was a computer screen, a printer, a telephone and numerous newspapers. Behind the desk was a large bookcase. The other room contained a television, a circular table with chairs, a burgundy leather couch and a recliner. There was also a portable bar with glasses and a bottle of Remy Martin atop it.

"Mr. Lowe will be with you shortly," announced the woman softly once the detectives were seated at the table. To Markie, who had probably seen too many old movies, her look seemed to project an air of mystery. Her English was perfect.

"Would you care for water or tea?" she asked politely,

"No thanks," replied Markie, answering for himself and Von Hess.

The detectives watched as the woman, assumed to be a secretary or personal assistant, bowed and left the room. Markie turned to Von Hess and raised his eyebrows. "

She reminds me of Anna May Wong," said the sergeant, referring to an actor of long, long ago. Von Hess offered no response. He was unfamiliar with Wong.

Chen Lowe entered his office a couple of minutes later. He was accompanied by his general counsel. The businessmen were similar in age and appearance. Of average height, both were potbellied and clean shaven. Each was attired in an expensive conservative suit and tie. Their wing top shoes appeared to be equally pricey.

Realizing they were in the presence of big money, Markie and Von Hess rose from their chairs to greet the men. Lowe's gold watch, diamond cufflinks and ruby pinkie ring supported their assumption of wealth. The general counsel was the first to speak.

"What can Mr. Lowe do for you gentlemen?" His tone was of the gentlest variety, but unmistakenly all business.

After Markie explained why he and Von Hess were there, Chen Lowe shook his head in remorse. He was genuinely sorry to learn of the fate of Dario Tengo.

"This is indeed a pity," said Lowe. "Mr. Tengo was a young man. He still had much living to do."

"What does Mr. Tengo's unfortunate death have to do with Mr. Chen?" asked the general counsel.

"We understand that Mr. Lowe may have had a business relationship with Dario Tengo," said Von Hess.

Lowe looked at his general counsel, waiting for his response.

"Mr. Lowe explored the possibility of entering into a business arrangement with Mr. Tengo, but nothing was finalized. They were only in the discussion stages."

"What was the discussion about?"

"They spoke of a new type of shoe under development."

"Was Dario Tengo representing the Frantellini interests?" Markie queried.

"Mr. Lowe's understanding was that Mr. Tengo was unhappy in the Frantellini association."

"So, he came to see Mr. Lowe?"

"Correct, Sergeant. They were endeavoring to align themselves with Mr. Lowe, where they'd receive a more generous share of the profits off the new shoe product."

"They, being who?"

"Mr. Tengo and his partner. The gentleman who created the Frantellini Sole."

"The new product is a shoe?" Von Hess asked.

"Yes, The Dynamic Shoe, is what Mr. Tengo called it.

"What's so special about this new product?"

"This shoe was specially designed to eradicate foot discomfort."

"Is that really possible?"

The general counsel shrugged before answering. "Who is to say what is possible. Mr. Lowe told Mr. Tengo that he was willing to be shown the proof."

"Have you people met the inventor of this shoe?" Markie queried.

"No."

"You never met Victor Spinello?"

"No. Is that the partner's name?"

"Yes," answered the sergeant. "Mr. Lowe, do you happen to know a woman named Mary Custer?" Lowe looked at his general counsel and answered in Chinese.

"No, Sergeant, Mr. Lowe has no knowledge of this person."

"Thank you, gentlemen," said Markie, after finding out what he needed to know. "We've taken up enough of your time."

After the detectives left Chen Lowe looked sad. He was just as disappointed with losing the brothel opportunity as he was with the shoe deal.

When the detectives returned to their vehicle, Markie had Von Hess telephone Detective Ellison. After apprising the precinct squad detective of the information gathered at the Chen Lowe Footwear Company, Von Hess asked if contact was ever made with Victor Spinello. It wasn't.

Detective Ellison explained what she had accomplished up until being consumed by a new priority case. The new matter involved an abducted child snatched off the street. Von Hess, knowing that child abductions were an all-hands on deck affair, understood. After hanging up the phone he conveyed to Markie that Detective Ellison wasn't able to accomplish much.

"Why not?"

"She got tied up with a kid snatch. You know what a megillah those can be."

"I guess it's all up to us for now, Ollie. Did she get to do anything?"

"She had intended to fingerprint people at the factory, but that created some drama."

"Like what?"

"The Frantellini family got into a big brouhaha."

"Over what?"

"According to Ellison, Richard Frantellini got excited over getting fingerprinted. He began complaining of chest pains. The daughter and stepmother started arguing over whether or not to call an ambulance or to drive him to the hospital themselves. The daughter wanted to call 911 and the wife insisted that she drive the old man to the hospital."

"That's the beef?" asked the astonished Markie.

"According to Ellison the two women hate each other."

"So, who won?"

"Father St. Denis, the department chaplain was there. He ended up making the call."

"Which was?"

"They called 911."

"Don't they understand that we need to compare fingerprints against the prints lifted from the murder weapon."

"Do you want to go and do that now, Sarge?"

"Nah, let it rest for now. Tomorrow we'll try and come up with this Victor Spinello. Once we get him, we'll grill him and print him. I also want to talk to the daughter and stepmother."

***

A GRIM LOOKING FATHER FIORELLO ST. DENIS sat Richard Frantellini's bedside at the hospital. The priest administered the last rites to his friend in the presence of Richard's daughter Maria, and his second wife. Not long after, the family patriarch passed away.

Father St. Denis did his best to console Maria, who surprisingly was holding up well. Richard's wife feigned distress. In order to make things look good, Ronnie actually managed to produce a tear or two in displaying her grief.

The priest spoke soothingly of their being light at the end of the tunnel. He explained how everyone would eventually reunite in a better place at some point down the road. The daughter nodded, smiled softly, and seemed to embrace the words of the priest. Ronnie thought otherwise.

Once Maria and Ronnie finished dabbing away at their tears and blowing their noses, they gradually began thinking of what was to come now that Richard was journeying home to the other side. Rather than coming together, their thoughts ran selfishly independent. The cutthroat adversaries saw each other as being in the way. The opposing agendas was something picked up on by Father St. Denis.

When the priest offered to assist in making the arrangements for Richard, both daughter and wife consented. Ronnie and Father St. Denis proceeded to the funeral parlor, while Maria was tasked with overseeing the continuity of the Frantellini businesses.

The ugliness resurfaced once Maria learned of the costs accrued in connection with her father's sendoff. She challenged her stepmother regarding the expenses charged to the Frantellini Shoe Factory.

Maria's frugalness caused her to find the purchase of a bronze casket with hand painted accents to be over the top. She also found fault with the expenditures concerning the floral arrangements, the days allotted for Richard's viewing and other miscellaneous death related costs.

"My father wouldn't have wanted all this," argued Maria, when the inevitable showdown came. "He'd never drain the company finances with such reckless spending. He was a humble man."

"Your father is not here to worry about what we do with his money," said Ronnie, dismissively.

"Are you looking to run my business into the ground?"

"Back up," countered Ronnie. "You're forgetting something. It's not your business. I'm the one with the biggest piece of the pie."

"My sister and I collectively vote as one. Dario is gone and Victor is going to side with us, so YOU REMEMBER THAT!"

"I promise you, that's something I'll never forget," said Ronnie icily. "And since we're counting pennies, who is covering the airfare of your sister and her husband to come here from Italy?"

Maria refused to dignify the comment. She simply stormed off muttering something under her breath. This altercation was the true turning point in their already strained relationship. Both women were of a mindset that some form of drastic action needed to be taken.

12

Fritzie's Last Round

BEFORE GOING HOME AFTER WORK to take a much-needed rest, Markie felt obligated to look in on his friend Fitzie, the Brooklyn bar owner. He asked Von Hess, who he had carpooled with, to drop him off after work at his car. Von Hess was curious why he didn't want to go home.

"You got someplace to go, Sarge?" Von Hess asked. "I can take you where you want to go, that way you won't lose your parking spot."

"It's okay, I've just got an errand to run."

"I don't mind, Sarge, I got nothing to do."

"Okay, drive me over to Fitzie's place."

This was something Von Hess hadn't expected. The detective was now worried because he believed that the sergeant still hadn't sufficiently recovered from the drunken binge he had been on. Not wanting to have to babysit Markie through another sobering up process, Von Hess voiced his concern.

"Look, Sarge, maybe you should wait before drinking again,"

cautioned Von Hess. "You're just starting to feel like yourself. Why give your liver a beating?"

"I'm not intending to drink, Ollie."

"Then why are you going to Fitzie's joint?"

"I want to check on him. The old man hasn't been right in the head lately."

"You had mentioned that he was slipping. Did he get worse?"

"That's what I'm looking to find out."

"He's got a wife, where is she?"

"His wife lives in their Staten Island house. Fitzie spends half his time in the apartment over the bar, so who knows what the story is with the wife. Fitzie always made it a rule to keep his business and his home life separate. He keeps that one apartment over the bar for himself. He rents out the other digs."

"Does he have a girlfriend?"

"No more now but he always had a squeeze on the side for many years."

"It's amazing how some guys can juggle that kind of a double life, Sarge. Not me."

"It's not for amateurs, that's for sure. But honestly, I don't think Fitzie kept any one woman around long enough to get serious."

"I don't know how he did it, Sarge."

"That's all over for him. Over the last few years, I think that I used his apartment for a love nest more than he did. I'll say one thing for Fitzie, the guy always took very good care of me."

"Fitzie has kids, right?"

"Yeah, his kids are married and live in Jersey someplace.

"I assume he must have a few bucks."

"He's in good shape that way, Ollie. The building that houses the bar is long paid for. Between the bar, the apartments he rents and the little shylocking he does, he's sitting pretty moneywise. I think he even may have been pushing a little swag now and then."

"It a shame how a lot of these ex-pugs get dementia. Those guys take way too many raps to the head."

"Yeah, Ollie, getting punchy is an occupational hazard in boxing. Anyway, I just want to see how he is."

When the detectives arrived at Fitzie's Brooklyn bar they were surprised to find it closed. Affixed to the front door was a yellow cardboard sign that reflected a printed notification made with a black magic marker. The sign indicated:

CLOSED INDEFINITEY

As the detectives wondered what happened, Markie heard his name being called. Both he and Von Hess turned to their rear to see who it was. Markie recognized the man who addressed him as a tenant in Fitzie's building. The tenant, an iron worker, was wearing a Yankee baseball cap. He was a large man with red hair and an exceedingly fair complexion. His voice was robust. His pronunciation left no doubt that he was a product of Brooklyn.

"What happened over here?" asked the sergeant.

"It's bad news for Fitzie, Sergeant," answered the man.

"Don't tell me he dropped dead...." said Markie, thinking the worst.

"You didn't hear what happened?"

"No, what happened?"

"Your boys from the precinct carted Fitzie off last night for beating the hell out of old Mike Mulrooney last night."

"The old man with one leg?"

"Yeah, Fitzie tuned him up pretty bad."

"I can't believe this," said Markie, addressing Von Hess. "Mulrooney was harmless. I think that he's even blind in one eye for Christ's sake. What was the beef over?"

"There was no beef. I wasn't there, but I heard Fitzie thought he was in the Polo Grounds boxing for the championship."

"Are you serious?"

"Yeah. Supposedly Fitzie was standing over poor Mulrooney yelling for the referee to start the count."

Markie had Von Hess drive him to the local precinct to find out the status of his bar owner friend. Once there he learned from the desk sergeant that Fitzie was being held in a psych ward for observation.

"The guy went off his nut," advised the desk sergeant. "He's not going home anytime soon, if at all."

"What about Mulrooney, the guy who got beat up?" "

He's in pretty bad shape, but their expecting him to pull through. They admitted him to the hospital."

"Does the family know?"

"Mulrooney has a daughter that we were able to notify."

"I'm talking about Fitzie's family."

"We notified his wife."

Markie nodded sadly and thanked the desk sergeant. He knew there was nothing he could do that would be of benefit to his friend.

"Tough break for Fitzie," commented Von Hess once they got back in the car.

"Yeah," answered Markie. "I just hope that poor Mulrooney doesn't die. That would make it murder."

"That poor bastard. I can't imagine taking such a tune up at his age."

"I can't either, Ollie. I guess Fitzie really did take too many punches in the head."

"Fitzie's a sick man, Sarge. They'll probably end up putting him in a padded room someplace."

"What could a guy do for him now, Ollie?"

"All you could do maybe is pray for him." Markie scoffed at the suggestion.

"Forget about that, I'd be jinxing him with the man upstairs."

"Where to now, Sarge?"

"Take me home. Tomorrow's another day."

When Markie arrived home his spirits were low. He felt a certain remorse for not having done something after first noticing that Fitzie' mental condition was declining. He went to the kitchen sink for a cold glass of water. After gulping down the fluid he remembered the unopened bottle of Johnnie Walker Black he had in the house.

Markie retrieved the bottle, thinking that he might crack it open. He stared at his answer to the blues for a few seconds before common sense finally won out. The sergeant knew that his stomach couldn't take it. Besides, he needed to go to work in the morning, and that was a priority.

Markie brushed his teeth, put on his pajamas, and slipped into bed. A collector of old school crime novels, he found such tales to be relaxing. On this particular evening, he opted to reread a Charlie Chan mystery, The Black Camel, which was written by Earl Derr Biggers in 1929.

Markie opted for The Black Camel because he recalled that there was something in there that reminded him of Rochelle Parrish, the love who dumped him for a professional wrestler. The sergeant didn't get beyond the third page. He fell asleep with the light on and the paperback on his chest.

An energized Markie rose the following morning early. Feeling refreshed physically, he faced the day with the intention of working hard. There would be no time for thoughts of Rochelle Parrish or Fitzie. Anxious to get started, he reached out to Von Hess telephonically at 6:00 A.M.

The ringing phone next to his bed jarred Von Hess, who had been woken from a dead sleep. His voice was raspy as he inquired as to who was calling.

"It's me, Ollie. Did I wake you?"

"That's all right, Sarge. Is everything okay?"

"Everything is fine. Can you pick me up at my house this morning instead of meeting me at work. I'll call us on duty from the field, that'll save us time."

"No problem," said Von Hess, yawning loudly. "What time do you want me to get you?"

"Can you be at my place at 7:00 A. M.? We can go for breakfast. I'm famished."

"Okay, Sarge, I'll see you soon."

"Is he crazy?" asked Mrs. Von Hess, who didn't appreciate the early wake up. "Why would the sergeant call you at this hour?"

"He's not crazy, just enthusiastic," answered Von Hess. "Go back to sleep."

13

The Long Arm Of The Law

THE CONFUSED VICTOR SPINELLO walked the Manhattan streets aimlessly in a trance-like state for miles. Upon arriving home, he managed to slip into his building unnoticed. Physically drained, he appeared to be a disheveled mess.

Once inside his apartment he immediately went directly to the kitchen sink to quench a burning thirst. Consuming several tall glasses of water alleviated the dryness in his throat. With achy legs riddled with stiffness, Victor limped to his bedroom. His weakened condition caused him to collapse onto his bed fully dressed. Before closing his eyes, he managed to use his feet to kick off his shoes. Seconds after, Victor was fast asleep.

Victor's sleeping was an uneasy slumber that came with frequent wake ups. Each eye opening reminded him that he had murdered a man. Some relief was found after Victor pulled the covers over himself. The blankets that reached over his chin provided a sense of security.

A throbbing pain in Victor's knee acted up to where he was unable to go back to sleep. The tenderness was the result of his wandering in the aftermath of a life and death struggle with Dario Tengo inside Dario's car. The struggle was something Victor vividly recalled.

The deafening gun blast inside the car that had caused his ears to ring was also recollected. Victor's jamming the inner sole of his shoe in his victim's mouth was another unforgettable element. Only Victor's wandering off aimlessly after the murder remained hazy.

During periods of regrouping, Victor began to justify his actions. *It was either him or me*, he thought, failing to put forth any other rationalization that would explain the uncontrollable rage that had consumed him. He loudly sighed at the thought of what he did with the inner sole of his shoe. Even Victor knew that this act was indefensible. *There isn't a jury anywhere that would be understanding to that,* Victor conceded to himself.

For what seemed like forever, Victor isolated himself in his apartment. He answered no telephone calls and refused to answer his door. As thoughts of a future of incarceration permeated his mind, true panic set in. Victor jumped up from his bed wide-eyed. Seated on the edge of his bed he grew desperate as to what to do. Glancing at the floor he saw the bloodied shoe he wore during the scuffle. Seeing that the shoe was without an inner sole didn't make things easier for Victor. It was a reminder of what he had done.

It's hopeless for me, Victor thought. The police probably have found Dario by now. They must have the gun with my fingerprints on it! Victor rose from his bed to look out his window onto the street. He gazed down at the people walking along on the pavement below. Everyone had someplace to go.

Where do I go? Victor thought. Then it came to him. *Italy! But not Milan, that's no good. Dario's family is there. I'll stay with my cousin in Liguria.* Victor began to gather the things necessary for travel. As he did this he thought through his game plan.

Once in Liguria, I'll continue my work on my Dynamic Shoe in safety. I can say that my cousin created the new shoe. No one will ever find me in Liguria!

Victor, once packed, hurriedly cleaned himself up. He tried to avoid looking at the common areas of the apartment he had shared with the man he murdered. The inventor planned to go to the bank to withdraw his money before heading to the airport. Working against the clock, Victor moved with the swiftness his aching body permitted. Just before leaving his apartment, he went to the window for a final look at the street below.

"One big ant colony," uttered Victor. "Arrivederci," he announced sadly, addressing the distant public beneath him. When Victor opened the front door to leave his apartment, what he saw caused him to come to an abrupt stop. It took a few minutes for the shock to wear off.

***

WHEN MARKIE AND VON HESS ARRIVED AT THE building that housed the Frantellini Shoe Factory they were fortunate to find parking close proximity to the location. The detectives entered the factory and asked a supervisor where the corporate offices were. They were informed that the executives weren't at work due to the unexpected death of Richard Frantellini. Markie and Von Hess hadn't figured on that.

On their way out of the building Von Hess took a second to look at the building's bells and mailboxes. What he saw reflected:

PH-Frantellini

5 -Tengo/Spinello

4 -Lowenstein

3 -Arnold-Perez

1/2-Frantellini Shoe Factory

"Do you want go knock on the door, Sarge?" asked Von Hess.

"Yeah. But I don't see any elevator in this place, Ollie."

"So, we'll take the stairs. It's healthier for us."

The detectives arrived at Victor Spinello's apartment just as he was leaving. Victor froze after seeing the two men blocking his path. He knew by their look that they were detectives there to arrest him for the murder of Dario Tengo. Victor's startled reaction made it obvious to the experienced lawmen that they had the man they were looking for.

"Relax, my friend," announced Von Hess. "We're detectives. Are you Victor Spinello?" Victor nodded weakly. Noticing the suitcase, the investigator asked, "Going someplace?"

"I, uh...."

"Turn around and face the wall," ordered the detective. "Put your hands up over your head and on the wall where I can see them." Once Victor complied, Von Hess patted him down for a weapon.

When questioned Victor responded in Italian, pretending that he didn't speak English. It was the only thing he could think of doing. Markie, who wasn't buying Victor's non-English speaking act, looked down at Spinello's small feet. The inventor's hoofs looked about the right size to match the inner sole recovered from Dario Tengo's mouth.

Markie, pointed to Victor's feet and said, "Nice shoes. Let's step back inside the apartment, pal," said the sergeant. Victor nodded, now seeming capable of communicating in English. Being unsure of his legal rights caused Victor to acquiesce.

Once the detectives entered the apartment Markie looked around as Von Hess began to question Victor. The sergeant spotted Victor's blood-stained shoes on the floor of his bedroom. Upon closer inspection, Markie discovered that one of the shoes was missing an inner sole. His examination of the existing sole revealed gold lettering that identified the item as a Frantellini Sole. Markie removed the inner sole and found it to be identical to the one removed from Dario's Tengo's mouth. At this point there was nothing to talk about. Victor was taken into custody.

"You should have never invited us into your apartment," voiced Markie, making it seem that he was under the impression that he was invited in. The remark went over Victor's head.

The handcuffed prisoner was removed to the precinct where the homicide occurred. Detective Ellison, who was on her day off, was notified at home. Since the child abduction case she was working on had been solved, she was instructed to come to work and process her waiting prisoner.

***

THE FUNERAL MASS FOR Richard Frantellini was held at St. Patrick's Cathedral. The service was a solemn one, with most attending receiving communion. Richard's daughters fought back tears, as Father Fiorello St. Denis spoke about their father. Ronnie, the grieving widow, declined to address those in attendance. Richard's daughters also declined the opportunity to talk about their dad.

Father Fiorello St. Denis was most eloquent in speaking of the generosity of his deceased friend. The priest concluded on an upbeat tone, referencing the Frank Sinatra song, *The Best Is Yet To Come.*

Maria Frantellini, despite the black suit she wore every day for a week, retired her grief quickly. Putting business first, she arranged for a private meeting with her sister. The topic discussed was the future of The Frantellini Shoe Factory and real estate holdings.

Dr. Caroline Frantellini, who was happy living in Milan with her physician husband, was more than willing to let Maria take the lead in this discussion of the family businesses. Caroline listened as Maria outlined her ideas moving forward.

"I have faith in you, Maria," said Caroline. Dad always said that you were the capable one when it came to business. So, whatever you decide is okay with me."

"What about you husband, Ettore?" asked Maria. "How will he feel about that?"

"Ettore is like me. He is going to be fine with whatever direction you decide to go. He's going back to Milan alone tomorrow morning."

"So soon? You don't intend to go also, do you?"

"No, we agreed that I should remain here until we conclude whatever business that needs addressing."

"That's good. How is Ettore doing?"

"Ettore needs more time. He is still grieving over his brother Dario. That's the reason why he wants to go home. He sees returning to work as therapeutic."

"Of course it is," said the younger sister. "Our only problem is figuring out what to do with our darling stepmother."

"What do you mean?"

"Ronnie is no good, Caroline. She's a gold-digger who got close to dad when he was vulnerable."

"He always seemed so happy being married to her."

"Yes, Caroline, he was happy with her because she made him feel young. But now, we're stuck dealing with her. Trust me, she is no good."

"I never realized how much you disliked Ronnie."

"I detest her."

"But you both live in the penthouse together."

"For right now, but that's going to change fast."

"You're moving out?"

"No, Ronnie is the one who is going to be moving once we find a way to get her out of our business."

"But isn't she is entitled to whatever dad left her," asked Caroline. This statement caused Maria to roll her eyes in frustration.

"She's entitled to SHIT!" Maria stated strongly, refusing to sugarcoat her feelings. "She's a conniver who schemed her way in to where she now owns half of everything Frantellini!"

"Take it easy, Maria. Don't get so excited."

"That's easy for you to say, Caroline. You'll be in Italy with a husband collecting checks from me here in New York. I'm the one who has to run the businesses and deal with this bitch every day."

"Perhaps we should contemplate selling off everything?"

"Absolutely not! The business is on the verge of developing a new shoe product that could revolutionize the industry."

"But Victor is in jail...."

"Victor is in jail, but not dead. I intend to get him out. Once I do, we'll do fine."

"What? Are you forgetting that he killed Dario, Ettore's brother? I don't understand you!"

"I'm well aware of what Victor did to Dario, Caroline. But this is business, and to be successful in business we have to put our personal feelings aside."

"So, Victor's killing Dario was okay with you?"

"I don't know how much you know about Dario, but trust me, he was no saint, Caroline. To be honest, Victor might have done us a favor. Anyway, Dario is dead and there is no bringing him back. It is stipulated in the contract they signed that their share reverts back to the Frantellini family in the event of the death of Dario or Victor."

"How could that be?" asked the perplexed doctor. "What about Dario's wife Gia and their children in Milan?"

"Dad and his lawyer were very shrewd. Thomas Beasley prepared the papers in a way that stated that upon the death of either Dario or Victor, their interest reverts back to the Frantellini family.

"Dario and Victor agreed to this?"

"Neither one of them was sophisticated enough to outmaneuver our father and Thomas Beasley. This was the way our father wanted it. He was looking out for us."

"Why, that's almost criminal, Maria."

"No, that's good business, Caroline."

"What about Ronnie, our stepmother?"

"I don't give a shit about her."

"So, what do you propose we do?"

"Ronnie has to go. If she remains in the family business, she'll end up destroying it."

"How do you propose that we get her out, Maria?"

"We'll have to try and buy her out. I'm afraid that it'll cost us plenty because she knows about the Dynamic Shoe that Victor was perfecting. She's probably going to look for a big number."

"What's the Dynamic Shoe again?"

"It's a product that addresses foot pain. If successful, it'll net us a fortune."

"This is all so bizarre to me," stated Caroline.

"Don't worry about a thing, Caroline. I'll handle everything for us." assured Maria. "I'll figure something out with the attorney. I just need you to go along with me."

"Of course I'll go along with you. Who is the attorney you are using?"

"I'm going to stick with Tom Beasley. We understand each other."

"All I need is for you to be available when I need you."

"I suppose that I'll have to remain in America longer than I planned."

"Let's see what the lawyer says. Right now, the priority is getting Victor out of jail."

"Ettore isn't going to be happy about that."

"He'll have to get over it, Caroline. This was our mom and dad's business, now it rightly belongs to us. Unfortunately, we must fight for what is ours."

Maria's comment struck a sentimental chord in Caroline. "I suppose mom would want that," said the older daughter wistfully.

"Of course she would," said Maria. "She'd never want her replacement taking over half of everything she and our father worked for. As far as your husband, time and money are a great cure for all ills."

14

Choosing Sides

THE CHIEF OF DETECTIVES bumped into Father Fiorello St. Denis at the NYPD Holy Name Mass and Communion Breakfast. For many people the breakfasts were affairs worth attending.

Aside from the religious aspect, it was a venue beneficial for those seeking to solidify relationships that would prove valuable down the road. This was especially true when a favor was needed. Many in the department fast tracked their career thanks to these communions.

Chief McCoy was glad to learn from Father St. Denis that the department chaplain was pleased with the apprehension of Victor Spinello. The chief smiled happily as the priest thanked him profusely for putting Markie and Von Hess on the case.

McCoy knew that Father St. Denis was sure to mention his good work to the cardinal. This could translate into great dividends for the chief. A favorable whisper by the cardinal into the ear of the police commissioner could propel Chief McCoy to greater heights. Thinking optimistically, McCoy hoped that word might even reach the mayor's office.

If the mayor hears my name mentioned in a good light often enough, McCoy thought, who knows what could happen. If something ever happened to the commissioner, I'd stand a chance of being his replacement! Such wishful thinking did much to put the chief in a good frame of mind.

Once back at his office Chief McCoy made it a point to express his satisfaction to Lieutenant Wright, who oversaw the handpicked detectives who worked out of the chief's office. The chief indicated that Markie and Von Hess deserved to be thrown a bone. After leaving the chief, the lieutenant called Markie into his office.

"How are you feeling, Al?" asked the lieutenant, aware that Markie had gotten out of a sick bed to work the case that was important to Father St. Denis.

"I'm feeling fine, Loo."

"You and Ollie did an excellent job in helping out the department chaplain. The old man is happy as a pig in shit over it."

"That's good, Loo."

"Look, things are quiet around here right now. You and Von Hess take a couple of days off. It'll be on the city. Just stay local in case something comes up, and I need you."

"Thanks, Loo,' said the appreciative Markie."

"Put in a request for two days off, so I have something on file. I won't submit it, and if nothing happens, I'll rip it up when you return to work without taking away the time from you guys."

The two days Markie and Von Hess took came directly after their regular days off, thus giving them an extended swing off. During this period the sergeant behaved himself. He ate healthy, drank lots of juice and water, exercised and avoided bars.

Much of the time Markie watched the old movies he loved on television. This form of entertainment, for a movie buff like Markie, was medicine. The storylines he viewed enabled him to escape to what he viewed as a better time and place.

Markie never missed a showing of the John Garfield-Lana Turner matchup in *The Postman Always Rings Twice*. Turner's powerful portrayal of Cora Smith was such that the sergeant understood the length some people would go to in the name love. The movie got him thinking of Rochelle Parrish, the woman who left him for the wrestler who passed himself off as an Indian when in the ring.

No longer inclined to drink, and not about to pursue Rochelle, the sergeant felt the need to do something. He chose to telephone Von Hess at his home.

"What's doing, Ollie?" Markie asked.

"Nothing, my wife and I are just watching television. Is everything all right?"

"I'm starting to feel kind of antsy. I'm ready to return to work."

"We still have another day, Sarge. Let's enjoy the time off while we can. When we go back, I'm sure they'll have a new caper for us to work on."

"Yeah, that's right," said Markie, who hoped that would be the case.

"Do you know what's on television in a half hour, Sarge?"

"What?"

"*Bataan*, with Robert Taylor."

Markie perked up at hearing this. He forgot all about the Lana Turner movie. Bataan was one of the war movies he loved.

"What channel, Ollie?" he asked.

***

THE ATTORNEY THOMAS BEASLEY sat at his desk leafing through an old issue of Playboy as he anxiously awaited the arrival of Maria Frantellini. When informed by his secretary that she arrived, the lawyer opened the door to his private office and greeted his visitor. The strong odor of the cologne that Beasley wore passed through the open door. It was an aroma significant enough to tickle noses.

"You're right on time," said Beasley, flashing a smile to his visitor.

Before closing his office door behind him, Beasley made it clear to his secretary that the business conference he was about to engage in was not to be interrupted for any reason. Clara Calhoun nodded, indicating that she understood. She then returned to her station.

After a few minutes passed, Clara rose from her chair and placed her ear to the door of Beasley's office. The secretary waited for the sounds of lovemaking to emanate. She was disappointed when there were no guttural grunts or moans of pleasure coming from the other side of the door. The noises that turned Clara on were replaced with what sounded like bickering. While the content of what she overheard lacked the spice she enjoyed, it nevertheless was of interest to Clara.

Maria Frantellini sounded clearly upset. Her annoyance was fueled by her father amending his will. From what Clara gathered, Maria was placing blame for the adjustment squarely at the doorstep of Thomas Beasley, the Frantellini family attorney.

"How could you have done this?" Maria demanded to know. "We went over this already, Maria. I already explained to you the circumstances."

"Tell me again, Tom."

"Your father and his wife came here one day out of the blue. He told me to change his will," advised Beasley. "His mind was made up. How could I have prevented that?"

"You should have talked him out of it!"

"I figured he'd change it again down the road. How was I supposed to know that your father had a bad ticker?"

"This is all your fault," accused Maria. "By you changing my father's will you put me and my sister in a bad position."

"That's unfair, Maria," countered Beasley. "If I didn't do it, some other lawyer would have. It was what your father wanted. It wasn't a matter of his having a feeble mind. Richard Frantellini knew exactly what he was doing. So how was I supposed to deny him?"

"You should have told him what a conniver his wife is."

"How could I do that? Ronnie was sitting right next to him. I did all that I could on your behalf."

"Like what"

"You and your sister would have been out altogether if it weren't for me," lied the attorney. "You should be thanking me. Your stepmother was angling to inherit the whole enchilada."

"That doesn't surprise me one bit."

"She would have gotten what she wanted if wasn't for me looking out for your interest."

"Seriously?"

"Sure, I'm serious."

"So, what can we do to straighten out this mess?" Maria asked.
"Well, the first thing we need to do is get you, your sister and Victor Spinello on the same page to act as a united front. As far as the real estate portfolio is concerned, the same goes for you and your sister. You two have to think as one."

"I understand all that, Tom. My sister Caroline is with me one hundred percent. What do we do about Victor? How do we get him with us?"

"Leave Victor to me," answered Beasley. "I'll get him off the hook on the murder rap and make him fall in line."

"You're awful sure of yourself."

"I am. Look, Victor is in a tight spot in a country he knows little about, so he has to be desperate for help. He'll go along once I explain to him that without your support, he rots in jail."

"You're sure that you can get him acquitted, Tom?"

"I haven't failed a client yet," replied Beasley. It'll cost you a little money though."

"I understand."

"Keep in mind that you're still going to have to pay Ronnie in order to get her out of the family business. I'll have to work on a formula for that."

"I'll call the accountant."

"Not yet. First let's start by getting Victor out of jail," said Beasley.

Maria let out a deep sigh before commenting, "It never ends."

"All this is going to take a little time, so relax, Maria," said the attorney, who stepped from behind his desk to wrap Maria in his arms. His amorous overtures were accepted.

Beasley's secretary had listened to the entire exchange taking place inside the office. Although intrigued by the conversation she overheard, it still took a back seat to the romantic antics of her boss and his client.

Clara Calhoun had a limited social life. Listening through the office door provided the thrill the secretary was missing. Her ear tightly pressed against the door caused it to redden. When the silence came inside Beasley's private office, she hurried to her workstation.

As she waited, Clara tried to visualize the sexual romp that had taken place in the next room. She thought of the couch inside the office, wondering which positions the lovers assumed when coupling.

He must be an animal for her to keep coming back for more, imagined Clara of Beasley. His staying power must be extraordinary.

Maria walked out of the private office alone. She straightened out her clothes as she passed Clara's station without bothering to look at the secretary.

Who does she think she is fooling, thought Clara. *I hope her stepmother gets everything*!

After a few minutes, Beasley telephoned Clara, instructing her to order lunch from a restaurant located near the office. Feeling in a good mood, he told Clara to order something for herself.

While having his lunch, the attorney reached out to a friend in law enforcement. Through this contact, he came to learn where Victor Spinello was being held.

While Beasley was doing this, his secretary made a call of her own. Clara telephoned the office of Ronnie Borden Frantellini at the shoe factory. After being transferred to voice mail, Clara left an anonymous message conveying that she should be aware that her stepdaughter Maria was conspiring against her. It was the secretary's way at taking a swipe at Maria, who she considered to be a snob. Once the call was made, Clara enjoyed the lunch her boss treated her to.

***

INCARCERATION ON RIKER'S ISLAND wasn't easy for Victor Spinello. He was facing a murder trial while locked up with people he had nothing in common with. Feeling alone, he often conversed with the correction officers to combat his isolation. Such friendliness with the gatekeepers didn't sit well with other inmates.

Victor was in constant fear of unsophisticated street hoodlums who took advantage of his lack of physically imposing presence. Forced to always be on his guard, there were few moments when Victor was stress free. Such pressure took a toll on Victor. This period behind bars transformed Victor into a man who looked older than his years.

When Thomas Beasley went to Riker's to see the man he was hired to represent he was taken aback by Victor's decline. His client's face was drooped, his mouth was turned downward, and dark shadows were visible beneath Victor's tired eyes. Beasley sensed that Victor was bewildered by his having a visitor. When told he was retained by Maria Frantellini to represent him, Victor perked up a bit. Beasley's assurances that he would be set free after the trial gave Victor a much-needed glimmer of hope.

Once put at ease, Victor was asked to recount the struggle with Dario Tengo that subsequently led to homicide. Beasley explained to Victor that in preparation of a defense he needed to know every detail, however minute. The lawyer stopped Victor early in his narrative to put forth questions relating to how the detectives had gained entry to his apartment to arrest him.

"You didn't invite the detectives into your apartment, now did you?" asked the defense attorney, who was leading the accused.

"Not exactly...." replied the prisoner. "I don't really remember...."

"Back up, Victor," said Beasley firmly. "Keep your answers simple and to the point. Let's try it again. Are you listening?"

"Yes."

The attorney now spoke in definite terms. "You never invited the detectives into your apartment, said the attorney. "Do you understand?"

"Yes."

"Now say it with conviction."

"I never invited the detectives into my apartment," echoed Victor.

"Good, now understand this. The detectives just took it upon themselves to visit you at your apartment without an invitation or appointment. They just bulled their way in. Right?"

"Bulled?"

"Yeah, bulled. It means they pushed you aside and entered, right?" "That's right," answered Victor, catching on. "They bulled their way in."

"And you gave no permission for them to snoop around your apartment, right?"

"Right. I gave them no permission."

"Good. Now, we are getting someplace. Tell me what happened with Dario Tengo." Again, Victor was prepped early on in his account. "Just listen to what I'm telling you, Victor. You had to defend yourself when you were in the car with Dario because he was beating you."

"Yes, Dario was abusing me."

"Physically beating you, Victor," corrected Beasley. "You hurt your leg right?"

"Yes, my knee."

"Okay, your knee. Dario pulled out a gun and threatened to kill you, didn't he?"

"He threatened to kill me with the gun."

"So, you had no choice other than to try and defend yourself." "Well I...."

"And during the struggle for the gun it went off," added Beasley emphatically, cutting off the prisoner.

"Yes, I suppose that's right."

"No supposing, Victor. I'm your lawyer now, so we're going to go over this again and again until you got it right."

"Please tell Maria thank you," said Victor, once the tutoring ended. "I am so grateful."

"Maria knows that, Victor. And you're going to have the opportunity to show her how grateful you are. One other thing. You've never been arrested before, correct?"

"That's right."

"Good. I may decide to put you on the stand. If I do, when it comes to putting the sole in Dario's mouth, you just say you have no recollection of doing that. Don't deny it, just say you lost all recollection of doing that."

"I just lost it," admitted Victor.

"That was temporary insanity," said Beasley, confidently.

"I guess it was," agreed Victor.

"Now listen, Victor. Have no doubts. I'll get you off," assured the lawyer. "But you're going to have to do something in return."

"Of course, what do you want me to do?"

"There is dissention among the Frantellini family. You must promise me that you'll stand by Maria Frantellini over her stepmother, Ronnie Frantellini. You must do whatever we ask you to do regarding the shoe factory. Are you prepared to do that?"

"Yes, of course. But what can I do behind bars?"

"You can sign this document," said Beasley, who removed papers from his briefcase.

"What kind of a document?"

""One that needs signing if you want to keep out of jail."

"Of course, I'll sign anything you say. But what am I signing?"

"The document indicates that the new shoe you're developing was co-invented by you and Maria Frantellini. That makes the shoe her property as well as yours."

"But the Dynamic Shoe is my pet project."

"We all know that you're the inventor, nobody will deny you that."

"But people on the outside won't know it."

"A lot of good their knowing it will do you if you stay behind bars," said Beasley. The attorney then reminded Victor of who was paying his legal fees.

"Yes but…."

"Look, Victor, wake up. You need Maria, and you need me. Sign this paper and you'll soon be free, or don't sign and rot in this jail. It's your decision to make."

"I'll sign." Victor would have agreed to anything for a chance at freedom. "Excellent. I'll start on your defense," said Beasley. "You're practically a free man right now."

15

Ronnie Gets Serious

EVERYDAY THOMAS BEASLEY'S SECRETARY took her lunch at her office desk. During these periods she usually could be seen reading something. Clara Calhoun was so engrossed in the book Last Exit to Brooklyn, the gritty Hubert Selby Jr. novel, that she nibbled on her lip instead of her sandwich. Absorbed in the account of a prostitute headed for trouble, she failed to notice Ronnie Frantellini enter the Beasley law office.

Ronnie had to clear her throat to get Clara's attention. Embarrassed to be seen reading the Selby novel Clara quickly slipped the paperback book beneath a yellow legal pad. This concealment came too late. The second wife of the late Richard Frantellini, having read the book herself, recognized the cover of the racy novel.

"That's one of my favorite books," commented a smiling Ronnie, who was glad to come across someone who shared her reading interests.

"It's not mine," responded Clara. "Someone happened to leave the book in the office."

"Sure, honey, I know," said the widow, who wasn't fooled by Clara's feigned innocence.

Ronnie might have been a lot of things, but the one thing she wasn't was an elitist snob. Clara's defensiveness sparked Ronnie's curiosity. She continued to chat casually with Beasley's secretary, gathering insights into Clara's history. Ronnie learned that Clara's father, like her own, was a hopeless alcoholic. The shared experience of dealing with similar demons forged a connection between the two women.

"We have lot in common, honey," said Ronnie, who pitied the secretary as someone starting out in the same place she crawled out of. Oddly, Ronnie, who was selfish by nature, wanted to do something for Clara. After a while she came up with a way to help herself and Clara at the same time.

Ronnie had a concern that Clara was in a position to alleviate. The concern had to do with Thomas Beasley, the Frantellini family lawyer who handled all legal issues. Ronnie needed to ascertain exactly where Beasley's loyalty rested. Whether or not the attorney was going to favor the Frantellini sisters over her was the question. In Clara, Ronnie saw a way to find the answer to this.

Determined to recruit Beasley's secretary to her side of the equation, Ronnie undertook a campaign to win Clara over.

"Because we have a lot in common I think we should be good friends, honey," advised Ronnie.

"But I'm just a secretary, Ms. Frantellini," said Clara, displaying her insecurity.

"Let me give you a piece of advice, honey. There is nobody better than anyone else. It's all about perception. If you look like you're a somebody, people will treat you like you're a somebody."

Ronnie could tell by Clara's perplexed look that Beasley's secretary didn't quite grasp where she was coming from.

"Let me explain it another way," advised Ronnie. "No one is going to give you anything. You have to get a seat at the table if you want to take it from those who have. It's as simple as that."

"But how?"

"By using the right bait, honey, that's how. With a little fixing you could be a pretty girl, Clara. You have to play the cards you were dealt." This remark drew a blank stare. "Look," continued Ronnie, "I'd be willing to help you, as long as you're willing to help me."

"How can I help you?"

"Let's talk about this later. Tell Beasley I'm here."

"Yes, Ma'am, he's been expecting you." After notifying Beasley, the secretary said, "Go right in, Ms. Frantellini."

After a minute or two Clara tiptoed to the office door of her boss. She placed her ear to the door so that she could listen in. It soon became clear to Clara that the purpose of Ronnie's visit was to get the Frantellini family attorney to assist her in seizing full control of the shoe factory and real estate holdings.

Clara listened through the door as Beasley explained to Ronnie that the only way she could take full control of the Frantellini operation was by buying out the interests of the Frantellini sisters and Victor Spinello.

"How much do you think it would it take to swing that?" asked Ronnie with directness.

"I'm afraid that you'll have an upward battle trying to pull that off," answered the attorney bluntly.

"Why is that?"

"Because Maria Frantellini wants to buy you out."

"Me?" asked Ronnie in a surprised tone, "I'm the majority owner. Did you remind her of that?"

"The two sisters, with Victor Spinello on their team, have just as much equity as you in the shoe factory," pointed out Beasley. "As far as the real estate goes, you are equal partners with the sisters.

"So can't you figure out a way to swing Victor to my side?" "Sorry, but I can't do that. I'm already committed."

"What do you mean, you can't do that?"

"Maria Frantellini beat you to the punch. She, her sister Caroline, and Victor are already acting as one. I already signed on with them."

"So, Maria is the one leading the opposition."

"As of right now, that's right."

"Did you talk Victor into going along with the sisters?"

"We spoke. I went to see him in jail."

"He'll never get out."

"Don't bet on that," said Beasley with confidence. "I'll get Victor out."

"You could swing that?"

"Naturally," replied the lawyer smugly.

"Are you happy as Maria's lawyer?"

"It has advantages."

"Would you like to be happier?"

"I would always like to be happier."

Ronnie smiled a straight-line smile. She recognized that she was sitting across from a man who would have no qualms about double crossing his own mother.

"You never know, things might change for you in the future," said Ronnie.

"Perhaps things will," stated Beasley, who wondered what Ronnie was plotting. He suspected that she likely had a plan up her sleeve.

When Ronnie opened the door to leave Beasley's private office, she noticed that Clara's hair was out of place on one side of her head. She also noticed that the secretary's ear was red. No phone did that, thought Ronnie.

Suddenly, it dawned on Ronnie where that mysterious phone call she received about Maria Frantellini had come from. Ronnie was now certain of Clara's value as a mole who could keep her one step ahead of Maria Frantellini and her attorney.

"How about us having dinner together tomorrow evening, Clara? Have you ever been to Barney Tendler's Steak House on West Street?"

"No, Ma'am."

"Meet me there at 7:00 P.M. It'll be my treat. Just remember to keep this between us girls."

"Sure," said Clara, accepting the invitation.

"Great! I have to run now and see an old friend."

***

ON THE SURFACE SMILEY ALLEN was an engaging man with a pleasant way about him. As the owner of his own business, the runtish Allen knew the value of getting on with people who entered his establishment. He made it a point to greet his customers cordially, more often than not by their first name.

What few knew about Smiley was that he spent four years in prison for a crime he didn't commit. Smiley took the weight for a guilty party who couldn't face another criminal conviction. In return for his sacrifice, he received substantial compensation in the form of cash. After serving the sentence imposed, Smiley used the funds to finance Smiley's Place, a waterfront Brooklyn eatery that became a go to place for truck drivers, longshoremen and other blue-collar types.

Aside from offering an affordable breakfast, lunch and dinner, Smiley had another way of drawing customers. The three joker poker machines in the back room of the restaurant provided a fine amusement for those who liked to gamble.

Smiley was standing outside his restaurant smoking a cigarette when Ronnie Frantellini came by. Upon seeing Ronnie, a childhood friend, Smiley threw his cigarette to the ground. The big smile on his face made it clear that he was glad to see her.

"Ronnie!" exclaimed the businessowner enthusiastically. "How the hell are you?"

"It's Ronnie Frantellini now," corrected Ronnie.

"You got married?"

"Yeah, but my husband died unexpectedly."

"I'm sorry to hear that. Who did you marry?"

"You've heard of the Frantellini Sole haven't you?" asked Ronnie. Smiley nodded. "Well, I married the owner, Richard Frantellini."

"You're shitting me,"

"No, it's the truth. Richard Frantellini was my husband."

"Man, did you hit the jackpot. That family is loaded. They're into real estate as well, right?"

"That's right. Look, I'm here because I've got a problem, Smiley,"

"What kind of a problem?"

"One that only you can help me with."

Smiley now knew that the matter to be discussed required privacy. He suggested that they move the conversation to a private table in Smiley's restaurant. Once settled, Ronnie expressed her need without mincing words.

"I want a couple of people to leave this world, Smiley."

"You mean gone, like in no coming back?"

"That's right, finito."

"What have they done to you?"

"They're in my way," answered Ronnie, without elaborating.

"Who are you looking to off?"

"My dead husband's two daughters. When they're gone, I'll be set for life."

"Are you sure this is a road that you want to go down,Ronnie?" asked the childhood friend, recognizing the gravity of her request. "I mean this is serious business we're talking here."

"Listen, Smiley," replied Ronnie, "I might never get another chance at something this big again. And Smiley, you know me. I know how to take care of my friends."

"I know that, Ronnie."

"So, who do you know that can help me?"

"I know a guy who can take care of this. He's a professional wrestler."

"A wrestler!"

"Don't laugh, I met him in jail. Trust me, he's a dangerous man, and capable."

"I trust your judgement, Smiley." Ronnie handed some money to her friend. "Take this," she said. "A lot more will come your way once I cash in. Set up a meeting."

Smiley Allen didn't procrastinate. He immediately telephoned his wrestler friend.

"It's me, Smiley."

"Hey, man, what's up," asked the wrestler.

"I got some special work for you."

"What kind of money?" asked the wrestler.

"Enough to satisfy. Are you around or on the road?"

"I'm in Baltimore now, tomorrow I'm wrestling in Virginia. After that, I'm back in New York."

"Can you come by my place when you get back."

"Yeah. What kind of job are we talking about?"

"A friend is in need of an exterminator."

"Your friend has money?"

"Definitely."

"I'm back the day after tomorrow."

"Okay, hang on a second." Smiley turned to Ronnie and asked, "Can you meet him here the day after tomorrow?"

"Yes," replied Ronnie. "What time?"

"9 P.M."

"That's fine."

Smiley then conveyed to the wrestler the proposed time and place."

"That works," said the wrestler. "See you later, pal."

16

Crippler

IN THE WORLD OF PROFESSIONAL WRESTLING financial success requires other skills beyond an imposing physical presence and the ability to wrestle. A large part of what makes a wrestler a marketable product was adeptness at communicating during interviews in a way that stirred fan interest. Also important was having a gimmick that would draw crowds to an arena and/or stimulate the purchase of closed-circuit presentations.

Factoring in promotional items, the right combination could net an athlete a fortune. Unfortunately, Crippler didn't fall into this category.

As a wrestler Crippler was average. He was just a tough thick necked guy who knew how to roughhouse and tumble. His communication ability was poor, often stuttering during televised interviews. He possessed no gimmick that would gain him traction in his career. As a result of all this, after a short push by the promoters, Crippler found himself relegated to jobber status.

Working as a jobber meant that he worked preliminary matches in which he was rarely scheduled to win. His role was to lose in order to build the reputation of the rising star performers. For adhering to the losing scripts put forth to him, Crippler was paid undercard wages.

Feeling the financial pinch due to a contentious divorce, Crippler resorted to using his brawn in ways that took him beyond the squared circle. He basically drifted into criminality to supplement his income. Saddled with alimony and child support payments made the embittered Crippler ornery enough to take on any form of wrongdoing for the right pay.

Years of ring work had left its mark on Crippler's appearance. His brutish look actually helped his sideline activities. Both of Crippler's ears were cauliflower. His nose was slightly bent to one side. Visible were a number of pronounced scars that ran east to west across Crippler's forehead. These creases across his brow were a product of blading, a process in which a wrestler cuts himself during a match with a razorblade that had been hidden in his trunks. The purpose for this coloring was to excite the fans during matches.

Crippler's voice was gruff, which seemed to fit his large imposing stature. Combined with a swagger, Crippler presented enough of a package to draw the interest of those in need of a thug with an intimidating presence. The wrestler proved to be a viable resource for many.

Moneylenders who wanted to collect money from deadbeats hired Crippler. Landlords looking to oust a difficult tenant also called upon Crippler as a solution. He was even an option for businessmen seeking to dissolve partnerships. In the majority of these cases a conversation with Crippler was usually sufficient for the targeted individuals to comply.

As this type of work became more common for Crippler his reputation grew. He gradually transitioned to more challenging assignments. These undertakings almost always entailed violence. For the right price Crippler broke arms, legs or even backs when called upon. He wasn't beyond taking a life if properly compensated.

Crippler's flexibility was something known to Smiley Allen, who was aware that Ronnie Frantellini would be willing to pay handsomely for what she wanted.

***

AS ARRANGED CRIPPLER MET WITH RONNIE FRANTELLINI at Smiley Allen's eatery. Once the introductions were made Smiley made himself scarce. He saw no upside to being involved in a murderous plot. Smiley convinced himself that he shared no culpability whatsoever for having facilitated the meeting between Ronnie and Crippler.

Over coffee Ronnie and Crippler wasted no time in discussing the work at hand. Crippler was taken aback at learning he was being asked to murder two women. Not that he was disinclined to do this, he was just surprised. Once they got beyond the hurdle of arriving at a mutually acceptable fee the two discussed strategy.

"How do you plan to do it?" asked Ronnie.

"That depends. Anyway, does it really matter how I do it?" Crippler questioned.

"Not really. I was just curious."

"I'll figure it out, but I need to know more," said the wrestler turned contract killer.

"Well, how long do you think it will take to get this done?"

"Again, it depends," replied Crippler. "Are you going to be able to get the sister from Italy over here?"

"I have a way."

"Can you arrange to get the sisters together someplace? That way I can take care of the two of them at the same time."

"That'll be no problem. Just tell me where you want them?"

Crippler thought for a few seconds before replying. "How about a busy restaurant?"

"I can definitely make that happen," advised Ronnie.

"Do you have a problem being there when the curtain comes down?"

"I prefer to be there."

"Good," said Crippler. "You get them to meet with you in a large busy restaurant. I'll do the rest. All I need is a couple of weeks preparation time in order to make my arrangements."

"Fine, I'll put together some dates and get back to you."

***

RONNIE FRANTELLINI TELEPHONED THOMAS BEASLEY to inform him that she wanted to see him for the purpose of assisting her in structuring a business transaction. She declined to discuss exactly what that transaction was over the telephone. Beasley was also in the dark as to the newly established friendship between Ronnie and Clara, his secretary. He would have been stunned to learn that Clara had told Ronnie all about the attorney's dalliances with her adversarial stepdaughter, Maria Frantellini.

When dealing with men Ronnie relied heavily on her attractive appearance. Experience taught her that playing up that angle went far in reaching whatever outcome she desired. Ronnie arrived at the Beasley Law Office looking her best. Her clothes flattered her figure, her hair was stylishly arranged, and her nails were freshly coated. Her makeup was impeccably applied, in short, she turned heads.

Ronnie greeted Clara with just a smile, revealing no further indication of their familiarity. Clara, having undergone some of Ronnie's tutoring, reciprocated by keeping the interaction professional. "May I help you, Ms. Frantellini?" asked the secretary, maintaining the distancing.

"Please let Mr. Beasley know that I'm here," answered Ronnie. Once Ronnie was inside Beasley's private office, the attorney's secretary placed her ear to the door.

Clara listened closely to the conversation inside the office. She was able to hear enough to get the drift of what was happening.

"Good to see you," said the attorney. "Have a seat."

"Thank you."

"So, Ronnie, what is this business that brings you here?"
Beasley asked.

"I've changed my mind," advised the wife of the late Richard Frantellini after taking a chair.

"About?"

"I've thought it over and decided that I'd be willing to sell out to my stepdaughters."

"You are?" asked the shocked attorney. "Why the sudden change of heart?"

"I'm just fed up and want out. If things are done fairly, I'll have enough money to do whatever I please. I can't see myself spending the rest of my life fighting with Maria Frantellini and smelling the stink of leather. There are better things to do while I am still young enough to enjoy doing them."

"I think that's a very practical way to look at things," advised the attorney, who was happy to hear this news. "But understand, you can't expect me to collude with you and take advantage of the Frantellini sisters. I mean, after all…."

"Save it, Tom," voiced Ronnie, silencing the lawyer. "I'm past looking to take advantage of anyone. Just get me the best price you can."

"That's fine then. I'll talk to Maria Frantellini and call the accountant to get a fair evaluation."

"You do that," said Ronnie, "and get back to me as soon as you can. I want this over and done with quickly."

Beasley smiled as he watched Ronnie rise from her seat to leave. Clara, once realizing that the meeting was concluding, scooted to her workstation. When Ronnie Frantellini passed by her desk, she gave Clara a wink.

Once Ronnie was gone, the attorney telephoned Maria Frantellini to convey her stepmother's willingness to sell.

"It looks like you win, Maria," said the attorney.

"Win what?"

"Your stepmother wants out. She told me that she is willing to sell off her end of things."

"For how much?"

"I can get you a deal. She isn't looking to make things difficult."

"All of a sudden she wants to play nice in the sandbox?" asked Maria, who was suspicious. "Why do you think that is, Tom? She has to have a reason."

"Who cares why," said Beasley. "Don't overthink this. She wants out, so let's accommodate her," emphasized Beasley. "I'm sure that we can get away with lowballing her."

"You do?"

"Yes, I do. If you can get the accountant to work with me, things will turn out well for us. All he has to is provide me with the right evaluation."

"He'll do as I ask."

"And your sister Caroline, she'll go along with everything and sign papers, right?"

"She'll be no problem."

"Excellent."

"What about Victor?"

"As long as I'm keeping him out of jail," advised Beasley, "I have him in the palm of my hand."

Maria wasted no time notifying her sister. The physician, who lived comfortably in Milan with her physician husband, voiced no objection to buying out her stepmother.

"I'm fine with whatever you want to do, Maria," said Caroline.

"What about Ettore?" Maria questioned.

"My husband feels as I do. We both have faith in your ability to manage our interests in America."

"You're going to have to stay in New York until we can settle things."

"But Ettore....is expecting me home"

"Ettore will be patient. He's better off in Milan where he can take care of things. You won't be here that long. Okay, Caroline?"

"I suppose it will have to be, Maria."

***

DR. ETTORE TENGO WAS sitting in his home library having a glass of red wine after a hard day of work. Childless, his house was always quiet. It was times like this that he felt lonely without his wife being in Milan with him. Still mourning the death of his brother, his melancholy mood was magnified by Caroline remaining in America. Spurred by his feeling sorry for himself he picked up the telephone after consuming his second glass of vino.

The conversation between the married couple began with a discussion of current events pertaining to their patients. Once this topic was exhausted, their catching up turned to happenings in New York City.

"I'm sorry I can't be there with you in New York, Caroline," said the doctor. "But one of us is needed here in Milan to tend to our patients. How are things going there?"

"I'm really not sure," she replied. "My sister is taking the lead in settling the family business mess."

"Do you think Maria would be interested in buying us out?" asked Ettore. "You know, I really wish she would."

"Is that wise, Ettore? Maria is convinced that Victor Spinello is on the verge of coming out with a great new product he's developing."

"Don't ever mention that name to be!" Ettore barked. "That bastard murdered my brother!"

"I know how you feel, but if this product is successful, it could mean a lot of money."

"I don't want a dime of his money! He's in jail where he belongs, and he should rot there!"

"But Maria said…."

Ettore, who was now highly agitated, didn't want to hear another word. He abruptly hung up on his wife. It was just as well. Caroline didn't have to tell him that the Frantellini family lawyer was representing Victor in his criminal case.

17

Wolfman Glass

THE MURDEROUS PLAN CRIPPLER HATCHED required the assistance of an accomplice. He found just the man he needed in an over the hill fellow wrestler. Wolfman Jack Glass had been a main event wrestler at his peak. Once reduced to undercard status, the amount of his pay was greatly diminished. He was now eking out a living often performing in the ring as the tag team partner of Crippler.

To minimize expenses, the two men traveled together when scheduled to appear in out of state wrestling venues. They passed the time when on the road by drinking beer in the car. Having the same mindset led to a bonding in which they trusted each other implicitly.

Both Crippler and Wolfman saw the prudence in taking an advantage wherever possible. In order to reduce expenses while on the road, they were in the habit of skipping out of diners without paying the bill. Their success in this larcenous behavior made both men more amenable to wrongdoing of a more serious nature.

Crippler set out to the Milford, Pennsylvania home of Wolfman Glass. Glass, a married man with children, was a big beer drinker who was all for having a good time. His cavorting while on the road left him habitually low on funds. His financial distress caused him to welcome any opportunity that would alleviate his economic difficulties. Generally speaking, the nature of the work mattered little. Be it a legitimate or criminal undertaking, if the payoff was there, so was Wolfman Glass.

Wolfman was memorable in appearance. A burly man who stood well over six feet, the three-hundred-pounder sported a long white beard and an ample head of snow-white hair. His pinkish complexion gave him something of a Santa Claus look.

Over a beer in Wolfman's home, Crippler put forth his proposition. Wolfman assumed a serious look when told that the work involved the execution of two women. Homicide was something new for him, as it was for Crippler. Glass stroked his long beard as he thought things over.

"What's wrong?" Crippler asked, sensing reluctance.

"Killing is something pretty serious," replied Wolfman. "What the hell is the difference?" Crippler asked. "Nobody lives forever. Besides, think of the money we'll be getting. The payoff is going to be big."

"I don't know about this," conveyed Wolfman. Wolfman's lack of enthusiasm for the work compelled Crippler to sweeten the pot.

"Look, I'm willing to split fifty-fifty with you on this. What do you say? "

The offer softened Wolfman's reluctance. "How much money are we talking about?"

Wolfman was advised of the money to be made. He found the number to be convincing.

"So, what's the verdict?" Crippler asked.

"I suppose that we don't always get to do what we like," said Glass, who now reconsidered. "I'm in."

"Now you're talking. Think of how many bumps in the ring we'd have to take to make this kind of money."

"Okay, I said that I'm in. So, what's the plan?"

Crippler explained how they were to go about murdering the Frantellini sisters. After working out the details of the intended crime, the wrestlers headed to the nearest pet shop. Being allergic to dogs and cats, Crippler remained in the car.

Wolfman entered the pet store and walked through the aisles in search of what he was looking for. He passed by turtles, fish, birds, lizards, puppies, and kittens before finding the mice he wanted. Glass purchased three, the limit that would fit in one of his large hands.

"Are you feeding a pet snake?" asked the fiftyish counterwoman, who looked at the ex-wrestler over glasses that hung low on her nose. "If yes, we also have nice large white rats available."

"This will do," stated Wolfman, as he took out his wallet. "My wife doesn't eat rats, only mice." he said tartly. The counterwoman ignored the remark. "What kind of snake do you have?"

"What snake?" asked Glass, sounding annoyed.

"Some snakes can eat poultry, depending on their type of course," explained the counterwoman.

"Look lady, I got no interest in the dietary habits of snakes," barked the customer.

"Then what do you want with mice? Do you plan to keep them as pets?"

"Me and the wife eat them for breakfast," answered the wrestler snottily. "Now what do I owe you?"

The wrestler's rude response put an end to the woman's inquisitiveness.

"How did you make out?" asked Crippler, who had been waiting behind the wheel of his car.

"I got three mice," answered Wolfman.

"Where do we go for the Kool-Aid?"

"Stay on this road. There is a guy I know who has a brother who works at a pharmacy. He can supply us."

Leaving Crippler behind in the car, Wolfman entered the office of a small carwash. A few minutes later, Wolfman Glass returned to the car.

"How did you make out?" asked Crippler.

"Sit tight, it's getting delivered. Let me have some money."

Twenty minutes later a Jeep pulled up to the car wash. The driver, a balding boney looking man, parked and entered the office. A few minutes later Wolfman's friend emerged from the car wash. He signaled Wolfman to join him. Wolfman walked over to his friend. In exchange for cash, Wolfman was handed a small package containing cyanide in a liquid form. The wrestler then returned to Crippler's waiting car.

"This shit is pale blue hydrogen cyanide," said Wolfman after handing the cyanide over to Crippler. "It works fast and its perfect for putting in a drink."

"Great," said Crippler, who then telephoned Ronnie Frantellini. "I'm all set to go," advised Crippler.

"I'll get us a restaurant," said Ronnie. "Me, my two stepdaughters and my lawyer will be at the table. Okay?"

"That's fine. Now listen, this is important. A very large man with a long white beard will pass by your table. He'll bend down to tie his shoe. When he does, all you have to do is look down at the floor and start screaming your head off.

"What am I supposed to be screaming about?"

"There will be mice under the table."

"I hate mice!"

"That's the idea. Now when you see them, you jump up from the table and start hollering. Make sure that you throw your arms around the lawyer's head while you scream blue murder. I don't want that lawyer to see anything. Do you think you could pull that off?"

"Don't worry about me," said Ronnie with assuredness. "I've pulled more than that off." Crippler wasn't quite sure how to take Ronnie's remark.

***

THOMAS BEASLEY, AT THE REQUEST OF RONNIE FRANTELLINI, made a dinner reservation at an upper westside restaurant on Columbus Avenue. On the evening of the dinner the attorney set a tone of reconciliation to those assembled at the table. He explained to the parties involved that whatever animosity existed needed to be set aside so that they could arrive at a palatable resolution. Everyone seemed amenable to this.

Beasley presented the acquisition deal he drafted. The proposition clearly was structured to favor the Frantellini sisters. Ronnie voiced not one objection. Her failing to pose questions was surprising to all at the table. Thanks to the ease in putting over the transaction, Beasley was in high spirits. He signaled for the waiter. Beasley ordered an expensive bottle of wine and told the waiter to keep the wine coming.

Crippler, using an alias, had made a reservation to dine alone at the restaurant in question. Upon arriving he was pleased to see that the restaurant was crowded. This was to his advantage. From a small table Crippler visually scanned the restaurant looking to see where Ronnie, two women and a man, were seated. Once he spotted them, he telephoned Wolfman Glass, who was waiting outside the restaurant a short distance away. Crippler provided Glass with a detailed description of the sisters and their table location. He then told him to stand by.

"Would you like something to drink?" asked the waiter, a small man with an accent.

"Let me have a Peroni," replied Crippler. "And let me have a salad, oil and vinegar."

"And for a main course?"

"Seafood Fra Diavolo."

"Very good, sir."

"Where is the bathroom."

"The restrooms are in the back to the right, sir."

This is perfect, Crippler thought, *Wolfman will have to pass by their table to get there.* Crippler telephoned his crime partner apprising him accordingly.

When a bottle of wine was delivered to the table of the Frantellini sisters, Crippler watched to see if they would drink it. After they took their first sip, the wrestler again telephoned Wolfman, advising him that the targeted women were drinking from wine glasses. Crippler then gave his associate the green light to proceed with their plan.

Wolfman entered the restaurant and walked immediately to where the restroom was located. On reaching the table where the Frantellini sisters sat, he noticed a woman at the table locking eyes with his. Her look alerted him that she was Ronnie Frantellini. Ronnie had no trouble recognizing the white bearded man who she had been awaiting.

Wolfman stopped alongside the table of the victim(s). He bent down, pretending to tie his shoelace. This was Crippler's cue to start heading toward the Frantellini table. It was also the cue for Ronnie to prepare to create a scene.

While down low, Wolfman reached into the large pocket of his coat and took hold of the three white mice he carried. He tossed the rodents under the table, one of which landed on Ronnie's foot. The stepmother's subsequent screeches were genuine. She flipped out at the feel of the mouse on her bare toes. Ronnie jumped to her feet and, as scripted, threw her arms around the head of Beasley. She began shouting that there were mice under the table.

This outburst caused the Frantellini sisters to also rise from their chairs and scurry about. In the midst of the chaos, Crippler was able slip liquid cyanide in the wine glass of each sister. As anticipated, the diversion enabled him to do this unnoticed. By the time things settled, Wolfman Glass had already left the restaurant, and Crippler was back at his own table.

Maria Frantellini, her sister Caroline, Beasley, and Ronnie Frantellini all eventually returned to their seats once the turmoil subsided. The Frantellini sisters reacted within seconds of each other, each succumbing to the effects of the cyanide. Beasley was stunned to see the sisters collapse at the table. He immediately went to their side in an attempt to revive them. Once realizing that his efforts were futile, he turned to glance at Ronnie. His gaze caused him to notice that Ronnie seemed calm, her lips taut.

The ambulance was promptly summoned, with all thinking that the sisters were felled by heart attacks prompted by the sight of the mice. The restaurant management provided no logical explanation as to how mice had made their way onto the floor of the restaurant. The toxicology reports would later reflect cyanide in the systems of the dead women. This now made the deaths a matter of homicide. A later police inquiry conducted by precinct detectives produced negative results.

***

WHEN FATHER FIORELLO ST. DENIS learned of the simultaneous death of Maria and Caroline Frantellini, he could hardly believe it. He wasted no time contacting Dr. Ettore Tengo, Caroline's husband, in Milan.

Father St. Denis was there to pick up Dr. Tengo at the airport when he arrived in New York. The distraught husband emerged from the airplane in a funky state. On their way to Manhattan, Ettore embraced the priest's offer to go and see his friend, the chief of detectives.

"I think that makes sense, Ettore," voiced the religious man. "I can't get over what happened, Father," said the doctor. "Who would want to kill them?" "The detectives, God willing, will uncover the answer to that question. We just need to give them some time."

The doctor went on to lament the ordeal of having to ship his wife's body back to Milan. Here again, Father St. Denis came forward with a suggestion.

"Since it was just you and your wife, Doctor, you should consider having Caroline's remains placed in the Frantellini mausoleum. She'll be with her sister and parents."

"Where is that?"

"In Brooklyn's Greenwood Cemetery."

"I suppose that would be easier. Do you think that Caroline would have wanted that, Father?"

"I really think so, Ettore," answered the priest. "And I'm sure that there is room there for you when the time comes."

"Resting in Brooklyn with my wife is as good a place as any."

18

Another Favor

CHIEF OF DETECTIVES HARRY MCCOY sat at his office desk shaking his head sympathetically at Father Fiorello St. Denis and Doctor Ettore Tengo. He listened without comment as the department chaplain articulated how Ettore had flown in from Milan in response to the execution of his wife and sister-in-law. The priest didn't ask for any favors. He didn't have to. His mere presence indicated that.

McCoy, being the good politician he was, saw pleasing the department chaplain as good insurance. The chief reasoned that a good word from St. Denis would go far with the higher ups.

Being a believer, the chief also couldn't help but think that doing right by the priest might do him some good when his time on earth expired.

Chief McCoy assured his visitors that he would have his best detectives support the precinct investigators in solving the double homicide of the Frantellini sisters. McCoy wasted no time in calling Markie to his office.

"What's up, Silvie?" Markie asked when he passed by the desk of Detective Silverlake, who had notified him that the chief wanted to see him forthwith.

"I guess the chief's has new work for you," replied Silverlake."

"What kind of job?"

"I got no idea. All I know is that he's got the department chaplain and some doctor from Italy in his office."

"Which chaplain?" "Father St. Denis."

"He's becoming a regular," said Markie to Von Hess, as he proceeded to the chief's office alone.

"Come in, Sergeant," said Chief McCoy upon seeing Markie standing in the doorway of his office. "Say hello to Father St. Denis and Dr. Tengo."

"Nice to see you again," said Markie, extending his hand to the visitors.

Markie remembered both men from the Dario Tengo homicide. After the handshakes, the chief got down to business.

"Doctor Tengo is here from Milan," reminded the chief. "You worked on that unfortunate business concerning his brother Dario and the Frantellini Shoe Factory."

"I remember, Chief."

"Well, now he's lost his wife and her sister. They were poisoned while eating dinner in a Manhattan restaurant. I want you and Von Hess to get to the bottom of it."

"I'm sorry for your trouble, Doctor," said Markie. "This is the first I'm hearing about this."

"This was not a shooting, so it didn't get a big splash," explained the chief to Doctor Tengo and the priest.

"When did this happen, Chief?" Markie asked.

"You were off, Sarge."

"Were the victims alone having dinner?"

"No, their lawyer and the stepmother were present at the table."

"It was only the sisters who were victimized?"

"I'm not sure of all the details," answered the chief. "That's why you're in here. Go out there and get a handle on things."

"Do we know the kind of poison used?"

"Get out there and find out the answers yourself," barked the chief, who disliked being asked questions he didn't have answers to.

"I believe it was cyanide, Chief," injected Father St. Denis, trying to be helpful.

At this juncture Markie was granted permission to interview Father St. Denis and Dr. Ettore Tengo individually in a private office at headquarters. After the sergeant and Von Hess completed the two interviews, they went to see the precinct detective who was charged with investigating the double homicide of the Frantellini sisters.

The precinct detective assigned to the case was a soft spoken, gray-haired man who made a distinguished appearance. In his late 50's, the six-foot detective looked very good for his age.

Having seen lots in his years with the department, he was too seasoned to feel that Markie and Von Hess were being intrusive by showing interest in his case. On the contrary, the investigator welcomed the assistance of the men from headquarters. Their presence meant less work for him to do.

After speaking with the precinct investigator, Markie and Von Hess reviewed the Frantellini case file.

"Ollie, let's take a ride over to the Frantellini Shoe Factory," announced Markie after reviewing the folder. "I want to talk to the stepmother who was at the restaurant when this went down. Let's hear what she has to say firsthand."

"Do you want me to call the shoe factory and see if she is available, Sarge?" Von Hess asked. Markie nodded his approval. Von Hess made an appointment for them to see Ronnie Frantellini at her factory office later that afternoon.

***

IMMEDIATELY AFTER AGREEING TO meet with the detectives, Ronnie Frantellini picked up the telephone and called the attorney Thomas Beasley.

"Beasley law office," announced Clara, after picking up the telephone. "How may I help you?" asked the secretary.

"It's me, Clara. I need to speak to Beasley." "Hold on, I'll transfer you," said Clara.

"We need to talk," said Ronnie once she had the attorney on the line.

"You sound tense. What's wrong?"

"A detective from police headquarters called me. He's meeting with me later this afternoon."

"This is probably about what happened at the restaurant."

"Duh!"

"Okay, relax, Ronnie. You already spoke to them once, let's see what else they want to know."

"These guys are from the chief of detective's office, not the precinct."

"That makes no difference," assured Beasley. "Just stick to the account you previously provided."

The tone of concern in Ronnie Frantellini's voice was as good as admission to the attorney. Beasley was relatively certain at this juncture that Ronnie had something to do with the double homicide.

"I want you there with me," said Ronnie, leaving no room for debate. "Meet me at the Poor Pep's across the street from my office in an hour."

"Very well, Ronnie. See you there."

Ronnie was seated in a booth inside the bar restaurant when Beasley arrived. She was drinking a Cosmopolitan. The attorney took a seat opposite his client and ordered the same.

"You're getting heated up about nothing, Ronnie," advised the lawyer, "Detectives ask questions, that's what they do. I'll let you know when to start worrying."

I should have expected something like this, thought the attorney. *Ronnie had everything to gain with the sisters out of the way. I must have been sleeping!*

The thought of Ronnie being involved in the commission of a double homicide irked Beasley. He wasn't outraged by the horrendous act itself because he, like Ronnie, was ruthless. His ire stemmed from the disappointment of not benefiting financially.

Perhaps it's not too late, he thought.

The attorney intended to try for a new arrangement with Ronnie Frantellini. With Ronnie now being partnerless, with the exception of a tiny piece of the shoe factory owned by Victor Spinello, Beasley saw a cash cow prime for milking.

"Nervous, Ronnie?" asked Beasley, with a knowing look about him.

"I don't understand why these detectives from police headquarters are coming around."

"You'll know once you talk to them."

"I don't see why they would involve themselves," stated Ronnie.

"Relax, you're in the clear."

Ronnie did a double take. "What's that supposed to mean?"

"If they just want to talk it means they haven't got anything that can link you to the killings."

"Link me to the killings!" Ronnie exclaimed, sounding shocked at what was said. "What have I to do with anything?"

"You stood the most to gain by the death of those two girls," said Beasley bluntly. "The detectives are limited, but they aren't morons. You're not fooling anyone, Ronnie. Certainly not me."

Ronnie stiffened at hearing this. "What are you trying to say, Tom?"

"You have nothing to worry about as long as you and I can arrive at an understanding."

Ronnie lifted her head up slightly and sat back as she stared at the lawyer. She now knew that the attorney knew. Realizing that a man of Beasley's ilk would stop at nothing, Ronnie had little choice other than to come to terms.

"So, you're shaking me down," Ronnie accused. "Don't forget, you were at that table too."

"I prefer to look at this in a business context," said Beasley. "The law will view me as someone having nothing to gain. If I were inclined to assist them, well that wouldn't be to your benefit."

"Assist them how?"

"Use your imagination, Ronnie. I can spin a pretty good tale when it comes to what I saw and heard."

Ronnie exhaled deeply before speaking. Her conclusion was to the point. "Now I know why they call you Sleazy Beasley."

"Now, now, no need to get nasty."

"Are you coming with me when I meet these detectives later?"

"I'll be there, if we come to an understanding."

Ronnie ordered another round of Cosmopolitans. Once the refreshments arrived Ronnie didn't bother to mince words.

"So, what's it going to take for us to get together?" Ronnie asked.

"I'm not a pig," replied Beasley. I just want ten percentage of whatever you pull down from the shoe factory and the real estate."

"You can't expect me to sign papers cutting you in."

"No, of course not. You'll just pay me my end in cash on a monthly basis."

"You realize that there are other ways to deal with people like you," threatened Ronnie, using a soft voice to convey her point.

"That road travels both ways," stated Beasley icily. The lawyer wasn't bluffing.

Ronnie was convinced that the attorney was her equal in terms of being dangerous. Feeling that she had no other options for now, she agreed to the lawyer's terms.

"Okay, there is enough to go around," said Ronnie. "I suppose you'll want to continue to represent the Frantellini interests, right?"

"Of course."

The attorney raised his glass to toast their unholy alliance. Beasley went on to explain the arrangement he had made with Maria Frantellini that pertained to getting Victor Spinello out of jail. Ronnie liked this, appreciating the upside of having Victor's Dynamic Shoe under the Frantellini umbrella. She authorized Beasley to continue in that direction, stipulating that he devise an incentive plan that Victor would agree to.

***

AS THINGS TURNED OUT, Markie and Von Hess got nothing out of Ronnie Frantellini. Her account, which was echoed by Thomas Beasley, remained as previously given to the precinct detective. They both claimed to have seen nothing other than mice in the restaurant. They knew of no one that would want to harm the sisters and so on. The detectives walked away from the interviews skeptically.

"I don't know about those two, Ollie," stated the sergeant

when alone. "She had good reason to see those women dead, Sarge. With the sisters gone, Ronnie's top dog."

"There is something about that lawyer that stinks as well. He seemed a little too damn confident."

Markie looked at Beasley's business card. Seeing two addresses, one in Brooklyn and one in Manhattan, on the card prompted him to visit the police precinct that covered each address. The squad commander in each precinct told the investigators what they knew of Sleazy Beasley. Based on this feedback, both Markie and Von Hess were now more suspicious of Ronnie Frantellini and Thomas Beasley than ever.

"What now, Sarge?" Von Hess asked.

"Let's go to that restaurant where the girls died."

"Do you want to interview the staff? "That, and I want to take a peek at their reservation log. Maybe that will tell us something."

19

Money Talks

THOMAS BEASLEY'S SECRETARY was looking into a small mirror when Teddy Leonard arrived at the lawyer's office. Realizing someone entered the office she instinctively began to touch her newly styled hair. The outfit she wore was new. It complemented her new figure. Her nails, colored a bold red, matched the toes hidden inside her shoes.

In a relatively short period of time Clara had made a dramatic transformation. Thanks to a physical trainer and a registered dietician the secretary had finally begun to feel good about herself. This progress was made possible thanks to the financing provided by Ronnie Frantellini. Part of the reason for Ronnie's generosity was to have a friend/informer inside Thomas Beasley's office who could monitor the activities of the attorney she didn't trust.

Clara had no thoughts of Teddy Leonard in a romantic sense. But she did want him, and others, to notice her improvement. She craved a complimentary word in recognition of her beautification efforts. The fitness center, the dieting and beauty treatments were now a part of Clara's routine. Unfortunately, her hope of a flattering word from Leonard wasn't realized.

Leonard's lack of acknowledgment was a blow to the secretary's ego. Clara found the retired detective's failure to even smile or engage the secretary in polite conversation to be disappointing. His apparent lack of interest turned out to be something positive in the long run. It served as motivation for Clara to intensify her self-improvement efforts.

"I'll let Mr. Beasley know you are here," advised Clara, addressing the private investigator.

"You do that, sweetheart," said Leonard.

The secretary cringed at being called sweetheart. She felt that the term was uttered without sincerity. With tightened lips she telephoned Beasley to tell him of the private investigator's presence. Clara made it a point to mention to her boss that the visitor arrived without an appointment.

"I'm telling you, Tommy," that secretary out there is a strange duck," said the private investigator.

"Clara is ok, leave her alone," said Beasley. "Did you ever get an office for yourself?"

"I don't need an office."

"I can rent you space here if you want," offered the attorney.

"No thanks, I don't need the overhead. I'm doing fine working from my house."

"You'll get more clients if you have a regular business address."

"I got enough work already. I don't need more."

"How much juice do you have in the Manhattan Criminal Court?"

"I got people I could talk to there," answered Leonard. "What do you need?"

"I need to get to a juror. There is big money in this for you if you could swing it."

"Give me what information you have, and I'll see what I could do."

Through his court connections Leonard was able to learn the identity of the jurors in the Victor Spinello trial. His subsequent research led him to identify jurors who might be receptive to compromise.

***

RUDOLPH PRISINSKI WAS A MARRIED BUSINESSMAN who resided in a Manhattan apartment in an upscale building that came with a doorman. He and his wife were the owners of a Manhattan based public relations firm that had seen better days.

While conducting research on the jurors he thought pliable in the Victor Spinello case, Teddy Leonard learned that the Prisinski business was linked to several addresses in recent years. Each relocation was to a less impressive building. This suggested hard times to the private investigator, who decided to probe further.

After conducting a discreet inquiry at a former address of the juror's firm the private investigator learned much. He found out that Mrs. Prisinski was confined to a wheelchair. He also confirmed that the Prisinski public relations firm had been spiraling downward, forcing the entity to move to less expensive office space.

At another former corporate address, the private investigator learned more. A cleaner for the building, after being incentivized, advised that he knew Rudy Prisinski fairly well. The source indicated that Prisinski and his wife were involved in a terrible automobile accident resulting in Mrs. Prisinski being paralyzed from the waist down. Their conversation was to the point.

"The wife was the one who wore the pants," said the cleaner. "Everyone around here knew that she ran the whole show."

"Who was driving?" Leonard asked.

"Rudy was. There was some talk going around that they were both drunk."

"Was he?"

"Probably. All I know is that they both drank. Rudy once told me that his wife would rather drink and watch television than work."

"Why would he tell you all this?"

"Because I'm a good listener. I ran into him in the bar around the corner one night. He was half-bombed and needed someone to talk to."

"Did he mention money problems?"

"Oh, yes. He went on about how big his business once was and how he had to downsize. Mr. Prisinski told me that at one time he had a dozen people working for him. When he was here he had only two people working part time for him."

What neither man knew was that Rudy Prisinski was now desperate enough to consider closing the business and looking for a job. Exasperating matters at home was his wife's continually blaming him for causing the accident that restricted her. Such peppering hardened Rudy to where there was no longer any self-guilt. Whatever sympathy he had for his wife had vanished.

Rudy's thoughts were blackest when drinking. If she hadn't been yapping that night that accident would never have happened! She was the cause! Sure, I had a couple of drinks that night, but so did she. She went on that talking jag and distracted me! Why doesn't God just take her?

The private investigator, his interest stirred, began shadowing Rudy Prisinski. He was waiting for the right opportunity to approach the fifty-year-old juror. Leonard watched as the glum faced Prisinski shopped in a supermarket. Seeing his man sift through discount coupons made it clear that Rudy Prisinski could use a financial boost.

Leonard's chance came after Prisinski finished food shopping. After dropping his packages off at his apartment, the public relations man went to a neighborhood bar. As Prisinski stood at the rail having his scotch and soda, Leonard assumed a position next to him. After ordering a beer the private investigator initiated a conversation with Prisinski. After some small talk Leonard tapped his index finger on the bar, indicating to the bartender that he was buying Prisinski a drink.

The surprised Prisinski looked at the private investigator and nodded his thanks for the drink. He then grew leery of Leonard. Prisinski suspected that the stranger was looking to hook up.

When Leonard began to expand their conversation the juror stiffened, responding curtly.

"Look, my friend," began Prisinski, "Thanks for the drink, but I'm not interested." Leonard found the comment amusing.

"Relax, pal," said the private investigator, "you got me all wrong.

I'm here to talk business with you."

"What kind of business?"

"The kind that will give you some financial relief."

"I don't follow you…."

"I got a sweet proposition for you, Rudy."

"How do you know my name?"

"I know all about you, Rudy."

"What's your game? What do you want from me?"

"I'm a private investigator. I'm here representing someone willing to put money in your pocket in return for you doing a small favor."

This interested Prisinski, who was desperate for money.

"Who is the someone, what's the favor and how much are we talking about?" Rudy asked.

"The who is my business," replied Leonard. "Me fattening you up to the tune of thirty grand in cash is yours end. And that's tax free, my friend."

"Well, what is the favor?"

"Not convicting an innocent man." "

Oh, I get it now."

"Let's take our drinks and go sit in a booth where we could talk," said Leonard. The two men resumed their conversation over another drink when seated.

"All you have to do is say that you believe that Victor Spinello is innocent and stick to your guns. It's as easy as that," explained Leonard. "A hung jury is as good as an acquittal."

Prisinski took a second before replying to the offer.

"You're asking me to take a big chance. Don't get me wrong, I'm interested because I could use the money. But you're asking a lot of me in return for peanuts."

Leonard was now certain that Prisinski was corruptible.

"Okay, so what's it going to take to get you on board?"

"More than thirty grand," said the juror without hesitation. "This is a murder trial. What value do you put on saving a man from decades in prison?"

"So, give me a number."

"A hundred thousand."

"Whoa!" Leonard declared. "That's way out of line. I'm not asking you to break him out of prison."

"Okay, so how close to that number can you get?"

"How about I give you thirty-five grand?"

"For the chance you're asking me to take? I'm afraid not," answered Prisinski, who rose to his feet, signaling that he was prepared to walk off.

"Sit down, Rudy," said Leonard, who could tell that Rudy knew how to haggle. "We'll get together on this. But, you have to work with me."

Rudy dropped back down into his seat and asked, "What's the counter?"

The private investigator produced ten thousand dollars in cash and rested it on the table. He pushed the money toward Rudy. As Leonard anticipated, the gesture went far in inducing Prisinski's to soften his position. With the cash only inches away from his grasp, the juror could only see money. After some further back and forth they eventually agreed to a total payoff of forty-two thousand dollars.

"Take the ten grand for now," said Leonard. "You'll get the rest after the trial."

"Okay, you got a deal," said the juror taking the money. "Exactly when and where do I get the balance?"

"The very next day after the verdict is rendered, you meet me right here at 6:00 P.M. for a drink. I'll have your money for you, and you're buying."

"How do I know if I could trust you to pay me the rest of the money?

"You got nothing to worry about. I'll be sitting in that courtroom practically every day during the trial. Here, you take my business card. On it is a telephone number and an address where you can reach me anytime." This satisfied Rudolph Prisinski.

***

THE PRIVATE INVESTIGATOR TELEPHONED the office of attorney Thomas Beasley the following morning. The call was answered by Clara, Beasley's secretary.

"The law office of Thomas Beasley," stated Clara into the phone.

"It's Teddy Leonard. Let me talk to your boss."

"Oh, it's you," replied the secretary. Her tone suggested that she wasn't exactly glad to hear from Leonard.

"I love you too, sweetheart. Just put me through."

"It's all arranged, Tom," advised the private investigator. "When can we get together?"

"Excellent! Meet me in front of my building at noon." "Okay, see you then."

When the attorney and the private investigator got together, they entered an eatery a short distance from where they met.

"The deal took a little doing, but it was cut," said Leonard. "I was able to get to…."

"Don't tell me which juror you got to," said the attorney, not allowing Leonard to finish his sentence. "I don't need to know that. All I need to know is that the case is in the bag."

"Don't worry, you're home free. But I have to tell you, it took a little negotiating."

"How much?"

"The guy drove a hard bargain. He asked for a hundred grand."

"You couldn't get him down from that?"

"I did get him down. We shook on forty-seven thousand," advised Leonard, tacking on an extra five thousand for himself. "He held you up," accused the attorney.

"Did you want me to risk losing him?" The investigator's counter was effective in ending the debate.

"Do I get any change from what I gave you?"

"No, I gave him the whole ten grand you gave me."

***

THE TRIAL OF VICTOR SPINELLO was a short one. Rudolph

Prisinski came through exceeding expectations. He proved to be a diamond when it came to his ability at persuasion. The public relations man managed to convince his fellow jurors that Victor, as outlined in Beasley's summation, had acted in self-defense. He cleverly articulated that Victor's stuffing an inner sole in the mouth of Dario Tengo was an aberration, something that any frustrated man placed in a life and death situation might do.

When the acquittal was announced the teary-eyed Victor, who was in the dark regarding the bribery, hugged Beasley emotionally. When released from custody, he swore his allegiance to Ronnie Frantellini, who he gave credit to for standing behind him in his time of trouble.

Victor's gratitude was so extensive that he signed the agreement drawn up by Beasley without reading the following stipulations:

- Victor Spinello's 5 percent interest in the Frantellini Shoe Factory remains in full effect.

- Victor Spinello is to be the recipient of an annual increase in salary of four percent for as long as he remains with the Frantellini organization, and providing that the entity exceeds the prior year's profits by ten percent.

- Victor Spinello is to be the recipient of a new company car every two years.

- Victor Spinello is to be released from having to pay rent in the apartment over the Frantellini Shoe Factory for a period of five years, providing the building remains under the ownership of Ronnie Frantellini and is resided in by Victor Spinello.

- Victor Spinello's employment responsibilities are restricted to solely working on the creation of new products for the Frantellini Shoe Factory.

The unmarried Victor thought he had struck a fantastic deal. He was guaranteed salary raises for doing work he loved, got to drive a new car every other year and lived rent free for five years. This was something he would never achieve in Milan.

Victor Spinello was also a free man. With the woe of incarceration behind him, and his having a small equity interest in a thriving business, he thought he died and went to heaven.

20

Shoes Off-Television On

THE OWNER OF GIARDELLO'S RESTAURANT was a congenial proprietor who made it a point to greet his patrons warmly when they entered his establishment. Even though he had never met Markie and Von Hess he approached them with a friendly smile, thinking that they were there to eat.

The smile evaporated when Von Hess advised the business owner that they were detectives from police headquarters to investigate the homicide of the Frantellini sisters. Giardello, while polite, was clearly defensive. He feared additional unwanted publicity and potential litigation issues.

"Detectives from the precinct were already here," said the businessman.

"We know," acknowledged Von Hess. "We're going to give things a second look."

"Nobody working for me had anything to do with poisoning those girls, Detective. And as far as those mice go...."

"Take it easy, you're getting yourself agitated over nothing, Mr. Giardello," voiced Markie.

"Then what brings you guys here? I mean, what is there to look at?"

"Sometimes a fresh pair of eyes looking at something could prove worthwhile in an investigation," explained Von Hess.

"I don't get it," commented Giardello, displaying his annoyance.

"Look, you're not here to get it, Mr. Giardello. We are," injected Markie, his patience also wearing thin.

The sergeant's tone caused Giardello to back off. Wanting no problems, Giardello became receptive to the wants of the investigators.

"I understand, Sergeant," he said with a shrug. "Call me Sammy. What can I do for you?"

Markie asked if a record existed that reflected the dinner reservations made on evening of the double homicide. The restaurant owner advised that a book was maintained to record reservations. He then fetched the journal. The book reflected the name and telephone number of those who made reservations at Giardello's on the evening in question.

Satisfied, the detectives thanked the owner after recording the names and numbers. They then returned to their unmarked vehicle and began making phone calls. The process was uneventful until they spoke to a restaurant patron with a son who happened to be a huge wrestling fan.

***

JERRY GELLER INVITED THE DETECTIVES into the Stuyvesant Town apartment he resided in with his wife and eleven-year-old son. The Geller family was interviewed by the detectives in the family living room. Things brightened for the investigators when told by Mr. Geller, the owner of a cleaning service, that on the evening in question he and his family were dining just a short distance from where the murdered sisters were seated.

"Did you notice anything unusual?" asked Von Hess. "Not really," replied Mr. Geller.

"We were pretty absorbed in our own conversation," injected Geller's wife. "We never noticed anything beyond our own table."

"Your husband indicated that he saw a wrestler near the victim's table when I spoke to him on the telephone," said Von Hess.

"I said my son thought he recognized a wrestler near their table," corrected Mr. Geller.

"What exactly did you see, son?" asked Markie, addressing the boy.

"I saw Wolfman Glass toss white mice under the table," answered the boy.

"Who?"

"Wolfman Glass is a professional wrestler, Sergeant," clarified Mr. Geller.

"Are you sure about this, Jay?" asked Mrs. Geller, who seemed skeptical. "You never mentioned anything to me about that."

"Please, let him talk, Ma'am," said the sergeant. "What exactly did you see, Jay?"

The youth looked at his parents for guidance. It was Mr. Geller who provided it. "Go ahead Jay, tell the detectives exactly what you saw."

"I saw Wolfman Glass bend down and throw a handful of mice under the table where the two women were sitting. At first I thought that he was tying his shoe, but then I saw the mice."

"You know Wolfman Glass because you watch wrestling on television, Jay?" asked Von Hess.

"Yes."

"We often go to the wrestling matches and have seen him in person," added the father."

"So, you recognized Glass as being there too, Mr. Geller?" questioned Markie.

"No, I wasn't paying any attention. I mean, I know who he is, but I was talking to my wife about something."

"What happened after Wolfman bent down and threw something under the table, Jay?" asked Von Hess.

"Everybody jumped up from the table and began running around and screaming."

"Did you see Wolfman put anything on the table where the women were, Jay?" "No, he just walked away real fast after he stood up"

"What direction did he go in?"

"I think he left the restaurant. He was headed that way."

"You don't know for sure?" Markie questioned.

"I lost track of him after I saw Crippler."

The detectives looked at each other in a puzzled way. "Crippler who?" Markie asked.

"Crippler is another wrestler," clarified Mr. Geller. "What was Crippler doing, Jay?"

"He stopped by the table where all the trouble was," replied the boy.

"Did you see Wolfman and Crippler talking to each other when they were in the restaurant?" asked Markie, leaning forward in his seat.

"No."

"But they were both there at the same time."

"Yes, but I didn't see them together."

"I see, Jay. When Crippler stopped by the table, what exactly did he do?"

"It looked like he put something on the table."

"He did this during the commotion?" Von Hess questioned.

"Yes."

"Did he put whatever he put on the table in one motion or two, Jay?"

"I don't understand what you mean," answered the youth.

"Show him, Ollie."

Von Hess then demonstrated by pretending to drop something in two glasses.

"Yes, that's just what he did," confirmed the youth.

"Jay, why didn't you tell us all this before?" asked the boy's mother.

"I told Dad."

Fearing domestic disruption, Markie quickly posed another question. “So, you saw Crippler drop something into two glasses, Jay?”

“I couldn’t really tell.”

“I see. But it looked like he could have been doing that, right?”

“I guess so.”

“Could you describe Wolfman and the Crippler to us, son?”

“Do you want to see their picture?”

“You have a picture of these guys?”

“Yeah, I’ll get it for you. It’s in my room.”

After a few minutes, the young wrestling fan returned to the living room with a wrestling magazine. After leafing through several pages, he stopped when he came to the photo he was looking for.

“Here they are,” said the youth, pointing to a photo of Wolfman and Crippler together in the ring.”

“Are your certain that these are the men you saw?” Von Hess asked.

“Yes. I’ve seen them lots of times as a tag-team.”

“He definitely knows them, Detective,” assured Mr. Geller.

“These two are great for taking their shoes off and watching wrestling on television,” injected Mrs. Geller.

“You didn’t happen to see the wrestlers eating together, did you?”

“No, Crippler sat at a table alone. After everything was over, he just finished eating.”

Seeing this as a big break in the investigation, Markie was grateful to the boy. So grateful that he wanted to show his thanks.

“So, you really like wrestling, Jay?” asked the Sergeant,

“Yes, sir,” answered the youth politely.

“You, know, I know some of these wrestlers. Maybe I could get you a few autographs, would you like that?” “The Wolfman and the Crippler?”

Markie laughed. “I don’t know about me getting their autographs for you. But I’ll see if I could get you some others.” After securing statements, the detectives thanked the family for their cooperation. They then returned to their vehicle. Once in the privacy of their car, they engaged in the difficult conversation each man knew had to take place.

"I guess you know who could help us with this, Sarge," conveyed Von Hess.

"Yeah, she's the right one to give us a line on these guys," replied a somber Markie.

"Are you going to be able to handle seeing Rochelle again? If not, I can see her alone."

The detectives were referring to Rochelle Parrish, Markie's former lover. Parrish, a rabid wrestling fan, was the woman Markie had fallen hard for. Her dumping Markie for a bogus Indian grappler who suited up in a headdress when entering the ring had caused the sergeant to go on the drinking spree that wreaked havoc on his body.

The detectives were aware that Rochelle's intimacy with the married, part-time Indian Chief positioned her to gather information on the wrestling performers who participated in the exhibitions on the east coast.

"Maybe you better go see her without me, Ollie," said Markie. "You can catch up with her at Mustang Harry's tomorrow at around six or six-thirty."

"How do you know that?"

"There is wrestling at the Garden scheduled for tomorrow night. Rochelle always stops over there for a drink with her sister before heading over to see the matches."

"You're not going in the bar with me to talk to her, Sarge?"

"Not a chance. You met her, so you know what she looks like. I'll wait in the car outside while you talk to her."

***

ROCHELLE PARRISH WAS AT Mustang Harry's with her sister before the two headed over to Madison Square Garden to attend the wrestling matches. There was some friction between the sisters. Rochelle was demanding to know if her sister had involved herself with her ex-beau, the married Chief Red Hawk. Once Rochelle's own romance with the wrestler ran its course, it got back to Rochelle through the grapevine that her sister began seeing wrestling's bogus chief.

Rochelle was in the middle of explaining to her sister the downside of engaging in a romance with a serial philanderer like Chief Red Hawk when Von Hess interrupted their conversation. "Excuse me, Ms. Parrish, do you remember me?" asked Von Hess, addressing Rochelle. Rochelle looked at the detective trying to place him. "I'm Detective Von Hess. We met a while back at your office when you worked for the producer, Enzo Baffi."

Rochelle froze. She feared that her involvement in Baffi's jailhouse suicide had come back to haunt her. "I remember you," stated Rochelle weakly. "Have I done something?"

"No, Ma'am, I'm only here to ask you for a favor." Rochelle, now relieved, was receptive.

"What kind of favor do you need?"

"Can we speak privately for a moment?"

"You can talk, this is my sister," said Rochelle, introducing her sister to the detective. "We have no secrets."

"Pleased to meet you," voiced Von Hess politely. "I can see the resemblance."

"So, what's the favor?"

"I'm trying to get a line on a couple of wrestlers. I know you are friendly with a lot of them, so I'm here to pick your brain."

"If they are in some kind of trouble, I want no part of it. I'm not an informer."

Von Hess, thinking fast, put forth a cover story. "It's nothing like that Ma'am. It's about my nephew. He's a sick little boy without much time left. Jay's a huge wrestling fan and I'm trying to see if I can get these two wrestlers to visit him at the hospital."

"Oh, I see," voiced Rochelle, who was now more amenable.

"Well, who are the wrestlers?"

"Wolfman Glass and Crippler." "Oh, those two. I wouldn't get my hopes up. They don't get out of bed unless there is a dollar in it for them. I might be able to get some of the other fellas to stop by the hospital."

"Thank you, Ma'am. But before I put you out, I'd like to give Wolfman and Crippler a shot. Do you know where I can meet up with them?"

"I don't know their schedule. They aren't on tonight's card. But I can call someone and probably get their contact information."

"That would be great, here is my business card. Their home address would be perfect."

"I think that I already have your card," conveyed Rochelle as she took the detective's card.

"You'll call me then?"

"Yes, I'll call you tomorrow."

"Can I buy you ladies a drink?"

"No thank you."

As Von Hess was about to leave, Rochelle posed a question to him. "How is Sergeant Markie doing?"

"He's fine," replied Von Hess.

"Tell him I was asking for him. Give him this," said Rochelle, handing Von Hess a business card that reflected:

THE SHOOTER SCHOOL
OF PROFESSIONAL WRESTLING
8 Avenue at W. 53 Street, NYC
Contact by Mail Only
Rochelle Parrish, Founder/C.E.O.
Yankee Phil Denim, Vice President/Trainer

"You're running a wrestling school now?" Von Hess asked.

"Yes, I just opened the business up with Yankee Denim."

"That's a name from the past. I remember him from when I was a kid. He's got to be up there in age."

"He's 83, but still capable of climbing between the ropes and teaching people how to wrestle. Yankee is one of the last experts in hooking still around. He knows all the promoters." "Hooking?"

questioned Von Hess, who wasn't familiar with the term as used in wrestling.

"A hooker knows all the crippling holds. He is what they call a shooter in the ring. Promoters used to match him with problem wrestlers who didn't want to follow the script. After Yankee got through with them, they did what they were told."

"I see."

"Here, take another one of my cards. Keep one and give the other to Sergeant Markie. Tell Al I was asking for him. Tell him to give me a call sometime."

"Will do."

When Von Hess returned to his vehicle, he found Markie thirsting for information.

"So how did you make out, Ollie?"

"Good. Rochelle was there with her sister. She said that she'd call me with information on the two wrestlers."

"Did she ask for me?"

"No, Sarge," lied Von Hess. "She never mentioned you."

"Oh," voiced Markie, obviously disappointed. "Did she say what she has been up to?"

"She's running a wrestling school. To be honest, we didn't talk very long because she and her sister were with two guys. They looked like they were coupled up."

Markie's reaction to the fib was peculiar. He offered no comment. He just turned his head to stare out the passenger side window of the car. His thoughts were his own.

21

Chasing Rainbows

RONNIE FRANTELLINI DIDN'T NEED ANYONE to tell her that Thomas Beasley was not a man to be trusted. She was able to see beneath Beasley's veneer of respectability and knew him for what he was. Ronnie saw a place for the lawyer in her affairs that would be beneficial to her. The only caveat was that Beasley needed to be watched. This is where Clara, Beasley's secretary, was useful.

Clara, who Ronnie was genuinely fond of, was a pipeline into the attorney's office. It was unlikely that there would be underhandedness going on that escaped Clara's attention. As a snoop by nature, Clara was ideal in serving as Ronnie's mole.

Being Ronnie's mentee was flattering to Clara. The secretary was in such awe of the Frantellini widow that she tried her best to deliver information of value. Since Ronnie was perceptive enough to know this, their relationship developed into an ironclad trust that is only found between the closest of friends. The emergence of this cohesive bond dismantled whatever protective walls that might have initially existed between the women.

Information began pouring into Ronnie immediately. Ronnie gained insights into the skullduggery that Beasley was capable of. His winning record in court, his concealed associations and unethical practices were all exposed to the Frantellini widow. Being a woman with a suspicious nature, Ronnie suspected there had to be a good reason why ex-detective Teddy Leonard had been dispatched to shadow Dario Tengo. She could only guess what motivated Maria Frantellini and Thomas Beasley to have Dario tailed.

"Clara, I want to help you," Ronnie conveyed in one of her rare tender moments over dinner. "You're the sister I never had."

"I feel exactly the same way about you," was the response Ronnie received.

"I'm going to build your confidence, Clara."

"You are?"

"We've already taken the first step. Look at how you've improved physically."

"I have, haven't I?"

"Of course. Trust me, honey, in this world a woman has to maintain herself if she expects to get anywhere," advised Ronnie, adding, "take it from a lady who knows. A woman who lets herself get too shabby ends up cleaning the underwear of some man who'll take her for granted."

Clara, embarrassed over the bluntness of the remark, looked down at her plate. She was unsure of how to properly respond to such a statement. Finally, she uttered, "I'm learning."

"You bet you are," assured Ronnie. "Look, honey, your biggest problem is that You don't give yourself enough credit."

"Credit? What have I accomplished?"

"It's not about yesterday, it's about today. With a little help you could be an oil painting, honey. All we have to do is bring out the colors. Trust me, just look at the progress we've already made. Just wait until a little more work is done to polish you up."

"I don't understand…."

"You are going to get the full treatment, honey. You already have the personal trainer, the beautician and the dietician. Next on the list is a little cosmetic surgery. When we're through, you're going to be a ten!"

"But I don't have the kind of money for that."

"Call me banker, honey. And don't worry, the money is coming out of the business. Trust me, there will be plenty to go around."

"I have to ask you, why are you being so good to me?"

"I know how stormy the weather can be in life, honey," replied Ronnie. "You started as my insurance, but now you're my friend. And everybody, including me, needs a friend."

The sentiment related by Ronnie brought tears to the eyes of the secretary. Ronnie watched as a tiny bubble began to roll down Clara's cheek. The heir to the Frantellini empire reached across the table and placed her hand over Clara's. The gesture was one of understanding and friendship, nothing more. It was a touching moment for a woman rarely touched.

"Don't start blubbering, honey," said Ronnie softly. "All that'll do is ruin the makeup."

***

TEDDY LEONARD BEGAN NOTICING began noticing the secretary's improvement. Leonard's eyes widened after entering Thomas Beasley's law office. His facial approval wasn't lost on the secretary. Leonard's crooked smile was a cross between admiration and lecherousness. Both were validation that Clara's hard work was paying off. More than anything the secretary was hoping that the private investigator would hit on her. She'd like nothing better than to shoot down his advances.

Clara pressed her ear to the office door of her boss once Leonard was inside. The conversation she overheard was of particular interest to her.

"What happened to your secretary, Tom?" asked Leonard. "Did she find a magic lantern?"

"Who, Clara?"

"Yeah, she's looking really good."

Beasley laughed. "She's been having some work done."

"Are you paying for it?"

"No, not me. Somebody must have deep pockets I guess. I don't ask."

"It's hard to believe it's the same woman."

"Clara's been on a health kick. I'm starting to think she has someone in her life."

"What have you got for me to do, Tommy?"

"Nothing right now, Teddy. I'll let you know when I need you."

***

ONCE VICTOR SPINELLO WAS A FREE MAN he returned to work at the Frantellini Shoe Factory. Once acclimated to his return, he found himself happier than he could have imagined. Under the regime of Ronnie Frantellini things were better than ever for him.

Ronnie, who had full faith in Victor's genius, had given him full authority to do whatever necessary to develop his Dynamic Shoe and whatever else he could dream up. With a hand on his hip, Victor looked around his office wondering what he should do first to further his project(s).

With Victor under her control, Ronnie acted on her next move. She invited Thomas Beasley out for lunch. Her purpose was to diminish the attorney.

Thanks to Clara, Ronnie possessed enough information about the Victor Spinello acquittal to throw a good scare in Beasley. Ronnie, who was skilled at reading people, was relatively certain that with this leverage, Beasley would ultimately cave to her demands. Their subsequent lunch conversation was to the point.

"Tom, you're a shrewd lawyer," began Ronnie. "That I have to give you."

"Why thank you," said Beasley, accepting the compliment. "I'm glad you appreciate my ability."

"But I know someone just a little slicker."

"Who is that?" Beasley asked, taken aback by the remark.

"Me."

"Why don't you get to the point," voiced the lawyer, who didn't appreciate Ronnie's cat and mouse approach.

"Don't get excited, Tom. I have every intention of continuing to use you as a lawyer to represent my interests."

"That's big of you. And let's not forget that I'm sort of a silent partner," reminded the attorney."

"Yeah, well, that's one of things I have to talk to you about, Tom. From now on you'll only be receiving money for the legal services you render."

"Wait a second, Ronnie. What are you trying to pull, we agreed…."

"That was yesterday, Tom. Today is today. You're out as a partner, silent or otherwise. Our deal died as soon as Victor was acquitted."

"My God, have you no ethics at all?" Beasley asked. "You can't pull this on me." Ronnie burst out laughing at the statement.

"You're talking ethics? That's really rich coming from you."

"I wouldn't be so smug if I were you, Ronnie. Are you forgetting that little episode concerning the Frantellini sisters, sweetheart?"

"Are you forgetting about that juror you had your private investigator bribe? His name was Teddy Leonard, I believe. I know all about that….and that kind of information could cut the legs out from under you."

"What are you talking about?" Beasley asked, pretending not to know what she was referring to.

"Save it, Tom. Just face the facts. Your edge is gone."

"Is that so?" Beasley asked, believing that Ronnie was bluffing. "I don't where know you're getting your information, but its inaccurate."

"I'm getting it from someone with very big eyes and ears."

"Who?" "Clara Calhoun," replied Ronnie. "Clara was privy to every dirty deal you ever did."

"That's impossible."

"Is it? Clara is a woman with very big ears. You'd be surprised at how much she knows. We became very good friends, you know."

"So, you were the one behind her dolling herself up," accused the attorney. "Well, Clara does what I say. She works for me!"

"No more, darling. You'll find Clara's resignation on her office desk. Clara works for me now full-time. You made the mistake of getting sloppy, Tom."

This revelation stopped Beasley cold. After digesting that Ronnie had succeeded in outmaneuvering him all he could say was, "I guess this levels the playing field."

"Not quite," voiced Ronnie. "I'm holding all the cards. You'll keep your mouth shut about the sisters. And I'll keep mine closed regarding that juror."

"So now I'm supposed to be out?"

"No, Tom, you're not out. You're a damn valuable lawyer and there is a place for you. As long as you follow the program you can stay on representing the Frantellini interests at the usual rate for your services. But that's all you get."

"Whatever you say, Ronnie," said Beasley, accepting defeat.

Seeing that Beasley lost his usual cockiness was pleasing to Ronnie. "Cheer up, Tom, things could be worse. At least you'll still be earning something."

"I'll live, Ronnie. No sense crying over spilt milk. I have to say one thing though."

"What?"

"You played your cards well, Ronnie."

"I always do. I learned how to play the game at an early age."

***

HAVING CLEARED THE AIR with Thomas Beasley, Ronnie wanted to celebrate. She set a time to step out with Clara Calhoun. Out for a fun night, the two women dressed appropriately for the occasion.

"You look great in that outfit, Clara," said Ronnie honestly. "It shows off that new figure."

"Thanks, Ronnie. I owe it all to you and our personal trainer."

"I told you that he was great. I like the way they did your hair too.

I'm thinking of doing my hair the same way."

The two women ending up spending the evening in an upscale Manhattan lounge called Berle's Blueprint. They were only at the bar five minutes before a man in his late forties approached Ronnie, offering to buy her a drink. He was a rugged looking sort who carried himself as only a man of great confidence would.

This impressed Ronnie, who had little tolerance for timid men. The stranger introduced himself as Carmine. Ronnie liked his look, so she accepted his drink offer.

"I'm Ronnie," she said, adding, "this is my friend Clara." "Hello, Clara, I'm Carmine. What are you girls having?"

As Carmine sought the bartender's attention to order drinks the woman locked eyes. Their exchange of smiles suggested that they were pleased. Ronnie then turned to check out her new friend. She liked Carmine's close-cropped salt and pepper hair, thinking it suited his face. The cleft in his chin and wide shoulders also were appealing.

When the drinks arrived, Carmine raised his glass to toast the women luck. As they clicked glasses, Ronnie noticed that Carmine had unusually large powerful looking hands. This prompted her to ask what he did for a living.

In answer to the question Carmine handed Ronnie his business card. The card reflected that he was the owner of the DeFaziolo Construction company. When Ronnie identified herself as the owner of the Frantellini Shoe Factory, Carmine immediately recognized the prominent Frantellini name.

"That's a big company. You folks are in the real estate business as well."

"That's right," answered Ronnie, "commercial and residential."

"Funny, but you don't look like a Frantellini."

"I was married to Richard Frantellini. My husband passed."

"So now you're the owner," said Carmine. "I give you a lot of credit, that's a big responsibility."

"I manage. I have Clara here helping me."

"I know your buildings well. How many do you own now?"

"Enough." As the conversation continued, Clara studied Ronnie closely. Her eyes were wide open, her face the epitome of seriousness. She was learning from the master.

"Our meeting like this is fortuitous," advised Carmine.

Ronnie smirked. "Is it?"

"I say that because I'm also an architect. My company does outside work, as well as interior work. We excel at drywall of course, but we also do exteriors. We should talk."

"We are talking," Ronnie said in her collected way.

"I mean we should sit down and discuss things over dinner. Are you hungry?"

"Clara and I could eat a little something." Carmine got the hint. "I mean with Clara, of course. My friend Mark is here with me. We should all sit down at a table."

Carmine summoned his friend, Mark, the owner of a waterproofing company. Mark, who was divorced, was a presentable man who seemed to have an affable way about him. It was clear by his smile that Mark liked what he saw in Clara.

Clara looked over at Ronnie to see her reaction to Carmine's friend. Ronnie nodded approvingly. Having received this encouragement from her tutor, Clara began to engage Mark with equal cordialness.

Once all were seated at a table Clara did her best to emulate the way Ronnie handled herself with Carmine. She proved herself to be a good student, with Mark displaying increasing interest in Clara as the evening wore on.

Mark was gentlemanly, polite and attentive. Clara saw Mark's crooked teeth as his only apparent flaw. Other than this he was attractive enough to be taken seriously. Clara was so intoxicated by the attention she was receiving that she refused to allow a few crooked teeth to undermine the best evening of her life.

When Ronnie and Clara caught up later in the restroom they compared notes. Ronnie expressed that she liked Carmine well enough to see him again. Clara admitted to liking Mark.

"Do you want to see him again, honey?" Ronnie asked.

"I'd love to. Do you think he'll want that?"

"He'll want to see you. Don't you worry about that."

"He makes me feel like....like Venus," said Clara, making her infatuation evident. Ronnie chuckled at hearing this.

"Forget Venus, honey. Think penis."

22

Choices

RONNIE FRANTELLINI HAD FINALLY met the goal she set for herself. She managed to secure the financial independence she always wanted without having to put in the labor. The components that made her wealthy were all in place. Her shoe factory staff was comprised of long-time employees that had been handpicked by Ronnie's late husband. Their loyalty translated into no heavy lifting for Ronnie.

As for the real estate portfolio, Ronnie made out well there also. A seasoned broker and her accountant took care of all property transactions. A management company took care of rent collections and maintenance. Legal matters were handled by Thomas Beasley. Now she had Clara, Beasley's former secretary, to pick up whatever the remaining slack was.

Having delegated much of the responsibility, Ronnie was left with plenty of time to focus on enjoying the perks that came with being an affluent business owner. Unlike Maria Frantellini, the stepdaughter she had murdered, Ronnie wasn't one to look for problems as long as the money was coming in.

One social benefit of Ronnie's position was her having the upper hand when it came to men. Her most recent love interest, Carmine DeFaziolo, entered into Ronnie's life unaware that all of Ronnie's romances had a shelf life. Carmine, blinded by what a long-term relationship would do for his company, underestimated Ronnie in this regard.

As a woman who bored easily, Ronnie remained open to meeting other men. She tended to grow melancholy whenever she heard the Peggy Lee tune, Is That All There Is. The vocalist's 1969 hit song was a reminder that it took lots to hold her interest.

Carmine was kept happy by having Ronnie's real estate representative award projects to his company. This flow of work gave Carmine a false sense of security. He erred when he started to take things for granted. Carmine's Waterloo came when he took it upon himself to start performing work that hadn't been first authorized.

Ronnie, who preferred doling out her treats, was irked by Carmine's boldness. Her subsequent iciness was beyond defrosting. The hammer she dropped on Carmine was designed to punish. Ronnie exacted her revenge with the intent of hurting Carmine's business. She had her lover start on several projects that required Carmine spending his own money. Once the labor, materials and equipment were in use, Ronnie cancelled the job without reimbursing Carmine.

Since Carmine commenced the work without a contract, Ronnie did not fear litigation. She correctly believed it likely that Carmine padded the invoices he submitted, making scrutiny of his work not in his interest.

As his world began to crumble, Carmine began pestering Ronnie for an answer as to why she turned on him. When she wasn't responsive to his overture he began showering Ronnie with flowers, candy and suggestions that they find time to get together.

All of Carmine's efforts to reignite the relationship was to no avail. His persistence gave a great deal of satisfaction to Ronnie, who delighted in seeing Carmine grovel. When she grew tired of tormenting him, Ronnie kissed off Carmine completely. The words used to express the termination of their connection came with brutal directness, minus explanation.

"You're out, Carmine," Ronnie conveyed. Her iciness was glacial, far beyond thawing.

While Ronnie's attachment to Carmine evaporated, such was not the case with Carmine's friend the water proofer and Clara. Their relationship continued on. This did not totally displease Ronnie because it was a testament to her ability to transform Clara into someone romantically desirable.

The water proofer was very different than Carmine. He was a respectful man who was genuine in his affection. In this respect Mark did much in boosting Clara's self-esteem. Mark's verbal attentiveness gave him staying power with Clara. However, there was one shortcoming. Although a bundle of compliments, Mark lacked the performance ability for Clara to reach the heights sexually. After sharing this bit of intimacy with Ronnie, the mentor's response came without hesitation.

"It sounds like it's time for a relief pitcher, honey."

"Do you think so?"

"Look at it in terms of singing, honey," said Ronnie. "When your vocal coach can't get you hitting those high notes, it's time for a new vocal coach."

"But I feel bad, Ronnie," expressed Clara. "Mark isn't terrible, he is just not the best. He has even offered to see a dentist to get his teeth fixed for me."

"Look, honey," began Ronnie, "do yourself a favor. Men think nothing of using women. So, you need to do the same." "I don't think Mark is like that," voiced Clara.

"If Mark's matches can't ignite that fire, it's time to find somebody with a Zippo lighter who can." \

"I don't know...."

"A word to the wise, Clara. If you love and leave them like I do, you'll never get hurt."

"But you married Richard Frantellini, didn't you?"

"That's right I did, and for good reason," replied Ronnie with a touch of defiance. "It got me where I am now, didn't it?"

"I suppose it did."

"What I'm trying to explain to you is that you have to pick your shots with men, honey. You have to always consider the gain. No gain, no marriage. The formula is as simple as that."

Clara took her hardened friend's counsel as seriously as one possibly could. Emulating her mentor, Clara resigned herself to think in a more calculating fashion. Mark was soon history.

***

BEING OUTMANEUVERED BY RONNIE FRANTELLINI was something that didn't sit well with Thomas Beasley. The attorney, who was accustomed to winning, was out to regain the revenue stream he felt cheated out of. In order to achieve this ambition Beasley knew that he had to once again gain the upper hand on Ronnie. The plan Beasley masterminded wasn't so very different from the strategy used by Ronnie to neutralize him. Both involved Clara, who he knew to be very close to Ronnie.

Beasley's initiative involved having someone pursue his former secretary romantically. He believed that Clara would be an ideal source of information concerning Ronnie's activities. The lawyer was banking on Ronnie taking part in some form of illegal, immoral or unethical activity that he could use to his advantage. To gain this leverage Beasley sought the services of Teddy Leonard, his private investigator.

When summoned Leonard promptly reported to Beasley's office. When informed of what was needed, the investigator thought of himself as the person to get close to Clara. This suggestion was discouraged by Beasley, who thought the gumshoe to be too old for such an assignment.

"I could be the right guy for this kind of job, Tom," said Leonard. "I don't think you'd be her type, Teddy," replied Beasley, being kind.

"What are you talking about? Leonard protested. "She's desperate for a man, so it's any port in a storm."

"You're forgetting how great Clara looks these days. She wouldn't even look at you twice."

"Don't underestimate me, Tommy. All I have to do is make with the charm. Believe me, she'll come around once I make nice with her."

"I wish I was as sure of that as you are. Do you really think she'll give you a tumble?"

"It's a cinch. I know just what to do."

"Okay, give it a shot, Teddy. You'll find her working over at the Frantellini Shoe Factory."

"By the way, what's the pay?" asked Leonard before leaving.

***

RONNIE ARRANGED TO HAVE DINNER with Clara at P.J. Clarkes on Third Avenue. She thought it a fun venue frequented by interesting people. Since Clara had never been there before, Ronnie shared some of the venue's history. "Frank Sinatra often sat at Table 20," in this place," said Ronnie.

"Really? Did you meet him?"

"No, I couldn't get close enough to him the time I saw him here. He was surrounded by too many of his friends. But I could tell that he was a fun guy."

"How did he look?"

"He looked like Sinatra," replied Ronnie, adding wistfully, "snagging him would have really been saying something."

"He's married, isn't he?"

"A wedding ring never stopped any man, honey. Never forget that. Did you know that Buddy Holly proposed to his wife in P.J. Clarkes?"

"Really?"

"Yes, and get this, he only knew her for just five hours. That was one gal who knew what she wanted."

"Maybe she was what he wanted," suggested Clara.

"Yeah, that too," conceded Ronnie. "By the way, did you ever hear from that water proofer anymore?"

"No. I took your advice and found somebody else."

"You did?" Ronnie asked excitedly, genuinely impressed. "Talk to me."

Clara told how she met Fernando, a part-time taxi driver. Ronnie let out a thunderous laugh upon hearing this.

"A taxi driver?" Ronnie asked, her eyes squinting with amusement.

"That's funny? "queried Clara. "What wrong with driving a taxi?"

"Take it easy, honey. I'm not putting down the profession," clarified Ronnie. "I'm only laughing because I once went out with a cabdriver myself."

"Not Fernando...."

"No, his name was Murray. He was from the Bronx. Murray was a riot who used to write funny lyrics to popular songs. He was actually pretty clever at it."

"What happened to him?"

"He was fun, but he had no money. So, rather than waste too much of my time, I cut him loose."

"Any word from Carmine, Ronnie?"

"Forget Carmine, tell me more about Fernando."

"Fernando's a real macho man. He's real rugged looking."

"You have to be a little careful with the he-man type, Clara," warned Ronnie.

"Why is that?"

"They can be hard to control. And trust me, you always want to be the one in control."

At some point during their dinner, Clara mentioned how she ran into Teddy Leonard."

"Beasley's investigator?" Ronnie asked. The suspicion was clear in her voice. "How did that happen?"

"I bumped into him on the street. You know, I always found him to be a creep, but after talking to him, I think that I may have misjudged him."

"Don't bet on that."

"He was really sweet to me. Full of compliments about how good I look."

"I suppose that he hit on you?"

"As a matter of fact, he did. He actually asked me to dinner."

"Did you accept?"

"I said maybe. We exchanged cards. I wanted to talk to you first."

"That was smart of you, honey."

"Did I make a mistake by talking to him?"

"The old bastard works for Tom Beasley, so there may be an ulterior motive behind his interest in you. Then again, he may just be horny."

"What kind of ulterior motive?" asked Clara.

"He may be looking to get close to you to get at me. Let's play it safe. You stay clear of him, why take a chance?"

23

Wolfman Howls

ROCHELLE PARRISH COULDN'T HELP but wonder why she hadn't heard from Markie. At first her ego would only allow her to assume that Von Hess, serving as her courier, had forgotten to convey her message to the sergeant. For a while this was a palatable thought for Rochelle. But as time passed she came to consider the possibility that Markie's had lost interest in her. This ego-shattering likelihood was quickly dismissed.

That detective probably never even gave Al my new business card, the bummed out wrestling school owner thought. I can't imagine Al not calling me after hearing that I asked for him.

That would be so out of character for him. Why, he always got right back to be when I reached out.

The truth of the matter was that Rochelle was now obsessed with connecting with the sergeant. She was between boyfriends and had plenty of time to miss Markie. Although Markie paled in comparison to the wild unpredictability of the Indian Chief posing arm twister, the sergeant did have his positives. For one, Markie was reliable. If he said he was going to do something, he did it. Then there was the gun Markie carried. That prop, along with the handcuffs, always added to the excitement.

Another positive thing about Markie was his availability. Managing a social calendar was something difficult to maintain with wrestlers, who spent the majority of their time on the road. A promotor's call offering an out-of-town opportunity on short notice was commonplace. Then there were the bookings that took wrestlers on tour to such faraway places as Canada, Japan, and Australia.

There came a point where Rochelle's curiosity got the better of her. Casting pride aside, she contacted Markie directly. Having gathered the information requested by Von Hess, she had the perfect excuse for doing so. When there was no pickup on Markie's cell phone, Rochelle left a message. When she received no callback, she began contacting the sergeant's office at headquarters. This too resulted in no callback.

Tired of Detective Silverlake advising that Markie was in the field, Rochelle had little choice other than to telephone Von Hess. She provided the detective with the addresses of both Wolfman and Crippler. Before ending the call with Von Hess, she inquired as to why Markie hadn't called her. Von Hess lied and said that he gave the sergeant her business card and informed Markie that she would like him to call her. For good measure he added that Markie might be seeing someone.

Rochelle wasn't sure how credible this information was. The information received from Rochelle enabled Von Hess to run background checks on both wrestlers. Crippler's rap sheet reflected that he had been incarcerated. Ever since his release from prison, the wrestler was careful to keep his criminal activity under the radar of law enforcement.

Wolfman wasn't as clever as his criminal associate. His checkered past in New York included serving time in Green Haven Correctional Facility, a maximum-security prison located in the Town of Beekman in Dutchess County.

"Let's start with Wolfman Glass, Ollie," said Markie after reviewing the arrest histories.

***

IT WAS EARLY MORNNG WHEN MARKIE AND VON HESS set out on their trip to Milford, Pennsylvania, located approximately 100 miles from New York City. While on the road the detectives stopped off at a diner for breakfast.

"How long do you think it'll take us to get there, Ollie?" asked the sergeant, as he chomped in his food.

"About an hour and a half, depending on traffic, Sarge," answered Von Hess. "I haven't been in the Poconos since my kids were little."

"I hope this Wolfman Glass is home."

"He probably is, he's scheduled to be wrestling in Atlantic City tomorrow."

During their drive Markie posed a question he had been meaning to ask Von Hess.

"Ollie, tell me the truth. Rochelle really never mentioned me when you spoke to her?" asked the sergeant.

"Not a word, Sarge," replied Von Hess. "She just gave me the information on the wrestlers and that was it."

"That's strange, because she's been calling me."

"You don't need her, Sarge."

"I know I don't. I was just wondering why she called me on my cell phone and at work."

"Did she say what she wanted?"

"She just left a message saying that I should call her." "Did you?"

"Nah, I'm through with her. I learned my lesson."

"Good for you, Sarge."

The trip to the Pennsylvania residence of Wolfman Glass was made with the name Rochelle Parrish coming up again. Markie was unable to suppress his desire to find out from Von Hess how Rochelle had looked when he last saw her. This was a tip off for the detective that his boss still had feelings for Rochelle.

The response Markie received from Von Hess wasn't complimentary.

"She looked like she slipped a little, Sarge." "

What do you mean by slipped?"

"She put on a few, Sarge. She's got more chins than in a Chinatown telephone book."

"Really?"

"Yeah, and she lost some of her polish. I guess hanging around those wrestlers rubbed off."

"Well, how coarse was she?"

"She curses like a drunken sailor."

Markie frowned and dropped the subject. He didn't want to hear more. When the detectives knocked on the door to the home of Wolfman Glass they were met by the wrestler's wife. She was a tired looking woman with long shoulder length hair. Her skin was pinkish, the top of her head a mix of blond and gray. There were traces of scalp psoriasis visible.

Mrs. Glass hailed from Humboldt, Iowa, a city with a rich wrestling history. She had met her husband years prior in the lounge of a Best Western that was known to be frequented by wrestlers when appearing in the city.

At the time of their first meeting Wolfman was at the top of his game professionally. He was making big money as a main event performer who was selling out arenas in the Midwest. The bearded wrestler's gimmick in the ring was biting the throat of his opponents, thus living up to the monicker Wolfman. Impressed by Wolfman's celebrity, the future wife was receptive to his advances. They eventually married and started a family. Wolfman's wife loved her husband deeply, remaining by him through the troubles he created for himself.

When Wolfman's wife asked why the detectives wanted to speak to her husband, she was told a fabricated story that conveyed that Wolfman may have witnessed a crime that was committed in New York City. The detectives had no problem justifying their dishonest account. They emphasized that they just needed to interview Wolfman about what he may have seen. Mrs. Glass accepted this as being the truth.

In actuality the detectives were there in an effort to get Wolfman to incriminate himself in the homicide of the Frantellini sisters. Even if Wolfman remained mum, the detectives had enough to take him into custody thanks to the eyewitness account of Jay Geller, the young wrestling fan. How Markie intended to proceed depended entirely on what Wolfman had to say. When queried as to the whereabouts of the Wolfman, Mrs. Glass conveyed that her husband was currently on the road. She advised that he was scheduled to wrestle in Atlantic City the following day, after which he would be appearing in Philadelphia.

"He drives to these arenas?" asked Von Hess.

"Yes."

"Will he be coming home after Philadelphia, Ma'am?"

"No, I believe that he's then off to Boston for a match."

"That's a hectic schedule he keeps," voiced Markie.

"It sure is," confirmed the wife. "I only get to see him one or two days a week."

"That kind of traveling could be expensive."

"He has it good sometimes. He always gets a comped room at one of the casinos when in Atlantic City. They give him the room because he spends time on the casino floor signing autographs and taking pictures with casino guests."

"Which casino?"

"I'm not sure. When he was an upper card wrestler, he was important enough to have that kind of deal with the best casinos. Now I'm not sure which one he stays at."

"What kind of a car does your husband drive, Ma'am?" Von Hess asked.

"Why do you ask that?"

"Just curious. I figure that a big man like your husband needs comfortable wheels considering all the driving he does to get to the venues he wrestles at.

"He's driving our black Jeep."

The detectives thanked Mrs. Glass and left. Once in their unmarked car, Von Hess telephoned his office and had Detective Silverlake determine what vehicles were registered at the address they visited. After securing telephonic authorization from their superior, the detectives planned to be in Atlantic City to attend the wrestling matches.

***

MARKIE AND VON HESS ARRIVED in Atlantic City early enough to ascertain the arena where Wolfman was appearing. They entered the arena with plenty of time to see the first match. While they had previously seen a photo of Wolfman in a wrestling magazine, the investigators wanted to be sure of what he looked like in person. They thought it possible that he might have shaved his whiskers to alter his appearance after the Frantellini homicides.

Von Hess identified himself to a security officer, asking for the person in charge of the arena. When a higher authority arrived, Markie advised that he and Von Hess were in New Jersey conducting a homicide investigation. When asked for further details, Markie explained that due to the serious nature of the inquiry he preferred not to provide too much information.

"I'm sorry sergeant, but I can't chance disrupting the show we're putting on," advised the man in charge.

"Nobody is looking to disrupt anything," assured Markie. "I promise you that we won't even talk to anyone."

"So, what do you need from me, Sergeant?"

"We just want to sit someplace where we could hear the introductions and take a good look at the wrestlers. Once we see our man, we're out of here."

"That's it?"

"That's it," assured Markie.

To accommodate the law enforcement officers, Markie and Von Hess were allowed to sit in ringside seats usually reserved for the press and photographers. Midway through the card, a shoeless Wolfman Glass appeared.

The bearded wrestler entered the ring wearing faded cut jeans and carrying an eighteen-inch dog bone. When Wolfman began getting clobbered by his opponent with his own dog bone, the detectives knew the end of the match was near. They rose from their seats and headed toward the arena exit as Wolfman's shoulders were being pinned to the mat. On their way they ascertained from security where the wrestlers parked their vehicles.

The investigators located Wolfman's black jeep in an open parking lot just a short distance from the arena. They waited patiently for their man to collect his car. When Wolfman finally appeared, he wasn't alone. He was with two females that had wrestled each other in one of the bouts the detectives witnessed. The women were dressed neatly in regular everyday street clothes. Even Wolfman seemed presentable. His hair was slicked back and in a ponytail. A rubber band was used to keep his beard manageable. The three wrestlers got into Wolfman's Jeep and drove off.

"Stick with them, I want to see where they go, Ollie," said Markie.

Von Hess followed the jeep at a safe distance. Wolfman proceeded to a building located in a seedy section of town. He exited his vehicle to engage in conversation with a man who appeared to be in his early twenties. It was obvious to the detectives that the two knew each other. "I think he's looking to score, Ollie," voiced Markie, referring to drugs.

"You're right, Sarge. They're doing a hand to hand right now."

The detectives next followed the Jeep to a liquor store where one of the women purchased a bottle of Southern Comfort. The Jeep was then tailed to the parking lot of a small Atlantic City motel. The trio remained inside the Jeep talking with the engine continuing to run. The smoke emanating from the exhaust made this clear.

"I thought this guy was supposed to be staying at a casino," commented Von Hess.

"Maybe he's got a better deal with the girls. He's probably going to hook up with one of them."

"Or both. What do you want to do, Sarge?"

"Let's keep watching and see what they do. If he goes in the motel with the girls, we'll have a little more leverage on him when we talk to him. I'm sure he doesn't want his wife to know what he does on the road."

"Are we pinching him?"

"Probably, but not right off the bat. I want to talk to him first and hear his story." After the passing of almost an hour the trio exited the Jeep. Wolfman, who seemed to be steady on his feet, stood next to his car taking swigs from a nearly empty bottle.

He passed the bottle to one of the wobbly legged ladies. She finished off what was left. The woman who took the drink was observed taking something from Wolfman. The detectives weren't quite sure what exchanged hands until the female wrestler brought her hands together and pointed upward.

Several firecracker-like pops and related muzzle blasts caused Markie and Von Hess to duck down and take cover within the confines of their vehicle.

When the shooting stopped the detectives raised their head in time to see the gun returned to Wolfman, who took his own target practice.

"These assholes are shooting out the overhead lights in the parking lot," said Von Hess. "Do you want to move in and take them, Sarge?" "No, Ollie. We're liable to end up killing them. There is no sense risking a shootout over property damage."

"Do you want me to call 911?"

"Yeah, do that. We'll keep an eye on them until the cavalry gets here."

24

Wolfman Croons A Tune

THE NEW JERSEY POLICE RESPONDED quickly to the 911 priority call. With guns drawn, four uniformed officers, supported by Markie and Von Hess, converged on the wrestlers. Wolfman Glass raised his hands over his head without having to be told. He was familiar with the routine. The women weren't. They followed suit only after being told to by the authorities. The police show of force had a sobering effect on all of the wrestlers. Those arrested offered no resistance.

The cold steel of the handcuffs on the wrists of the ladies was something they never before experienced. Their emotions were ignited as they contemplated the unknown consequences of their actions. The disturbing thought of embarrassment, possible loss of employment and the expenses connected to legal representation ran though the minds of the women.

Wolfman presented a cooler picture. An experienced hand at being busted, he was aware of the repercussions he was facing. He was screwed and he knew it. Memories of life behind bars caused Wolfman to frown. He glanced around as the police bracelets were placed on his wrists. There was no escape. The realization caused him to let out a loud frustrated sigh, after which he accepted his situation in silence.

The wrestler with the white beard knew that with his past record it was likely that he'd have to serve time in prison. At his age this wasn't a pleasant thought. I can't go back in the can, thought Wolfman, who went on to convince himself that he couldn't do anymore time. Wolfman and the two female wrestlers were isolated and placed in the back of separate police cars. They were then transported to a police facility where they were booked on charges of criminal possession of a loaded gun, possession of a small quantity of cocaine and causing property damage.

Once at the station Markie and Von Hess took a back seat to the New Jersey authorities. They patiently waited for their opportunity to interview Wolfman Glass in connection with the murder of the Frantellini sisters. The New York City detectives chatted and drank coffee, paying little attention to what was unfolding around them. Had they been more alert they would have detected that something was going on behind the scenes. One of the female wrestlers was a fan favorite being groomed by the wrestling promoter to be the lady champion. Due to her being on good terms with the promoter, the future champion notified the promoter of her trouble in the hope that she'd keep her job.

Since the promotion was already on the radar of the media due to the alleged steroid use by the talent, the promoter saw damage control as being paramount. Fearing a scandal that would be amplified in the press the promoter came to the rescue quickly. He contacted his corporate attorney in the hope that his exposure could be contained. The promoter's attorney was a New Jersey former state prosecutor with strong ties to his former office. Once apprised of the situation the attorney immediately took steps. While it was impossible to completely make the matter disappear, the attorney's efforts did meet with significant success.

Arrangements were made for restitution to be made for the damage caused at the motel. Receiving an inflated repair cost made things palatable to the owner of the motel. There were also incentives afforded to those responsible for enforcing the law. The understanding arrived at called for the female wrestlers to be cut loose without any publicity or documentation of their involvement in the out of hand partying. Since Wolfman's wrestling career was on the downswing anyway, it was decided that he should be the one to take the weight. Another arrest added to the wrestler's record would matter little.

Markie and Von Hess stood by quietly as Wolfman was charged with criminal possession of a weapon and public intoxication. The cocaine charge somehow was no longer in play. The New York detectives just looked at each other without saying a word. Since they had what they were after, a vulnerable Wolfman, they saw the behind-the-scenes manipulations to be none of their affair.

Markie and Von Hess took advantage of the opportunity to look at Wolfman's vehicle. They discovered that there was cyanide in the glove compartment of the wrestler's Jeep. While this meant nothing to the New Jersey authorities, it meant plenty to the sleuths from New York City. The cyanide was potent ammunition to use during the effort to break Wolfman Glass.

The grilling of Wolfman by Markie and Von Hess started out slowly. Eventually the exchange intensified.

"You're going away on this Jersey gun rap, Wolfman," advised Von Hess. "It looks like you were left holding the bag."

"I don't what you're talking about," replied Wolfman.

"I'm talking about you doing a stretch."

"Jail don't scare me," the wrestler declared, putting on a brave front. "I've done time before."

"Educate him, Ollie," injected Markie.

"You're not looking at just this New Jersey rap," pointed out Von Hess.

"I'm not?"

"We found the cyanide in the glove compartment of your Jeep."

"That stuff is legal," said Wolfman, who was a bit more concerned than before.

"What do you think is going to happen when that cyanide is matched to what killed the Frantellini sisters in New York City?" Markie asked.

On this Markie was running a bluff. He had no idea if cyanide comparisons were feasible or could prove anything. Luckily, Wolfman had no idea either.

"You're looking at a double murder in New York, on top of the charges here in Jersey, my friend."

Wolfman stiffened. Not knowing what to say he processed the words in silence.

"You'll be doing your wrestling in the can for the rest of your life if you don't wise up" warned Von Hess.

"Then there is the domestic front to consider," said Markie. "I don't see your wife being very happy with you swapping bearhugs with a couple of babes out here in Jersey."

Wolfman did a double take as a result of this comment. "You aren't telling her are you?"

Markie shrugged. "Those things have a way of leaking out," answered the sergeant.

Wolfman was now thinking hard. He began to see his life crumbling as he envisioned a future of incarceration and a destroyed marriage. Since this wasn't the first time he had been caught straying, exposure of his infidelity was a woe that he knew would carry a grave consequence domestically. With no one on the outside to support his commissary needs, incarceration would be that much more unbearable.

Von Hess sensed the wrestler's weakening. "So, what is it going to be?" Von Hess asked. "Do you want to help yourself or not?"

"How can I help myself?" Wolfman asked, his energy drained.

"Sing us an aria about the Frantellini sisters, and then maybe we can help dig you out of this hole."

"Can you guarantee that?" Wolfman asked hopefully.

"There are no guarantees in this life, my friend," said Markie. "If you play ball, you got my word that we'll work with you. If you bullshit us, you can count on getting buried."

"What do you want to know?"

"Start with the Frantellini sisters getting poisoned."

Wolfman nodded his understanding. He then customized a story that he believed to be to his advantage.

"Okay, look, it was like this. I don't know anything about any poisoning. All I do know is that some guy I met in a bar wanted to play a prank on the people at that table in the restaurant."

"For what reason?"

"I don't know the reason why. Anyway, I did the guy a favor and dropped some mice under a table in that restaurant. That's all I did."

"Did you get paid?" Von Hess asked.

"Yeah, I got a few bucks."

"From whom?"

"I don't know the name of the guy."

"What about the cyanide in your glove compartment?" Von Hess asked. "Is that supposed to be a coincidence?"

"That's not illegal to have," reminded Wolfman, "you can get that shit a lot of places legally."

"And you gave some cyanide to who?"

Wolfman was taken aback. Unsure how to reply, a frown formed on his face, making it clear he was uncomfortable with the question.

"This is the time to come clean, if you're looking to help yourself," reminded the skeptical Von Hess. Wolfman looked down without responding, making it obvious that he wasn't being truthful.

"Cut the shit, you aren't fooling anybody," said Markie finally, losing patience.

"What do you want from me?"

The question posed by Wolfman smacked of frustration. At this point, the detectives knew they were getting close to breaking their man.

"We want the truth."

"I already told you that I put the mice under the table. I swear that's all I had to do with anything."

"Do you think we're a couple of farmers?" questioned the sergeant. "Now, for the last time, I want to know who was involved. Who paid you to put the mice under the table and who slipped the cyanide in the drinks. Either you give, or you are on your own to face the music."

"I need to use the bathroom," said Wolfman, stalling for time to think."

"In a minute."

"I'm going to piss my pants if I don't go."

"Piss your pants or shit your pants?" asked Markie. "Do him a favor, Ollie."

Wolfman was at the urinal with Von Hess at his side. The veteran detective continued to work on the wrestler.

"Listen," said Von Hess, who assumed the good cop role. "You do what you want, but I'll tell you right now, you're not helping yourself in there."

"I told you everything," said Wolfman, trying to remain firm.

"Well, there is something you ought to know before you stick to that story," countered Von Hess.

"What's that?"

"Let me wise you up," voiced Von Hess calmly. "We already know who your friend is. We got a witness who's a big wrestling fan, so you guys were both recognized. It's not like you're somebody invisible. You guys are both well known to the public."

"I look like a lot of people," said Wolfman.

"Maybe that's true," acknowledged Von Hess. "But your friend is getting booked for homicide. When that happens, there is no more deal for you on the table. Do you really think that your pal Crippler isn't going to take the deal we offer him? He's a cinch to tell us all about you to save his own ass. Think about it. If you can't see that, you've taken too many bumps in that ring."

"If you know about Crippler, why were you asking me who I was working with?"

"We wanted to test your truthfulness," answered Von Hess. Remember something, misery loves company. Your friend is going to give you up in a New York minute. Doesn't it make sense to beat him to the punch?"

By the time Wolfman returned to the interview room with Von Hess his head was riddled with thoughts of betrayal. *The detective is right*, thought Wolfman. Crippler is bound to snitch, sure as rain.

Wolfman indicated that he was now willing to cooperate. He began rattling off details.

"Look, it was like this. Crippler paid me to toss the mice under the table. Some rich lady was paying him to take out the two women."

"That's what we wanted to hear from you," said Markie.

"Now you heard it, Sergeant."

"Keep talking."

"All I know is that Crippler wanted me to create a scene at the restaurant. So, I got the mice."

"What about the cyanide?"

"He asked me to get him some cyanide, so I did."

"And the cyanide didn't give you a clue as to what he was up to I suppose?" asked Von Hess, picking up the questioning.

"How could I know for sure what he was going to do with the cyanide?" asked Wolfman. "He didn't say and I didn't ask."

"Why didn't he get the cyanide himself?"

"I got no idea why. You'll have to ask him that question."

"Okay, Ollie," interrupted Markie, "take his statement down."

"I have to make a statement?"

"Yeah," confirmed Markie. "And you're going to sign it too."

"And if I refuse?"

"What do you think?"

These bastards got me by the shorthairs, thought the prisoner.

"You win, Sergeant, I'll sign," said Wolfman. "You guys aren't going to tell my old lady are you? She'll forgive me for getting arrested for the gun, and maybe even being an accomplice in a murder that I had no idea was going to happen, but she'll never ever let me off the hook for another infidelity."

"Don't worry, Wolfman. That's a secret we'll take to the grave," assured Markie.

25

If At First You Don't Succeed....

TEDDY LEONARD DIDN'T FIND it easy to tell Thomas Beasley that his advances toward the attorney's former secretary failed to gain traction. His admission was ego shattering as well as professionally disappointing.

Beasley didn't find this news surprising. The attorney threw it up to Leonard that he had initially thought the private investigator to be too old for such an undertaking. Besides that, the reinvented Clara wasn't likely to jump at the chance to go out with just any man.

"I honestly thought Clara would be easy pickings," said Leonard. "I can't believe that she'd ever play hard to get."

"I told you, Teddy," reminded Beasley.

"You did tell me. I'll give you that. At first I thought she showed interest," explained the private investigator. "But she fooled me.

"You should have listened to me."

"Do you think somebody may have smartened her up about me?" The question gave Beasley pause. The attorney never factored in Ronnie Frantellini's influence over Clara.

"If so, I got a good idea who," answered the lawyer.

"Who?"

"Ronnie Frantellini, who else. Well, whatever the case, go find somebody capable of worming his way into Clara's heart. And don't look in the senior citizen center."

"Just curious, what makes you think Ronnie Frantellini might be engaging in a shady activity?"

"Trust me, that gal is diabolical. She's a demon who can't help herself from stepping over the line. Ronnie makes us look like a couple of altar boys."

"She's that bad?"

"Forget how bad Ronnie is, just concentrate on getting somebody close to Clara."

"If you want to get Ronnie pinched we could go about it another way."

"No, no, no. I just want to know what she's up to," answered Beasley. "Once I get the goods on her, I'll be in a position to restore my original agreement with her."

"Which was?"

"Never mind."

"But you're her lawyer, don't you already have enough dirt on her?"

"I got plenty, but I can't use what I already have. She found a way to neutralize me, so I need more."

"I don't get it, Tom," voiced the perplexed Leonard. "If you can't use whatever you already got on her, how could you use anything new?" "Because I'm not the one who is going pop her little bubble....you are."

"Me?"

"Yes, you. You're going to shake her down."

"Do you really think so?" questioned Leonard, believing that Beasley was now taking a lot for granted.

"Don't worry Teddy. I got you covered," Beasley replied.

"When she's up against it with you, she'll come running to me to make you go away. I'll broker a deal which will take care of you and get me back what was mine."

"Talk about diabolical, you should be in one of those James Bond books!"

"All you have to do is figure out a way to get somebody close to Clara. Through Clara we'll find everything there is to know about Ronnie. Trust me, girls talk."

"You know, Tom, I'm thinking. Clara probably didn't give me a tumble because she knows I'm close to you."

"Either that or she noticed the bags under your eyes, Teddy," commented Beasley, shaking his head.

"Very funny. I did everything except kiss her ass in Macy's window!"

"So, what happened?"

"I don't know," replied Leonard. "I could have sworn that I had Clara hooked. When I followed up with a call, I was shocked by the way she brushed me off."

"Did she happen to give you a reason why she soured on you?"

"No, there were no explanations."

"Then they might have smelled a rat," concluded Beasley, "and it wasn't Clara who got the first whiff. She's not bright enough for that, Teddy. My guess is that she spoke to Ronnie about you, and Ronnie put the kibosh on things."

"I see."

"Go out and find us a pretty boy that nobody knows. Look for a boy-toy type, or even someone who could pass as a respectable businessman. You have to get close to Clara without arousing Ronnie's suspicion. Do you know of anyone?"

"Offhand I don't. But I'll find somebody."

"So go and find the right fit."

"I'm on the clock, right, Tom?"

"Yes, you're on the clock."

"Hey, wait a minute, I have an idea," said Leonard with enthusiasm. "That juror we got to might be the right guy for getting close to Clara."

"Do you think so?"

"Absolutely. He's smooth, a regular Joe College type who owns his own business. And he is desperate for money. I think he'd be perfect!"

"He can play the role?"

"He conned all those other jurors in voting for an acquittal, didn't he?"

"That's true."

"The guy has a sick wife, so he probably isn't getting any. That makes him a natural for us."

"So, what are you waiting for, Teddy?"

"Let me have some money and I'll go see him today."

***

RUDOLPH PRISINSKI STOOD ALONE at the bar drinking scotch. As he drank he kept an eye on the entrance. Rudy was anxiously awaiting the arrival of Teddy Leonard. He wasn't exactly sure why the private investigator wanted to meet with him. All Rudy knew is what Leonard had indicated telephonically. Leonard had said that he had something good for him.

Since Prisinski had exceeded expectations in the Victor Spinello homicide trial he was hoping that he was going to receive a bonus for the performance that led to Spinello's acquittal. Or, could there be a problem? Rudy thought.

The private investigator entered the drinking emporium with his head held high. He was attired in an expensive brown tweed overcoat. Leonard confidently approached Rudy. The smile on his face was broad. The two men greeted each other with a handshake. Rudy, ever wary, maintained a serious look.

The private investigator took out a fifty-dollar bill and placed it on the bar. He then raised his hand to summon the bartender. "Scotch on the rocks," ordered Leonard. "And set up my friend here with whatever he's having."

Once the drinks were placed before the men they clicked glasses wishing each other good luck. When the bartender placed the change on the bar, Leonard picked it up.

"C'mon, Rudy, let's move to a booth where we can talk," said the private investigator, leaving a five-dollar tip atop the bar.

Once seated Leonard removed an envelope from the inner pocket of his overcoat and placed it on the table. This gained a reaction from Rudy. Seeing the thickness of the envelope caused Rudy to begin licking his lower lip in anticipation of what was to follow.

"What's this?" Rudy asked.

"Two grand in twenties."

"For me?"

"It could be. I like the threads you got on, Rudy. It's perfect for the job I have in mind for you."

"I wear a suit and tie for business. What is the job you need me for?"

"It's a nice project," said Leonard, pushing the envelope closer to Rudy. "Count the money."

The private investigator was being shrewd. He knew that once Rudy touched the cash he would be hard pressed to return it and likely accept the opportunity being offered.

"It's all here," announced Rudy, after counting the contents of the envelope.

"This money is just for openers. You're gonna make out like a bandit on this, Rudy. Finish your drink. I'll go buy us another round and then I'll give you the layout."

Over a fresh cocktail Rudy grew more comfortable.

"So, what's the story?"

"You really do make a nice appearance dressed up, Rudy. That's gonna be important on this job."

"Maybe you should tell me what the job is."

"The first thing you need to do is put that envelope in your pocket."

"I haven't agreed to anything yet, Mr. Leonard."

"What's with the Mister Leonard? Call me Teddy."

"Okay, Teddy. What's the deal?"

"First, I have to ask you a few questions."

"Go ahead and ask."

"You don't have any out-of-control vices, right?" "None."

"Do you gamble?"

"A little, but I got no money for that right now."

"That's good. And you're no rumpot, right." "Nah, I drink but I can handle it."

"What about girls? Do you fool around on your wife?"

"I wish I had the money to fool around with someone. My wife is, let's just day, incapable."

"Well, that's fine. This proposition just might provide you with relief in that department, Rudy."

The private investigator went on to explain that he was contracted to find out if a Manhattan businesswoman was engaged in any illegal, immoral or unethical activity. Leonard explained that he was to accomplish this by getting someone romantically involved with the close friend and employee of the targeted woman.

"So, let me understand this. You want me to be a secret agent who has to get the goods on some woman by getting close to her friend?"

"Exactly."

"I have one concern, Teddy. I can't be testifying in court on any of this. I mean, I'm a married man with a reputation to protect."

"Don't worry about that, there will be no court involved in this. That is something you can bank on."

"Do you think this woman will go for me?"

"Sure, it'll be a cinch for you."

"I'm curious, why don't I just make a play for the woman you want me to get the dirt on?"

"She's too smart to be taken in. Her friend will be easier for you."

"So, this lady I have to take up with, what does she look like?"

"That's one of the bennies with this job. She's a honey, not the brightest light maybe, but a honey."

"How old a honey?'

"Age appropriate for you."

"And you think that she'll like me?"

"You're a charmer with a convincing line of shit, Rudy. Don't worry, she'll like you. You'll just have to be nice, be attentive and wine and dine the woman. The information we want will come once you start snuggling up under the sheets with her."

"You'll finance me for all expenses, right?"

"Definitely."

"How much money do I get beyond the two grand you gave me?" Leonard smiled at the question. He took out a pen and wrote a number on a napkin. He passed the napkin to Rudy and said, "You get this every day you work on this job."

"This works," said Rudy, agreeing to the pay. "What if these women check me out? I can't have them coming to my house or giving me grief."

"Relax, I'm getting you phony credentials. She'll never know who you are or where to find you."

"Where are you getting the identification from?"

"Leave that to me. It may be a good idea to grow a beard. The whiskers will alter your appearance. Once this assignment is over you could shave it off and nobody will ever recognize you."

"What am I supposed to tell my wife when I'm out all night?" asked Rudy. "Tell her the truth, that you're working for me," answered Leonard. "But remember this, never tell her any details of the work you're doing. As long as the money is coming, she should be okay, right?"

"That's for sure. So, how should I kick this off?"

"Don't worry about that for now Rudy. I'll figure something out once I do a little surveillance."

Once the deal was finalized. The men ordered another drink. The additional libations removed any awkwardness, creating a chumminess that led to other discussions.

"Do you think you could help me drum up some new business for my public relations firm, Teddy? I could use the help."

"I worked in Manhattan my whole police career. I know lots of corporate people from when I was a detective. If I deliver new business to you, I get a slice of the pie, right?"

"Of course. How big of a slice do you expect?"

"I ought to stick you up for half, but since we're friends now I won't. I'll just take twenty percent."

"That's very generous of you, Teddy," said Rudy with a trace of sarcasm.

"Ain't that the truth."

"I was thinking more like ten percent," countered Rudy.

"Let's split the difference and make it fifteen percent."

"You got a deal." The two then shook hands. "Another round?"

26

A False Hero

TEDDY LEONARD'S SURVEILLANCE OF Clara Calhoun proved productive. The private investigator took note that during the workweek it was Clara's habit to walk to a nearby market that featured a salad bar.

The salad bar, which fit nicely into Clara's dietary routine, was located not far from the shoe factory. Seeing that Clara always reached into her purse for cash to pay for her food was inspirational for the private investigator.

Leonard's idea centered on his belief that most women could be swept off her feet through some act of heroism. I'll make Rudy a Prince Charming that comes to the rescue of the fair maiden, Leonard thought. If that doesn't make her heart flutter, nothing will.

The private investigator mapped out a scenario that would put his theory to the test. His plan required the assistance of an accomplice. After mulling over several candidates, Leonard decided on a criminal he knew from his days on the force.

Tex the Thief was a pill-popper who described himself, when asked, as an actor between roles. His claim to fame on the screen was occasionally appearing as an extra in western movies. The thirty-seven-year-old Tex met his expenses by committing burglaries and selling the swag he walked off with. The most noteworthy thing about Tex was that he could always be seen wearing Luchese cowboy boots.

To find Tex, Leonard went to see the proprietor of a junk shop where people sold things they didn't want anymore. The junk shop was operated by Scarface, a nasty baldheaded man with a severe pockmarked face. Scarface was standing behind his cash register when Leonard entered his business.

Upon seeing the former NYPD detective Scarface stood erect. As a fence who took in stolen goods, he was naturally wary of Leonard even though they had a loose understanding. Since Scarface was of the school that believed a cop, retired or not, could cause him grief, he feigned friendliness.

"Did you get that watch for me?" asked Leonard.

"Not yet, but don't worry an Oyster Submariner will eventually come in. I remember what you want."

"I thought you said you were expecting some."

"I had a couple of Rolex watches in the back, but you want an Oyster Submariner. You have to wait."

"Have you seen Tex?"

"He'll be around. What did he do now?"

"Nothing. I have a proposition for him that'll make him a few bucks."

"I expect him to come by in a little while."

Leonard was in his car when he spotted Tex walking down the street thirty minutes later. The thief was coming from the far end of the block. Tex was recognizable from a distance due to his unique walk. His right foot pointed outward with each step taken. A hand, as always, was in his pocket as he walked.

As Tex advanced the private investigator emerged from his vehicle to have a word with him.

"Hey, Tex," called out Leonard. "Hold up a minute."

"What's up?" asked Tex innocently.

"I got a job for you that's right up your alley."

"You got an acting job for me?" The question Tex posed caused Leonard to grin.

"Matter of fact I do."
"You do?"
"This is sort of a private gig."
"I don't do any kinky shit, no role playing for somebody looking to get their jollies."
"This job is nothing like that. I need you to stick up a woman."
"I'm no stickup man!"
"Relax, this is all in fun," expressed Leonard, laughing loudly. "This isn't going to be a real robbery."
"I don't understand."
"It's going to be staged. My friend is trying to make an impression on this girl he likes, so we're trying to make him out to be a hero. You pretend to be sticking up her up, and my friend will intervene and chase you off."
"I get it now," said Tex. "But where do I run to?"
"Anyplace you want, nobody is going to be chasing you."
"I don't have a gun."
"You don't any gun, you can use a knife. When my friend comes to the woman's rescue he'll give you a kick in the ass. All you have to do is run off."
"No cops, right?"
"Definitely no cops."
"How much do I get?"
"Two hundred clams for a minute of work."
"Okay, I'll do it," quickly agreed Tex.
"Good," said Leonard, putting forth his hand. The men shook on it.

***

RUDOLPH PRISINAKI WAS just twenty feet away from Clara as she walked from work to the store to get her lunch. Rudy watched closely as Tex began to walk alongside Clara. Rudy could see that Tex was saying something to Clara.

Tex produced a small folding knife and raised it so that Clara could clearly see it. He then demanded her money. Seeing the blade, Clara immediately stopped walking. She was removing cash from her purse when Rudy suddenly sprang into action. As scripted, the public relations man in the blue suit and black tie took hold of Tex by the collar. Rudy spun Tex around with force enough for Tex to fall to the ground and lose control of the folding knife.

Clara watched in awe as her rescuer lifted Tex to his feet and violently shook him. Rudy completed his heroic act by kicking Tex in the buttocks, sending the pretender on his way. Once Tex had run off, Rudy picked up the knife and placed it in his own pocket.

"Are you alright?" asked Rudy, addressing the victim.

"Yes, I think so," Clara replied, still shaken. "Do you think I should call the police?"

"No, I wouldn't bother doing that. The guy is gone, and as long as you're not hurt, the police are probably not going to waste their time."

"I suppose you're right."

"Where were you heading to?"

"I was on my way to pick up lunch."

"You're still pretty shaken, how about I walk with you until you settle down."

"Thank you, I'd appreciate that."

When they reached the corner Rudy removed the knife from his pocket and dropped it down the sewer. As they passed a restaurant, he suggested they go inside and have lunch.

Clara responded just how Teddy Leonard figured she would. Open-eyed and impressed, Clara agreed to sit down with the Prince Charming that she believed rescued her. The lunch went exceedingly well with Clara agreeing to see Rudy again.

After lunch Clara rushed back to the shoe factory. She was anxious to share her experience with Ronnie Frantellini. Ronnie listened without comment as Clara communicated what had occurred. Ronnie grew curious when informed that the assailant allowed himself to be manhandled, disarmed and humbled in such fashion without putting up a fight. She also wondered about Clara going to lunch with the man who intervened on her behalf.

"Did you call the cops?" Ronnie queried.

"No, we didn't bother. The man who helped me felt that it would be a waste of time."

"This guy who helped you, is he a big man?"

"Not especially. Walter is about average."

"The man who accosted you, how big was he."

"He was about the same size as Walter, only thinner."

"Walter is the name of this guy who came to your rescue?"

"Yes, Walter Quigley."

"Did Walter say what his business was?"

"He's into real estate. He was dressed nice in a suit and tie, so he must do pretty well for himself."

"I see. Did Walter ask to see you again?"

"He did. We hit it off. I mean, I could hardly say no after how he helped me."

"Did he say when he was going to call you?"

"He actually asked me out already. I told him yes. We've set a date to have dinner at the Minetta Tavern in the West Village. I've never been there, so I'm looking ahead to it."

***

THE WIFE OF RUDY PRISINSKI FOUND the noise coming from the blow dryer annoying. She hated to be distracted when watching television. An avid fan of Jeopardy, she was having difficulty hearing the answers to the questions.

"Close the damn bathroom door, Rudy," she shouted to her husband.

When it became apparent that Rudy couldn't hear her, she turned her wheelchair to throw a paperback book in the direction of the bathroom. This also drew no response from Rudy, who was happily singing Blondie's hit song, *Heart of Glass*.

When Rudy stepped out of the bedroom, the aroma of his cologne permeated the room. Finding the cheerfulness of her husband out of the ordinary, Mrs. Prisinski grew suspicious.

From her wheelchair she watched her husband closely. *This son of a bitch is up to something*, she thought. Mrs. Prisinski moved her wheelchair closer to her husband. Hearing Rudy warble the lyrics of the Blondie tune had meaning for her. His singing caused her to reflect back on when she had her mobility. Back then whenever Rudy sang it meant he was preparing for lovemaking. The wife convinced herself that Rudy was going out to meet someone for romantic purposes.

Feeling helpless, Mrs. Prisinski sat in silence. She stewed as her thoughts turned to life before the accident. She had been a successful woman in business who had gained the admiration of many by starting her own public relations firm. She let out a sad sigh as she thought of the men who had once sought her affection. While flattered, she always repelled their advances, remaining faithful to her husband. Her love for Rudy was now thought to have been foolish fancy.

"And for what?" she suddenly shouted aloud.

"What's up with you?" Rudy asked, his tone was far from cordial. *I'm helpless in this damn chair*, thought the wife before replying. If I take a stand now, he's liable to leave me, then where will I be?

"I just said for you to have a good time," she answered without a shred of sincerity.

"There is no good time to be had," answered Rudy, knowing full well that wasn't what his wife had blurted out. "I told you I'm going to work for that private eye I know. This is business."

"Dressed like that?"

"I have to do surveillance at some club, so I have to fit in," lied Rudy. "There is a good chance that I'll be very late getting home. It'll all depend on how things go."

"How late is very late?"

"That's hard to say," answered Rudy.

"I don't know about you, Rudy."

"Look, do you think I'm working a parttime job because I like it?" asked the husband. "I am doing it because our public relations business is in the toilet. We have bills to pay due to your mounting needs. So, please, just cut out the attitude."

"You dare talk about my needs?" Mrs. Prisinski shot back. "You were the one driving that night, Rudy," reminded the wife. "You were the one responsible for putting me in this damn chair!"

Rudy detested how his wife always threw up the accident to him. Drawing a deep breath, he held his tongue. He remembered that he and his wife weren't alone in the apartment. The cleaning woman they used weekly was in the kitchen. On this evening, she was there to tend to the needs of Rudy's wife in his absence.

The additional help was an added expense, but an unavoidable one. A grandmother in her early sixties, the woman couldn't help but overhear everything.

"I have to get going," said Rudy, looking to terminate the ugly scene.

Rudy stepped in close to kiss his wife goodbye. The nearness enabled his wife to get a better whiff of the cologne he wore. The powerful fragrance, and Rudy's feigned act of affection, only fueled her animosity further.

"Just go," said the wife harshly.

"Please see that my wife eats something," said Rudy to the sitter who now entered the room.

"Of course," replied the woman softly.

"After dinner, find a movie on television to watch," suggested Rudy. "She likes television."

This remark was particularly irking to Rudy's wife, who felt like she was being treated like a child. It sparked a response.

"Enjoy yourself," commented the wife with bitterness.

"This is no picnic that I'm going on," countered Rudy. "We need the money. I don't hear you complaining when I bring home the bacon."

"Whatever. Just go."

“You should be grateful for the sacrifices I make for you.”

“Grateful to you? For what, putting me in this damn chair?”

“Why don’t you change that record?” cried out Rudy, who was sick and tired of being blamed.

The hired woman’s eyes widened as she looked at the angry Rudy. Finding him frightening, she was relieved when Rudy stormed out of the apartment. The awkwardness of the situation caused the aide to try and settle the climate.

“Would you like a nice hot cup of tea, Ma’am?” asked the older woman softly. “

Yes, please. Put some Jack Daniels in it. You’ll find the bottle in the kitchen cabinet.”

27

Ronnie's Test

IT JUST DIDN'T PASS THE sniff test for Ronnie Frantellini. She couldn't digest why anyone would endanger themself by interrupting a street robbery to benefit a total stranger. By her logic, she could only envision a young blue collar working man heroically stepping up to take such a risk, but an older man in a suit and tie seemed farfetched to her.

As a rule, Ronnie relied heavily on her gut instincts, which to date had never failed her. As far as Clara's rescue, she had her doubts. Once suspicious, Ronnie began searching for a motive as to why someone would come to the aide of Clara. She arrived at only one feasible possibility.

Clara had nothing to offer this Walter Quigley other than her looks, thought Ronnie. What businessman is going to risk his life for a pretty face? There must be an angle behind this, and it probably has something to do with me.

With this thought circulating in Ronnie's mind, Walter Quigley was now viewed as a potential threat. Ronnie reasoned that anyone capable of ingratiating themselves with Clara would be in a position to gather enough information to shakedown a well-heeled woman like herself.

Clara is still very naïve, thought Ronnie. She's green enough to let something slip that might be best unsaid. I could be wrong, but better safe than sorry. I'll have to figure this guy Quigley out before things go any further. Ronnie knew that in order to dissuade Clara from dating a man she liked she would need to articulate a reason why the person was a wrong fit. To do this Ronnie needed ammunition to bolster her argument. At first the Frantellini widow thought that having a background check conducted on Walter Quigley was the prudent thing to do at some point. Such work was usually referred to Thoms Beasley.

Since the Frantellini attorney couldn't be discounted as a prime candidate for double-dealing, Ronnie thought it best to keep the family lawyer out of the loop for the time being.

Ronnie decided that before doing anything, she'd arrange to have a face-to-face interaction with Quigley. Ronnie was a fast worker with a keen mind when it came to scheming. She went to the office of the creative arm of the Frantellini Shoe Factory to see Victor Spinello. When Ronnie arrived at Spinello's office she found him hard at work with a pen in one hand and his shoe in another. He had resumed his work on his Dynamic Shoe. Ronnie cleared her voice to get Victor's attention.

Looking up from his desk, Victor smiled broadly upon seeing Ronnie. His indebtedness to her knew no limits. As a result of Ronnie's role in securing his freedom, Victor's loyalty to Ronnie was unwavering. Plainly put, in the eyes of Victor Spinello, Ronnie walked on water.

"How are things going, Victor?" asked the owner of the Frantellini Shoe Factory, smiling happily.

"It won't be long now, Ronnie," replied Victor. "I am finally nearing completion of my work. The Dynamic Shoe will soon be ready for public consumption."

"That's great, Victor, you just keep plugging away on our shoe," encouraged Ronnie, who liked using inclusive terminology. "But I don't want you killing yourself. You're no good to the company if you collapse from overwork."

"Don't worry about that, I love what I do."

"I know you do. But I still worry," lied Ronnie. "Tell you what, let's get together for dinner one evening this week. We'll go to a nice place."

"Why, that would be fine," answered the surprised Victor. "When do you want to go."

"Let me check my calendar and I'll let you know the details later."

Ronnie intended to arrange to have their dinner at the same place, day and time Clara would be dining with the man who called himself Walter Quigley.

***

THE STORYBOOK RESCUE INVENTED by Teddy Leonard was, although cliche, nevertheless effective. The private investigator had accurately sized Clara up as someone apt to have a fairytale notion of love, as opposed to being an assertive woman capable of defending herself.

Clara was so impressed by what she believed to be Walter Quigley's act of gallantry that other men paled in comparison. She began comparing her hero to the other men she knew.

Clara doubted that the water proofer would have placed himself between her and danger. Even the courageousness of Fernando the taxi driver was in question when it came to his risking his life. As Teddy Leonard forecasted, Clara's reaction to being saved by Walter Quigley was that of the classic damsel in distress.

On the evening of their scheduled dinner Clara was so eager to be picked up by Walter that she shamelessly waited on the sidewalk in front of her home for him to arrive. With eyes gleaming happily and a toothy smile she greeted Rudy Prisinski with a warm embrace. It was clear that the deceptive man she believed to be Walter Quigley had made his mark on her emotions.

Aside from making headway on his mission, Clara's warm reception was rewarding to Rudy/Walter in another way. It had been a long time since Rudy held a woman with passion. The feel of Clara's breasts pressing against his chest sent a signal throughout his body that demanded more. Neither participant wanted to unlock their hold on each other. They held hands as they taxied to the West Village restaurant they planned on having dinner at.

Rudy made all the right moves while sitting with Clara at the restaurant bar having a pre-dinner quaff. He held eye contact as they spoke. He listened attentively to her spoken words as if they mattered. Such seemingly trivial things went far with Clara as the alcohol went down.

I really like this guy, thought Clara wistfully when Rudy left to use the restroom. *But I really must find out more about him*. When Walter returned to the bar she began her probe.

"So, Walter, you mentioned that you were involved in real estate."

"I'm a property owner," replied the fraudster. "I have a portfolio consisting mostly of B-buildings."

"In New York City?"

"Yes, here and I own a few in New Jersey."

"Do you live here in the city?"

"No, I have a house in Red Bank," he replied.

She's quizzing me, thought Rudy, *that means she's really going for me. Once I get a couple of drinks in her I'll steer the conversation to Ronnie.*

"I hear that Red Bank is beautiful, Walter," said Clara, who now wondered if he was married.

"It is. Did you know that Ernest Hemingway used to come here?"

"I can see why, this place is lovely, Walter" said Clara, who had never been at the eatery before. "Do you come here often?"

"I come enough. It's one of the restaurants I like. I like to experience different places."

After Rudy said this he began thinking back on a time when his business was profitable enough to wine and dine clients. In those days he went only to the best places.

"A penny for your thoughts," announced Clara, picking up on his distant look.

"I was just thinking of how fortuitus our meeting was," replied Rudy, thinking quickly.

"You risked your life to save mine, Walter. That makes you special."

"You were worth saving."

Their conversation continued to progress along this lovey-dovey line until interrupted by the unexpected presence of Ronnie Frantellini and Victor Spinello.

Shocked to see Victor, Rudy froze. He feared that Victor would recognize him as one of the jurors in his trial. To his amazement, somehow Victor didn't.

"Ronnie!" declared Clara, "What brings you here?" she asked, already knowing the answer to her question.

"I just had to pull Victor out of that office," said Ronnie. "He needed a break. You mentioned that you would be here, so I decided to surprise you. I hope you don't mind," added Ronnie, now addressing Rudy.

"Not at all," said Rudy, smiling nervously.

"Walter, this is my best friend and boss, Ronnie Frantellini. You have no idea how much I owe this woman."

"Now, now, Clara," said Ronnie, who seemed genuinely pleased at being appreciated.

"It's my pleasure to meet you, Ronnie," conveyed Rudy politely. "And this is Victor," said Clara.

"I'll be back," stated Ronnie, "I'm going to freshen up."

"You look familiar to me Walter, have we ever met?" questioned Victor, unable to place Rudy.

Rudy bristled, fearing that Victor might yet come to remember him as being a jury member at his trial.

"No, I don't think so," answered Rudy. "I have that kind of a face"

"I suppose you're right. "What are you having, Victor," asked Rudy, quick to change the subject. "Scotch on the rocks."

"You can order Ronnie the same," said Clara, aware of what her best friend drank.

"Excuse me, I need to use the rest room myself," Victor announced.

"They seem like very nice people," said Rudy, feeling somewhat relieved to be alone with Clara.

"They are, Walter. I really love Ronnie. She has done so much for me. And that Victor, well he's simply a genius. What a nice man!"

"What makes him a genius?"

"He's the one who invented the Frantellini Sole. Now he's on the verge of introducing a new product. Ronnie expects the company to make a fortune on The Dynamic Shoe."

"That's very interesting. Tell me more."

"Do you want to hear interesting?"" asked Clara, moving closer to her date. "Victor was arrested for murdering a man. But don't worry, he is no axe murderer. It was self-defense. He was acquitted in court."

"I don't think we should bring that up now." The last thing Rudy wanted was talk of Victor's trial.

"No, of course not. Ronnie thinks…." Clara stopped talking when she saw Ronnie returning to the bar.

When the four were all together again, Ronnie suggested that they all be her guest for dinner. This worked for Rudy because he'd now be able to pocket the money he was advanced by Teddy Leonard.

"So, Walter, Clara told me that you are in the real estate business," said Ronnie.

"I own a number of properties," answered Rudy.

This was the sort of opening that Ronnie was waiting for. She waited until Victor again needed to use the restroom before spreading misinformation.

"I've been thinking of selling the Frantellini Shoe Factory and real estate holdings," announced Ronnie, adding, "but please don't breathe a word of this to anyone. I haven't told Victor of my plans."

"That is interesting," said Rudy. "Why sell?"

"It's time, Walter. It's just time."

Ronnie went on to make it a point to convey that she was limited concerning the real estate end of her affairs. She noted that it was her late husband and stepdaughter who tended to such matters.

Ronnie's test was threefold. If Walter proposed a business proposition with an eye toward taking advantage of someone who he believed to be unsophisticated in business, that would speak of his true character. If he failed to express an interest, then perhaps Walter wasn't all that successful. Finally, and most importantly, if she was later approached by someone making her an offer, that would mean Walter spoke to someone about her selling out. It would be of interest to see who that someone was.

"You're really thinking of selling, Ronnie?" asked Clara, who was stunned to learn of this.

"I'll sell, but only if the right offer comes along. I don't mind admitting that I'm looking for plenty of cash under the table. I don't need Uncle Sam to be more of a partner than he already is. Don't you worry, Clara, you'll be fine because you're with me."

Rudy sat in silence thinking. Money under the table! This is exactly the kind of stuff that Teddy Leonard is after!

It was Clara who drew Rudy further into the conversation.

"Walter owns lots of properties," announced Clara.

"I have some commercial properties," answered Rudy, now hoping to find a way to change the conversation because his sophistication in the area of real estate was limited.

"Walter owns B-buildings in Manhattan."

Relief for Rudy came when Ronnie spotted Victor returning to their table. "But let's not talk about this now," said Ronnie. "Remember, not a word to Victor. I don't want to upset him."

There came a point in the evening that Clara and Ronnie got to speak privately. Ronnie wanted to know if Clara was going to take Walter home. When Clara answered that she was thinking of having Walter over her house for a nightcap, Ronnie frowned.

"What's wrong?" inquired Clara.

"Have you forgotten my advice already?"

"What do you mean?'

"Didn't I advise you that you don't give yourself too easily unless there is something there for you."

"You didn't say that with Fernando."

"Fernando is an oasis in the desert, and not someone to be taken seriously. He fills a need and that is it. However, with this Walter, it's an entirely different story. If he is what he says he is, he represents a future for you. If he isn't, well, that is something else."

"So, I shouldn't take him home?"

"I advise that you make him work for it. He'll appreciate you more."

"What's the big deal?"

"Look, Clara, I'm just saying that we should have a better understanding of Walter."

"What is there to understand?"

"I want you to think about something, honey. What kind of businessman would dare put himself in harm's way? Facing off with a knife wielder is more in line with a different sort of man. Walter may have some kind of motive."

"Do you really think that?"

"Trust me on this, Clara. Don't jump in with both feet. Give it some time for us to know Walter better."

"But why would Walter want to do anything harmful to me?"

"It may not be about you, Clara. He may be using you to get to me."

"But why?"

"Business is a treacherous game, honey. If you have a need for intimacy, ring up Fernando."

As a result of their conversation Rudy never made it up to Clara's apartment for a nightcap. However, Ronnie's late-night call to Fernando prevented the night from being a washout for her.

***

RUDY ARRIVED HOME without understanding what went wrong. He had mixed emotions. On the positive side, his learning of Ronnie Frantellini's plan to sell her assets and engage in tax evasion was something that would please Teddy Leonard and whoever Leonard was working for. On the negative side of the equation was the disappointment of his returning to his own apartment unfulfilled sexually.

Rudy entered his apartment to find the senior citizen he hired to watch over his wife asleep on a couch. Seated in her chair in front of the television was the sleeping Mrs. Prisinski. Her chin was pitched downward, resting against her upper chest. Her right hand grasped the empty glass that rested on her lap.

Rudy placed his ear close to his wife's face. He was sorry to see that she was still breathing. He was hoping otherwise. Mrs. Prisinski reeked of alcohol consumption.

Rudy, not wanting to deal with either sleeping woman, took out a pen and quickly scribbled a note which he left on the lap of the sitter. The note read:

I got home and went right to bed.
If my wife wakes up before you leave come and get me up.
If she doesn't, just go without waking her up.
Rudy

28

A Strategy Proves Fruitful

RONNIE SAT AT HER OFFICE DESK thinking about who to call first in her inquiry into Walter Quigley. She picked up the telephone and dialed up the real estate agent who did business with the Frantellini family. The agent indicated that she had never heard of any commercial property owner named Walter Quigley. Before hanging up the phone the agent promised to ask around about Quigley.

When word came back to Ronnie that Walter Quigley was a total unknown, Ronnie took pride in her ability to short circuit what could potentially be trouble for her. She immediately requested that the real estate person put her in touch with the investigative firm she uses to vet prospective tenants. Ronnie ordered a background check be conducted on a Walter Quigley of Red Bank, New Jersey. Ronnie indicated that she would make payment for this service in cash, adding that no invoice was to be generated. Ronnie wanted to assure the secrecy of the transaction.

The investigative agency that conducted the database research reported that they identified no Manhattan or New Jersey commercial properties owned by anyone named Walter Quigley. The researchers also checked Walter Quigley's name for business ownership. This effort proved negative. A review of newspaper articles and media outlets was also fruitless.

The investigative firm, working off the subject's approximate age, advised Ronnie that they assembled a list of all people named Walter Quigley residing in New Jersey and Manhattan. Their offer to conduct background research on these individuals was rejected by their client. Ronnie believed that she found out all she needed to know.

"We could always conduct surveillance on Quigley," said the man from the investigative firm, not giving up hope for more work. "That could tell us a lot." Ronnie, thinking that this might be a good idea, was somewhat receptive.

"Not right now," replied the client. "Perhaps down the road we could do that if necessary."

Ronnie was now certain that there was more to Walter Quigley than met the eye. Somebody must be behind this Walter Quigley in order to get dirt on me, she thought. But who?

Ronnie ran through a list of people who might have an interest in knowing more about her. One name that came to mind was Carmine DeFaziolo, her former lover who owned the construction company.

I wouldn't put it past that ambitious son of a bitch to want to shake me down for work, Ronnie thought when considering Carmine. A second suspect that came to mind was her attorney, Thomas Beasley. He's another one, thought Ronnie.

Ronnie knew that she needed to be patient. She was confident that eventually someone was going to approach her regarding her plans to sell her holdings. When that happened things would be clearer. Her wait wasn't a long one.

***

RUDY PRISINSKI CONVENED WITH TEDDY LEONARD at their

usual watering hole. Both men liked to discuss their business over drinks. The alcohol relaxed them to where they were comfortable speaking plainly to each other. They sat in what was now their usual booth. The private investigator leaned forward and listened carefully as Rudy began to convey what he had found out.

"I ended up having dinner with Clara, Ronnie Frantellini and Victor Spinello."

"Victor Spinello! How did you let that happen?" Leonard asked with concern.

"I had no control over it. Clara and I were in a restaurant having a drink at the bar when Ronnie Frantellini and Spinello just showed up unexpectedly."

"Did Clara know they were going to be there?" "She seemed as surprised as I was."

"Don't tell me that Spinello recognized you…."

"If he did he never let on. I think that we got lucky. Let me tell you, I almost died when he showed up with Ronnie."

"And they weren't invited?"

"No, definitely not. Dinner was supposed to be just me and Clara. The other two just showed up."

"Somebody had to have told her where you guys would be."

"I think that Clara did mention it to Ronnie."

"Jeeze, that was a close shave. So, what did you find out?"

"Ronnie Frantellini said that she had plans to sell her factory and properties."

"She said that?"

"Yes, she told us when Victor went to the bathroom. She didn't want him to know anything about it."

"I wonder what made her confide that," commented the suspicious minded Leonard.

"She mentioned it probably because I passed myself off as somebody with substantial real estate holdings. I think that might have got her talking."

"Did Ronnie say that she had a buyer?"

"She didn't say that. But what she said is that she wants cash as part of the deal so that she could avoid the tax bite. She was quite emphatic about that."

"That's tax evasion! It's what put Al Capone away," voiced Leonard, referring to the legendary former Chicago crime lord. "What else did she say?"

"That was about it. We dropped the subject when Victor came back to the table."

"You did a good job with this, Rudy," complemented Leonard.

"But just so you know, I had to spring for dinner for four at the Minetta Tavern in the West Village."

After being told the amount, Leonard peeled off the money owed from the wad of cash he carried.

"What do you want me to do next on this, Teddy?"

"Sit tight. Let me talk to the man I work for. Once I do that, I'll get in touch with you. Let me ask you something, Rudy, how did Clara look?"

"She was very attractive. To be honest, it's not going to be hard on me to snuggle up to her."

"Clara wasn't always such a honey. She's been working hot and heavy at improving herself. Did you get to first base?"

"I told you everything I found out."

"That's not what I mean. I'm asking if you're going to be bending Clara over."

"I thought that I had a good shot at getting an invite up to her apartment that night."

"What happened?"

"Things were going along fine. The romance dampened when Ronnie and Victor arrived."

"Ronnie might have said something to her. Were they alone at any point?"

"Well, they did go to the lady's room together a couple of times."

"Things chilled after that?" "I suppose they did."

"That's what happened," said Leonard, who began scratching his chin. "Ronnie put the kibosh on it."

"Why would she do that?"
"She probably doesn't trust you a hundred percent yet."

***

TEDDY LEONARD SAT ACROSS from Thomas Beasley in the lawyer's office. The grin on Leonard's face made it clear that he had good news to communicate. Leonard, feeling comfortable in the lawyer's office, looked at Beasley as he helped himself to a cigar from the box resting on Beasley's desk.

"May I?" Leonard asked.

"Go ahead, help yourself. So, what have you got for me?"

"My man hit the long ball. He had dinner with Clara, Ronnie Frantellini and Victor Spinello. He found out that Ronnie is looking to sell both the factory and the real estate holdings."

The look on Beasley's face was obviously one of alarm. "Victor Spinello!"

"Relax, Tommy, the juror was never recognized by Victor."

"Are you certain of this?"

"Definitely."

"What is this about Ronnie selling out?"

"My man got it straight from Ronnie's mouth."

"What was Victor's reaction to this?"

"Victor wasn't privy to that part of the conversation. Ronnie mentioned her plans when Victor went to the head. She instructed Clara and my man to keep her intention to sell in the shade."

The wheels in the scheming attorney's head began turning. Now armed with this information, he was envisioning a cleaner path, one that didn't involve the extortion of Ronnie. Leonard could see that the attorney was pensive.

"It gets better, Tommy," said Leonard. "Ronnie wants cash incorporated into any deal she makes. She's out to beat the taxman."

"This is something I can work with," said Beasley. "I could broker the deal."

"You'll be able to collect on both ends, right? From the buyer and the seller."

"Let me worry about how I make out, Teddy."

"Touchy, touchy," said Leonard, realizing he spoke out of turn. "So, I got you good information right?"

"You did very good."

"You could bury Ronnie for tax evasion." He received no response to his comment. "Anyway, you owe me money," stated Leonard, switching subjects. "My man incurred some extra expenses."

After being told how much he owed, the attorney asked, "Why did it come to so much?"

"The dinner was for four people."

"Did you get a receipt?"

"No, my man forgot to get one," lied Leonard. "Where did they go, to Europe for this meal?"

"Hey, he delivered for you, didn't he?"

Beasley nodded without smiling. "I'll have to write you a check."

"No problem, Tom. Make it to cash."

The attorney took out his checkbook and squared the account with the private investigator. The amount covered in the check exceeded the expenditure submitted by Rudy Prisinski.

"Okay, you better go now, Teddy. I have some work to do. I'll be in touch."

"Can I take another cigar?" Beasley nodded his approval.

Once alone in his office, Beasley began making phone calls asking around if anyone knew of a potential buyer for the Frantellini interests. One attorney friend indicated that he knew the general counsel of the Chen Lowe Footwear Company. The attorney friend agreed to send out a feeler.

Since Chen Lowe was a significant player in the shoe industry, it was no strain for Beasley to see the Chen Lowe Footwear Company as the ideal entity to speak to.

Beasley's lawyer friend telephonically contacted Chen Lowe's general counsel. The conversation spurred interest. Arrangements were made for Thomas Beasley to go to the Chen Lowe Footwear Company and meet with the entity's owner. Present for the meeting with Beasley and Lowe was Lowe's general counsel.

"Mr. Beasley is here to propose to us what he believes is an opportunity," said the general counsel. Chen Lowe smiled without expressing himself verbally. "Tell Mr. Lowe what that opportunity is, Mr. Beasley."

"I can get the Frantellini Shoe Factory sold to you, lock, stock and barrel, for a lowball number."

"Explain to Mr. Lowe how that is possible," said the general counsel.

"I've represented the Frantellini people for years," explained Beasley. The woman who now owns the firm is the widow of the founder. She relies on me heavily."

"We read about Mr. Frantellini's passing," said Lowe's general counsel. "A tragedy indeed."

"Yeah, well there is an upside to everything. Anyway, she has no one other than me to advise her. I could put over a deal that would be favorable to Mr. Lowe."

"You would be willing to betray your client?" Lowe asked in a soft voice.

"This is strictly business for me, Mr. Lowe," Beasley countered, answering Chen Lowe's question.

"You will be the attorney handling the transaction I assume?" injected Chen Lowe's general counsel.

"No, our mutual attorney friend will be the lawyer on the deal." Chen Lowe looked over at his general counsel without speaking. Once their eyes met the business owner nodded his approval.

"This acquisition would include the rights to the Frantellini Sole and whatever else they have in the works I assume," voiced the general counsel.

"Absolutely," replied Beasley. "By the way, the Frantellini Shoe Factory is getting ready to launch a new product called The

Dynamic Shoe. It's expected to be a sensation."

"This is of interest to me," commented Chen Lowe, without revealing that he knew all about the pending introduction of The Dynamic Shoe from his prior dealings with the murdered Dario Tengo.

"So, tell us, what are your personal expectations, Mr. Beasley?" questioned the general counsel.

"I expect the usual commission to go to the other attorney. All I want from you is one dollar on every Dynamic Shoe sold once it goes on the market."

"For how long?" asked Chen's general counsel.

"Perpetuity."

The stone-faced Chen Lowe took a pen in hand and began jotting something down on a piece of paper. After a moment Lowe spoke to his general counsel in Chinese. The general counsel responded to Beasley in a manner that made it quite definite that Lowe was inflexible in his position.

"Providing the sale price for Frantellini Shoe Factory is favorable to Mr. Lowe's interest, he's prepared to pay the standard commission in cash. Mr. Lowe is also willing to pay you personally twenty-five cents on every Dynamic Shoe sold. Those are his terms.

"We need to negotiate this further, Mr. Lowe," said Beasley, addressing Lowe.

"That is Mr. Lowe's only offer, Mr. Beasley," said Lowe's general counsel. "If you can deliver on what you say, and remain interested, call me directly and we shall proceed accordingly. Here, take my business card, Mr. Beasley."

"Okay, wait a second, you guys have a deal," said Beasley, accepting the terms. "There is just one condition regarding the sale. I can get the price down only if Mrs. Frantellini receives some of the sale money in cash. The seller is not looking to fatten up the tax man."

The general counsel looked at Chen Lowe for his decision. Lowe nodded in the affirmative. "If you can bring the deal to the table, we have an agreement Mr. Beasley," said the general counsel.

The meeting concluded with Beasley indicating that he would talk to Ronnie Frantellini and use his influence to convince her that it was in her interest to sell her factory to Chen Lowe.

Once Beasley returned to his office he got in touch with his closest friend in the real estate business. Their conversation was fortuitous. Beasley's contact indicated that the owner(s) of Cromie and Linwood, a property management/building ownership firm, was actively looking for opportunities to purchase both commercial and residential buildings in Manhattan.

"Will they take care of us?" asked Beasley.

"Definitely. They've been in the business for a long time. They know the score."

"Okay, go and talk to them."

"I'll do that."

"Good. While you tend to that, I'll work on the seller and get you a list of the properties they are looking to unload."

29

Ronnie Strikes Again

RONNIE FRANTELLINI DIDN'T have to wait long for the bait she put out to get nibbled on. Word of her looking to sell off her businesses resulted in the first overture coming from her attorney, Thomas Beasley. Ronnie was hardly surprised. When she thought things over it all made sense to her because it wasn't in Beasley's nature to let getting bested go unanswered. Beasley's telephone call was received warmly even though Ronnie was onto his chicanery. The shifty lawyer spoke enthusiastically of his being approached by an attorney he was acquainted with. Beasley related that his friend was affiliated with a serious player in the shoe industry. Beasley conveyed that there was an interest in acquiring the Frantellini Shoe Factory, and possibly the Frantellini real estate holdings.

"Who said that I had any interest in selling out?" Ronnie questioned.

"Nobody," replied Beasley.

"My friend approached me out of the blue," lied Beasley. "He knows that I've represented the Frantellini family for years."

"What did your friend say?"

"He said he had the opportunity of a lifetime, and I agree with him. If this deal could be put together, you'll be financially set for life." This gave Ronnie food for thought. While she initially had no interest in selling, she had to admit that being set for life was something to think about. Beasley could sense that Ronnie was pondering the opportunity.

"Think of it, Ronnie," said Beasley, now pitching hard. "This deal means no more worries. Your biggest headache will come from deciding how to spend all your money!"

"This does sound interesting," admitted Ronnie.

The two agreed to meet the following day to discuss things further. Their meeting took place over lunch at a Chinese restaurant a few blocks from the Frantellini Shoe Factory. The venue was selected by Beasley for a reason.

Once seated they ordered cocktails. The drinks arrived in short order, giving Beasley the opportunity to comment on how efficient the restaurant staff was. The lawyer then began praising the industriousness of the Chinese in general. This conversation was designed to set the stage for a discussion about Chen Lowe.

Ronnie, you'll never guess who the interested party is," said Beasley.

"Who?"

"The Chen Lowe Footwear Company. Like I said over the phone, the owner is looking to expand and wants to buy your factory and maybe even your real estate portfolio."

"Why didn't they call me directly?"

"Chen Lowe's general counsel does his talking for him. Anyway, he happened to mention Chen's interest to my attorney friend, who told him that he knew me and that I represented the Frantellini family," said Beasley, who enhanced his fabrication.

Will you just listen to this son of a bitch, thought Ronnie, who knew that the rumor she spread prompted Beasley to act on what he believed to be inside information.

"This Chen Lowe has plenty of money, Ronnie," advised Beasley. "Give me the green light and I'll sit with them and structure a deal for you."

Beasley's words were enticing. Ronnie's desire to determine if Clara's robbery was a staged affair was now secondary. Beasley's coming forth with an actual deal with Chen Lowe was too big not to be taken seriously.

"It's funny how things happen, Tom," said Ronnie, "I've actually been considering liquidating and living happily ever after."

"That makes perfect sense," voiced Beasley, encouraged by Ronnie's comment. "There aren't many people in a position to take their money while they are still young enough and healthy enough to enjoy it."

"How much do you think I'll get for the business, Tom?"

"Well, you have to realize a couple of things. Let's face it, the shoe business isn't what it once was in New York, Ronnie. That'll make the amount of the acquisition seem lower than expectations. But you'll make up some of the difference by taking money in cash under the table."

"What's in this for you, Tom?"

"Me? Just my normal commission, Ronnie. I'm entitled to that. I'm really doing this for you as a favor."

"I see," acknowledged Ronnie. *I wonder what this bastard will be getting from Lowe*, she thought.

"This could be a grand slam for you, Ronnie."

"What about the real estate?"

"Don't worry about the properties. If Lowe has no interest in the real estate, I have contacts with clients willing to purchase buildings."

"Give me a little time to think things over, Tom."

"Of course, but don't take too long. We need to strike while the iron is hot."

"I don't think it's in my interest to appear too anxious either."

"You're a shrewd operator, Ronnie," complimented Beasley.

"You're exactly right. We probably need to let Lowe wait a bit. But we can't wait too long."

I'm a lot shrewder than you think," thought Ronnie who said,

"Let's order the food, Tom, I'm hungry."

***

IT WASN'T IN RONNIE FRANTELLINI'S DNA to let anyone get over on her. While the idea of selling the factory to Chen Lowe was appealing, she simply couldn't bring herself to include Thomas Beasley in any transaction after what he had pulled with Clara. Tampering with her friend's affection was Ronnie's excuse to exact revenge on the lawyer.

There was one common denominator between Ronnie and Thomas Beasley. Both saw the world as a jungle in which one had to eat or be eaten. In the case of Thomas Beasley, Ronnie saw a predator.

I don't need to keep high stepping around a slithering snake always looking to bite me, thought Ronnie. *I'd be doing the world a favor by erasing him. As far as Chen Lowe, If I decide to sell, all I have to do is call him myself. If he's interested he'll talk to me.*

Once the dark side of Ronnie emerged there was no stopping her ruthlessness. She once again contacted her childhood friend Smiley Allen. After being assured that he would be properly compensated, Smiley wasted no time in reaching out to Crippler, his wrestler friend.

***

"I HAVE ANOTHER JOB if you want in on it, Crippler," advised Smiley telephonically.

"What kind of job?" Crippler asked.

"Same as last time. Are you interested?"

"I'm willing to listen."

A meeting between Crippler and Ronnie was set at Smiley's

place of business. Upon getting together with the wrestler, Ronnie quickly articulated that she wanted Crippler to eliminate the attorney Thomas Beasley.

Crippler's head went back, displaying surprise. He paused to look at Ronnie oddly.

"Now you want me take out a lawyer?" Crippler asked. "Are you sure you aren't nuts?"

Ronnie, rather than being insulted, found the remark amusing. "I'm no crazier than you are," she replied. "I have my reasons. And I have the money to get what I want."

"What did the lawyer do?"

"Let's just say that he poses a threat to me, and leave it at that," replied Ronnie.

"Fair enough. Just the one guy has to go, right?"

"That's right."

"The fee is the same as last time," said Crippler.

"This is just one person," pointed out Ronnie.

"Makes no difference. One or two, it's the same fee."

"Very well, when can you take care of this for me?"

"This week I'm on the road wrestling. I can probably take care of it early next week. Tell me about this guy."

"Like I said, he's a lawyer. You'll be able to find him at his office. I know that he still hasn't found a secretary, so he'll probably be alone there."

"How big a man is he?"

"No where as big as you. He certainly won't give you any trouble. His office is…."

"Hold on a second," interrupted Crippler, "let me grab a pen."

***

ONCE CRIPPLER AGREED TO MURDER Thomas Beasley, the time had come for Ronnie to appraise Clara of what she learned about Walter Quigley. Their conversation took place in the privacy of Ronnie's office at the Frantellini Shoe Factory. Since Ronnie knew that her protégé had developed feelings for the man purporting to be Walter Quigley, the task at hand wasn't going to be pleasant.

"Sit down, Clara," invited Ronnie. "I'm sorry to have to tell you this, but you need to understand the truth about Walter Quigley."

"What about him?" Clara asked.

"Walter, or whatever his name is, was using you to get information to use against me."

"How could you be certain of that, Ronnie?"

"I set a trap in order to get to the truth."

"What kind of trap?"

"Listen, Clara, I had Walter checked out. So, just take my word for it when I say he's no good. Is there really a need for me to go into details."

"No, that's not necessary," Clara said with disappointment. "I believe you. But I'd love to know who Walter was spying for?"

"That's not something you need to know Clara. Trust me, you're better off not knowing."

Ronnie would never reveal the name of Thomas Beasley to Clara because Beasley was the man Ronnie marked for execution.

"So, what should I do about Walter if he calls me?"

"Don't take his calls, Clara. Ignore him. If you see him on the street, just keep walking and don't engage him. Don't worry, he'll get the hint and fall off the radar screen sooner than you think."

"You seem very sure, Ronnie."

"I am sure, Clara. Do you know what I think you should do?"

"What?"

"Give Fernando thc cabdriver a call. He'll take your mind off Walter Quigley quick enough."

"But what about Walter's gallantry in saving me from the robber? He didn't have to do that."

"C'mon Clara, can't you see that it was all staged? Walter was paid to get close to you, to get to me."

This statement silenced Clara, who had no more questions. At this point Ronnie began to feel a little sorry for Clara.

"Cheer up honey, things could have been worse. You could've fallen in love with Walter. Right?"

"That's true."

"Do yourself a favor and give Fernando a call. He'll take your mind off Walter. That's what the cabdriver is there for."

"What do you mean?"

"Fernando is there to drive the blues away, silly."

30

Crippler Gets Crippled

MARKIE HAD DETECTIVE VON HESS drive to the wrestling school operated by Rochelle Parrish. The Sergeant offered a flimsy explanation for this. He claimed to have a hunch that Crippler might be at the school.

"So, are you coming in with me, Sarge?" Von Hess asked after parking the department car.

"No way," replied Markie, pretending that seeing Rochelle was the farthest thing from his mind. "I'll wait in the car, Ollie. If Crippler is inside don't confront him. We'll take him when he leaves."

"Whatever you say, Sarge."

"And Ollie, if Rochelle asks for me, tell her I'm outside in the car and that I don't want to see her."

"Sure thing, Sarge."

Von Hess shook his head as he exited the car. He initially figured that Markie was probably just hoping to get a glimpse of Rochelle from afar in order to curb his curiosity as to how his former flame was looking. What the detective didn't realize was the depth of the sergeant's lingering affection for Rochelle. Markie' pining came with an intensity that caused him to wish that Rochelle would come running to him once Von Hess told her that he was outside in the car.

Von Hess entered the second-floor training school that was located in an old building on 8th Avenue. The ceiling of the gym was made of tin. In the center of the large room was a raised wrestling ring. Several folding chairs were situated around the ring for spectators.

Among those seated were a handful of aspiring wrestlers, all of whom were attired in appropriate wrestling togs. These students were fixed on the instructor who was explaining the importance of histrionics when engaging in a wrestling exhibition.

Von Hess scanned the room for Crippler. There was no sign of him. The detective, who found the training interesting, paused to watch for a few minutes.

"Remember that you start out in this business as a preliminary boy," declared Yankee Phil Denim. "That means your job is to put your opponent over. So, it's up to you to make it look good to the paying customer. When a hold is applied on you, you have to grunt, grimace and show that you are in pain. And believe me there will times when there will be true pain."

Th old veteran grappler then pointed to his ear. "This cauliflower ear of mine didn't come without pain. So, be prepared to take your lumps."

Yankee Phil called a student into the ring and began demonstrating how to apply and react to basic wrestling holds. With each hold Denim made it a point to explain how important it was to know a counter hold. He showed his audience how to roll properly when thrown and how to take a fall when slammed to the mat.

"Can I help you?" Denim asked after noticing the visitor."

"I'm looking for Rochelle Parrish," replied the detective, flashing his badge.

"Okay, folks, take five," said Denim, as he stepped out of the ring to talk to Von Hess. "Is there a problem, Detective?"

"No, no trouble. I just need to speak to her."

“She’s in the office. C’mon, follow me.”

Rochelle was seated at her desk and talking on the telephone when Denim and Von Hess entered her office. She held up one finger, indicating that they were to stand by.

“Detective Von Hess,” said Rochelle, after concluding her call. “What brings you here?”

“I’m looking for Crippler,” said the detective.

“Did you think you’d find him here?”

“Do you need me here, Rochelle?” interrupted Denim, feeling that his presence was unnecessary.

“No, Yank, the detective and I have become old friends,” replied Rochelle. She then turned to address Von Hess. “What can I do for you now, Detective?”

“Can you find out when and where Crippler Jackson is going to be wresting?”

“I just got off the phone with the promoter. He’s hiring a couple of my students as standby wrestlers in case somebody doesn’t show up for a Long Island show.”

“Is Crippler scheduled to wrestle here in the city?”

“I’ll tell you in a minute.” Rochelle telephoned the promoter’s secretary to inquire about the upcoming Madison Square Garden Card. After getting the requested information she thanked the secretary and hung up the phone.

“Crippler is wrestling Skull Fagan at Madison Square Garden,” advised Rochelle. “It’s an early show, so the first match should go off at around 2:00 P.M.”

“I thought they wrestled in the evening.”

“Not always, now and then they’ll put on an afternoon show on a holiday.”

“Thank you,” voiced the detective, who then reached into his wallet to give Rochelle two Detective Endowment Association courtesy cards. “Give one of these to Yankee,” said Von Hess.

“What are they?”

“DEA cards. They may help you get out of a driving ticket one day.”

“But I don’t have a car.”

"Stick it in your purse, you never know when you may need a break from the boys in blue."

"Thanks. Speaking of boys in blue, did you tell Markie that I was asking for him?"

"I did," lied Von Hess.

"How come he never bothered to call me?"

"I don't have an answer for that. I think he might be seeing somebody now," said Von Hess, tacking on another fib."

"Oh, I see. Well, that doesn't mean he can't find time to say hello to an old friend."

"That's true. I guess that I'll have to say thanks for the both of us."

"Tell Markie that I want him to thank me personally."

"Will do."

Von Hess returned to his car, where Markie waited. The sergeant was anxious to hear how things went. Once the detective was behind the wheel, Markie's first question came. "Did you see Rochelle?"

"Yeah, Sarge. Crippler is wrestling at the Garden this Thursday afternoon."

"That's good, the plan will be to grab him then. By the way, how did Rochelle look, Ollie."

"Same as always."

"Did she ask for me?"

"She never mentioned you, Sarge."

Markie's face turned serious. "She could be a cold bitch sometimes that one, Ollie," said the sergeant.

"I'd say so, Sarge. Her side of the waterbed must be frozen."

"In all honestly I can't agree with that," Markie declared, wistfully recalling his intimate moments with the woman he still had a thing for."

***

CRIPPLER HAD JUST FINISHED wrestling a seventeen-minute

match in Madison Square Garden. The action was strenuous enough for Crippler to sweat profusely. The engagement came with the price of a dangerously blackened eye for Crippler. The injury was the result of a miscalculation by his opponent when delivering a roundhouse punch. By the time Crippler reached the locker room to shower the injured eye was completely closed.

After getting dressed Crippler was met by his opponent, who expressed his remorse for having inflicted such a serious injury.

"Sorry about that potato I handed you, Crippler," said the less experienced opponent, referring to the landed punch.

"Forget it, kid. Accidents happen in this business."

"Can I treat you to dinner to make up for it?"

"That's not necessary, getting banged up is all part of the game. Besides, I got business to take care of," said the injured wrestler touching his bruised eye. Crippler's business was murdering the attorney, Thomas Beasley.

"Did you hear what happened to Wolfman?"

"No, what happened?"

"I heard that he got busted when partying in New Jersey with a couple of the lady wrestlers."

"That sounds like him," commented Crippler, not thinking any more of it.

Crippler found his injured eye to be an excellent excuse to introduce himself to Thomas Beasley. The wrestler telephoned Beasley's office to make certain that the attorney was there. He was.

Crippler identified himself as a Manhattan doorman who sustained a severe injury on the job due to his being bitten by a tenant's dog. Seeing this as the type of lawsuit that translated into easy money, Beasley entertained the caller.

"Where is the injury?" asked the lawyer. "My eye. I can't see out of it, it's shut closed. It looks like a bubble."

"You got bit in the eye by a dog?"

"Yeah, the guy's got a Great Dane," fibbed Crippler. "The dog just missed my eyeball."

"Did you go to the hospital?"

"Not yet, I wanted to talk to a lawyer first."

"How did you come to get my name?"

"Somebody in the building where I work said that you were a top lawyer who gets things done."

"Where is the building?'

"It's in Carnegie Hill, near the Metropolitan Museum. Can I come and see you now?"

"Certainly," said Beasley, aware that Carnegie Hill was an enclave of very old money. "Come and see me. We'll talk and then get you to a hospital." The lawyer then gave Crippler his address.

"Okay, I'll be there in a little while."

"Who was it that referred you to me? I don't remember having any clients in that area."

"It was a friend of a friend who gave me your name."

In the privacy of the men's room Crippler opened up the brown leather gym back that housed his wrestling shoes and tights. Also contained in the bag was a loaded .22 caliber handgun wrapped in a towel, a jump rope and a lead pipe.

Crippler exited the Garden unsure of exactly how he was going to kill Thomas Beasley. It would all depend on how physically formidable Beasley seemed to be.

***

MARKIE AND VON HESS WAITED FOR Crippler Joe Jackson by the designated parking area for athletes appearing at the Garden. Accompanying them was the precinct detective who was assigned to investigate the murder of the Frantellini sisters.

"Thanks for helping out on this case, Sarge," said the precinct sleuth as they waited in their department car. "I'm sorry that I wasn't available when you took down the other wrestler. You guys did great work on that."

"No problem," answered Markie. "We know how hectic it can be keeping up with a precinct caseload."

"You said it, Sarge. Nobody cares that we're understaffed," grumbled the detective. "The cases just keep coming. What gets me is that the brass expects…."

"Here he is," announced Von Hess, interrupting the precinct detective's complaining.

"Let's take him before he gets to the car," said Markie. "You two take him from the front. I'll get behind him."

When the precinct detective produced his gold shield he announced to Crippler that he was under arrest. The wrestler, taken aback, protested.

"Arrested for what?" Crippler defiantly asked.

"Homicide. Now put your hands behind your back, pal."

"What homicide?"

"The Frantellini sisters," answered the detective, reaching out to take hold of Crippler's wrist."

Crippler, knowing that he had a loaded gun in his bag, wasn't going easily. He pushed the precinct detective to the ground. This caused Von Hess to step forward and seize Crippler by his arm. The contact further triggered Crippler. The wrestler, reacting violently, swung his gym bag at Von Hess. The brass buckle on the bag caught Von Hess on the cheek, dropping him to the ground. Blood began leaking freely.

Von Hess, who had been rocked, nevertheless managed to rise to one knee. The groggy Von Hess drew the blackjack he carried in the pocket of his coat. As he gathered himself, Von Hess watched as Markie began yoking Crippler's neck from the rear. Instinctively the wrestler stepped to his side. He swung his hand back and took hold of Markie's testicles and twisted. Von Hess winced, knowing that the pain felt by the sergeant was excruciating. Markie was left writhing on the ground in pain.

Things were unfolding too quickly for the veteran precinct detective to get into the fray. He acted by drawing his revolver just as Von Hess was rising to his feet.

"Freeze!" ordered the precinct detective.

In answer to this order Crippler turned and took a step toward the precinct lawman. His advance was menacing, causing the precinct detective to fire twice. Both bullets found a home in the wrestler's midsection. Crippler held his abdomen with both hands. After a second or two he sank down to his knees. Crippler then slowly fell onto his side, where he remained. He was promptly rear cuffed by the precinct detective.

Von Hess went to assist Markie in getting to his feet. The precinct detective produced a radio and called a 10-13. This was the code that requested immediate assistance.

By the time the responding uniformed reinforcements arrived, the precinct detective was experiencing chest pains. The uniformed force transported all of the combatants to the nearest hospital. Once there, Crippler and the precinct detective were admitted. Crippler became a hospitalized prisoner in a private room. He was being treated for the bullet wounds he sustained. The precinct detective, who was also in his own private room, was being doctored for a major heart attack.

Markie and Von Hess were both treated and released. The Sergeant was given a pain reliever and received a wrapped ice pack to soothe the ache below his belt. He was advised by the medical staff to wear supportive underwear. He hobbled around for a period. It took three stitches to close the wound sustained by Von Hess. The former Marine sported the scar proudly. It was Mrs. Von Hess who was outraged by her husband's injury. It rekindled her desire for her husband to put in his papers and retire.

"What are you waiting to get killed, Ollie?" she nagged, hoping this time she'd get through to her husband. Her question fell on deaf ears.

When Crippler was well enough to realize that he was expected to fully recover from his gunshot wounds he did lots of thinking while convalescing in the hospital. Aware that he was facing the prospect of spending serious time behind bars, he opted to cooperate with the authorities in the hope of securing a reduction in his sentence.

It's all I could do, reasoned Crippler as he thought things over. *I'm not spending the rest of my life rotting in some jail cell.* Of the quartet involved in the street battle, the precinct detective was thought by many in law enforcement to have made out the best. In their eyes being eligible for a tax-free disability pension for the rest of his life was akin to hitting the lotto.

31

Finding A Way Out

AFTER CONSULTING WITH LIEUTENANT WRIGHT, the chief of detectives had his lieutenant fetch Markie and Von Hess. When they arrived at the chief's office, Wright was gloating. The lieutenant, and the chief, both found Markie's shuffle and the bandage on the face of Von Hess to be amusing.

The chief covered his mouth with his hand in an attempt to conceal his chuckle. Both the chief and lieutenant saw humor in the detectives having scuffled with a professional wrestler.

Chief McCoy cleared his voice before communicating as a superior. He asked the men to have a seat at the table that touched his desk to form a T shape arrangement.

"How are you men feeling?" asked the chief.

"We'll live, Chief," answered Markie.

"I'm glad to hear it," said McCoy. "Are you both back to full duty?"

"Yes, Chief. As of this morning."

"There are no restrictions, correct?"

"None, we're both good to go," said Markie.

"You seem to still be in discomfort, Sergeant. Are they doing anything for that?" "They told me to wear new underwear."

"I suppose it'll take time to get better. How about you, Ollie?" "I'm fine, Chief," replied Von Hess. "The stitches will be coming out soon."

"The scar will eventually fade, Ollie," said Lieutenant Wright.

"I'm not worried, Loo," voiced the detective.

"I'm surprised that you let that guy get the drop on you," critiqued McCoy.

"He was a big boy, Chief," replied Markie.

"He was as big as a house," echoed Von Hess.

"So, why didn't you shoot him?"

"He was shot," answered the sergeant."

"I know that. But one of you should have shot him. Think of the prestige that would have given to this office. It would have shown everyone that my special squad is out there in the thick of things."

Markie and Von Hess glanced at each other after hearing the chief's remark. Lieutenant Wright, who realized how bad this sounded, thought it appropriate to redirect the conversation.

"Crippler is lucky to be alive," said Wright. "I heard from the DA's office that he wants to cooperate on the Frantellini homicides."

"We already have an eyewitness saying he killed the girls," advised the chief.

"Apparently there is more to the story. He wants to spill who put him up to it. Here, Al, this is for you."

The lieutenant then handed Markie a piece of paper that reflected the name and telephone number of the assistant district attorney prosecuting the wrestler.

"Go and see the ADA."

"The DA's office is willing to make a deal with a cop fighter, Loo?"

"Apparently they are, Al. Crippler has a former Jersey prosecutor in his corner who knows people. The lawyers have been talking. Go see what the story is."

"Will do."

"When you get together with that wrestler don't forget to protect your nuts, Sarge," joked the Chief.

"I'll remember to do that, Chief."

***

THE HOSPITALIZED PRISONER WAS in his hospital bed

watching television when Markie and Von Hess arrived to interview him. Crippler's thick wrist was handcuffed to the bed railing. The uniformed police officer guarding Crippler was seated not far away in a chair. He was reading a newspaper. Things were peaceful. "I'm Sergeant Markie from headquarters, announced the sergeant.

"We're here to interview the prisoner. Go get some coffee for yourself, Officer. Take your time, we'll be here for a while."

No problem, Sarge. I'll be in the cafeteria. Do you want my phone number? You can call me when you want me back."

"Good idea. Take his number, Ollie."

Once alone with the detectives, Crippler grew uneasy. He hadn't expected that he would again see the men he had assaulted. Unsure of what was going to happen, he braced himself for what he suspected might follow. He feared that one of the detectives would shoot him and claim that he made a reach for his gun while being taken to the bathroom.

"Now look you guys, I'm handcuffed to the bed here. And I'm not getting out of this bed for nobody."

"Nobody is asking you to," said Von Hess, who began touching his bandaged face.

"So, why are you guys here?"

"You called us," reminded the detective.

"I never called you."

"Relax," said Markie. "The lawyers said that you want to roll over. We're here to listen to the story you have to tell."

"I want to talk to my lawyer," said Crippler.

"Here, call him," said Markie, handing the wrestler his cellphone. Once receiving the okay from his attorney Crippler handed the cellphone back to Markie.

"It's okay for me to talk to you. My lawyer said that he worked things out with the prosecutor's office."

"So, let's talk."

"Look, about what happened with us...." began Crippler.

"Forget ancient history, today is a new day."

"Yeah, I know, but that detective didn't have to shoot me,"

bitched the prisoner.

"And you didn't have to twist my nuts," said Markie with abruptness. "So, let's just move on. What have you got to spill?"

"I'm being charged with a double murder and a gun, so I have to help myself. I just finished wrestling a match when you guys jumped me coming out of nowhere and...."

"Alright, look, just change the record, will you," said Markie. "Ollie, you try talking to him. Maybe you can get through."

"Righto, Sarge. Look Crippler," said Von Hess softly, "why don't you just start by telling us why those two sisters had to go. We know all about what happened when you got pinched."

Crippler nodded, indicating that he understood. "Some rich woman wanted them dead. I killed the wrong people."

"What do you mean?"

"I should've killed that rat bastard who ratted me out." "Who was it?" "Wolfman Glass, right? Am I right or wrong?"

"Alright, let's stay on point," injected Markie. "Stick to the dead sisters."

"Who is this woman who hired you to bump them off?" Von Hess asked.

"All I know about her is that she paid me plenty to do it, so how could I say no?"

"Her name?" Von Hess asked.

"I only know the bitch as Ronnie. I don't know anything else about her."

The two detectives looked at each other after hearing the name Ronnie mentioned.

"If you didn't know her, how did you get together?"

"A friend of mine knew her and introduced us."

"Who is he?"

"Smiley Allen. I know him from the can. Smiley and Ronnie were kids together I think, or something like that."

"Where do we find Smiley?"

"He owns small restaurant on Hamilton Avenue in Brooklyn."

"Why did Ronnie want the sisters killed?"

"I don't know, I never asked. I'm in it for the money and that's it."

"You got paid in cash?"

"That's right."

"I'm curious about something," injected Markie. "Why did you call Ronnie a bitch? She paid you didn't she?"

"Yeah, she paid."

"Then why is she a bitch?"

"I called her to let her know I was busted, and that I could use some relief to pay a lawyer."

"She got you your lawyer?"

"She got me shit! My wrestling promoter got me the lawyer. That bitch Ronnie made out like she didn't even know me."

"So that's why you're cooperating now....to get even with Ronnie."

"Yeah, that, too. Look, I need to get some kind of a break for killing those sisters. With a kid eyewitness against me, my lawyer said I haven't got a shot at winning in court."

"I'd say that's about right."

"Look, I got even more information that will interest you."

"Hold up a second," said Von Hess.

"Do you have Ronnie's telephone number?"

"Yeah, I know it."

"Let me have it."

After taking the number Von Hess stepped away. He reached out to Detective Silverlake over at police headquarters. Silverlake ran the number with a contact he had at Verizon. Ten minutes later he was able to confirm that Ronnie was in fact Ronnie Frantellini.

"So, what other information do you have for us?" asked Markie, once Von Hess returned to the bedside of the prisoner.

"Before you guys busted me I was on my way to clip a lawyer for Ronnie. I was heading to his office to take care of business, when you guys jumped on me. That's why I had the gun."

"What lawyer?"

"Thomas Beasley." Markie, recognizing the name, let out a laugh.

"You know him?" asked Crippler.

"Yeah, we know him," said the sergeant. "You knew where to find him?"

"I made an appointment to see him at his office. I told him I was an injured doorman and wanted to sue somebody. He jumped right on it and told me to come right over."

"How long are you going to be in the hospital for?" Markie asked. "Did the doctors say?"

"The doctor said that I should be out of here early next week."

"You're going to have to wear a recording device for us. We want you to go see this Ronnie and get her on tape."

"If it's going to help me, I'll definitely do it. I just have to talk to my lawyer first."

"No, problem. We have to talk to the ADA as well. The two lawyers will work out the legalities regarding your case."

"What about this Smiley Allen, Sarge?" asked Von Hess. "That's right, Ollie," answered Markie, who then turned to Crippler. "Where do we find Smiley again?"

"He has a restaurant on Hamilton Avenue in Brooklyn. Ask anybody on the waterfront where Smiley's place is."

Markie intended to do just that after Von Hess conducted a background check on Smiley.

***

IT WAS ABOUT NOON WHEN the detectives arrived at Smiley Allen's eatery. The investigators parked their unmarked car and observed the location for twenty minutes. During that time the detectives could see that Smiley did a robust business with longshoremen lined up to get in. It was shrimp day, the one day of the week that Smiley sold fried shrimp Italian bread sandwiches and/or hot plates.

Outwardly, the apron wearing Smiley Allen gave every appearance that he was reformed and running a legitimate business. Now married with children, Smiley came to appreciate the peace of mind that came with making an honest living.

However, because he was an ex-con in good standing with others of that ilk, he couldn't remove himself entirely from his past associations.

"What can I do for you, Detective?" asked Smiley, after Von Hess identified himself.

"We're here to talk to you about Ronnie Frantellini."

"Sorry, but the name doesn't ring a bell."

"Try giving the bell another press," said Markie.

"I already told you, Sergeant, I don't recognize the name."

"What about Fred Weston?" asked Markie, making up a name.

"Fred who?"

"Fred Weston, he's my brother-in-law the IRS Agent. I could arrange for you to meet him."

As a businessman who gets over on his taxes, Smiley didn't need things spelled out further.

"Look fellas, I don't want any trouble. I've had some. I'm a married man with kids now."

"Then tell us how you know Ronnie Frantellini."

"We grew up together. I know her since we were kids."

"And Crippler the wrestler you know from where?"

Smiley let out a sigh. He now had a good idea where this was going.

"You know where I know him from."

"Tell me."

"I met Crippler in the can," advised Smiley. "A guy like him is good to know when you are in the joint."

"Your friend Crippler has been pinched for murder," said Markie. "Just do you know, he's singing an aria" The statement caused Smiley's mouth to drop open.

"I got nothing to do with anything like that!"

"Look, Smiley, make it easy on yourself. What do you prefer, being on the side of the prosecution or the defendant's side?"

"What the sergeant is saying," injected Von Hess in a calm tone, "is that Crippler is implicating you as the go between with him and Ronnie. So, you have to declare where you stand."

Smiley was now convinced that it was in his interest to cooperate. He admitted to the authorities that he was the one who introduced Ronnie to Crippler. However, he stubbornly refused to acknowledge that he knew that Ronnie wanted Crippler to commit murder.

"How did the introduction come about?"

"Ronnie called me. She said that she was having a problem with somebody and needed someone to convince the person to fall in line," lied Smiley. He added, "Ronnie married into money and when her husband died he left her sitting pretty with a business and property. I assumed her problem was a landlord-tenant issue or something along those lines. So, I introduced her to Crippler."

The detectives remained expressionless upon hearing Smiley's fabrication. The ex-con picked up on their skepticism.

"Look, I'm telling you the truth," insisted Smiley. "Crippler was the right fit for Ronnie because he presented the intimidating figure Ronnie was looking for. Whatever their arrangement was, I don't really know. I just arranged for them to meet in my restaurant, and that's it. I wasn't privy to their private conversations."

The detectives were fairly certain that Smiley was withholding information. However, Smiley's statement provided enough of what the detectives were after. He supported Crippler's account as to how he met Ronnie. This served as proof that Crippler was being truthful.

"Okay, Smiley. Keep your powder dry," said Markie, concluding the interview.

"Does this mean that I'm going to be called to testify?"

"That all depends on the DA's office."

"How do you figure it?"

"They may put us on the stand to testify as to what you said, rather than have you take the stand."

"What are the odds of that?"

"It's about 50-50," said Markie, "that they may not want you on the stand."

"Why?"

"You may get tripped up on the stand or might change your story. I have one last question for you, Smiley."

"What?"

"Do you know a lawyer named Thomas Beasley?"

"I never heard of him."

"Square business?"

"Square business."

***

MARKIE AND VON HESS SAT in their unmarked police vehicle rehashing their interview with Smiley Allen. Once they finished discussing Allen they kicked around their next move.

"So, what next, Sarge?" asked Von Hess.

"You have to do a report on what Smiley had to say. After that, I think we need to go see the ADA who is handling this. I want to make sure everyone knows that Thomas Beasley was the lawyer who got the acquittal for Victor Spinello in the Dario Tengo murder."

"All roads lead to the Frantellini Shoe Factory," commented Von Hess.

"I wonder why Ronnie wanted Beasley clipped, Ollie."

"It could have something to do with that murder trial. Or, maybe she doesn't want to pay the lawyer's fee."

"I doubt that, Ollie. She's got to have money coming out of her ears. Besides that, the Frantellini family got what they wanted in the Victor Spinello case. If Ronnie was the one who hired Beasley to represent Spinello, then why wouldn't she want to pay?"

"You know, Sarge, I was always a little curious about the outcome of that case. I mean, the acquittal and all." "Maybe we should take a closer look at that Victor Spinello acquittal. There might be something to learn from a little digging."

"It can't hurt, Ollie. I'll run that idea by the DA's office."

Markie's conversation with Assistant District Attorney Kim Smyther met with enthusiasm, as was his conferral with his superiors over at headquarters. Markie and Von Hess were given the approval to follow whatever path they chose in relation to the Victor Spinello acquittal.

With the assistance of the investigators at the district attorney's office Markie and Von Hess were able to get information on those serving on the jury that acquitted Victor Spinello. They also learned that Thomas Beasley was known in the legal profession as an attorney with a less than stellar reputation.

Further inquiry at the DA's office concerning Beasley resulted in their learning that a former NYPD detective named Teddy Leonard was the private investigator who the lawyer often worked with. When Detective Von Hess began asking detectives he knew about Leonard, he soon gathered that Leonard's reputation was no better than that of Thomas Beasley.

After interviewing several jurors, the detectives gained insights into the trial. They came to understand that one juror in particular was ardent in his effort to convince the other jurors to vote for an acquittal. Successful in his influence, the juror in question was described by one person on the jury as being hellbent on exonerating the defendant. Armed with this information, Markie decided that the time had come to interview the persuasive juror named Rudolph Prisinski.

32

Rudy's Regrets

RUDY PRISINSKI WALKED INTO the crowded pizzeria to pick up the food his wife ordered. He was greeted by the counterman with only a simple nod. The fiftyish pizza maker was busy slicing a pie he just removed from the oven. He was a balding man with a thick brown and gray mustache. The heat from the oven allowed him to wear only a white V-neck short sleeve T-shirt in the winter. His white pants were loose fitting. An abundance of chest hair spilled over the top of his shirt. His arms were exceedingly hairy.

"I'm here to pick up my wife's order," announced Rudy after a minute of waiting.

"I got you," said the counterman who looked up from his work. "It'll be ready in a minute."

"It's not ready yet? Rudy asked. "She called it in a half hour ago."

"I'm here alone tonight," explained the worker.

"Let me have another Sicilian," said a pimpled faced teen who bellied up to the counter.

"Here you go, son," said the counterman, handing the teenager a square slice and taking his money.

This delay annoyed Rudy, who was in a hurry. At this point two new customers entered the pizzeria looking to place orders. Rudy flashed an unpleasant look. It was his way of warning them not to cut the line.

"Here you go," said the counterman after placing Rudy's pizza in a cardboard box. "Fresh out of the oven. Do you want a bottle of soda with it?"

"No, I'm good."

When Rudy returned to his apartment he was immediately questioned by his waiting wife who wanted to know what took him so long.

"The place was jammed with people," exaggerated Rudy. "I thought I was going to be there all-night waiting for this pie."

"Let me have one of the calzones now, Rudy. I'm famished."

"What calzones?"

"I told you to get me a two calzone with the pie. Don't tell me you forgot to get it."

"I didn't forget anything," replied Rudy, who was now agitated.

"You never told me to get you any calzone."

"I did so! Now go back to the pizzeria and get me my calzone. Two of them!"

Rudy placed a food tray onto his wife's wheelchair. "Here, start on the pizza," he said, "placing two slices on the tray. I'll be back with the calzones."

"Get me a fork and a coke with ice before you go, Rudy." Rudy got the fork and soda for his wife. "What's this? You know I only use two cubes with my soda, why on earth did you fill the glass with ice?"

Rudy looked at his wife with disdain as she sat in her wheelchair. He then reflected on what intimate time with Clara Calhoun might have been like. His mental comparison caused Rudy to have dark thoughts. For the first time he seriously thought of how much he'd love to rid himself of Mrs. Prisinski.

"I'll be back," said Rudy, heading for the door."

"What about this ice?"

"I'm going to get you your calzone."

"Oh, just go. And stop off to get yourself a drink why don't you!"

On his way for his wife's calzones Rudy did just that. He stopped off at a nearby tavern to have a drink. He needed one to take the edge off. As he enjoyed his quaff Rudy looked around at his surroundings. His eye caught that of a woman seated alone at the bar. Liking the view, Rudy ordered himself another drink and one for the stranger. She accepted the drink with a polite smile. The calzones had now become a secondary concern.

If she's hungry she could eat another slice of pizza, thought Rudy. He then sauntered over to the chestnut-haired woman who drank alone.

***

RUDY PRISINSKI'S WIFE hated to be home alone. As a rule, whenever her husband was away from the house for any length of time arrangements were made to have someone keep her company. Hours had gone by since her husband went for the calzone. She began to wonder if she may have pushed him too hard.

Mrs. Prisinski had long finished her pizza and had grown tired of waiting for Rudy. Since her telephone calls to her husband's cell phone were going unanswered she seethed inwardly. With no one to vent to she turned to drink. She wheeled herself over to where her bottle of rye was kept. Mrs. Prisinski had just poured the rye into her glass when she heard the knock at her apartment door. After taking a healthy sip, she rolled herself to the front door.

"Who is there?" she asked loud enough to be heard through the closed door.

"Police Department," announced Von Hess.

"Wait a minute." Mrs. Prisinski telephoned the lobby desk to verify the identity of her visitors. "Why did you send people up without announcing them first?" Mrs. Prisinski demanded to know.

"They flashed their badge and whisked by me, Ma'am. I didn't know where they were going," lied the man posted in the lobby. Mrs. Prisinski reacted by rudely hanging up the phone.

Von Hess had flashed his gold shield to the man assigned to the lobby desk and inquired about the location of the Prisinski apartment. After being given the apartment number, the detectives took the elevator up without waiting to be announced.

"Who are you looking for?" Mrs. Prisinski asked after opening the front door.

"We're here to see Rudolph Prisinski."

"My husband isn't home right now. What did he do?"

"Will he be home soon, Ma'am?" asked Von Hess without replying to the question posed.

"He was supposed to be home a long time ago," answered the annoyed wife. "Is my husband in some kind of trouble?"

"There is nothing to be alarmed about, Ma'am. We're just here to ask him a few questions about the jury he served on."

"What about it? They found the guy innocent, is there something wrong with that?"

As this conversation was taking place in the doorway, Rudy came off the elevator. The odor of alcohol on his breath was noticeable. Startled to see two men talking to his wife, he inquired as to what was going on.

After introducing themselves the detectives asked if they could enter the apartment to discuss a matter with Rudy. Before the husband could respond his wife spoke up.

"So where is the calzone?" she asked.

"They ran out," answered Rudy, who had forgotten all about it.

"But the bartender didn't run out of Scotch, did he?" Mrs. Prisinski queried sarcastically.

Rudy had no intention of getting into it with his wife in the presence of the authorities. Instead, he invited the detectives into the Prisinski home. Rudy shut off the television so they could talk without distraction.

"It's our understanding that you were quite emphatic in your belief in the innocence of Victor Spinello," voiced Von Hess.

"The guy was an innocent man," stated Rudy without hesitation. "I was no more emphatic than anyone else. Why are you here asking me about the trial all of a sudden?"

"Let us ask the questions, Mr. Prisinski," said Markie. "Do you happen to know an attorney named Thomas Beasley?"

"I never heard of him."

"You don't know Thomas Beasley?"

"Should I?"

"Beasley was the defense attorney in the Spinello trial," advised Von Hess.

"Oh, that's right," stated Rudy, who now recalled Beasley. "Sorry, I forgot. I did have a couple of drinks a little while ago and I'm not thinking as clearly as I should."

"What does all this have to do with my husband?" asked Mrs. Prisinski. "I want to know."

"Please," interrupted Rudy, cutting his wife off. Let the detectives do their job."

"Thanks," said Von Hess. "We're trying to find what exactly made you so adamant in finding Victor Spinello innocent," said the detective bluntly.

"I believed that the man was innocent. The evidence was insufficient to convict Spinello. I mean, c'mon, how could you expect me to convict an innocent man?"

"We have no expectations, Mr. Prisinski."

"Are you trying to accuse me of something?" asked Rudy, who now got aggressive.

"No one is accusing you of anything," said Von Hess calmly. "We are looking into all angles because someone targeted Thomas Beasley for death."

In his confusion Rudy's mouth dropped open. At this point he still couldn't see how the detectives were connecting him to Beasley, a man he had never seen outside the courtroom. Rudy could only now assume that Beasley might have been behind the bribe he received. But since the private investigator Teddy Leonard never mentioned who he was working for, Rudy couldn't be sure.

"Do you know a man named Teddy Leonard?" Markie questioned. "He's a private investigator."

"Why no," lied Rudy. The question caused Rudy to fluster.

"Isn't that the name of the private investigator you work for?" asked Ms. Prisinski, again entering the conversation.

Rudy turned to face his wife. The dirty look he gave her expressed his anger at her interference. Unable to contain himself he responded in a harsh tone.

"Will you please mind your own damn business," barked the agitated husband. "Excuse me, Detective," he said, "I'll be right back." He then wheeled his wife into the bedroom and placed a chair beneath the doorknob thus preventing her exit.

"How dare you do this to me!" Mrs. Prisinski shouted through the door. "I'll let you out when I finish my business with the detectives," said Rudy. "We can't keep having you interrupt us."

"Hold on a second," said Markie. "That's not called for. Let her out of that room." Rudy reluctantly did as he was told. Mrs. Prisinski emerged from the room livid.

"I want that bastard arrested," demanded the irate wife, pointing to her husband.

"Take it easy, Mrs. Prisinski," said Markie. "Let us finish what we started."

"Look, Mr. Prisinski, we spoke to Teddy Leonard," fibbed Von Hess, now aware that Rudy was connected to the private investigator.

"You spoke to him?" asked Rudy, the blood now seeming to have drained from his face. Being no hardcore criminal, Rudy began to see his life crumbling before him.

"Yeah, we spoke to him," answered Markie, the hard edge to his voice evident. "He told us all about you and him."

Rudy remained silent, not sure how to proceed. Such wasn't the case with his wife. Mrs. Prisinski turned to her husband and began questioning him. After receiving a few clumsy replies to her questions Mrs. Prisinski warned, "You better start talking, Rudy, if you know what's good for you."

"I think I may need to talk to an attorney," said Rudy weakly.

"We can't afford any attorney!" exploded the angry wife. "And I want the truth now, Rudy. Either you fess up or so help me the only lawyer you'll be talking to is my divorce lawyer," she threatened.

"I think it may be in your interest to get on board the bus, Rudy," advised Markie. "If you don't, your silence may end up costing you a lot more than you bargained for."

"The sergeant is giving you good advice," added Von Hess, almost sounding fatherly. "Things will go a lot easier on you if you sit on the right side of the table while the sitting is good."

"I don't understand…."

"We're talking about you doing less time in jail if you play ball, Rudy," said Markie. "The secret is out. We know why you pushed for an acquittal in the Victor Spinello case."

"Just tell them what they want to know, Rudy. You're making it worse for both of us," urged Mrs. Prisinski.

Rudy finally caved in to the pressure he was receiving. "I only did it for us," he said, addressing his wife."

"Explain yourself, Rudy," said Von Hess.

"My wife and I have a lot of expenses to pay since her accident," began Rudy, who was now speaking directly to the detectives. "We needed money badly. Our business has been falling apart. I have bills to pay, and my wife's medical condition is bleeding me dry. She's not a healthy woman."

"Never mind about me," injected the wife.

"Please, Mrs. Prisinski. We understand," said Von Hess.

Getting Rudy to fess up was easy from this point on. Unable to stand up to his having been triple-teamed, Rudy was a defeated man with no viable path to take other than rolling over for the law. The former juror ultimately confessed to accepting bribe money from Teddy Leonard in return for ensuring that Victor Spinello would not be convicted.

"And what else did you do for money?" Von Hess asked, sensing there was more to tell.

"I was paid to get dirt on Ronnie Frantellini."

"Did you?"

"I got close to Beasley's old secretary. She's close to Ronnie."

"Leonard paid you?"

"That's right, Sergeant."

"And you know nothing about the murder of the Frantellini sisters?"

"I already told you, I know nothing about that."

Detective Von Hess took down Rudy's confession. At Markie's direction the detective then contacted the assistant district attorney they were working with. After that conferral Rudy Prisinski was arrested for the crime(s) he committed in connection with the Victor Spinello prosecution.

Before carting Rudy off to the local precinct for booking, the law waited for Mrs. Prisinski's sister to come by the Prisinski apartment. She was to stay with Rudy's wife. During the wait Markie addressed Mrs. Prisinski.

"Excuse me Mrs. Prisinski, I'm going to have a word in private with your husband," said Markie. "Detective Von Hess will keep you company."

"What's that about?" asked Rudy's wife after her husband and the sergeant stepped into the hall.

"I'd say it's about you never getting locked in a room again," replied Von Hess.

"I should have never done that, Sergeant," said Rudy, expressing remorse after receiving a tongue lashing from Markie.

"If you ever abuse you wife like that again, I'll personally see to it that you get yours .I'll be on you like stink to shit."

"I swear not to, Sergeant," said Rudy nervously. "Do you think that I'll have to serve much time in prison?"

"The court looks on taking a bribe as serious business. More than likely you'll have to do a stretch."

"Any idea how long?"

"That's entirely up to the judge. But if things pan out they might go easy on you," conveyed the sergeant.

"You'll tell them how I cooperated, right?"

"Yeah, I'll put in a word in for you with the prosecutor. But remember this, I'll bury you if you ever abuse your wife again."

33

Looking Out For Number One

BEING A MAN WITH VICES, money in the pocket of private investigator Teddy Leonard didn't last long. Flush with the proceeds from his work for the attorney Thomas Beasley, he treated himself to a day at the races. After having had a couple of drinks at one of the Aqueduct Racetrack bars he got ambitious with his wagering. Leonard bet the pick six.

Winning a pick six required selecting the winning horse of 6 races. To his amazement Leonard managed to accomplish this. The payoff netted the private investigator just under twelve thousand dollars. Not wanting to push his luck, Leonard left the track with his winnings tucked away in his front pants pocket.

Once home in his apartment Leonard sat down in front of the television. Undecided as to what he wanted to do to celebrate his winnings he turned on the TV while thinking things out.

While channel surfing Leonard came upon the actress Sharon Stone being interviewed on the evening news. While Stone answered the questions being put to her, Leonard thought of her performance in Basic Instinct, the movie that established the actor as a sex symbol. The former NYPD detective now knew how he wanted to spend the rest of the evening.

Leonard telephoned the Kingly Castle to determine if Mary Custer, the Sharon Stone lookalike, was working. When informed that she was, the private investigator showered and put on fresh clothes. He then went to a steakhouse located not far from the Kingly Castle. After consuming a tenderloin steak Leonard strolled over to the strip club. Once there he sought out the companionship of Mary Custer,

"Long time no see, stranger," greeted Custer, who remembered the private investigator. "Where have you been hiding?"

"I've been kind of busy. How about we reacquaint?" After a series of lap dances Leonard got around to propositioning Custer. "What do you say to us getting together in a more private setting?" Leonard asked.

"That could be arranged. We have a room for special customers," replied the strip club worker.

"I was thinking more along the lines of you coming over to my place and spending the night."

"Sure, but I don't come cheap."

Once the financials were agreed on, arrangements were made for Custer to meet Leonard at his apartment when she finished work.

When the private investigator returned to his apartment he found the business card of Detective Oliver Von Hess in the door jam. Although this gave him pause, he didn't allow it to dampen his romantic plans.

Leonard began to straighten out his apartment in preparation of the arrival of his guest.

***

THE INVESTIGATORS MADE a second visit to Teddy Leonard's apartment the following morning. Seeing that the business card left by Von Hess was no longer where it was left, the detectives assumed that the private investigator was home.

Von Hess knocked on the door to Leonard's apartment. When no one came to the door, the detective began to bang away with his blackjack. This got Leonard's attention. The barefooted private investigator went to the door attired in a white terrycloth bathrobe. The bags under Leonard's eyes were large, suggesting he had little sleep. Although he had never met either detective before, Leonard could tell that they represented the law. They had that cop look.

"Are one of you Von Hess?" asked Leonard.

"I'm Von Hess," acknowledged the detective. "This is Sergeant Markie. We're from the Chief of D's office."

"I know where you work, I saw it on the business card you left me."

"Can we come in?"

"This isn't exactly a good time. I got company over, know what I mean?"

"What time is your company leaving?" Markie questioned.

"I don't know, she's still asleep."

"Let her sleep. We'll be quiet."

With all parties coming from a law enforcement background, there was no need for anyone to pull any punches. The sergeant informed Leonard that they were there to arrest him. Understanding the role of the men confronting him Leonard remained civil.

"What am I being charged with?" Leonard asked.

Once apprised accordingly, the private investigator knew he had a problem. Leonard, after sizing up the two detectives, thought it unlikely that he'd be able to bribe his way out of trouble. He tried anyway.

"How about I buy the three of us breakfast, Sarge. We could go to a nearby joint down the street and talk this over."

"No dice," stated Markie flatly. "Get dressed, we're going for a ride."

"Can't you extend me a little professional courtesy, Sarge? I didn't retire from the post office you know. All I want to know is what the cards stacked against me are and if I have wiggle room."

"You'll find out soon enough, pal," said Markie icily. "Get dressed."

"Can I at least get rid of my company first?" Leonard asked in an agitated tone.

"Don't you trust her here alone?"

"Not really, Sarge. She's only rented."

"Okay, get rid of her. Ollie will help you."

Leonard, followed by Von Hess, proceeded to his bedroom. He gruffly rousted Mary Custer from her slumber. The Sharon Stone lookalike jumped up abruptly. Seeing another man in the bedroom, caused her to wonder what was next on the agenda.

"What the hell is this?" Custer asked, wiping the crust from her eyes.

"Time for you to go, sweetheart," said Leonard curtly. "I got business."

"Who is this guy?" she asked, referring to Von Hess, who wore a small smile. While Von Hess seemed familiar to her, she couldn't place him.

"C'mon, get your ass up and get out," barked Leonard, who was in no mood to answer questions posed by a hooker. "You already got what you had coming to you, so be a good girl and scram."

Once alone in the apartment with the detectives, Leonard prepared himself to leave.

"So, who ratted me out?" Leonard asked Von Hess, who was supervising Leonard's preparation to go.

"Rudy Prisinski," replied Von Hess.

"I suppose you guys pinched him."

"Yeah, we did. And now the dominos are starting to fall."

"Rudy didn't have to open his big trap," said Leonard. The guy was never arrested before, right?"

"Don't kid yourself. The court takes bribery of a juror seriously. He'll do a stretch."

"Are you trying to tell me that Rudy wasn't thrown a bone for squealing?"

"He'll receive a consideration for playing ball."

"So, what happens with me?" asked the private investigator.

"For you, things aren't pretty," said Von Hess. "The DA is looking to throw the book at you"

"That'll change. They'll loosen the screws if I spill what I know," shot back Leonard with confidence.

"I guess that all depends on who you have to offer."

"I got plenty to tell. But in return, I want a pass. What do you think, Sarge?"

"We can't guarantee you anything," advised Markie. "Maybe it does make sense for us to have that breakfast before we put the cuffs on you."

"So, you do have professional courtesy," declared Leonard heartily, when Markie agreed to go for breakfast.

"With limitations," replied Markie.

Once at the diner the men ordered their food before getting down to business. "Okay, start talking, my friend," said Markie.

"I got your word that you'll fix things up with the DA if I spill what I know, right?"

"You got my word that I'll talk on your behalf. I can't promise more than that. Leniency will all depend on what you bring to the table."

"Fair enough."

Teddy Leonard went on to admit that he bribed the juror Rudolph Prisinski in the murder trial of Victor Spinello. He explained that he was paid by the attorney Thomas Beasley to do this. This revelation came as no great surprise to the investigators.

"So, let me get this straight," said Markie. "You were paid money to bribe Rudolph Prisinski by the lawyer for Victor Spinello".

"Correct."

"So Spinello retained the services of Beasley to get him off?"

"I don't know that for sure, Sarge. I can't be sure who retained Beasley on behalf of Spinello."

"Could Ronnie Frantellini have had something to do with it?"

"That is possible. I do know that her and Beasley had some side agreement."

"What was the agreement?"

"Tommy Beasley never told me. But I'm certain they had something going."

"What makes you so sure?" Von Hess asked.

"Tommy Beasley's secretary went to work for Ronnie Frantellini," advised Leonard. "Tommy hired me to get somebody close to her. Tommy wanted information that could be used against Ronnie so that he could recoup whatever it was he felt cheated out of. These aren't exactly honorable people that I was dealing with."

This last remark caused the detectives to chuckle.

"I can tell you something else. Tommy Beasley had something on Ronnie. Somehow he lost that leverage and wanted to regain it. That's why he hired me to get someone close to the secretary."

"So, he wanted dirt to regain the advantage. And you hired Rudy Prisinzki to help you do it."

"Now you got it."

"And you hired Rudy specifically to get close to Beasley's former secretary."

"Correct, Sarge."

"You're willing to testify to all this?" asked Markie.

"As long as I get to slip through the net, you can bank on it. What other choice have I got, Sarge?"

"You are going to have to talk to Beasley while wearing a wire."

"If I must, I will. But I hate to do it. You know as well as me what wearing a wire does to a guy's reputation." This remark caused all three men to laugh aloud.

On last thing, Can you tell us anything about the Frantellini sisters getting whacked in a restaurant."

"Not a damn thing. Beasley never mentioned that once to me."

Markie assessed Leonard's truthfulness. He believed the former detective was being truthful.

"Okay, Teddy," said the sergeant. "You sit tight and be sure to keep your nose clean. I'll talk to the DA and see what could be done on your behalf."

34

Leonard Gets Lucky

MANHATTAN ASSISTANT DISTRICT ATTORNEY KIM SMYTHER sat alone in her One Hogan Place office. She was deep in thought. An ambitious woman with a pale complexion, she came to the realization that she was working long hours for what she considered inadequate compensation.

Once she acquired her law credentials, Smyther immediately secured employment with the DA's office. This smooth transition was thanks to the influence of her uncle, a politically connected judge. Now, after several years of prosecuting cases, Smyther grew disenchanted. She perceived herself as being in a job that was stalling her career. Her feeling of unappreciation caused her to consider going into the private sector.

Smyther penned a letter of introduction to the managing partner of Pemberton, Banks and Stocker, a high-end law firm. Along with the letter was a copy of her resume. Before sending off the documents she had a telephonic conversation with her uncle.

The judge felt that it was his duty to be brutally honest with his niece. Over a drink later that evening he informed Smyther that she fell short in the one area that mattered most with big firms. The judge explained that access to corporate clients and/or high net worth individuals ruled supreme. He emphasized that the ability to bring new business to a firm towered over all other factors.

Smyther was unconvinced of this. All her life she had been led to believe that a law degree from an ivy league institution was all one needed. She voiced her skepticism to her uncle's position. At this point the frustrated judge took off the gloves with his niece. He made his point in two sentences:

"Look Kim," said the judge, "it's all about the money. The dumbest lawyer from a billionaire family is more valuable than the brightest candidate from the greatest school."

When the phone went silent, the judge realized that he may have devastated his niece. To get back on track the judge began to point out the advantages of his niece staying where she was in the DA's office. He communicated that her work ethic would catapult her career in time. He assured the ADA that at some point down the road she would be elevated to bureau chief and then after, something greater.

Smyther's conversation with her persuasive uncle energized her. After hanging up the phone she tore up the letter of introduction she penned. Now, thirsting for more work, she welcomed the appearance of Markie and Von Hess at her office door.

"Do you have results for me, Sergeant?" Smyther asked hopingly.

"We made some headway," replied Markie.

"Well?"

"Crippler is now playing for our team. He's agreed to wear a wire."

"Excellent," said the ADA.

"He told us all about the plot hatched by Ronnie Frantellini to murder the lawyer Thomas Beasley."

"I want you to get Ronnie Frantellini on tape talking about that. I'd love to see that sleazeball lawyer getting what he deserves."

"I hear you," said Markie.

"See what you can get on Beasley regarding the Victor Spinello acquittal. There is no way that I should have lost that case."

"We already got the scoop on that."

"You did?" From whom, Crippler?"

"No," replied Markie. "Crippler knew nothing about that."

"From whom then?"

"We broke the juror Rudolph Prisinski. He admitted that Beasley's private investigator paid him off."

"I knew it!" Smyther exclaimed, slamming her hand on her desk.

"How did you manage to get him to fess up?

" Prisinski is no hardened criminal. All it took was a little squeezing and a push from his wife."

"So, what did the juror say?"

"He said that an ex-detective named Teddy Leonard worked for Thomas Beasley. Prisinski said that it was Leonard who paid him off."

"I knew I didn't lose that trial legitimately!" exclaimed ed the ADA triumphantly"

"That's right, the fix was in," said Markie.

"The chickens are now going to come home to roost," declared Smyther. "I'm going to crucify both this private investigator and that juror!"

Markie's eyes were now open to just how vindictive ADA Smyther could be. "You may want to rethink some of that," said the sergeant.

"Why should I?"

"We were also able to turn Teddy Leonard the private investigator, so he's cooperating with us."

"So?"

"So, he told us how Thomas Beasley paid him to pay off the juror in the Victor Spinello case. He's willing to testify to that."

"So, we finally got Sleazy Beasley!"

"That's right, we do. But Leonard is only going to play ball if he gets a deal," advised Markie. "He'll testify or do whatever you want, but he's expecting to walk."

"I'm putting every last one of these bastards away," declared the ADA, her tone communicating her determination.

"I know you want blood, but if we want to win the war, we might have to lose a battle here and there."

"I don't need you to remind me of that, Sergeant," shot back the ADA, who took the sergeant's statement as being preached to.

"All I'm trying to convey is that Rudy Prisinski is a ground ball. He's a scared rabbit who knows that he'll have to serve some time. But this Teddy Leonard is another story. He has been around the block."

"Leonard's the only guy who can serve up Beasley," injected Von Hess. "Prisinski never dealt directly with Beasley."

"Never?"

"No, never. Everything went through Leonard." "Oh...."said Smyther, who was now reconsidering her adamance.

"Leonard's an ex-detective," said Markie. He knows exactly how the game is played. If we want Beasley, then we need Leonard on the team. Just give him what he wants. We'll wire Leonard and then we'll rope in Beasley really good. We can always get Leonard at some point down the road. He'll never change his ways."

"I can't see myself letting him off altogether, Sergeant," conveyed the ADA.

"There is a major piece that we're forgetting about," voiced Von Hess.

"There is?"

"Ronnie Frantellini. She was the one behind the murders of her stepdaughters in the restaurant. Beasley can probably add to what the wrestlers already told us about that. He can probably supply an actual motive."

A ringing telephone on ADA Smyther's desk interrupted the conversation. The ADA picked up the phone.

"What?" asked the ADA. Her face then changed to one of grave seriousness. "I'm coming right over." ADA Smyther jumped from her seat and bolted from her office. "You two stay here, I'll be back," were her parting words.

"Where do you think she scooted off to, Sarge?" asked Von Hess.

"Something must have happened. Either that or she had to go take a good dump for herself."

An hour had passed before Markie and Von Hess realized that the ADA wasn't coming back anytime soon. Upon learning what caused the ADA to rush out of her office, the detectives came to understand that no further business would be discussed that day.

***

THE MANHATTAN DISTRICT ATTORNEY was standing at the podium addressing the crowd that attended the Police Athletic League luncheon. Suddenly, in mid-sentence, he paused.

Appearing confused, his eyes rolled upward, and he collapsed to the ground. Just like that, in a matter of seconds, the district attorney was no more. He fell dead before a stunned audience.

The death of the DA left the governor tasked with appointing an interim district attorney. The man in Albany saw the vacancy as an opportunity to take care of Bernie Miller, an assistant district attorney in the office of the Manhattan District Attorney. The appointment of Miller, who happened to be the governor's brother-in-law, raised more than a few eyebrows.

However, since the governor had just won reelection he had nothing to fear politically.

Among those unhappy with the appointment was ADA Kim Smyther, who felt such nepotism had no place in her chosen profession. Smyther openly voiced to whoever would listen that one of the bureau chiefs, or even herself, would have made a more palatable choice for the prestigious post. She cited Miller's lackluster performance as a prosecutor and poor attendance record to support her position.

In truth, Smyther's strong opposition to Miller was actually rooted elsewhere. She held a personal grudge against the new appointee that bordered on the ridiculous. Miller had once referred to Smyther as Him instead of Kim when engaging in a conversation with several male attorneys at an office event. The slight, amplified due to the cackling of the male attorneys, caused Smyther to confront Miller about it head on. The ugly exchange of harsh words that unfolded created an animosity that was beyond repair. The appointment of Miller reopened an old wound.

***

MARKIE, VON HESS AND TEDDY LEONARD sat in an unmarked car around the corner from the law office of Thomas Beasley. The cooperating private investigator needed no guidance in heading the tape recording he wore while seated in the back seat of the vehicle. Leonard stated in a clear voice the date, time, mission and who he was going to see. After emerging from the unmarked police vehicle, he walked to Beasley's law office with a spring in his step.

As Leonard proceeded to Beasley's office, he kept in mind Markie's parting warning that if he tipped off Beasley that he was wired, there would be serious repercussions to face. The admonition caused Leonard to snicker.

I can't believe Markie would think that I'd be stupid enough to do anything that would blow my deal, thought Leonard. *I like Tommy, but not enough to go to jail for him.*

If he were being totally honest with himself Leonard would admit that he wouldn't go to jail for his own mother.

Upon entering Beasley's office, the private investigator found the attorney working at his desk. Leonard flashed a happy smile and greeted Beasley pleasantly.

"Still no secretary, Tommy?" asked the police cooperator.

"It's not that easy finding the right fit."

"Did you ever think of calling a temp agency?" Leonard was making small talk before getting down to his purpose.

"Don't worry, I'll find what I'm looking for. So, what's up?"

"That juror I bribed for you on the Victor Spinello trial has been bugging me for more money. I told him I'd talk to you."

The comment immediately raised Beasley's antennas. Leonard's words were too exact, too direct."

"I don't know what you're talking about, Teddy," replied the cautious attorney."

"I'm talking about Rudy Prisinski, the public relations guy you paid me to bribe. You know, the juror we got to."

Beasley held up one hand to silence the private investigator. As he did this he jotted down something on a yellow legal pad with his free hand. He then turned the pad to face Leonard. Beasley's jottings scolded Leonard for mentioning the bribed juror's name and bringing up the bribery incident. The message included a reference to the walls possibly having ears.

"I got it," said Leonard. "I was just saying…."

"Look Teddy, I'm a busy man," interrupted Beasley, not allowing the private investigator to finish his sentence. "If you don't mind, I'd appreciate it if you left me to my work."

"Sure, I understand, Tommy. You're a busy guy. But what do you want me to do about Rudy?"

"I have no work for you right now, Teddy," said Beasley abruptly, silencing Leonard. "When I do, I'll call you."

All Leonard could do at this point was exit the attorney's office. Once on the street he telephoned Markie to inform him of what had transpired with Beasley.

"We'll have to figure another way," said the disappointed sergeant. "Come back to the car."

"Give me a little time, Sarge. It's near lunchtime. I have an idea." Leonard waited on the opposite side of the street until Thomas Beasley left his building. When he did, Leonard reentered the office building. Once inside the building he located a cleaner to inform him that he had forgotten something inside Beasley's office. Being a familiar face as the attorney's private investigator, the cleaner used his key to gain access to the office.

"I'll be out in a minute," advised Leonard, slipping a twenty-dollar bill in the cleaner's hand.

Upon gaining access into the lawyer's office, Leonard began looking for the sheet of yellow legal paper that Beasley had written on. He found the paper in question in the wastepaper basket by the lawyer's desk. It was torn into small pieces.

Leonard scooped up the scraps of paper and placed them in his pocket for future reconstruction. Before departing the private investigator took another yellow sheet of paper from the yellow legal pad. He tore the blank sheet into small pieces and dropped them into the wastepaper basket. Leonard then returned to the waiting Markie and Von Hess.

Once safely in the unmarked car, Leonard explained to the waiting detectives that he had the note that had been passed to him by Leonard.

"Where is it?" asked Markie.

"I got it in my pocket. It's in pieces, we have to piece it together."

The detectives didn't ask how he retrieved the note. They didn't want to know.

***

WHEN THOMAS BEASLEY returned to his office he happened to glance at his wastepaper basket. What he noticed was disturbing. Seeing no ink on any of the yellow pieces of paper contained in the basket, he inspected further. To his dismay he found that the note he tore up was no longer there.

The attorney now knew that he had something to worry about. Unable to concentrate on business, he left work for the day. He stepped into the first bar he passed while walking on the street. Once inside, he began to drown his concerns. With Teddy Leonard believed to be cooperating with the law, Beasley felt that it was only a matter of time before the law would come down on him.

***

AFTER THE INVESTIGATORS pieced together the handwritten note authored by attorney Thomas Beasley, they photographed the document and then vouchered it as evidence. The detectives then briefed ADA Kim Smyther accordingly. With Smyther's okay, and after conferring with their superiors at headquarters, Markie and Von Hess set out to take down Beasley.

The detectives began looking for the attorney at his place of business. Several failed attempts caused Markie to suspect that Beasley hadn't been coming to work. The sergeant verified his suspicion after speaking to several people at the building where the lawyer's office was.

"Call up Silverlake at the office, Ollie," said the sergeant. "Have him get us a home address for Beasley."

"Righto, Sarge."

Detective Silverlake ascertained a home address for Thomas Beasley by conducting a database search. The detective conveyed this information to Detective Von Hess telephonically.

"He lives at 252-First Avenue, NYC, Ollie," advised Silverlake.

"That's around the East 20's, right?"

"I think so, Ollie. Hold on a minute, let me check."

"Don't bother, it makes no difference. Where did you get the address from?"

"That's the address on Beasley's driver's license."

Markie and Von Hess proceeded to the First Avenue address, which was located within the complex known as Stuyvesant Town.

35

An Elusive Esquire

THE INVESTIGATORS WERE STARTLED at the appearance of the man who answered the door to his apartment. Expecting to see a professional man, they were instead greeted by a clammy representation of the legal profession. Thomas Beasley was unshaven, disheveled and emitted the distinct stench of alcohol. Despite all this, Beasley remained functional.

The attorney had entered into a state of depression. His downward spiral was attributable to his inability to figure out a way to counter the damage caused by Teddy Leonard's cooperation with the law. The defection of the private investigator likely meant the downfall of Beasley's legal career. The attorney was facing humiliation, disbarment and likely incarceration.

"Are you Thomas Beasley?" Von Hess asked. Receiving nothing but a blank stare for an answer, the detective repeated his question. This time he received a weak response that came in a low voice.

"You wasted no time," answered the lawyer, assuming his visitors were law enforcement.

"You're Beasley?"

"Yeah, I'm Beasley. Where are you guys from?"

"We're detectives from police headquarters." Von Hess then identified himself by producing his gold shield.

"Put your tin away," said Beasley. "I know a detective when I see one. You guys all look the same."

"Yeah, well, I can't say that you look like a typical lawyer."

"Why don't you just state your business," said the weathered attorney, taking offense to the detective's remark.

"You've got a case," announced Markie tartly. "Get your coat."

Beasley, in attempt to project dignity, straightened up to his full height and asked, "Do you have an arrest warrant?"

"Are you coming or not?"

"Oh, so that's how it is," said Beasley.

"That's how it is," echoed Markie.

"Can I at least clean up before we take our ride?"

"Yeah, you'd be doing us all a favor."

It took close to an hour for the attorney to make himself presentable. However, no amount of polishing could conceal the look of Beasley's fatigue. He was the picture of a ruined man when placed in the back seat of the unmarked police car. The silence during the lawyer's transport was broken when he asked where he was being removed to.

"We're going to the District Attorney's office," replied Markie, who turned to face the prisoner in the back seat.

"You guys work in the DA's squad?"

"No, we work directly for the chief of detectives," answered Markie.

"That's right, you said that. Why are you taking me to the DA's office instead of a precinct? And how come I'm not cuffed if I'm under arrest?"

"Do you want to be cuffed?"

"I'd like to know what I'm being charged with, Sergeant."

"Bribing a jurist in a homicide trial."

"So, how come I'm not in handcuffs?"

"We want you to play ball with us, that's why you aren't cuffed."

"But I'm arrested, right?"

"That you are."

"What kind of evidence have you got besides Teddy Leonard's lies?"

"We got that note you wrote to him in your office," advised the sergeant.

"How do you intend to prove that I wrote any note?"

"Handwriting comparisons will prove that."

"Good luck trying to get a credible handwriting expert to testify. They'll just say that they need more handwriting samples before making any determination. They'll stall until you run out of samples."

"Let us worry about that," chimed in Von Hess. "We have a reliable resource."

"What else have you got besides that ingrate private investigator?"

Von Hess looked over at Markie. "Tell him, Ollie," said the sergeant.

"A contract was put out on your life," said Von Hess.

"Says who?"

"Says the hit man contracted to clip you. He's pitching for our team."

"Who hired him?"

"Ronnie Frantellini."

Beasley let out a deep sigh. The prisoner sat back in his seat thinking. The wheels in his head were turning slow. He closed his eyes in defeat.

Once they arrived at the district attorney's office Beasley was placed in an office for a formal interview. Once the prisoner learned who was prosecuting him, he knew for certain that he was in for a hard time.

"ADA Smyther hates me," commented Beasley. "She thinks that she is holier than thou!"

There came a point when things brightened for Beasley. This came after he learned that ADA Bernard Miller had been promoted to be the new district attorney.

"Well, what do you know about that," said Beasley, who now seemed invigorated.

There was hope in what was once thought to be a lost cause. The detectives sensed the exuberance in their prisoner.

"Do you have a history with the new DA?" asked Von Hess.

Unknown to the detectives, Miller happened to be a classmate of Thomas Beasley. The two had elevated their grades through both college and law school by bribing office workers who had access to the school computer system.

"We've met," answered Beasley, playing it cool. "What happened to the old DA?"

"He dropped dead while giving a talk someplace."

"I'll shed no tears for that son of a bitch. That was another guy never liked me for some reason."

"So, what is it going to be?" Markie asked. "Are you going to play ball?"

Beasley saw his relationship with Miller as his ticket to freedom. In Miller, Beasley now had the leverage needed. He knew enough dirt about his old friend that could prove embarrassing, if not criminal, for the interim appointee.

"We need to talk about all this, Sergeant," said Beasley calmly, his confidence now fully restored. "I want guarantees."

"You're in no position to dicker," reminded Von Hess.

"Perhaps. Look, I'll tell you what you want to know," advised Beasley. "But only after I get some assurances."

"Let's hear what you got to put on the table."

"I can prove that the person who paid to get Victor Spinello off also paid for the commission of a double homicide. Does that tickle your interest? I'm sure the new DA would appreciate it. When can I make my phone call?"

"Who do you want to call?" Von Hess asked.

"My Aunt Josie in Canarsie. I'm entitled to a call, remember?"

"Ollie, give the man his due."

"Righto, Sarge. What's the number you want called?"

"Thank you, Sarge," said Beasley with a smirk.

Von Hess dialed the number. The call was to the cell phone of Bernard Miller, the new interim district attorney. At the request of the DA, their conversation was a private one.

***

ADA KIM SMYTHER ENTERED THE office walking as if she had a two by four strapped to her back. Her lips were sealed tight, projecting the sternest look possible. She faced Thomas Beasley with fire in her eyes.

"Okay, Mr. Beasley," said the ADA. Her tone was direct and stiff. "District Attorney Miller is only interested in prosecuting one person, Ronnie Frantellini."

Smyther then turned to Markie and added, "And that's regardless of who we have to let walk."

After some back-and-forth negotiations between ADA Smyther and Thomas Beasley, the agreement reached favored Beasley. In return for his cooperation, Beasley's prosecution was declined.

Markie and Von Hess looked on in silence as Beasley was advised by the ADA that he had to share all he knew without embellishment.

"This includes whatever evidence you have to support your claim that Ronnie Frantellini orchestrated the double homicide of the Frantellini sisters," said Smyther.

"Was Ronnie Frantellini the one who had be marked for death, right?" Beasley asked.

"How do you know that she had you marked for death, Mr. Beasley?" Smyther asked.

"They told me," Beasley said, indicating the detectives. "Look Smyther," replied Besley, "this isn't about revenge. My only objective is to stay out of jail and keep my license."

"That's an ambitious objective."

"But obviously an attainable one," Beasley shot back. "How about we stop the cat and mouse. I'll start telling what you want to hear, and you start generating the paperwork that lets me walk away clean."

"You'll have your deal," said Smyther, her unhappiness evident. "I'll have the papers drawn up now."

Markie and Von Hess both looked at Beasley realizing that he had pulled a rabbit out of his hat.

"Okay, Mr. Beasley, spill it," said Markie once the ADA left the room. "Just remember one thing," added the sergeant, "if you're caught in one lie, there is no deal."

"Understood. Don't forget that I'm a lawyer. I understand these things completely. Where do I start?"

"From the beginning."

Beasley explained how he was retained to fix the Victor Spinello trial. He made it clear that Ronnie's ambition was to secure full control of the Frantellini businesses. Beasley didn't stop there. He communicated that in order for Ronnie to achieve her ambition, she needed the Frantellini sisters to be done away with.

The unethical lawyer stated that Ronnie admitted to him that she hired an assassin to commit the double homicide. Beasley emphasized that he only learned of this after the fact. He acknowledged that he was present in the restaurant when the Frantellini murders went down, reiterating that he had no prior knowledge that murders were on the menu at the time.

"What is your proof of all this, Mr. Beasley?"

"Between me and that private eye of mine, you already have all the proof you need regarding the bribery matter," answered Beasley. "As far as Ronnie hiring an assassin to kill the sisters, she told me what she did in no uncertain terms after the girls were dead," lied the prisoner.

"Why would she admit that to you?"

"I was the Frantellini family lawyer. She trusted me."

"Do you know who Ronnie hired to commit the murders?" asked the ADA.

"No, she never told me that, and I didn't ask."

"I still don't understand why she felt the need to admit to you that she committed murders," voiced Smyther, who had returned to the room.

"Look," said Beasley, sounding frustrated. "I was there at the table in the restaurant, remember? I was her lawyer, so she confided in me. Remember this, Ronnie is no fool. She probably figured that I had her number anyway concerning the murders."

"And you told no one about this?"

"I'm telling you now, aren't I?"

"Why did Ronnie Frantellini all of a sudden want to have you clipped," queried Markie.

"Ronnie is a treacherous lady. She probably later realized that I was the only person who could finger her in the murder of the sisters. So, I had to be eliminated in order for her to protect herself. I'm telling you, that the woman is pure evil. Do you want to hear what else she did?"

"Go on."

"She befriended my secretary and hired her away from me!"

"Why?"

"That's anybody's guess. But it gives you an idea of what kind of person Ronnie Frantellini is."

"Did you challenge her on that?"

"Of course not. I was angry of course, but what was I going to do? She was still a client."

Hearing this, Markie and Von Hess looked at each other having their doubts.

"Don't forget that we interviewed Teddy Leonard," reminded the sergeant, "and that juror you bribed." A grimness now crossed the face of Beasley. "So, you might as well tell us exactly what you did after your secretary switched her allegiance.

Remember, if you lie, there is no deal."

"Okay, okay," said Beasley, who went on to reveal how he hired Teddy Leonard to get someone close to his former secretary in an effort to compromise Ronnie Frantellini. When he finished with his account Beasley was permitted to leave.

ADA Smyther offered no comment. She was disgusted that District Attorney Miller orchestrated things so that Thomas Beasley was able to walk away a free man.

Wanting to protect the reputation of her office, this was something she didn't want to talk over with Markie and Von Hess.

"What's your next move?" asked Markie, addressing the ADA.

“I don’t really know,” admitted Smyther. She then waved the detectives off, dismissing them.

When alone Markie and Von Hess discussed the situation among themselves.

“Do you know what I noticed about that shyster son of a bitch lawyer, Ollie?” Markie asked.

“What’s that, Sarge?”

“Beasley was crapping his pants when we first picked him up. Everything changed after he made that phone call to the DA. I only wish we could have listened in on the conversation.

36

Crippler Is Put In Play

WHATEVER THE BOND THAT EXISTED BETWEEN Thomas Beasley and the interim district attorney remained a puzzle to Assistant District Attorney Kim Smyther. The uncertainty of the connection hampered the ADA's ability to do her job as she saw fit. Fearing the retribution attached to stepping on toes, Smyther was left with little choice other than to go along with the interim district attorney's program.

In accordance with DA Miller's edict, the focus was to prosecute Ronnie Frantellini to the fullest. To achieve this end, an ironclad case needed to be put together. This was possible with the cooperation of the wrestler known as Crippler.

After being released from the hospital Crippler was sent to Riker's Island while presumably awaiting trial. Unable to meet the exorbitant bail set, he remained on Rikers marking time until he was called upon by the authorities he agreed to cooperate with.

With the help of ADA Smyther, Detective Von Hess secured a takeout order that enabled him to temporarily take charge of the inmate. Once pulled out of Rikers, Crippler was taken to a nearby Queens police precinct by Markie and Von Hess. It was there that the wrestler was familiarized with the recording device he was expected to wear. Once wired up for sound Markie and Von Hess then drove the prisoner to the Frantellini Shoe Factory where he was expected to engage Ronnie Frantellini in conversation about her hiring Crippler to commit murder(s).

Markie and Von Hess parked their unmarked vehicle in the vicinity of the shoe factory. While in the back seat of the vehicle Crippler was coached regarding heading the recording device he wore. Before exiting the vehicle Von Hess felt it necessary to remind Crippler that he had a bullet with the wrestler's name on it should he dare attempt to escape.

Crippler, who was satisfied with the terms he entered into with the law, had no such intention. Furthering Crippler's compliance was the wrestler's recollection of being shot by a detective at the time of his apprehension. Having no intention of taking another police bullet, Crippler nodded his head conveying understanding.

Markie and Von Hess trailed behind on foot a short distance to Crippler's rear as the wrestler made his way to the shoe factory. "

Do you think maybe we should have brought along a couple of more guys with us on this, Sarge?" asked Von Hess, as they walked. "If this guy decides to get cute, we very well might have to shoot him."

"You got your blackjack with you, right, Ollie?" Markie asked.

"Always. But I can't see the two of us ever taking Crippler down physically, even with my convincer."

"That's why they give us guns to carry, Ollie," said Markie. "If it comes down to it, it'll be Crippler's funeral, not ours."

The detectives assumed a position across the street from the shoe factory once Crippler entered the building. Due to the high volume of pedestrian traffic walking on the commercial block, the law enforcement officers were able to blend in without notice.

Since there was no security or access controls in place at the Frantellini Shoe Factory, Crippler was able to make his way to

Ronnie Frantellini's office without being challenged. The wrestler found Ronnie sitting at her desk with a cigarette in one hand and a pen in the other. In front of her was a large black seven ring checkbook binder. She was paying bills.

The wrestler stood quietly in the doorway of Ronnie's office. His hulking frame took up the entire opening. Ronnie looked up from her work only after Crippler cleared his throat to make his presence known. Startled at the sight of Crippler, Ronnie's mouth dropped open.

"What are you doing here?" Ronnie asked with directness. "I thought you were supposed to be in jail."

"I was. We need to talk."

"What did you do, break out?"

"No, I had been in the hospital," replied the wrestler. "I was shot by one of the detectives, remember?"

"I remember. So how did you get out?"

"Because I got shot for no reason, the judge set a bail that I could make."

"So, what brings you here?"

"I need money. Right now, I have a legal aid lawyer, and that's not good enough. I need a good lawyer and relief with my expenses. I figure you owe me for keeping my trap shut."

Ronnie's reaction came in the form of a frown. Her face made it clear that she wasn't sympathetic.

"What's with the look?" Crippler asked. "Look, bitch, you owe me."

"Let's get something straight right now," said Ronnie firmly, as she discreetly opened her desk drawer where she kept pepper spray. "You don't scare me. And furthermore, I don't know what you're talking about."

"Look, you paid me for killing two women," declared Crippler in a voiced designed to menace. "And you still owe me for trying to clip that lawyer Beasley. That's what got me pinched."

"You're delusional," said Ronnie, who suspected a set up. "Go and tell your troubles to a priest."

"Don't give me that. I need money," repeated Crippler. "You wanted that lawyer Beasley killed and I…."

"Okay, okay, can it," said Ronnie abruptly, producing the pepper spray. "Did you tell the cops such gibberish?"

"What's that you got there?"

"Pepper Spray with a special solution in it," answered Ronnie. "One squirt of this stuff in your eye and you'll be blinded for life," lied Ronnie.

"Okay, okay, take it easy," said Crippler, who took Ronnie's threat seriously.

"So, what lies did you tell the cops?' Ronnie asked, believing she secured the upper hand.

"I never spoke to the cops. I'm nobody's snitch. All I want from you is enough money so I can take off for good."

"That's probably a good idea just to be rid of you and your ravings," conveyed Ronnie.

"You got the checkbook out, write me a check."

"You'll get cash, not a check. I'll have to go to the bank. Meet me at 6:00 P.M. tonight at 42nd Street and Avenue of the Americas. Be in front of Bryant Park. I'll have enough money for you to disappear. Do you have an up-to-date passport?"

"Yeah, I travel to Japan and Australia sometimes when I wrestle." "Good. Go someplace far and stay there."

"Are you giving me enough? Remember, I did your killings for you."

"Stop," Ronnie barked. "No more talk. You'll get your money and I'll be done with you. Just forget my name and talk of this killing business.

With Markie and Von Hess walking to his rear, Crippler returned to the unmarked police car. Once all were inside the vehicle Markie placed his index finger to his throat and moved it along the front of his neck, signaling the wrestler to shut off the recording device he was wearing.

Crippler apprised the investigators of the information that was memorialized on the recording device. After listening to the recording, the detectives were satisfied. They took the prisoner to a restaurant, where they remained until it was time to head for Bryant Park.

After conferring with ADA Smyther, Markie received the green light to arrest Ronnie Frantellini the moment she handed the money to Crippler by Bryant Park. The sergeant then telephoned his headquarters office requesting Detective Silverlake to meet him in the field. Silverlake was needed to take charge of Ronnie Frantellini while Markie and Von Hess returned Crippler to Rikers.

***

SMILLEY ALLEN REACHED for the cell phone in his pants pocket several times without success. It was almost as if some invisible power was preventing him from grasping his phone. After much contemplation he finally permitted himself to take hold of the device. Smiley knew that what he was about to do might come back to haunt him one day.

I don't know why I'm getting involved, Smiley thought. I mean, this isn't even my problem.

Even though Smiley saw no upside for himself by contacting Ronnie Frantellini, his misguided loyalty won out. He made the call. As the phone rang he thought, *I have to be nuts. If I had any brains I'd be steering clear of this whole mess.*

"Hello?"

Smiley didn't answer immediately. After a second or two he spoke.

"Ronnie, it me, Smiley."

"Smiley?"

"Yeah, Smiley. Look, you've got trouble coming your way. Two detectives were at my place digging for information."

"About what?"

Crippler got busted. They know I introduced you to him," advised Smiley. "I figure that he must be cooperating with the law."

"I think you're right. Crippler was just here at my office."

"He was?"

"Yeah. You didn't say anything to the detectives I hope."

"I had to tell them something. They threatened to put the IRS on my ass, what else could I do?"

"You could have lawyered up!" Ronnie answered tartly.

"Look, Ronnie, I've got a family and a business to protect now. I run all my expenses through this joint, and that includes season tickets to the Yankee games, my car, my clothes and the toilet paper that wipes my ass. I can't afford to get nailed by the IRS, Ronnie."

"Okay, I hear you, Smiley. So, what exactly did you tell them?"

"I invented a story they would swallow. I told them you needed to put out a tenant and needed someone imposing to serve as a convincer."

"That's it?"

"That's it, I swear it. But you have to figure that Crippler is spilling his guts to get out from under."

Ronnie didn't comment. She was having worried thoughts.

"Ronnie are you still there?"

"I'm here, Smiley. That cauliflower eared son of a bitch was just in my office crying for money. I was just on my way to the bank for him. I'm supposed to meet him later to give him an envelope."

"That cinches it then," advised Smiley. "If he's out of the can, then Crippler had to have gone bad. You were being set up. Our friend is working for the cops now."

"Your friend, not mine," corrected Ronnie with bitterness.

"What are you going to do?" Smiley questioned.

"What else can I do? I've got to drop out of sight while I still can."

"Where are you going?"

"Do you really want to know, Smiley?"

"No, of course not, Ronnie. It's none of my business."

"You have to do me a favor, Smiley."

"I don't know, Ronnie...."

"All I want you to do is talk to my friend Clara if you hear anything. She works for me at the factory. She'll know how to reach me wherever I am."

"Who?"

"Clara, you can find her at the Frantellini Shoe Factory."

"Sure thing, Ronnie," lied Smiley, who had no intention of getting involved further. "Good luck."

***

AT RONNIE'S REQUEST, Clara met her mentor inside of Our Lady of Pompeii Church on Carmine Street in Manhattan's West Village. Clara was surprised to see that Ronnie was carrying a large suitcase. The two sat in the last pew in a corner of the church. Their conversation was whispered.

Without going into detail, Ronnie explained that trouble was brewing. She indicated that circumstances compelled her to immediately relocate overseas for an undetermined length of time. When Clara questioned why, Ronnie remained vague. All she would convey was that the time had come to test Clara's loyalty. Ronnie made it a point to remind her friend of all she had done for her.

"I know that I can count on you, Clara," Ronnie said. "You aren't going to disappoint me are you?"

"Of course not," replied Clara. "Tell me what I have to do."

"I want you to take charge of my businesses in my absence. You will have full authority."

"I don't understand, Ronnie," said the baffled Clara. "What happened."

"All you need to understand is that you are the only person in this world who I trust enough to turn the keys over to, Clara. Can I depend on you?"

"Of course you can. But you'll have to explain to me what I need to do. Afterall, I have no experience....

"I already spoke to my accountant. He'll be available to help you whenever necessary. Here, take this," said Ronnie, handing her friend a manila envelope that she produced from a large canvas bag. "Inside this envelope is your copy of my last will and testament.

It's been notarized by my accountant and witnesses. This document makes it clear that in the event of my death, regardless of how or when I die, all of my assets will go to you, Clara.

"Oh, my God, Ronnie!" exclaimed the shocked Clara. "Are you in some kind of danger? Are you sick?"

"I think they may be looking to put me in jail for something I had nothing to do with," fibbed the mentor. "I'd rather die, so I'm not taking any chances. I'm going far away and intend to stay there. That's why I need your help."

Clara didn't know what to make of things. Her perplexed look was obvious. "But…."

"Inside the envelope you will find all you need to know pertaining to operating the shoe factory and the real estate that I own. I'm giving you full authority to act on my behalf. And don't worry, we will be talking regularly over the phone."

"Yes, but…."

"There is nothing more for me to explain now, Clara. I have to move fast. C'mon, let's go."

"Where are we going? "

We have to make a stop to put everything in order." Ronnie could see that Clara was getting nervous. "Don't get nervous, honey. All you have to do is stand by me and you'll live a beautiful life. C'mon, we'll talk more in the cab."

Ronnie took Clara to the bank where she arranged for Clara to have the authority to write checks. Clara was empowered to withdraw and deposit money from Ronnie's business and personal accounts. Clara was also now in a position to decide on all banking and business-related matters.

Ronnie advised Clara that she would be traveling extensively while in search for a place to settle down. She went on to assure Clara that her operation of the businesses would run smoothly, noting that she should work closely with Victor Spinello at the factory. Ronnie described Spinello as one of the few people who could be trusted. Ronnie made it a point to add that the conversations between the two women should remain confidential, noting that although Victor was trustworthy, he was not to be in the loop when it came to the communication arrangements made between Ronnie and Clara.

"Victor already knows about my entrusting you to run my business affairs in my absence. He's only a minority owner in the factory, so he was fine with it. Victor must never know how to contact me."

"Where are you going to go?" Clara asked.

"Right now, to the airport," replied Ronnie. "It's lucky that I have an up-to-date passport."

"You're definitely leaving the country?"

"I'm taking the first plane to Europe," said Ronnie, I'll be safe overseas."

"What do I tell people who come to the factory looking for you?"

"Tell them I left you in charge and that you don't know where I went. Let them try and find me."

"How do I communicate with you if I don't know where you are?"

"I'll call you once a week and tell you where to send me cash. I'll be receiving mail at different addresses in the beginning. Now listen to me, Clara. No one is to know that we are in contact. Not the cops, not anyone. Do you understand me?"

"Of course, Ronnie."

"Remember, no checks, just cash. When you're sending me money, wrap up the cash in a newspaper and place it a heavy a duty envelope." "How much should I send every week?"

"It'll vary depending on circumstances. I'll let you know when I call you," advised Ronnie.

"When will that be?"

"Without fail I'll call you every Sunday at 6:00 P.M. sharp. We need to establish a telephone number where I could reach you other than the office line and your cell phone."

"I have no other phone," voiced Clara. "

What about that cabdriver beau of yours?"

"Fernando?"

"Yes, where does he live?"

"On Avenue C in Alphabet City. You want to call me there?"

"No, wait a minute, I have an idea. Fernando has a mother who lives in Manhattan right?"

"Yes, she lives alone."

"That's even better. Let's use her phone."

"What do I tell Fernando?"

"Tell him nothing other than you need to use his mother's private line every Sunday at 6:00 P.M."

"He'll want to know why…. how do I explain this to him?" "

Just say that you're worried about competitors tapping into your phones. Tell him there are confidential conversations going on with international investors looking to buy an interest in The Dynamic Shoe. Make sure to tell him you're giving his mother a chance to make a hundred dollars every time you use her phone. They'll go along. If they balk, offer them more money." 0

"How should I send you the cash, Ronnie?"

"Like I said, wrap the cash in a newspaper and then put it in a big envelope. Fed Ex it to me. Make sure that you don't always go to the same office. Mix it up."

"Are you ever planning to come back?"

"Maybe someday. I really don't know."

"You mean I might never see you again?"

"No, of course not. We have to cash out little by little. Then, you can come and stay with me wherever I am. I'll let you know where I'm settled when the time is right. Don't fail me, Clara. Remember, not a word to anyone about our arrangements, and that includes Fernando."

"I'll remember."

"Now call Fernando and get me his mother's number. I'll call you Sunday, at 6:00 P.M."

Ronnie embraced Clara once their business was concluded. She left after kissing her friend's cheek.

Once Ronnie was gone, Clara found herself in charge of the Frantellini Shoe Factory, the real estate holdings and access to more money than she ever imagined possible.

37

Clara Gets A Gift

WITH TIME TO SPARE, before having to meet with Ronnie Frantellini by Bryant Park, the detectives decided to take Crippler for something to eat. They had their meal at a bar restaurant off Avenue of the Americas. The detectives couldn't get over how fast the cooperator ate his meal. After devouring a burger and fries, Crippler announced that he was still hungry. He asked for another burger.

"Another burger?" Markie asked with surprise. The sergeant had only eaten half of his BLT at this point.

"I'm a growing boy," replied the wrestler.

"You'll get a belly ache," said Markie, trying to avoid adding to the tab.

"Not a chance."

Markie signaled the waitress. Another burger with fries was ordered. "How about you, Ollie?"

"I'll just have more coffee, Sarge."

"How about letting me have a cold beer?" asked Crippler, pressing the envelope. The waitress stood by waiting for a decision to be rendered on the beer. Von Hess looked at the sergeant, who would have to make the call. Markie surprisingly agreed.

"Okay, bring him beer," said Markie, addressing the waitress.

"Budweiser," voiced Crippler.

The beverage came at the same time Detective Silverlake from headquarters arrived at the eatery.

Silverlake, who was no stranger to hoisting a few in the office with Chief McCoy, looked at Markie in a wanting way. "Is a beer in order, Sarge?" he asked.

"This isn't a party, Silvie," reminded Markie. "We're here on business." Silverlake offered no reply. The look of disappointment on his face said it all. After a moment Markie loosened up. "Ah, what the hell," he said, calling over the waitress. "Four beers," he ordered.

"Make mine Coke," said Von Hess, canceling his beer.

When the time came to head to Bryant Park, Crippler had grown accustomed to being in the company of the detectives. He had spent enough casual time with them to almost feel as if he were a peer. This was not an unusual development. Familiarity often went far in removing barriers that exist between a law enforcement officer and a criminal.

Crippler stood alone at the southeast corner of 42nd Street and Avenue of the Americas waiting for the arrival of Ronnie Frantellini. Silverlake was positioned about five yards away. Markie and Von Hess eyeballed Crippler from within the confines of Bryant Park.

After forty-five minutes of waiting, it became clear that Ronnie Frantellini wasn't keeping her appointment with Crippler. Efforts to telephonically contact Ronnie proved negative. While no one knew for sure, all could only conjecture as to what might have gone wrong.

"Do you think that she could have spotted us, Ollie?" asked Markie.

"I doubt it, Sarge," replied Von Hess. "This an active location with lots of people coming and going. We don't stand out. Maybe there was a miscommunication as to where to meet."

"No way," piped up Crippler. "She picked the corner. She must have smelled a rat and took off."

"What now, Sarge?" Silverlake asked,

"We go look for her," answered Markie.

"What about me?" Crippler asked.

"You go back in stir."

***

THE DETECTIVES SPENT SEVERAL DAYS discreetly trying to locate the whereabouts of Ronnie Frantellini. They monitored her place of business and residence to no avail.

Finally, the frustrated investigators gave up. Markie conceded that Ronnie was in the wind.

"Let's go rattle some cages, Ollie," said the sergeant.

Markie and Von Hess entered the Frantellini Shoe Factory and asked a worker where they could find the person in charge. They were directed to the office of Ronnie Frantellini, which was now being occupied by Clara Calhoun, the former secretary of attorney Thomas Beasley.

"Can I help you?" asked Clara when the detectives appeared at the entranceway to the office.

"Detectives," announced Von Hess, displaying his gold shield.

"What can I do for you?" Clara calmly asked. She anticipated the visit.

"We're looking for Ronnie Frantellini."

"She is not here."

"Where is she?" "

"She's traveling."

"Traveling where?" Markie asked.

"She didn't say where she was going."

"Well, that's kind of unusual, isn't it?"

"Not really."

"When is she scheduled to be coming back?"

"She didn't say."

"Get her on the telephone," said Markie abruptly, losing patience.

"I'm sorry, but I have no way of getting in touch with her."

"Wait a minute," said Von Hess, "are you saying that she left her business without leaving a number?"

"I'm sorry, but that's the way she wanted it. I don't even know if she took her cell phone with her."

"So, who is running things over here?"

"I am," answered Clara.

"And who might you be?" Markie asked. "Clara Calhoun."

"And you got no idea where she went?"

"None," replied Clara. "All she told me was that she'd call me at some point."

"What are you supposed to do in an emergency?"

"Handle it. Ms. Frantellini gave me full authority to address any issue," replied Clara, sounding proud.

"So, if this joint burns down, you can't get hold of her?"

"That's right, Sergeant. That's the way Ms. Frantellini wanted it."

"And you didn't find this to be odd?"

"I'm not paid to question my boss, Sergeant."

"She must have great faith in you," said Markie, with a trace of sarcasm.

At this juncture it was clear to the investigators that Ronnie had absconded. Before leaving the factory Markie asked Clara to notify him whenever she heard from Ronnie. It was a request that the sergeant had no expectation of being complied with.

Once they were alone in their vehicle, the sergeant instructed Von Hess that the time had come to put out a wanted card for Ronnie Frantellini.

"There is little else we can we do, Sarge," commented Von Hess. "It's a sure bet that Clara knows more than she's telling us."

"No question, Ollie. We'll have to chill out until the warrant pops or Frantellini decides to come back."

"How about we spend a little time surveilling this Clara. Ronnie Frantellini could be holed up right here in the city under our noses. If that's the case, Clara might lead us to her."

"That's an idea, Ollie," agreed Markie. "Dollars to donuts, Ronnie has to be talking to her. And she has to be drawing money from the business."

"Do you want me to reach out to a contact in the phone company?"

"No, not yet. Let's give it a week or so before we do anything. After that, I want you to ring Clara up. Ask her if she heard from Ronnie. When she tells you she hasn't, you tell her that she needn't bother to call us even if Ronnie returned. Say that the case we needed to talk to Ronnie about fell through and that we have no need to see her. Once Ronnie gets wind of that, she might show her face."

"That's an old trick that worked before for us," noted Von Hess.

"Let's hope it'll work again, Ollie."

Markie then telephoned his office to post Lieutenant Wright and Chief of Detectives Harry McCoy accordingly. The Chief, after hanging up with Markie, telephoned Father Fiorello St. Denis as a courtesy. The department chaplain was informed as to where they stood. Father St. Denis agreed to notify the chief in the event he learned of the whereabouts of Ronnie Frantellini.

38

Easy Money

FERNANDO'S MOTHER, ESPERANZA, WAS A GOD-FEARING widow of modest means. At sixty-eight she traveled about with unusual peppiness. Her positive attitude and congeniality made her popular with all people she came into contact with.

Esperanza earned a few dollars off the books by sewing. Her clientele consisted of neighborhood residents who were aware of her ability with a sewing machine. This revenue supplemented the small monthly pension check she received thanks to her late husband, who had been a city employee.

Esperanza resided alone in a tidy two-bedroom apartment in a public housing project on Avenue D. When not sewing she kept busy by regularly volunteering at her church. She helped feed the homeless, participated in clothing drives and ran errands for those lacking the mobility to do for themselves.

Unfortunately, Esperanza's fine traits did not rub off on her son Fernando. When it came to integrity, Fernado was asleep at the wheel. He was the sort who would put slugs in the collection basket at Sunday Mass.

Fernando, an only child, lived in a small studio apartment a few blocks away from his mother. His living close was reassuring to his mother. The widow, who was in the dark as to her son's true character, had just one concern. This worry had to do with Fernando not being married. She prayed regularly for Fernando to meet his soulmate. Her prayers were so intense that she wore the shine off her black rosary beads.

The questionable ways of the street proved to have a greater influence on Fernando than his righteous mother. Esperanza's son developed into a self-centered opportunist. When it came to work, Fernando found driving a taxi to be the least intrusive form of employment. The one thing he liked about driving a cab was that he was pretty much his own boss. The occupation also afforded him the luxury of working where and when he wanted to.

Fernando never missed the opportunity to take advantage of naïve passengers. Particularly vulnerable were women drawn to Fernando's rugged handsomeness. Many inadvertently revealed their interest by commenting on the strong resemblance Fernando had to the actor Anthony Quinn. Hearing this compliment delighted Fernando. It meant that he had another woman to potentially sponge off.

The smooth-talking Fernando had little trouble adding Clara Calhoun to his scorecard. At first Clara was merely an attractive tryst who was good for sex, clothes and a free meal. This changed in scope once Clara made it known that she ruled over the Frantellini Shoe Factory and real estate holdings.

Recognizing a good thing, Fernando began devoting all of his attention to Clara, who was now suddenly marriage material. This delighted Fernando's mother, who believed that her prayers had been answered.

At Fernando's urging, Clara put him on the Frantellini payroll. The position she created for him came with an impressive title and salary. This appointment somewhat concerned Ronnie Frantellini, who had little choice other than to approve the hire telephonically. Ronnie knew that she was in no position to deny Clara anything. The only stipulation insisted on by Ronnie was that Fernando was to remain in the shade as to her whereabouts and the arrangement between the two women. This understanding later proved to be overly ambitious. Fernando informed his mother that she would receive cash every time her telephone was used on Sunday. Such good fortune Esperanza could hardly object to.

Fernando never let on that he was pocketing half the money that Clara gave him for his mother. Fernando would accompany Clara to his mother's apartment to receive the pre-arranged telephone calls from Ronnie Frantellini. At first, Clara stood by her promise to never discuss the content of her telephonic weekly conversations. Fernando, not buying the cover story he was told, felt the need to get to the bottom of all the mystery.

Since the only telephone in the apartment was located in the kitchen, Fernando and his mother had to wait in another room until the call that came in for Clara was completed. Clara's speaking in a low voice made efforts by Fernando to listen from afar unproductive.

However, on one occasion he was able to hear Clara address the caller as Ronnie. Not one to remain uninformed, Fernando picked up a small recording device at Radio Shack. He then planted the recorder in the kitchen where it couldn't be seen by Clara. Although limited to capturing just one side of the conversation, the cabdriver gathered enough to want to know more about the arrangement between Clara and Ronnie.

The information gathered by Fernando via the tape recorder came in sections. The first eye opener for Fernando arrived when he learned of the amount of money Clara was sending to Ronnie. Another revelation surfaced when he gathered that Clara was in Sligo. Fernando was at a loss as to where Sligo was. He had to ask several people before finding out that Sligo was in Ireland.

Realizing the amount of money that was now within his reach, Fernando ratcheted up his selfish campaign to lure Clara to the altar. His ardent attention was unwavering. This, coupled with his virtuosity between the sheets went far in removing whatever hesitation Clara may have had.

Blinded by love, Clara consented to Fernando's marriage proposal. Once captured emotionally, Clara was putty in the hands of Fernando. She provided her new husband with all the details of her arrangement with Ronnie. Fernando was staggered as he began to consider the possibilities that were now before him.

The new husband, who had been functioning as the security manager of both the Frantellini factory and properties, now saw far beyond what he was currently doing.

The former cabdriver grew outrageously ambitious. He began absorbing all he could about the workings of the Frantellini businesses. Snooping around offices after hours proved informative. He was particularly impressed by the potential connected to Victor Spinello's Dynamic Shoe, which was nearing completion.

Fernando's diabolical side peaked over dinner one evening when Clara mentioned that she stood to inherit the Frantellini motherlode in the event of Ronnie's death. This information caused Fernando to sit straight up in his seat. He then began to have dark thoughts.

Why wait? Fernando thought. That bitch over in Ireland could live for another fifty years!

"Is everything alright?" Clara asked, taken aback by Fernando's gazing off someplace other than where they were. "Fernando?"

"Oh, I'm sorry, Clara. I was just thinking."

"Of what?"

"Of how life brought us together. Isn't it wonderful?"

"Yes," answered Clara. "I've never been so happy. I only wish I could tell Ronnie that we married."

This revelation was something Fernando was adamantly against. He didn't want anything to upset what he thought was a great situation. His greatest fear was Clara being sidelined by Ronnie.

"We already discussed that, Clara," said Fernando. "Ronnie would never approve of me. She'd think you could have done better. Let me prove myself before you fill her in."

Clara went along with Victor's wishes. She voiced no objection to the gifts Fernando afforded himself. The new car, the clothes and fancy jewelry were all just fine with her. Clara's acquiescence was practically assured as long as Fernando continued to behave like the perfect husband. That, and his ongoing efficiency in bed, protected his position.

Their marriage came with enough pocket money for Fernando to take care of his mother. Buying Esperanza a new stove, refrigerator and furniture eased his conscience. Fernando even sprung for a new sewing machine for the old lady.

Fernando eventually began considering the feasibility of making a big move. It was one bold enough that, if successful, it would net him control of the Frantellini empire. But first, he needed to gain insights into Victor Spinello, the genius behind The Dynamic Shoe. Fernando's familiarity with Victor alleviated any concern he might have had. Fernando accurately sized up Victor for what he was, a workhorse genius lacking the strength to create waves.

The fact that Victor had once murdered made little impression on Fernando. He recognized that geniuses, like artists, were apt to be emotional characters capable of going off at any given moment.

Fernando's strategy called for keeping Victor content by not interfering with his creative juices. Once Fernando became more acclimated to the operation of the shoe factory and real estate business his entrepreneurial side began to take shape. Seeing a way to build upon these enterprises, he contacted a family member who resided in Spain. Fernando and the family member, who was an attorney, explored the feasibility of forming an import/export entity that would complement the Frantellini Shoe factory. The lawyer also proposed they then consider selling and/or leasing Frantellini properties to high-net-worth Spanish investors he was acquainted with.

The only fly in the ointment when it came to these initiatives was Ronnie Frantellini. Fernando suggested to Clara that she pitch these concepts to her mentor. This wasn't received well. It didn't take long for Fernando to realize that his wife didn't have it in her to pitch horseshoes, let alone a business deal to the woman who did so much for her.

Clara tried to explain to Fernando that Ronnie would perceive such an overture as overstepping. When Fernando voiced otherwise,

Clara vehemently fired back. She conveyed that her mentor would see such a proposal as an attempt to take advantage of her in her absence.

Fernando, driven by greed, knew the time had finally come to embark on the vile path he had been thinking of. He planned to permanently remove Ronnie Frantellini from the equation.

Fernando was the sort of man who could justify anything. He likened Ronnie's death as some kind of public service that would be of societal benefit. Fernando saw murdering Ronnie as doing his wife a big favor. After all, thought Fernando, once Ronnie is out of the way, Clara comes into the works. She'll thank me later....that is, if she ever finds out.

Fernando had no doubt that if he could keep Clara and Victor Spinello happy, they'd let him do whatever he wanted when it came to business. This included directing the future of the Frantellini Shoe Factory and the real estate assets. If Fernando could ascertain where the packages of money were being sent to Ronnie, he knew that he'd be able to figure out where Ronnie was harbored in Sligo. All he needed to do was get his wife to reveal to him the most recent mailing location. Fernando's ability to influence Clara made this doable.

39

Guinness On Air Lingus

FERNANDO FOUND THE MAN HE WAS looking for hanging out with a group of men on the southwest corner of East 9th Street and Avene D in lower Manhattan. The two shared a history that dated back to their teenage years.

Back then they were close friends who spent four evenings a week playing basketball at a local high school. Engaging in halfcourt roundball provided a diversion that kept them out of trouble most weeknights. However, exceptions did exist. Friday evenings in particular offered temptations to engage in mischief.

After several hours of basketball on weekday evenings the two boys always found themselves hungry.

Fridays, with no school causing them to rise early the following day, they washed down their food with beer purchased at an agreeable bodega.

When short on money the youths concocted foul schemes to finance their wants. Fernando and Luis got comfortable committing

Friday evening knifepoint robberies after basketball. All was going well until they underestimated an elderly woman walking on a dark street who they believed to be an easy mark.

The woman, frail in appearance, dropped her handbag to the ground when accosted. This wasn't out of nervous clumsiness. The bag was dropped in a deliberate attempt to thwart the robbery. Luis, who held the knife, made the mistake of watching Fernando bend down to pick up the handbag. The spunky victim, seeing her chance, quickly reached into the pocket of her brown overcoat for the canister of pepper spray that had been given to her by husband for self-protection.

Two squirts of the inflammatory agent to the face of the distracted Luis neutralized him. Temporarily blinded, Luis fiercely began rubbing his eyes. The crime victim then turned to give Fernando his dose of pepper spray. However, with Fernando, the woman was too slow on the draw. He had already fled the scene, leaving his friend Luis to stagger about blindly.

The incapacitated Luis was subsequently arrested by the local police patrolling the area. Since his victim was a senior citizen, Luis was treated harshly by the courts and received a stiff sentence. When released from prison Luis was hard pressed to find work.

Thanks to connections he made in jail, Luis turned to selling heroin on a street corner for economic relief. His clientele consisted of junkies visiting his corner to cop smack. Luis was on the job when approached by Fernando, who he hadn't seen in years. Despite the passing of time, their reunion was a cordial one.

"Hey, look who it is," said Luis, upon seeing his old crime partner. "How you doing, man? It's been a long time."

"I've been looking for you," said Fernando.

"You been looking for me?"

"You're not pissed off at me are you, Luis? I mean, I had to book that night you got busted or get busted myself."

"Nah, I understand, man. I'd have probably done the same thing."

"You're looking good, Luis."

"I know how to take care of myself," stated Luis with confidence. "Somebody said you've been driving a cab. You don't look like no cabdriver."

"I stopped doing that shit after getting married. I got it good now."

"I can see, look at you," said Luis, eyeballing Ferando's apparel.

"Thems nice threads, man. And look at that car! That's yours?"

"Yeah, it's mine. Look, I'm here because I need a favor, Luis.

"You looking to cop some shit?"

"Nah, nothing like that."

"So, what favor can I do for you? It looks like you got it better than me, man."

"Let's talk business, Luis." Fernando then handed his friend two crisp one-hundred-dollar bills. "If you can help me out there is more where this came from."

"I don't do no violence," advised the drug dealer. "I just push H. I'm clean, I don't even chip, man."

"It's nothing like that. I need a passport, driver's license, you know legit identification to borrow for about a week."

"I don't think I know anybody who will give up that kind of shit easy, Fernando."

"And the guy has to look something like me."

"You know, man, you do look a little like my cousin."

"Does he have a passport?"

"Definitely. He works in a hospital. He takes his wife on a big vacation every year. They have no kids and she works, so they've been all over. If you take good care of him, maybe he'd be willing to do it."

"That's perfect. How much do you think he'll want?"

"I have to talk to him. But he's going to ask me what you need his shit for."

"Tell him it'll only be used to get me someplace overseas. When I return he can have his stuff back."

"What happens to him if you get in trouble over there?"

"He can report his stuff stolen or lost. That'll cover him with the cops if something goes wrong."

As it turned out the drug dealer's cousin wanted no part of renting out his passport and identification for any amount of money. Although this was a setback, Fernando was not one to be discouraged. The reward at the end of the rainbow was too tempting not to take a chance. He'd travel under his own name.

***

FERNANDO PROMISED CLARA that he would call her the minute the plane landed. Fernando's wife was under the impression that her husband was visiting relatives in Barcellona, Spain. Fernando's deception had everything to do with his plan to dispose of Ronnie Frantellini in Ireland.

Not a big fan of flying, Fernando ordered a Guiness when a stewardess came around to take his order. Soon after he switched to Irish whiskey. Once the edge was off he put on headphones, closed his eyes and began listening to music. As Fernando relaxed he began thinking of the money he'd have access to once Ronnie was gone. With the benefits connected to his evilness in mind, he eventually dozed off smiling happily. When he awakened, Fernando began leafing through a tourist magazine one usually finds on an airplane. During his browsing he came to learn that Sligo was a big attraction destination for those wanting to surf the wild Atlantic. This caused Fernando to remember that Ronnie's money was being mailed to the Sligo Atlantic Surf House, a small ocean resort in Sligo. If she's there, thought Fernando, maybe I can figure out a way to drown her."

Fernando's flight into Shannon Airport in County Clare was a smooth one. Feeling relieved after landing safely, he hired a car to take him to Sligo. He recruited the driver to assist him in finding a suitable bed and breakfast. Using the alias of Fred Ricardo, Fernando secured lodging in a private home owned by a middle-aged couple who welcomed him warmly.

Since Fernando paid the homeowner cash in advance, there was no need for verifying his identity. The cover story Fernando invented was a plausible one. Claiming that he worked for a production company, he indicated that he'd be staying in Sligo for about a week. The American explained that he was there to examine the landscape for an upcoming movie that was in the planning stages. The couple never doubted Fernando's fabrication.

The sole question the elderly couple posed had to do with transportation. Realizing the renter would need transportation to get around, they offered to provide Fernando with access to their second car for a reasonable fee. A financial agreement was soon reached.

Fortunately, Fernando knew how to drive a stick shift. He found that operating a 1981 Ford Escort with a steering wheel in the right side of the car took some getting used to. Shifting gears with his left hand was also something of a challenge. However, the future assassin adapted without incident.

***

OF ALL HER TRAVELS IN IRELAND, Ronnie Frantellini found Sligo to be most to her liking. A large city such as Dublin was tempting from a social standpoint. However, Ronnie wasn't taking any chances. Acting prudently, she decided to remain low key for a couple of years, tucking herself away in a country setting. Having Clara handling things in New York, she was able to sleep easily. Ronnie's intent was to wait until things settled before considering any return to the United States.

Ronnie took residence in the Sligo Atlantic Surf House. The first two nights spent at the small hotel on the Atlantic Ocean were eerie. This was because the hotel owner, an Englishman named Henry, was a peculiar man in both appearance and demeanor. His forehead was broad, his teeth yellowish and his eyes penetrating. He spoke while displaying a crooked smile that made him seem quite untrustworthy.

Adding to the mystery of Henry was his being the only person working at the site. Henry, acting alone, prepared breakfast, lunch and dinner in the main dining room. In the evening, he served as the hotel bartender for guests residing at his establishment. Although Henry made no inappropriate overtures, after a couple of cocktails Ronnie began to think that she was in some kind of an Alfred Hitchcock movie. To offset her uneasiness, she slept with a steak knife she stole from the kitchen under her pillow.

Things improved with the arrival of additional hotel guests. Hotel staff suddenly began appearing and the owner was now only seen in the bar area during the evening hours. Henry seemed less intimidating to Ronnie as she watched him mingle with the other hotel guests. It was at the bar that Ronnie came to meet Sean O'Flaherty. A handsome six-footer, O'Flaherty served as the hotel entertainment director. Now that's someone I could go for, thought Ronnie, as she began smiling shamelessly at the good-looking blond-haired hunk of man. Her friendliness received a return smile.

Once learning that Ronnie was staying at the hotel alone, O'Flaherty made it a point to convey his availability. As far as Ronnie was concerned, Sean O'Flaherty was a rental item who would meet her companionship needs while stranded in the country.

At the urging of her new friend, Ronnie tried her hand at surfing. O'Flaherty assured the hotel guest that he could teach Ronnie all she would need to know to tackle the recreation.

Since Ronnie was a good swimmer, she decided to give surfing a whirl. Attired in wetsuits, the pair ventured playfully into the briny. Before long, the two were together whenever possible.

The romance that blossomed became something of an item at the hotel. This was met without argument from the hotel owner. Henry loved the security of having a full-time hotel resident who promptly paid in cash. To him, it made no sense to judge the morality of a cash cow.

The combination of daytime fun, evening dinners and cocktails, capped off by torrid romantic interludes left Ronnie in no hurry to move out of the Sligo Atlantic Surf House.

***

FERNANDO'S SEARCH for Ronnie soon led him to where she was residing. With the aid of binoculars, he was able to spot Ronnie with her blond-haired boytoy on the beach from afar. At this point it was only a question of Fernando shadowing Ronnie until the opportunity arose to assassinate her.

Fernando's surveillance led him to notice that Ronnie carried her handbag wherever she went. He also gathered that she took drives with the blond-haired man in his beat-up 1974 white MGB convertible. The existence of a romantic connection was clearly obvious.

Fernando's chance finally came when he observed Ronnie venture off alone on a Sunday morning. Sean O'Flaherty, who had promised to take Ronnie on a hike, backed out of their planned day trip at the last minute due to inclement weather. The two had intended to go to Slieve League Cliffs, also known as Sliabh Liag, Ireland's Majestic Sea Cliffs Rising. The location in question was almost 2,000 feet above the Atlantic Ocean, making it one of the highest sea cliffs in Europe.

Not one to tolerate disappointment, Ronnie decided to venture outdoors unescorted in the rain. She walked to the Glen Horseshoe area near Benbulbin. Unbeknownst to Ronnie, she was being followed by Fernando, who remained behind her at a safe distance.

Ronnie proceeded to a dangerous area without realizing that steep climbs and slippery terrain were ahead. Fernando was vigilant to the conduciveness of his surroundings. With no one else on the trail, he saw this as the perfect venue for murder. Fortuitously for Fernando, Ronnie paused to take a breather at a site known for tragic falls. She stood at the edge of the cliff and inhaled deeply to invigorate herself. Ronnie placed her handbag and umbrella on the ground so that she could stretch her arms out to fully embrace the dampness.

Fernando, from his vantage point, was able to see that a fall off the cliff would be unquestionably fatal. He set upon his victim from the rear and unleashed a two-handed shove. Ronnie never saw her doom coming. Fernando then kicked her umbrella off the cliff. He was about to do the same with the handbag, when an idea suddenly came to him. I could use this, he thought.

Fernando took the handbag and secreted it under his coat. He then made his way back to the Sligo Atlantic Surf House in search of Sean's MGB convertible. Finding the car door open and no one around, he dropped the handbag onto the passenger floorboard.

Fernando then returned to where he was staying. Upon arrival he advised the landlord that his work was completed. He then inquired if the husband would be willing to drive him to the airport in Shannon.

"That's a three-hour drive," said the wife.

"I'm more than willing to compensate your husband for his trouble," said Fernando, producing his bankroll.

"Why, sure it'd be no trouble at all," said the husband upon seeing the money. "What else have I got to do? When do you want to head out?"

"I'd like to go as soon as possible."

"Well then you go pack. While you do that my wife will prepare us a sandwich for the road."

"Great," said Fernando. "How much do I owe you for the ride?"

"See my wife about that. I'll go gas up the car."

On the drive to the airport Fernando thought of the murder he perpetrated. Satisfied that he committed a perfect crime, he was in high spirits.

Let the pretty boy try and explain what Ronnie's bag was doing in his car, thought Fernando. Fernando was safely back in New York City by the time Ronnie Frantellini's body was discovered. The authorities in Ireland had conducted a search for Ronnie after Sean O'Flaherty turned in the purse he found in his car. As a result, the law overseas focused their initial attention on O'Flaherty. This was playing out just as Fernando figured.

40

News Travels Fast

THE IRISH AUTHORITIES found Clara's contact information in Ronnie's purse. With the intent of notifying a next of kin, they telephoned Clara at the shoe factory. Clara was devastated when informed that Ronnie was dead. The shocking news was met with a high-pitched wail that carried far beyond Clara's office.

Victor Spinello, who was in the next office came running to investigate the cause of the alarming screech. Seeing the distraught Clara caused him to enter her office to determine what was wrong.

"Ronnie's dead!" Clara shouted upon seeing Victor.

"Oh, no!"

"I've lost my best friend," lamented the weeping Clara, opening her arms to Victor as would a sobbing child seeking comfort from a parent.

"What happened?" asked Victor, taking Clara to him. He began to pat her back as he tightened his squeeze. After a minute or two of weeping, Clara regained her composure.

"Victor, please go and get Fernando," she said.

When Fernando arrived in his wife's office he pretended to be shocked by the news. He immediately placed his arms around his wife to soothe her pain. Fernando, expressing no emotion, looked over Clara's shoulder at Victor as he comforted his spouse.

"Give us a few minutes alone," said Fernando, dismissing Victor.

"No one ever treated me better than Ronnie did, Fernando," conveyed Clara sadly.

"I know. She even remembered you in her will, right?"

"Yes, Fernando. She left me everything. And I never expected anything from her."

"I know you didn't. Don't worry, we'll make it all work," said Fernando confidently. "Ronnie would want us to carry on." As he conveyed this Fernando's eyes were raised toward the ceiling. A look of satisfaction was evident by the crooked smile on his face.

The Frantellini empire is as good as mine, he thought. Once the emotions subsided Fernando wasted no time taking charge. He went through Ronnie's office, and then her penthouse apartment, with a fine-tooth comb. During his search he came across the number of Father Fiorello St. Denis. He telephoned the priest, seeking his help in making the arrangements for Ronnie.

Father was alone in his office at the rectory going through his calendar when his phone rang. The priest could tell that there was something wrong by the somberness in the caller's voice. "Father, my name is Fernando. I work at the Frantellini Shoe Factory. My wife is...."

"I know who you are," said the priest, who kept abreast of things pertaining to the Frantellini family.

"You do?"

"I've been a close friend of the Frantellini family for many years. Is everything alright?"

"Ronnie Frantelli was found dead in Ireland. I found your number among her things."

"Oh, my God!" St. Denis blurted, finding it unbelievable that another Frantellini related tragedy came about.

"How did she die? What were the circumstances?"

"I know little, Father," replied Fernando. "I didn't know who else to call."

"You did the right thing calling me. Please tell me what you know."

Fernando's account lacked many details. The priest asked for the identity and telephone number of the authority overseas who notified Clara of Ronnie's death.

"I'll call Ireland and circle back to you, Fernando," advised the priest.

Father Sr. Denis learned that Ronnie's death was still under investigation in Ireland. He further learned that Ronnie's purse was found in a male friend's vehicle. This made the man a person of interest in the investigation into whether or not Ronnie's death was accidental, an act of suicide or the result of foul play.

After getting off the phone with Ireland, St. Denis contacted Fernando apprising him accordingly. He reminded Clara's husband that Ronnie remains would have to be shipped back to New York City. He offered to assist in making the necessary arrangements.

"Thank you, Father, we'd appreciate that," advised Fernando.

"Can you perform the Mass?"

"Of course," replied the priest. What are you going to do about the funeral arrangements?"

"Do you have someone?"

"Yes, of course. I'll take care of everything. How is your wife doing?" "Not very well. My wife and Ronnie were very close."

"I see. I can talk to her if you like."

"It might not be a bad idea to spend time with her, Father."

"I'm on my way."

When St. Denis arrived at the shoe factory he found Clara alone in her office. Their conversation was informative. Father learned that Clara never told Ronnie that she married Fernando. Father St. Denis found this to be quite odd.

"Why the big secret?"

"Well, Father, Ronnie was my best friend. She was protective of me. She didn't exactly see Fernando as marriage material."

"I suppose she thought you could do better."

"I suppose, Father. I owed so much to Ronnie that I just couldn't go against her on anything."

"What does your husband do?"

"He works for the company."

The priest found this interesting. "Ronnie hired him?"

"Not exactly, I hired him," Clara replied, quickly adding, "but Ronnie approved it."

"I see, how is that working out?"

"Very well. Fernando is ambitious and has taken a real interest in both businesses."

"Has he a background in business?"

"No, actually he has no formal education. He was a cabdriver when we met. But he's a fast learner."

Father St. Denis grew more curious with every new fact being conveyed to him. His questions, carefully posed, continued.

"What was Ronnie doing in Ireland anyway?" asked the priest, fishing for information. "Vacationing?"

"That's a long story Father. All I can tell you is that Ronnie had some kind of trouble that involved the police."

"In Ireland?"

"No, here in New York City."

"What kind of trouble?"

"She never shared that with me. But it must have been something serious because she left me in charge of everything," advised Clara, adding, "she gave me full authority to run the businesses in her absence."

"When did she plan on coming home?"

"She had no definite plans to return. We spoke weekly and I'd send her whatever money she needed."

"And you had no idea what her trouble was?"

"Not a clue, Father. All I was told was that she was being wrongly accused of something."

This information inflated the priest's suspicions. "So, I wonder what happens to the business now?"

"According to the will she prepared before she left, I'm to inherit all she had."

"Everything?"

"Yes, Father, everything. The shoe factory, the real estate and everything else she had."

"What about Victor Spinello? I believe he has an interest in the shoe factory."

"Victor does have some equity in the Frantellini Shoe Factory. That won't change."

"Do you need help with all that's on your plate?"

"No, Father, I'll be okay. Thank God for Fernando, without him I don't know what I'd do."

The priest could only express himself with a nod.

The following day the police department chaplain went to Police Headquarters to meet with his friend, Chief Harry McCoy. The priest conveyed what he had learned concerning the death of Ronnie Frantellini. He also communicated his suspicions.

"This is very interesting," commented the chief, who agreed that there might be foul play behind the death of Ronnie Frantellini. At this point he called Markie, Von Hess and Lieutenant Wright into his office. After conveying the facts, the chief instructed his detectives to look into the matter. "See what you boys make of all this," said the chief.

"Do you know the name of Clara's husband, Father?" Markie asked. "I only know his first name, Sergeant. It's Fernando. I can get it for you."

"Thanks, Father. That'll be helpful in our getting a line on him," said Markie.

***

FATHER FIORELLO ST. DENIS, at the request of Clara's husband, performed an abbreviated funeral Mass for Ronnie Frantellini. The service drew few people to the church. The scant number of people present in the house of worship was a sad reminder to the priest that the ranks of the faithful were dwindling. More accurately, the poor turnout could be attributed to Ronnie having no family or friends other than Clara.

Smiley Allen, who had read Ronnie's obituary in the newspaper, decided that it was in his interest to stay away. Out of sight out of mind, he thought, thinking the funeral might be attended by members of law enforcement.

After the service a party of four went for lunch at a nearby restaurant. Present at the table was the priest, Clara, her husband Fernando and Victor Spinello.

Father St. Denis had a bad feeling about Fernando. He sensed that Clara's husband exerted a controlling influence on his wife. Furthering his negative opinion of Fernando was the way Clara's husband passed him a gratuity for performing the Mass. It was done in a very indiscreet way which the priest interpreted as Fernando playing the big shot.

After the pre-lunch cocktails were served, Fernando stood up at the table and raised his drink to toast the deceased.

"Here is to Ronnie Frantellini," announced Fernando, "a very generous woman. May she rest in peace." He then happily sipped of his libation.

A very generous woman indeed, thought Father St. Denis, who pondered the words. His opinion of Clara's husband sank further once Fernando asked the priest to give everyone at the table a general absolution. *What does he need to be forgiven for*, wondered the suspicious priest.

"What do you say about that, Father?" Fernando asked loudly. "Are you going to cleanse us from our sins?"

"I'm afraid that this doesn't fit the criteria necessary for a general absolution," answered the priest politely.

"But you could do it if you wanted to, right?"

Fernando persisted because he believed in heaven and hell. He wanted to rid himself of having to answer for the murder he committed when it was his time for reckoning.

"I do have the authority."

"That's what I thought. So why not do us all a solid."

"I'm sorry, Fernando, but unfortunately the answer is no."

Fernando's reaction to being told no was revealing. His annoyance was made obvious by the snarl on his face. Father St. Denis interpreted Fernando's look as pure evil. The priest saw Clara's husband as someone to be wary of. Father feared that the unwitting Clara, and Victor Spinello, were both destined for future trouble.

After the lunch Fernando approached Father St. Denis from a different angle. Hellbent on receiving his general absolution, he asked the priest what he could do for the benefit of the church. While the priest's dislike of Fernando was unyielding, he didn't allow his personal feelings to stand in the way of improving the parish house of worship.

"Our church is in need of some improvement," said Father St. Denis.

"Such as?"

"We could use a bathroom installed in the back of the church. Many of our parishioners are elderly and often in need of access to such a facility."

"How much will it cost for a new bathroom, Father?" asked Fernando.

After the priest conveyed the number Fernando reached into his pocket for his checkbook. The ability of Fernando to cut such a sizable check on the spot was astounding to St. Denis. *He already has seized great authority*, thought the priest.

Before handing the check over to St. Denis he posed one question. "Now how about that general absolution, Father? I think this entitles me to it."

The priest's smile came with a grimness after hearing the request.

"Why don't I just hear your confession?" St. Denis asked.

"I don't think we need to go through all that when you can just give me what I'm asking for," replied Fernando.

Something terrible must be weighing heavily on his conscience, thought Father St. Denis. *Something that he's afraid to confess.*

"You know, Fernando," said Father St. Denis, "a general absolution is only used to grant forgiveness of sins to a group of people simultaneously. It's done without confessions and restricted to situations of grave necessity," explained the priest.

"I'd call churchgoers needing to avoid pissing in their pants a grave necessity, wouldn't you, Father? Do you really want to deny them a restroom?"

"Of course not," was the only reply to the question that the priest could offer. At this point the man of the cloth recognized who really benefitted from the death of Ronnie Frantellini.

Father St. Denis gave Fernando his general absolution. The priest did so with his fingers crossed.

***

OVER COFFEE IN HIS OFFICE CHIEF OF DETECTIVES HARRY MCCOY and his detectives listened to the department chaplain's Frantellini update. The suspicions aired by the priest couldn't be discounted.

"How about you, Sarge, did you turn up any information?" McCoy asked.

"Some, Chief," answered Markie. "We spoke to the authorities in Ireland. Ronnie was last seen by the owner of the hotel where she was staying. He said she was taking a hike in the rain. He recollected her carrying an umbrella and a handbag at the time. "

"That's it?"

"That handbag turned up in the car of a hotel employee she took up with."

"It was definitely the same handbag?"

"Yes, the hotel owner identified the handbag. It was the same one."

"So, they probably got their man if there was foul play, right?"

"Not exactly, Chief. The Garda I spoke to indicated that the boyfriend turned in the handbag to the law himself. He was the guy who reported Ronnie missing. Would a guilty man do that?"

"He could be clever, couldn't he?"

"He could, Chief."

"What did they establish as the cause of death?"

"Ronnie went off a cliff. The weather definitely made the footing slippery, so it's possible that she accidently fell to her death."

"Did they grill the boyfriend?"

"They did. Apparently he was credible. Without evidence ,they're leaning toward an accidental death."

"So that's it then."

"I don't know, Chief. There are aspects complicating all this. Clara Calhoun is the secretary who once worked for Thomas Beasley. He's the lawyer we flipped. Beasley represented the Frantellini business interests. Beasley arranged for the juror in the Victor Spinello murder trial to be bribed."

"Hold up, Al," interrupted McCoy, who was confused. "Go slow. Tell me who these people are again."

"They're all intertwined, Chief. Ronnie Frantellini left everything she had to Clara Calhoun. The two women were tight. Clara once worked for Beasley, the Frantellini lawyer. She left Beasley to go to work for Ronnie. Are you following me?"

"Got it," said the chief. "Keep going."

"Victor Spinello has a piece of the Frantellini Shoe Factory. He was acquitted in the murder of Dario Tengo, who also had a piece of the shoe factory. Victor was represented by Beasley in court."

"And Beasley had the juror bribed," injected the chief.

"Correct. Beasley flipped and said that Ronnie put out the murder contract on the Frantellini Sisters."

"Okay, now I remember," stated Chief McCoy. "Are you getting all this, Father?" Father St. Dennis nodded in the affirmative. "So now Ronnie is dead," said the chief, "and that's that."

"Pretty much, Chief."

"But what about Clara's husband, Fernando?" Father St. Denis asked. "I have a bad feeling about him."

"Look into this Fernando," ordered Chief McCoy, addressing Markie. "I already did, Chief," replied Markie. "I had Ollie do a workup on him."

"Their marriage was kept a secret from Ronnie," chimed in the priest.

"Fill everybody in, Ollie," said Markie.

"The husband is Fernando Cruz," advised Von Hess. "He was a cabbie who comes from the lower eastside. He has a minor arrest history, nothing serious. Thanks to his marriage, now he's riding high."

"Fernando has taken over the reins of the business from his wife and Victor," chimed in St. Denis. "He's writing the checks and everything."

"Okay," said Chief McCoy. "Al, I want you and Ollie to stay on top of this. See if there is an Ireland tie in with Fernando."

41

The Emerald Isle Delivers

MARKIE AND VON HESS attempted to gather information from the airlines to see if Fernando had traveled to Ireland. Frustrated by the red tape involved in going through proper channels on this side of the Atlantic, the sergeant had Von Hess reach out to the authorities in Ireland in the hope of expediting the process. This was a wise decision.

Once Von Hess apprised the Garda he was dealing with of what he wanted, results were forthcoming. Fortunately, someone among the Garda had a family member who was an executive at Aer Lingus. It wasn't long before the New York City detectives learned that a man named Fernando Cruz had flown into Shannon Airport just days before Ronnie Frantellini's death. They also learned exactly when Cruz flew out of Ireland.

Possessing this knowledge caused Von Hess to go to the NYPD photo unit for the purpose of securing Fernando's old arrest photo. Von Hess was a little disappointed upon receiving the photo he requested because it depicted Fernando as a teenager. "What do you think, Sarge?" Von Hess asked. "He's too young in this photo, Ollie. People in Ireland might not recognize him."

"We could get a more up to date photo," suggested Von Hess.

"Before we do that, let's show the picture to the priest." After viewing the photo Father St. Denis indicated that he didn't recognize the young man in the photo.

The detectives were now certain that they needed a more recent photo of Fernando. Rather than go to the Department of Motor Vehicles or the Taxi and Limousine agency for a photo, Markie opted to photograph Fernando for an up-to-date image.

Using a camera with a zoom lens Von Hess wasted no time in taking several surveillance photos of Fernando as he walked on the street. The photos were developed and sent to the Irish authorities, who in turn showed these photos to people residing in the general area of the hotel where Ronnie Frantellini had been staying in Sligo.

Their hope that someone would recognize Fernando was realized. The Irish authorities hit paydirt when they knocked on the door of the Irish couple that housed Fernando at their bed and breakfast. Both husband and wife identified Fernando Cruz as being known to them as Mr. Ricardo, a man who stayed in their home.

The positive results achieved fostered further cooperation between the two law enforcement agencies. Von Hess was informed by his Irish counterpart that fingerprints of three people were lifted from the recovered handbag of Ronnie Frantellini. As expected, the fingerprints of Ronnie Frantellini and Sean O'Flaherty were on the handbag. The third fingerprint on the bag belonged to someone yet unidentified.

Von Hess proceeded to the police identification section at police headquarters and arranged to have the fingerprints of Fernando Cruz sent to Ireland for comparison purposes. The end result of this was that the third fingerprint on the handbag belonged to Fernando Cruz.

***

IT WASN'T LONG BEFORE MARKIE AND VON HESS responded to the Frantellini Shoe Factory with two members of the Irish Garda. The Irish authorities were in America for the purpose of apprehending Fernando. When they arrived at the factory the law enforcement officers were informed by Clara that her husband was not there. When asked where he was, Clara questioned the detectives as to what they wanted with her husband.

The New York City detectives saw no reason why the Guarda shouldn't speak for themselves. The law enforcement officers from Ireland didn't pull any punches. Their way was polite, but firm. They advised that Fernando was wanted in their country for murder. It was explained that Fernando had traveled to Sligo for the purpose of murdering Ronnie Frantellini. This got a heated rise out of the skeptical Clara, who challenged the veracity of the claim.

In defense of her husband Clara pointed out that Fernando was in Spain at the time in question. When concrete proof was produced to the contrary, Clara was stunned. Feeling lightheaded she felt it necessary to take a seat.

"Can I get you some water, Ma'am?" asked Von Hess.

"Fernando wouldn't do such a thing," Clara stated weakly. "I mean, could he?"

"I'm sorry, Ma'am, but I'm afraid he could."

Needing support, Clara asked if she could have Victor Spinello, the minority partner in the shoe factory, come to her office. The investigators voiced no objection. When Victor entered the office the detectives explained that Fernando was going to be taken into custody and extradited to Sligo to face murder charges. Victor stood open mouthed as he digested this. All he could think to do was just listen.

By the end of the meeting, everyone learned of Fernando's past arrest history. This caused Clara to reevaluate her relationship with her husband. It had finally become apparent to her that Fernando had been using her for the purpose of seizing control of the Frantellini holdings. Surprisingly, with the mystery of Fernando now unraveled, Clara no longer showed signs of falling apart emotionally. If anything, she presented a stoic front. Fernando was out.

Ronnie's mentoring had lots to do with Clara's resilience. She thought of Ronnie's words which still resonated. Fool me once, shame on you. Fool me twice, it's shame on me!

The more Clara thought things over, the more convinced she became of Fernando's treachery. *I made a big mistake marrying that man,* thought Clara, now reflecting on Fernando's past behavior. *Ronnie was right all along. I was too blind to see that Fernando wasn't right for me. The bastard was no damn good from the beginning.* At this point, any feelings she had for the husband who deceived her had now vanished.

When the detectives began to query Clara about Ronnie Frantellini, there was no longer a reason to withhold information. Clara was forthcoming about the arrangement that existed between her and her late mentor.

At the request of the detectives Clara telephoned Fernando, who was occupied visiting one of the Frantellini properties. Clara, as instructed, told her husband that she needed him at the shoe factory right away due to a labor-related incident.

While awaiting the arrival of Fernando, Clara came to appreciate the supportiveness of Victor Spinello. Although Victor remained quiet, his remaining at Clara's side throughout the ordeal spoke volumes. He was there for her. Victor's arm around Clara's shoulder came from a man with no agenda. This was reassuring. Victor made Clara feel safe.

Comforted by Victor during the wait for Fernando to arrive at the factory gave Clara time to think. She began comparing the differences between a nurturing man like Victor and a selfish taker like her husband. This reflection caused Clara to feel like a fool.

When Fernando arrived at the shoe factory the authorities immediately took him into custody. The law spread him eagle, frisked him and then handcuffed him. Clara and Victor stood by quietly as this unfolded. The shocked Fernando, once realizing that he had been set up, unleashed a barrage of profanities that were all directed at Clara.

Upon learning from the lawmen in Ireland that he was facing murder charges overseas caused Fernando to flip out. His eruption magnified to where he lashed out in an attempt to kick Clara. It took a crack in the face from one of the Irish investigators to still him. Clara wished she was the one striking the blow.

"I didn't do anything," protested Fernando weakly as he licked the blood from his lip. For the first time Clara saw her husband pathetically humbled.

"Save it your energy, bucko," said one of the Irishmen. "You'll need it where you're going. We know you killed Ronnie Frantellini."

"I didn't kill anyone," protested Fernando emphatically.

"Sure, you didn't. You'll be taking a nice plane ride back with us to prove how innocent you are," said the other Irishman, the older of the two law enforcement officers. The devastated Fernando offered no reply other than demanding to speak to a lawyer.

"Clara call me a lawyer," ordered Fernando.

"Call your own lawyer, big shot," said Clara, turning her back on Fernando. At this moment she reflected on Ronnie, believing that her act of defiance would've made Ronnie proud of her.

"Victor, get me a lawyer," Fernando ordered.

Fernando reacted in solidarity with Clara. Saying nothing, he turned his back on Fernando. With the iron gate now closed, Fernando went along quietly with the detectives. Once on the street Fernando paused to look back at the Frantellini shoe factory. What he saw was a shattered dream.

"It could have all been mine," he said sadly.

"C'mon, pal, keep moving," ordered Von Hess, who tugged on the prisoner's arm to move him along.

"I almost had it all," lamented Fernando.

"Is that why you killed that woman on the other side of the pond?" Markie asked. Fernando didn't acknowledge the question. "Did you honestly think that you were going to get away with it?"

"I want a lawyer," answered Fernando, not knowing who that might be.

***

OVER DINNER WITH FATHER FIORELLO ST. DENIS, Chief McCoy apprised the NYPD chaplain of the fate of Fernando Cruz. Father St. Denis shook his head sadly as he rehashed the history of the Frantellini family.

"It seems a shame how things worked out for that family," lamented the priest. "In the end everything landed in the hands of non-family members."

"You never know about things in this life, Father," said Chief McCoy.

"Richard always said that he wanted his factory and real estate to stay in the family. Everything seemed to go bad once Richard married that woman."

"How did he meet Ronnie anyway?"

"We were on a plane coming back from Italy. Ronnie happened to be sitting next to Richard. I only wish I had been paying more attention."

"Are there any Frantellini family members left in Italy?" "The only one left married into the family. Richard's son in law, the doctor, is over there."

"Maybe you should give him a call, Father. He might want to talk to a lawyer about the business."

"I'm not sure of his interest. But I think that perhaps a call to Dr. Tengo is in order, Chief."

42

All You Need Is Love

DOCTOR ETTORE TENGO WAS more than a bit apprehensive when he received a long-distance call from Father Fiorello St. Denis. Since prior calls from America as of late had been death notifications he feared hearing more awful news. Still reeling after the murder of his wife, brother, and sister-in-law, the physician took a deep breath in preparation of what he was about to be told.

When Father St. Denis voiced, “Ettore, I’m afraid that I have some unpleasant news for you,” the doctor’s knees buckled. A sick feeling began to come over him.

“What now, Father?” Doctor Tengo asked.

“Your father in law’s wife was found dead. I’m sorry, Ettore.”

“Ronnie is dead?”

“Yes, her body was found in Ireland.”

“What was she doing in Ireland?”

Father informed Doctor Tengo of the circumstances surrounding the murder. After concluding his narrative, the priest imparted what he believed to be appropriate wisdom.

“Life in this world comes with many highs and lows, Ettore. We must accept whatever our Lord brings our way. His plan is beyond our comprehension. We must accept, remain strong and continue forward."

Doctor Tengo was flabbergasted. "La famiglia è maledetta," he uttered into the phone, implying that the Frantellini family was cursed. "What is expected of me to do in America, Father?"

"Nothing, Ettore. You may want to speak to your brother Dario's wife and a lawyer. You both may be entitled to something from the Frantellini businesses. Victor has a small interest in the shoe factory."

"That bastard who murdered my brother could choke on his interest," said the doctor bitterly. "I don't want a Frantellini penny! I'm only too glad to be done with the whole damn family."

"I understand, Ettore," said the priest, "But you must consider your brother's family. His widow and children may be entitled to something."

"Really?"

"I have no knowledge of any contractual agreements that may exist. All I do know is that it seems like Ronnie Frantellini had inherited everything, and she left it all to her friend. There may be wiggle room."

"This is all too complicated for me, Father. My brother Dario was a very private man when it came to his business affairs, and my late wife had absolutely no interest in the family business. She left all decisions to her sister. Now everyone is dead."

"But Ettore, surely you should confer with an attorney. I must again remind you of Dario's family."

"Gia is being well provided for, Father. I am looking after her and the children. Thank God, I am doing very well here in Milan. America represents bad memories for us, Father. We've turned the page."

"But perhaps Gia...."

"Of course you had no way of knowing, Father, but Gia and I married. We came to console each other in our time of grief," advised Ettore. "My wife is a righteous lady, and her children get along well with me. Together we are expecting a child of our own. Life in Milan is good. Whatever is in America, can stay in America as far as we're concerned."

"Buona fortuna," said the priest, wishing the physician good luck. He understood.

"Molte grazie, Father," thanked the doctor.

Father St. Denis hung up his office phone and turned in his seat to face the crucifix hanging from the wall behind his desk. He crossed himself and began praying, thanking his God for a happy ending in Milan.

***

NOW ON HER OWN, CLARA found herself nervous over her responsibilities. Taking charge of the Frantellini businesses without guidance was challenging for her. Ronnie had provided Clara with more than just business advice. There was the accounting firm who could fill that void. What they lacked was the ability to instill confidence in Clara the way Ronnie did.

The certified public accountant who handled the Frantellini Shoe Factory and real estate holdings suggested that Clara retain the services of a reputable law firm he knew of. She accepted the CPA's recommendation without hesitation. Clara, in the dark, sat back and let the professionals handle everything. From the sidelines she watched her businesses push on as if operating on remote control. Then Victor Spinello stepped up.

While the creative Victor fell short in terms of business acumen, he possessed the intelligence to learn. He suggested to Clara that they, taking baby steps, should gain a full understanding of their business interests. Victor proved to be the support Clara needed in terms of building her confidence. Their collaboration enabled them to garner the knowledge necessary to operate their business efficiently. The time eventually came when they no longer merely squeaked by operationally.

As hurdles were being overcome, Clara came to see Victor as

more than just a business partner. Victor was appreciated for his genius, patience and considerateness. Clara recognized the minority partner to be a rare gem. Since Victor never made a pass at her, Clara began to wonder why. She knew that Victor had feelings for her, he showed that in many ways. He's probably just shy, she thought. I doubt that he's gay.

Wanting more, Clara began spending time with Victor after office hours. It began with dinner after work. As things progressed Victor began cooking Italian meals for Clara. They took long walks, engaged in much revealing conversation and then the inevitable emotional attachment took hold. Love had planted its flag.

Although it took Clara to make the first overture, once Victor felt comfortable, he proved to be quite creative in his romantic pursuit. His method in communicating his amorous feelings impressed Clara.

Appalling to her was when Victor took pen in hand to profess his love in verse. He mounted his poem on a plaque, then gift wrapped it and presented it to his object of affection over a home cooked dinner. When Clara began to open the package, Victor prevented her from doing so.

"Open it at home, Clara. I think that might be best," said Victor, who wanted to avoid an emotional scene that would likely result in tears. Clara couldn't wait to go home so that she could tear open the package that had kept her wondering. Just as Victor thought, tears flowed profusely when Clara finally got to open her present. She sat in her living room as she read the poem Victor wrote for her. Digesting Victor's words once wasn't sufficient. It took several reads before Clara first put the poem aside. Then, after a few minutes, she again looked at the poem that was addressed to Tesoro Mio, which meant my treasure in English. It read:

Tesoro Mio

My deepest desire is no longer forbidden,
My feelings within are not to be hidden.
I profess my love to a once distant star,
Who stole my heart from afar.

Your inner beauty, I can clearly see,
As well as the things, I want to be.
Titles and riches are not my goal,
Tis a life together, that will make me whole.

Lighten the weight of this torch I carry,
Relieve my burden, let us marry.
I pledge my love to you, Clara, the one I adore,
and vow to cherish you, forever more.

All my love tesoro mio,
Victor

Clara was still wiping her eyes when the telephone rang. It was

Victor. Within the hour they were reunited in Clara's penthouse apartment, the abode that was once occupied by those named Frantellini. Since Clara's divorce from Fernando was finalized, a decision was quickly made that the couple would marry. The pair began to make wedding plans. The honeymoon came early.

***

SMELLING OPPORTUNITY, THE HARD-NOSED BUSINESSMAN Chen Lowe saw his chance to broaden his footprint in the shoe industry. Not satisfied with mere expansion, Chen's long-term goal was to dominate all things having to do with footwear. The businessman believed that if his company was the one to introduce Victor Spinello's Dynamic Shoe, once developed, he'd be able to realize his lofty ambition.

Through a well-placed bribe to an employee of the Frantellini Shoe Factory, Chen's general council learned that the Dynamic Shoe was close to completion. Chen had his in-house lawyer set up a lunch meeting with the happy newlyweds Clara and Victor Spinello. The foursome broke bread at the Yi Ming Gardens in Manhattan's Chinatown district. The offer Chen made to purchase the Frantellini Shoe Factory was attractive enough to warrant serious consideration. Included in the purchase price were the rights to Victor's Dynamic Shoe.

When neither Clara nor Victor jumped at the offer, Chen's general counsel conveyed that there was also an interest in the Frantellini properties. This made an impression. Both Clara and Victor knew that the money to be made by selling all would be enough to free them from ever having to work again. Chen was told by the couple that they would get back to him after conferring with their accountant.

Later that evening over cocktails the CPA recommended that Clara and Victor accept the offer made by Chen Lowe. The accountant explained that the upside overshadowed the downside of selling out. At this point Clara's accountant and lawyer, out to sweeten the pot, took charge of the negotiations with Chen Lowe. An agreement was reached thanks to Chen Lowe wanting to become the dominant power in the shoe business. Chen's exuberance was over the top. He was so thrilled that he threw a dinner party in honor of Clara, who had announced her first pregnancy. Life was good to Clara and Victor from this point on. Having plenty of money, they purchased a home in East Hampton, New York. At first there was some social awkwardness. However, this changed once more children came. Clara's participation in school-related activities enabled her to make friends and fully acclimatize to the playground of the rich.

Victor's transition to living in East Hampton materialized with even less difficulty. Once it became known that he was the inventor of the Frantellini Sole and Dynamic Shoe, Victor became socially acceptable. Having children diminished Victor's need to invent. Now devoted to his family, he was content to rest on his laurels. Oddly, adding to Victor's acceptance was the fact that he murdered a man. This provided an element of mystery and danger that many found exciting, once people were confident that Victor was no psychopath.

Victor developed an affinity for shooting pool, practicing hours on the table in his home. Having won a charity tournament gained him the friendship of the owner of a vineyard who was also an avid pool afficionado.

Through his new friend Victor gained membership to a country club where he began playing golf. While only an average player, he embraced the challenges that the activity presented. Even Clara and their children availed themselves of the club's amenities.

When reflecting back on her life, Clara found it hard to fathom that she once was the love starved secretary of a shyster lawyer. In time, that part of her life journey was erased altogether.

43

Follies Of The Squared Circle

THE DEATH OF RONNIE FRANTELLINI was a major setback for Crippler. With Ronnie gone, the wrestler lost his bargaining chip. Once valueless to the prosecution, the murderer was basically abandoned by prosecutors. This meant that Crippler had to face the music without hope of leniency. He entered prison
a bitter man.

Being no stranger to incarceration, Crippler knew he had to be wary once on the inside. There was no mystery to the fact that snitches were not warmly received behind bars. With survival in mind, Crippler entered prison prepared battle with a hostile inmate population who might be aware that he had cooperated with the authorities.

As it turned out Crippler's concerns were for naught. The reality was that his reputation stood him better than expected. Being a double murderer of substantial physical prowess garnered him a degree of prestige behind bars. Further enhancing his reputation behind bars was the skirmish he had with the detectives who arrested him.

Crippler's former profession also made him popular among inmates. He used his wrestling background to his advantage by graciously answering questions pertaining to the wrestling business. His criminal audience remained rapt whenever Crippler communicated the little-known secrets of the ring. Tales of how blood in the squared circle was used to build drama during a wrestling match proved to be fascinating to those with an interest in wrestling. Crippler shed light on how color, attained via self-inflicted wounds made with a razor, fired fans up.

Crippler told stories out of school concerning the big stars of the mat when holding court. He revealed how champions were determined and how big paydays were earned in wrestling. All of this appealed to some of the brawnier inmates, who had thoughts of breaking into the grunt and groan business upon their release.

Crippler instructed these aspirants, teaching them how to apply wrestling holds and how to avoid injuries when taking falls. For those with actual potential, Crippler wrote letters of introduction to the promoters he knew. The former wrestler also put aside time to exchange letters with well-wishing wresting fans. For Crippler, all of this was therapeutic.

Crippler made it a point to write letters to the wrestlers he knew explaining why he had become a snitch. He justified his actions by citing how Wolfman Glass had ratted him out. This outlet for venting was good for Crippler's mental health.

The sole visitor who trekked to the Green Haven Correctional Facility, a maximum-security prison located in Dutchess County, to see Crippler was Smiley Allen. Smiley's visits were greatly appreciated because Smiley never came to see Crippler empty handed. His arrivals came with the food Crippler liked and the latest gossip.

Smiley never held a grudge over Crippler having brought him to the attention of the detectives. In this the men were more or less similar. Crippler never blamed Smiley for introducing him to Ronnie Frantellini.

Crippler only complained of one lingering thorn in his side. It had to do with the long sentence he was serving. Smiley appeased his friend by agreeing that he had received shabby treatment. All he could do was urge his friend to try and stay positive

Crippler possessed the resilience to serve his long sentence one day at a time. When his release date finally came Crippler was faced with a world that had undergone many changes. The former wrestler found the new technology baffling. He couldn't understand how technology advanced to where it impacted every aspect of life. Crippler found it all frustrating.

The one constant that went unchanged was Crippler's woes concerning his lack of funds. Now old and not having a family that wanted any part of him, Crippler came to think that he might have had it better incarcerated.

Convinced of this, Crippler went into a bank with the intention of getting caught robbing it. As he planned, he got caught and subsequently returned to living as a guest of taxpayers. For Crippler, prison was now viewed as a retirement home that fed him regularly and addressed whatever medical needs arose.

***

SMILEY ALLEN FOUND OUT about Crippler getting busted by reading about it in the newspaper. As he sipped coffee at the breakfast table he commented to his wife, "Well what do you know about that."

"Know about what, dear?" asked Smiley's wife, who sat on the other side of the table.

"An old friend of mine got caught robbing a bank."

"Oh, my God! Who?"

"You don't know him."

"Why did he do it?" Smiley shrugged and replied, "I don't know, it's just one of them things I suppose."

"So, who is the guy?"

"Nobody important," answered Smiley, rising from the table. "I'll see you tonight. I have to go to work."

Smiley went off to work that morning and continued to do so for many years. By the time he turned sixty, his children had received their education, married and were out of the house. At the age of sixty-five he sold his business. Smiley and his wife then retired to a Naples, Florida condo.

Years later, long after outliving his wife, Smiley began to show signs of dementia. Unable to live alone any longer, one of Smiley's children placed him into a care community. He lived in an apartment-like home with safety features and staff to look after those experiencing mental decline.

Smiley was waxing nostalgically one afternoon while conversing with a fellow resident, a former Ohio liquor salesman. He was reminiscing about living in New York City. The listener remained silent during Smiley's narrative, only nodding occasionally. He was oblivious to the names being dropped.

Names such as Crippler and Ronnie Frantellini had no significance to the transplanted Ohioan with the far-off look of a man with a mind elsewhere. His audience made no difference to Smiley, who was himself in another place and time.

When Smiley began injecting vulgarity into his narrative, a staff member who had been walking by overheard him. He approached Smiley to ask what was agitating him.

"What's wrong, young man?" asked the staff member in a condescending voice.

"I got nothing to say to any screw," replied Smiley, thinking he was incarcerated.

The staff member smiled, finding Smiley's remark amusing.

"What's your name?" he asked.

"You know my name," came the gruff reply.

"Do you know where you are?"

"Yeah, I'm in God's waiting room."

"That's right. Try to watch your language, the angels don't like profanity."

Smiley watched as the staff member walked off. "These freaking screws," he said in a raspy whisper, "they're always asking questions."

***

WOLFMAN GLASS MANAGED to slip through the net in terms of serving a long prison sentence. Not knowing how he would be received once out, he returned to his wrestling career with trepidation. His worries were justified. Crippler's letters to wrestlers he was friendly with damaged the already soiled Wolfman's reputation in the industry. In short, few people cared for a snitch who was only out to save his own skin.

Wrestlers who were sympathetic to Crippler embarked on a campaign of coldshouldering Wolfman. Some made snide remarks behind his back, others openly referred to him as a snake or rat to his face. Entering a locker room in any arena had become a challenge because Wolfman never knew who might confront him. Wolfman needed money so he sucked it all up.

The wrestling promoters saw an upside to all this. Collectively they came up with a way to cash in on Wolfman's tarnished reputation. Wolfman was asked to wear a mask and wrestle under a new name. Hence came the introduction of The Secret Informer from parts unknown.

Agreeing to be billed under this new monicker and advertised as the most despised wrestler in the world, Wolfman received a national push by the promoters. Making up Judas-like storylines as they went along, the promoters publicized feuds that resulted in a series of grudge matches between The Secret Informer and opponents who genuinely disliked him.

Since the ring action was extraordinarily fierce, fans came out to see opponents try to unmask The Secret Informer. The formula clicked, making Wolfman a headliner who was selling out at big arenas throughout the country.

The matches were stiff, grueling affairs for Wolfman, who was often the recipient of savage poundings. The blows administered to him were heavy handed. The holds applied by his adversaries were meant to cause hurt. The vicious slamming to the mat Wolfman received came with a thunderous thud that shook the ring. Despite all this, The Secret Informer was never unmasked.

The promoters, wanting to protect their investment, put forth a couple of restrictions. The word from the office was that all this punishment was justifiable in the ring, just as long as the mask worn by Wolfman wasn't removed and that there were no broken bones that would prevent him from showing up for his next ring commitment.

However, despite the punishment he was taking, there was one satisfaction for Wolfman that couldn't be denied. The compensation he was receiving far exceeded any other earnings he made previously. As long as Wolfman maintained upper card status, he was okay with the battering.

With inadequate time to heal his injuries, the wrestler billed as The Secret Informer was on a path that inevitably led to physical decline. The strain on his ligaments and muscles, coupled with no break in the punishment he was receiving, left Wolfman incapable of performing in the ring with credibility. Finally, the wrestling promoters concluded that time had come for The Secret Informer to be unmasked in the ring.

This decision left only preliminary under card gigs available for Wolfman at a fraction of what he had been earning. There were no other viable options for Wolfman other than to terminate his wrestling career.

With no legitimate skills to fall back on, the out-of-work wrestler was fortunate to be married to a woman who knew how to save for a rainy day. Thanks to Wolfman's successful run as The Secret Informer, his wife was able to save enough money to last them for a long time.

Once he retired, Wolfman began spending time drinking beer at a local bowling alley not far from where he lived. The owner of the bowling alley was impressed enough by the former wrestler's celebrity that he offered work on a per diem basis. The job, depending on need, required Wolfman to act as a greeter, bartender and bouncer.

After conferring with his wife, Wolfman accepted the position. Both had thought it a good idea for him to stay busy. Unfortunately, Wolfman couldn't separate himself from his past vices. Once comfortable in his new position, the former wrestler reverted back to his philandering ways.

Wolfman proved weak when faced with temptation. The allure of a woman who belonged to a bowling league caused him to redirect the affection that was supposed to be reserved for his spouse. The other woman was the wife of a long-distance truck driver who spent much of his time on the road. The cure to her loneliness was found in Wolfman.

After months of trysts, the traveling truckdriver got wise. Upon first setting eyes on the scary looking lover his wife took up with, the husband realized he was no match physically for Wolfman. The truck driver turned to an equalizer to achieve the revenge he sought.

The official police report reflected that Wolfman was shot outside the bowling alley by an unknown assailant who unleashed a close-range blast from a 12-gauge shotgun that blew off the shooting victim's right leg. Those in the bowling alley who responded to the sound of the fired shot found Wolfman alive, but in a state of shock.

Wolfman claimed to the authorities that things happened so fast that he was unable to identify who shot him. It was a story he stuck to because he wanted to keep his wife in the dark and his marriage secure. Since there were no witnesses to the shooting, the shooter went unidentified.

Those on the bowling team could only whisper among themselves as to what caused their team mate to be walking around with two black eyes. Hers was a tale that Wolfman's former mistress wasn't about to share with anyone.

The wanderings of the one-legged Wolfman had finally come to an end. Now domesticated, he resigned himself to spending his days peeling the potatoes his wife intended to cook for him. Together they watched television, drank coco and turned in early.

Wolfman was in front of the television one evening watching a game show with his wife. As he eyeballed the television he gobbled up left over frog legs, one of which went down the wrong way. When the former wrestler began choking on his food his wife began frantically slapping her husband's back in the hope of his spitting out what was troubling him. Her efforts failed. She learned of the Heimlich maneuver only after her husband died while seated in the living room love seat.

44

Business As Usual

THOMAS BEASLEY'S ABILITY TO CIRCUMVENT her prosecutorial efforts was something that ADA Smyther took personally. She was perturbed enough to conduct an inquiry into the relationship between Beasley and the interim District Attorney. To protect her position, she was discreet in this endeavor.

Smyther began by contacting those in the legal profession she was friendly with. While no one provided concrete answers, the consensus was that Beasley must have something on DA Miller.

Smyther next turned to her politically connected uncle for his wisdom on the matter. The retired judge was responsible for her securing a position with the Manhattan District Attorney's Office as an ADA.

Smyther visited her uncle, a widower, at his home on Manhattan's West 96th Street one evening after work. The judge sat back in his chair gazing at the ceiling with his fingers meeting in steeple fashion. It as if he was listening to a proceeding. After being informed of the facts he calmly responded to his niece. It was all perfectly understandable to him. He went on to explain how things worked in political circles.

"Nepotism is a part of business," advised the uncle. "That what got DA Miller his job in the first place with the DA's office. That's not the worst thing. Let's face it, I got you in didn't I?"

"I know," said Smyther. "But what is the connection?"

"Miller is related to the governor though marriage," answered the judge in a matter-of-fact way. "Care for a brandy, Kim?"

"No thank you. But what about this business with Beasley?"

"Obviously there must be a prior relationship between Miller and Beasley. Otherwise, Beasley would never catch such a break. Are you sure you won't have a brandy? I'm having another one."

"No, thank you," answered Smyther. "But what could the connection between them be?"

"Hold on a second, let me go in the next room and make a call." The retired judge returned five minutes later with the answer to Smyther's question. "Thomas Beasley and DA Miller were classmates."

"Really?"

"According to my source the two are thick as thieves. They were roommates."

"So that's the connection."

"One hand washes the other, Kim. Who knows what they've got or had going on together."

ADA Smyther looked at her uncle, a man she always looked up to, in awe. It was as if she were seeing him for the first time.

The judge found the answer to her question by simply picking up his phone. Smyther eyes were now open. Where her uncle lived, the brandy he drank, the car he drove and his expensive taste in clothes had now all come into question. What was the origin of the money the judge used to pay for these things, she wondered. He must have been doing his own favors in return for financial considerations! Smyther concluded mentally.

Finding all this disturbing, the disillusioned ADA banished the unpleasantness from her mind. She returned to her work with a renewed passion to put wrongdoers in jail.

ADA Smyther was destined to listen to her uncle, who had been espousing the important role of politics when it came to advancement. Under the tutelage and influence of the judge, ADA Smyther was eventually promoted to being a bureau chief in the DA's office.

Smyther's uncle lived long enough to see his niece become a judge in the Manhattan Criminal Court. Once there, she established the reputation of being a hanging judge. She, like her late uncle, looked at the ceiling with her fingers forming a steeple as she listened from the bench.

Smyther remained vigilant in her belief that fair play must prevail on all matters before her court. However, having a long memory, this was challenging when it came to defendants being represented by Thomas Beasley. To her credit, the judge would excuse herself from Beasley's cases rather than test her resolve to maintain objectivity. In this respect it could be said that Beasley, who had continued on with his long career, had emerged the winner once again.

***

MARKIE WAS AT HOME ON HIS DAY OFF reading the morning paper. He had just finished having a breakfast consisting of oatmeal and a banana. As he sipped the remainder of his coffee, he noticed a headline that grabbed his attention. The reported account told of a member of the city council who faced forgery charges for allegedly falsifying documents related to a business transaction.

The sergeant reacted to the story with minimal interest until he read that the politician in question was a cousin of Bernard Miller, the interim Manhattan DA. This tickled Markie's curiosity. A couple of days later, acting on a hunch, Markie had Von Hess drop him off at the Manhattan Criminal Court.

"Wait in the car, Ollie," Markie said. "I'll be out in a minute."

Once inside the court Markie looked up a court officer he was friendly with. His purpose was to inquire about the council member's case. Markie came to learn the attorney representing the council member was Thomas Beasley. While this was hardly surprising, he was taken aback after being told that Beasley's private investigator was Teddy Leonard.

"Are you sure about that?" Markie asked. "Leonard was the private investigator working for Beasley?"

"It looked that way to me, Al," replied the court officer. "He stood in court with Beasley and the councilman."

Now this really is hot shit, thought Markie.

The sergeant returned to his waiting vehicle shaking his head. When he entered the unmarked car he began to share what he found out with Von Hess.

"You're not going to believe this, Ollie."

"What's that, Sarge?"

"Thomas Beasley is defending that city council member who got pinched for forgery. The councilmember is related to DA Miller."

"They're all in bed together those crooked bastards."

"And you know what else, Ollie?"

"What?"

"Teddy Leonard is still on team Beasley. Birds of a feather."

"I guess Beasley let bygones be bygones."

"Now that I think about it, maybe it's not all that surprising. Finding another shifty investigator willing to do his bidding wouldn't be that easy."

"Sometimes I think the whole damn system is in need of a house cleaning," voiced Von Hess, adding, "beginning with the top people on down." Markie couldn't disagree.

"It's really incredible how they get away with the crap they pull, Ollie."

"The system is rigged to the benefit of the lawyers, Sarge. They make the laws to suit their interests."

"You said it, Ollie," agreed Markie. "The judges are lawyers. They bend the rules all the time and don't have to give any explanation. And you know what the killer is?"

What?"

"The hypocrite bastards will bang that gavel down and put you or me away for sneezing in church. Meanwhile they'll let their pals off left and right."

"I wonder what Judge Kim Smyther thinks about all this, Sarge."

"She's a tough cookie, but fair. If she's presiding over this case she'll hang that councilman for sure."

"I agree. She's tough, but at least with her everybody gets stung by the bee the same way."

***

THE LAW PRACTICE OF THOMAS BEASLEY continued to thrive. Beasley continued to be the lawyer believed to have a Midas touch, a legal wizard who settled cases to the advantage of his clients. Minimum sentences, favorable plea deals and declined prosecutions abounded when it came to a client of Thomasa Beasley. Between his criminal caseload and handling the affairs of non-criminal clients, Beasley found himself in need of support. For relief he decided to hire someone that would be amenable to his way of doing business. Such a candidate needed to be resourceful and streetwise, like Beasley himself.

Beasley identified such an attorney at his high school reunion. After a few cocktails the attorney, a solo practitioner with few clients, admitted to cheating his way through law school. This was impressive to Beasley, who believed that he found someone who wouldn't be above chicanery in order to attain desired results.

Beasley's secretary was an attractive gum chewing woman with a rough edge who came to him with experience working for a shady lawyer who had passed away.

Within six months the secretary became sexually involved with the attorney Beasley took into his firm. Engaging in office trysts when Beasley was in the field, their love nest was upset when Beasley caught them doing the very same thing he often did. Beasley's reaction was harsh. In a fit of anger, the man with a short memory fired both employees on the spot. When Beasley later discussed the situation with Teddy Leonard over drinks in a tavern, his private investigator appeared unsurprised. He summed up his feelings with brevity.

"Some people got no respect," said Leonard.

"Precisely," voiced Beasley in agreement. "I can live without another lawyer for a while, but a good secretary is something I need."

"Maybe an answering machine makes the best secretary for you, Tom."

Beasley pondered this for a few seconds. His thoughts were interrupted when Leonard elbowed him. The private investigator raised his chin in the direction of the entranceway to the tavern.

Finding the two women who entered worthy of his attention, the lawyer sent over drinks once they settled in at the bar. Soon after he and Leonard joined the ladies. There was no more shop talk.

***

IT WAS JUST BEFORE DAYBREAK when Teddy Leonard arrived home. Tired after drinking and frolicking at the apartment of the woman he picked up, he immediately went to bed. Five hours later he rose. He did so out of necessity. Through puffy eyes he brushed his teeth and shaved. After jumping out of the shower his eyes were still puffy.

Leonard got himself dressed in preparation for a client meeting. As a rule, the private investigator shied away from marital cases. However, since this investigation involved the wife of an affluent Wall Street type, he took advantage of the opportunity to jack up his rates substantially.

After his client meeting the private investigator took in a movie. Having arrived early he purchased a bag of popcorn and found himself a seat in the back row where he waited for the next showing. The houselights were on leaving the movie house well lit.

The private investigator passed the time by scanning the theater.

To the far-left Leonard noticed a boy of about twelve sitting next to a bespectacled man in his late thirties. The man was thin, neatly dressed and clean shaven. His straight brown hair was combed with a rigid side part. The adult man seemed to be doting on the boy. The boy's look was difficult to interpret.

His antennas now up, Leonard kept an eye on the pair. This kid is either brain dead or scared shitless, thought Leonard. Leonard watched as the man and the youth rose from their seats and walked up the aisle. They returned a few minutes later with the boy carrying popcorn and a large soda. They then took their seats and waited for the movie(s) to start. When the house lights went out, Leonard began to see behavior that infuriated him.

Unable to stomach what was occurring, Leonard got up and interrupted the action. He took hold of the youth by the collar and pulled him out of his seat. He then kicked the boy in his butt and sent him running toward the exit. Leonard then turned toward the pedophile.

The private investigator sat down next to the stunned bespeckled man. Leonard produced his revolver and poked it in the boy lover's ribs.

"Police, get your ass up, you're coming with me," hissed Leonard. The man, thinking he was up against the law, offered no resistance. Leonard took the pedophile to the men's room and forced him to belly up to an old-fashioned standing urinal. He then ordered him to face the wall and not turn his head. This prevented the man from seeing Leonard face to face. Once Leonard determined that he and his man were alone, the private eye unleashed a vicious assault from the rear.

The ex-NYPD detective smacked off his victim's glasses, causing the cheaters to fall into the yellow stained urinal. Leonard then took his man down to the tiled floor by yoking his neck. This was followed by vicious stomps with the heel of Leonard's shoe landing on the pedophile's face. Once satisfied that the pedophile was sufficiently beaten, Leonard relieved himself on the assault victim's glasses. He didn't bother to flush.

After leaving the movie theater Leonard hustled to a bar several blocks away feeling upbeat over his violent performance at the movie theater. Once at the ginmill he ordered a double Scotch. As he sipped his intoxicant he went down memory lane recollecting how long it had been since he last gave someone a tune up of such magnitude. It was reassuring for Leonard to know that he still had what it took to administer such a thrashing. In his distorted view, he saw it as a validation that he was aging well.

***

MARY CUSTER, THE SHARON STONE LOOKALIKE from the Kingly Castle Review, again crossed paths with Teddy Leonard. The two were at a convenience store on a line to purchase Lotto tickets for a huge jackpot.

At first Leonard didn't recognize Custer due to the darker hair she now sported. He finally realized who she was after overhearing the counterman address his regular customer by the name of Mary.

Leonard, who stood behind Custer, eyeballed her from top to bottom. Liking what he saw, the private investigator reacquainted himself with the good time girl.

"Hello, Mary," said Leonard. It took a few seconds for Mary to recognize the ex-NYPD detective. When she did she wasn't exactly cordial in acknowledging him. "Oh, you," she said cooly, vividly remembering the time she was hustled out of Leonard's apartment.

"It has been a while," agreed Leonard. "You're looking well."

"Thanks," Custer said.

"Still working at the same place."

"Yeah, I'm still there." "I've been spending a lot of time out of town on a business deal," lied the private investigator, continuing the illusion that he was a man of means. "Did you ever do anything with that celebrity lookalike idea you had?"

"No, that never got off the ground," answered Custer. "You know, I was hoping to see you again."

"Why? To tell me off over that day I rushed you out of my apartment?"

"No, to get you to invest. I knew that you were keen on my business idea."

"I still am," replied Leonard, playing along. The two decided to go for coffee at a nearby diner. Once there Leonard reignited his feigned interest in financing Custer's business dream of launching a celebrity lookalike brothel. His motive for showing interest was to get intimate with the Sharon Stone clone without having to spend money for the privilege. This was a stretch because Custer, a working girl, wasn't about to give anything away for free.

As the pair continued to reconnect there came a point in which the private investigator suggested that they relocate to a more private setting. Custer agreed to accommodate him if properly compensated. Leonard checked his wallet to see how much money he had on him. Having sufficient funds to cover the entertainment the two finished their coffee and set out to Custer's apartment.

After satisfying his desire, the private investigator offered to treat Custer to Chinese takeout. She laughed at this proposal believing that her trick was joking. At this juncture Custer was still under the impression that Leonard was a very wealthy man who had the funds to rejuvenate her brothel idea.

Custer countered the Chinese takeout offer by suggesting the two go to an upscale steakhouse. Leonard quickly mulled this over before agreeing. He incorporated one stipulation, that they would return to Custer's apartment for a free of charge second round of lovemaking. Since Custer was famished, she consented.

The meal got off to a bumpy start at the restaurant. Leonard was taken aback when Custer ordered a bottle of expensive red wine without first consulting him.

Leonard's intent was to order house wine. When he voiced this he was met with Custer's disapproval.

"I hate the house wine here," she said, adding, "I thought you were supposed to be a sport."

The tension mounted when Custer went on to order the most expensive steak on the menu. When the former NYPD detective conveyed that she'd never be able to finish such a large steak, the comment he received came tartly.

"Let me worry about what I eat," said Custer.

In an attempt to offset what he saw as a huge tab coming, the private investigator ordered roast beef hash, the cheapest offering on the menu. Thinking of money, Leonard's lust for Custer had now begun to wane.

As for Custer, she stepped up her campaign to get Leonard to commit to financing her dream of operating a brothel. Her application of pressure totally soured the private investigator, who now had enough of Custer. Leonard removed the cloth napkin from his lap and threw it on the table in disgust.

"C'mon we're leaving," Leonard announced abruptly. Fed up, he then called for the bill.

"But I haven't had dessert," reminded Custer.

No longer wanting anything to do with the Sharon Stone replica Leonard offered no explanation for his behavior. When pressed for an explanation, he pulled no punches in responding. He concluded his verbal tirade by conveying in no uncertain terms that Custer stood a better chance of getting nuked than his spending money on the pipe dream of a skanky whore.

Things really began to spiral downward after Custer was called a skanky whore. Mary Custer responded in kind with choice words of her own. Containing his anger, Leonard paid the bill without saying another word. He intended to do his talking on the street. Once outside retaliation came swiftly. The former lawman took hold of Custer's long hair, yanked her head downward and spun her head in a circle. This motion caused Mary to fall to her knees. Upon releasing his grip Leonard had a clump of Custer's hair between his fingers.

The assaulted woman reached into her coat pocket for the knife she always carried. Custer plunged the blade deep into Leonard's abdomen. A second sticking resulted in the knife entering Leonard's throat.

Leonard, his eyes bulging in disbelief, placed both hands on his neck. He stared at his attacker in silence as he began to slowly fade, ultimately falling to the ground dead. Thinking fast, Custer picked up off the ground the hair that was yanked from her head. With no place to run, she stood her ground waiting for the police to arrive.

When they did she claimed self-defense, showing the authorities the hair that was plucked from her head. She communicated that the knife belonged to Leonard, who she managed to disarm.

When queried by the police as to what sparked the confrontation she purported that Teddy Leonard, who she claimed to know from the Kingly Castle Review, was a wannabe pimp who was pressuring her to engage in prostitution for him. She insisted that she killed Leonard because she feared for her life.

While the self-defense fabrication seemed plausible to Custer, it failed to impress the jury that found her guilty of murder. Her conviction resulted in decades behind bars. During her incarceration she came to rely on religion to help see her through. When finally released from jail Custer found work as a cleaner in a church rectory.

Custer lived her life in relative obscurity until she was found dead one August morning. The senior citizen ex-convict had been vigorously scrubbing the pastor's bathtub when felled by a heart attack.

Teddy Leonard, who had been an only child, died without ever having made prior arrangements. Since Leonard had no will or family to leave anything to, whatever assets he had accumulated in his lifetime were taken by the State of New York. He was buried in a potter's field on Hart Island in the Bronx.

45

Another Day, Another Dollar

RUDOLPH PRISINSKI HAD DIFFICULTY acclimating to incarceration at first. Facing prolonged confinement led to his entering into a state of deep depression. Rudy's somberness was reflected by eyes that often stared out blankly at nothing in particular. Concealed within his mind were inner thoughts that were obviously not pleasant.

Even on occasions when Rudy could be overheard talking to himself, he revealed little. His mumbles were always laced with profanity. The best that others could decipher was that Rudy's words had something to do with his sentencing and the steep fine he received.

Eventually the time came when the former public relations man learned to accept his situation and settle down. Once communicative, Rudy would air his discontent in a casual fashion to anyone willing to listen. He'd complain that he had been unfairly persecuted, citing Victor Spinello, the killer of Dario Tengo as an example of his mistreatment.

"They let a killer walk free, and me they put behind bars for taking a few bucks," was Rudy's most often repeated lament. Rudy neglected to ever mention his cooperation with the authorities. That aspect of his tale of woe never entered into his narratives.

"Why wasn't Victor Spinello retried?" Rudy had asked his attorney. "Why wasn't he retried for the murder he committed?"

The answer Rudy received was curt and to the point. "The DA's office declined prosecution," came the reply. This was hardly the explanation the inmate was looking for.

In need of someone to blame his predicament on, Rudy pointed his finger at his wife. She's the one who put me here, he thought. Her and that damn wheelchair ruined my business. She drained me physically and financially.

Refusing to look within as the cause of his troubles was somewhat helpful. It was far more palatable for Rudy to shift blame rather than admit to his own poor decisions.

Responsibility for the accident that restricted his wife was something he firmly refused to acknowledge. Time had erased an accurate recollection of the incident altogether.

Rudy, over time, came to massage the crimes that led to his incarceration. He found a degree of peace by immersing himself in positive, although inaccurate, recollections of how things went down. He rewrote the past and incorporated adjustments that made for a more pleasing tale. In one particularly artificial retrospect he justified his bribe receiving as doing what was necessary for the survival of his family. In explaining this to fellow inmates Rudy elevated his wife's condition to near death.

"Without my providing the financial wherewithal to meet her needs, she'd be dead," Rudy would say. This fabrication played nicely in his mind. "I was too good!" Rudy would declare convincingly. "Why, she owes her very life to me....what else was I to do?"

When Rudy's wife showed up at the prison one visiting day unannounced he was stunned. But there she was, wheelchair and all. Mrs. Prisinski was able to make the trip thanks to the assistance of her sister, who accompanied her on the pilgrimage. Rudy looked at his wife as she sat in her chair and lectured him on how he ruined her life. Mrs. Prisinski put forth no inquiries as to how her husband was doing or if he needed anything. She expressed no concerns as to his treatment. Rudy's wife was unwavering in venting her anger. Blasting Rudy was her sole purpose for being there. Now, having a captive audience, she was able to verbally abuse him until she grew tired of doing so. As he took his medicine Rudy focused on the movements of his wife's thin, unforgiving lips. He maintained his silence throughout. What Mrs. Prisinski failed to realize was that Rudy had ceased listening to her, his mind was elsewhere. Rudy was thinking of how swell it would be to push his wheelchair bound spouse down a flight of stairs.

"You find this to be funny?" asked Rudy's wife loudly, after realizing that her husband bore a crooked smile.

"What was that you said?" Rudy asked, snapping out of his pleasant daydream.

"Aren't you listening?"

"Why did you even bother to come here?"

"To remind you of what you did to me!" The back-and-forth exchange was typical of the prison conversation the couple had every six months or so.

When Rudy received an early release from prison he never informed his wife. He emerged from jail vowing never again to return to the life he once knew. Instead, he made his way to Port St. Lucie, Florida where he took a job working in a supermarket. What little money he made he spent in a bar he came to frequent. It was there that he met a sort of soulmate, a functional alcoholic who he enjoyed drinking with.

The two entered into a relationship that ultimately led to their living together. After several years the union unexpectedly ended when Rudy's girlfriend found him dead one morning.

Prisinski had been sitting on the bathroom bowl when discovered. Ironically, he had been reading, *The Lost Weekend*, by Charles R. Jackson, a tale of an alcoholic writer.

In Rudolph Prisinski's pocket his girlfriend found thirty-two dollars and sixteen cents. In a dresser drawer there was a pint of cheap whiskey resting atop his underwear. In Rudy's wallet there was his social security card, driver's license and a photo of the wife he abandoned, which reflected an inked in mustache below Mrs. Prisinski's nose.

As for Rudy's wife, she fared well. She gave up drinking after moving into her sister's home. With the animosity that poisoned her mind now removed, she began to think productively. She, with the help of her sister, started a small advertising business. The two worked well together. Their efforts provided them with a healthy income well into their retirement years.

***

MARKIE TELEPHONED JERRY GELLER, the father of the boy who identified the wrestlers involved in the restaurant slaying of the Frantellini sisters. Mr. Geller was impressed that Markie remembered the promise he had made to his son.

Arrangements were made to meet with Markie the next time that wrestling was being staged at Madison Square Garden.

"Who was that?" asked Mrs. Geller, who had overheard part of the conversation.

"That was Sergeant Markie," replied the husband.

"What did he want?"

"Remember when he offered to introduce Jay to some of the wrestlers backstage at the Garden?"

"Yes."

"Well, he wants to make good on it."

"Really? Why would he want to do that?"

"I guess because he's a man of his word."

"You're going to go with them, right?" Mrs. Geller asked, the caution in her voice evident. "He might be some kind of a sicko. You know, just because he's cop, that doesn't mean he can be trusted."

"Stop, he's just being decent. But not to worry, I'll be with Jay."

When young Jay Geller learned of this treat he began thinking of what it would be like to grow up and be a cop. The badge, gun and perceived thrill connected to the occupation was enticing to the youth. Jay was also influenced by Markie having access to the wrestlers he followed on television and in the magazines.

Fortunately, Jay withheld his interest in law enforcement from his parents. They had always instilled in their son the importance of aiming high when considering a career.

Emphasized was the necessity of earning a good enough living to comfortably take care of a family one day. Jay had listened to the preachings of his parents long enough to realize that it was best to keep his future ambitions to himself.

On the evening of the wrestling matches Markie took time to walk by the bar that Rochelle Parrish frequented prior to going to the Garden show. Unable to resist the temptation to take a peek inside, the sergeant took a step into the establishment. He hesitated to proceed further upon spotting Rochelle.

Rochelle was seated at the bar with another woman, who looked enough like Rochelle, that it was easy to assume they were siblings. Standing next to the women was Yankee Phil Denim, Rochelle's partner in the training school they operated. Yankee was drinking beer from a mug.

Conflicted emotionally, Markie struggled in deciding what to do. Much of him wanted to make his presence known, yet he feared once again falling victim to an aching heart. Markie decided to play it safe. He abruptly left the establishment unnoticed.

Once outside in the cool air, the sergeant looked at his watch. Seeing that he had plenty of time before meeting Geller and his son in front of the Garden, he found himself a place to have a drink. Ending up at tavern a block away, Markie stood at the bar and ordered his usual libation.

As he consumed his whiskey and beer, the sergeant began to visually scan the bar. He noticed a woman, not far where he was positioned, that appealed to him. She was age appropriate, fair skinned and in line with his physical preferences.

Markie was particularly impressed with the woman's hair. Her tresses were shorter than a bob, but longer than a classic pixie. Markie perceived this as the earmarks of someone employed in a corporate setting. The dark pants suit she wore seemed to support this assumption. When the sergeant failed to realize that, aside from the hair, his attraction had much to do with the stranger being similar to Rochelle.

After ordering a glass of wine the woman happened to turn in Markie's direction. She offered a friendly smile when their eyes met. The grin projected was a passing one, not of the variety that lingered or suggested interest. This got Markie thinking.

After ordering another shot for himself, Markie stepped up and sent a drink over to the object of his attention. The stranger was receptive. When Markie relocated to where she was he introduced himself. Soon after it came out that he was an NYPD Detective Sergeant. Feeling safe, the women's interest heightened. This wasn't surprising to Markie. Experience taught him that many women felt safe talking to law enforcement officers.

Further conversation revealed that Markie's new acquaintance was from Florida. She was in New York City on business and scheduled to remain in the Big Apple for several days. Markie also gathered that the woman was married. The sergeant questioned the woman regarding her employment. He was impressed when informed that she was the senior vice president of a national pharmaceutical concern. Suspecting that the executive might be out for a good time, Markie inquired as to where she was staying. She advised that she was stopping at the Sheraton in Times Square, making it a point to mention that she was in town alone.

The two hit it off well enough for Markie to feel comfortable excusing himself for an hour. He explained that he had to run an errand on behalf of a crippled eleven-year-old boy wanting the autograph of his favorite wrestling stars. He added to his story to elevate his image.

As anticipated, the crippled boy yarn had the results that the sergeant hoped for. It was agreed that the two would reunite at the tavern in one hour.

After parting, the sergeant hurried to Madison Square Garden where he met the father and son Geller. Mr. Geller gained entry to the arena after producing tickets for himself and Jay. Markie got in by flashing his shield to the ticket taker.

Markie escorted the father and son to the access point where the wrestlers emerged from when heading to the ring. This entry/exit was under the control of a Garden security officer. Markie, followed by the father and son, pulled out his tin and strolled past the security officer without issue. The three made their way backstage. Once there several wrestlers, who Markie had previously met when he was seeing Rochelle Parrish, remembered the sergeant. The warm greeting he received from the grunt and groaners was impressive to both Mr. Geller and his young son.

When Markie told of Jay being a loyal fan, the athletes were only too glad to extend themselves for the youngster. Mr. Geller, who had brought along a camera, took pictures of his son alongside his favorite wrestlers. Even the reigning champion was agreeable to being photographed with the boy. One thoughtful performer passed around Jay's wrestling program for the athletes to autograph for the youth.

When Rochelle Parrish suddenly entered the off-limits area with her sister and Yankee Phil Denim, she stopped short upon seeing Markie. Appearing happy, Rochelle approached her former lover without hesitation. Her cordial greeting came complete with a smile. Protective of his emotions, Markie's remained distant. He acknowledged Rochelle with just a stiff nod of his head.

Rochelle was perceptive enough to detect Markie's cautiousness. Keeping things light, she attempted to rekindle their connection with casual conversation. Her efforts proved unfruitful. Frustrated, Rochelle wasted no further time in getting to the point. She asked Markie why he never called her. The sergeant seemed bewildered by the directness of the question. Sensing his confusion, Rochelle asked the sergeant if Detective Von Hess had told him that she was asking for him.

Markie responded in the affirmative, never letting on that Von Hess never mentioned a word to him about Rochelle's interest. Markie knew Von Hess well enough to know that the detective was only trying to protect him from rekindling a relationship with someone who callously broke his heart by taking up with others. When Rochelle insisted on an explanation as to why Markie never called her, the sergeant had no reply to offer. Feeling cornered, he simply thanked Rochelle for her assistance in the Frantellini case and excused himself, claiming that he had business to attend to.

Rochelle watched as Markie said goodbye to Mr. Geller and his son before making his departure. Once Markie left, Rochelle approached Mr. Geller. After introducing herself as a friend of the sergeant, Rochelle began digging for information about the sergeant's private life. To her disappointment, Mr. Geller communicated that he only knew Markie on a professional basis. Rochelle found herself now realizing just how much she missed what was no longer hers. Her sister, who had been occupied elsewhere, noticed the troubled look on Rochelle's face. She asked what was wrong.

"Nothing is wrong," answered Rochelle grimly. She then stormed out of the room.

Yankee Phil Denim, observing this abrupt exit, approached the sister to find out what happened.

"What's going on?" Denim asked.

"I don't really know, but I'm thinking that partner of yours might have feelings for that cop, Yankee," answered the sister.

While Yankee was pondering this, Markie was on his way to see the woman he had promised to meet. As he strolled along briskly he was envisioning how nice a cure it would be if he got lucky.

Just before reaching the tavern, Markie's cell phone went off. Seeing that the caller was Lieutenant Wright, his superior at police headquarters, he answered.

"Yeah, Loo. What's up?"

"I have a new job for you," advised Wright. "What's it all about, Loo?"

"We got us a serial killer on the loose."

"Are you starting a task force?"

"Chief McCoy isn't quite there yet. He doesn't want to draw too much attention to this. He's hoping that you and Ollie could wrap this thing up before it goes any further."

"He's got a lot of faith in us."

"That he does. Come in the first thing in the morning with Von Hess and I'll fill you in on what we know so far. Just so you know, this caper is one for the books."

"Really? I what way?"

"Our perp is a psycho with a fixation for famous monsters. I'll explain when I see you."

"You got it." After hanging up Markie checked his watch for the time. I'll give Ollie a call later, he thought.

When Markie arrived at the tavern as planned, he saw no sign of the stranger he was to meet up with. Eventually he got tired of waiting for her. Markie asked the bartender what happened to the woman he had been talking to earlier. The sergeant was told that she had left with an off-duty detective who worked in the local precinct.

Disappointed, Markie's thoughts reverted back to Rochelle as he traveled to his apartment with a newspaper instead of a woman. When he got home he dialed Von Hess to notify him they had to be at their office in headquarters early. Their new adventure would one into the world of a madman hellbent on settling old wrongs. "The Case of the Yearbook Killer," would prove to be one of the most bizarre cases of Markie's career.

THE END

www.ingramcontent.com/pod-product-compliance
Lightning Source LLC
LaVergne TN
LVHW052335100826
845147LV00020B/1069

* 9 7 8 1 9 4 2 5 0 0 9 8 8 *